MW00962261

RIPPLE

By
Michael C. Grumley

i.i

Books by Michael C. Grumley

BREAKTHROUGH

LEAP

CATALYST

RIPPLE

AMID THE SHADOWS

THROUGH THE FOG

THE UNEXPECTED HERO

ACKNOWLEDGMENTS

Special thanks to Frank, Donna Tim, Dale, Jim, Rob, John, and Les. For all of their expert help and advice.

And to the best group of beta readers a writer could hope to have.

1

Les Gorski stared through his dark-framed glasses with a weary expression. Most of the men before him were not the normal soldiers he was used to working with—those with a grizzled toughness and the ability to endure extreme conditions.

This group was very different. Instead of fighters, these men were engineers. Smarter in some ways, but greener. Navy engineers who, along with Gorski and his own team, were there for one reason and one reason only.

Watching as the row of men donned their gear, Gorski turned around and glanced out over the emerald waters of the Caribbean Sea. Gorski stood firmly on an oil platform approximately one hundred miles off the island of Trinidad. All of it was nothing more than a cover, he mused. A smoke screen.

A story concocted by the U.S. Navy, in which the obsolete oil platform had experienced a technical malfunction on its way back to the scrapyard. But in reality, the *Valant* had been stopped precisely in its current location to conceal something discovered in the waters beneath it. Something astonishing. Something that could have been ripped straight from the pages of a conspiracy handbook.

But there was no conspiracy.

This time, it was real. No painted stories or embellished eyewitness accounts. In an ironic twist, it was much simpler than that. The first verifiable extraterrestrial craft ever to be found on Earth. Underwater and buried hundreds of feet beneath the coral.

That was why Gorski and the team were there. Which now included his new group of soft and inexperienced divers. There was however, one exception.

Gorski glanced back from the rising sun, down to the

large face of his wristwatch. They had to hurry. They had precious little time to find out just what they were dealing with. Before anyone else did.

***

Two stories above Gorski, Will Borger sat in a ratty old chair, staring at an even older CRT-style computer monitor. The quarters module of the aged oil rig left a lot to be desired, both in terms of comfort and technology. But it was good enough. At least for this mission.

Borger's large, overweight frame remained motionless as his eyes darted to a second monitor with a live feed of the dive team below him. They were the engineers from the naval research ship *Pathfinder*, now anchored less than a thousand meters from the edge of the giant rig.

What they were doing had to be done quietly. With the least amount of resources possible. Not because of a lack of funding—Admiral Langford and Secretary of Defense Miller were making sure of that. It was to avoid attention. They couldn't risk being noticed. By anyone. The official explanation for the oil rig and the *Pathfinder* ship was thin but just enough to keep the operation quiet and away from the attention of any other U.S. government entities. And from the rest of the world.

Borger's tired eyes returned to the first monitor, and back to one of the recordings the team had made beneath the surface. Detailed images capturing large sections of the alien ship's dark gray hull; smooth and unblemished.

So far they had only traced a small portion of the structure through the maze of coral and vegetation. Two things had immediately become obvious, given its position and orientation. The first was that the ship was *big*. The second was that it hadn't crashed. It was buried. Intentionally.

Borger crossed both arms over his large stomach, which rested beneath a loose-fitting blue and green Hawaiian shirt.

His steely eyes stared at the visible portion of the hull in the underwater video.

Dozens of questions raced through his mind. Questions that couldn't be answered. Not yet.

Borger twisted slightly in the chair, causing it to squeak. The room around him remained silent, much of its faded interior paint now peeling and giving way to dozens of small patches of rust. However, the one thing Borger was extremely thankful for was the air conditioner. Although on its last leg, it was still pumping out enough cool air to keep his perspiration to a minimum.

He leaned forward and began typing on the keyboard, zooming in on the video and playing the last part of it back. Steve Caesare, one of the divers, could be seen touching the alien ship's hull, brushing his hand firmly against it. Each time he did so, a green glow appeared and traced his motion before fading again. None of them, including Borger, had ever seen anything like it. The effect was so strange that every time Borger watched it, the same thought ran through his mind: *What the hell was that?*

2

Half a mile away, aboard the *Pathfinder*, Neely Lawton had a similar thought. As a systems biologist, Neely was staring at her own monitor, observing something very different taking place. She was far more interested in the plants and vegetation surrounding the alien craft than the ship itself. Or more precisely, the genetic behavior of those plants.

She breathed in, barely moving, watching the image on her screen with fascination. A small dark-green tube from a sea whip lay on a flat glass Petri plate, positioned beneath a large Euromex biological microscope. Its powerful lens focused in on the severed end of the fibrous tube.

In silent amazement, Neely watched as the damaged cellulose fibers moved like tiny searching fingers. Then very slowly, and one by one, the microscopic fingers found each other and began rebuilding, weaving themselves back together. At a speed that was simply stunning.

It was only the second time she had ever seen it. The first time happened with a different plant, pulled from the jungles of Guyana. A plant that was very different. But their structures, or more specifically their DNA, were very similar. Both plants possessed the same incredible healing properties she was now witnessing.

The testing of the plant's genetic behavior was easy to replicate. And like the first sample, this one's behavior also mimicked one of the smallest and most sinister living organisms known to man: the human cancer cell.

Yet, unlike a cancer cell, these plant cells were not dedicated to the growth of a deadly tumor. The reconstruction witnessed here applied to all parts of the plant's biological structure. And it worked just as fast.

Another difference was that cancer cells were the result

of a more natural biologic breakdown caused by damage to DNA base pairs of a cell's genes. The plant's cells, on the other hand, had mutated as the result of a compound from the alien ship. A catalyst they had yet to fully identify, let alone understand.

Neely bit her lip, keeping her eyes on the monitor. From a scientific standpoint, the process she was witnessing was…almost magical. Far beyond anything she ever expected to see in her lifetime.

But there was no denying it now. Test after test showed the same behavior: *a holy grail* of modern biology. The rapid-growth behavior of a cancer cell, without the horrific repercussions.

Yet as quickly as Neely Lawton's excitement grew, a worry was also building.

Yes, the plant cells had a very similar DNA sequence to cancer, with none of the side effects. At least none she could detect. But the strain had yet to be studied in a larger, more complex environment.

Neely relaxed, then took a deep breath and stood up. The small room had become uncomfortably quiet since the rest of her research team was abruptly reassigned to another ship.

It was all part of the ruse.

She faced another table with neatly organized testing equipment, including a small matrixed tray with thirty-six shallow Petri dishes, all containing a small amount of pink liquid.

In each, a small sample of the bacterium had been injected into a common microbiological nutrient broth. And just as it had done previously aboard the *Pathfinder's* sister ship *Bowditch*, the bacteria began to replicate. Rapidly.

She reached down and pressed a button on her keyboard, causing the powerful electronic microscope to zoom out slightly. The culture she had been watching was already growing too large to fit within the dish. Splitting, and then in just thirty minutes, splitting again.

By tomorrow, the new cells would take over the broth and consume the entirety of the medium, exhausting its food supply.

As Neely continued staring down at the metal table, the same nagging question surfaced again: *What was the catch?*

Every breakthrough came with a cost. Nothing was free in this world, especially in the field of science. Each discovery, no matter how small or how profound, came with its own set of limitations. Its own set of complications, and more specifically, its own *rules*.

Her overarching question was simple. What was the bad news?

She folded her arms and frowned. Pushing the thought away, she then glanced up through the front glass door of the short laboratory refrigerator where several stacks of test tubes were held firmly in place inside. There, more of the bacteria were divided into small sample groups and held at near-freezing temperatures.

They had nearly lost it all—if not for the last remaining trace of extracted DNA, retrieved by a single man in one of the greatest acts of courage she had ever seen.

3

The man's name was John Clay.

Considered attractive by most measures, and above average in height and build, Clay sat quietly on the edge of the large seawater tank in Puerto Rico. He wore a slight frown on his face, his eyes closed. Above him, the sky was filled with muted gray clouds.

"Are you okay?"

He nodded and opened his eyes, peering into the face of Alison Shaw, who sat near him. Both had their legs dangling into the cool water of the research center's giant tank.

"Can I help?"

"I'm okay," he responded quietly. With some effort, he pushed himself up straighter and grimaced at the pain. His body was badly battered, deep purple bruises covering much of his chest and arms. The exposed areas of his legs didn't look much better.

Alison touched his arm gently. "Are you sure you're ready for this?"

"I don't know that I'm sure of anything at the moment."

She smiled. "You can be sure about me."

Through the lacerations on his face, his lips parted to reveal a warm smile. His tanned jawline remained lean and strong. "That, I know."

His eyes stared back at her with deep affection before finally returning to the water. Several feet away, two dolphins waited, their heads bobbing out of the water excitedly.

It had been almost a month since Clay had found himself literally moments away from death. Saved only by his wits and a monumental stroke of luck.

He had only recently been released from the hospital in Honolulu and traveled back to Alison's research center in Puerto Rico.

It was her idea.

Alison shared with him what had happened with a young girl named Sofia, who was suffering from leukemia. It might have been easy to dismiss the event if it had not also happened with Juan's younger sister. *And* if Clay and Alison hadn't known what was really behind the miracles. Which was their discovery near Trinidad.

Now Clay sat on the concrete edge of the tank with Dirk and Sally waiting.

You come now.

The translation emanated from a computerized vest worn by Alison.

Clay grinned and replied, "Easy, Dirk. I'm feeling rather old at the moment."

Dirk opened his mouth and wiggled his head, and the vest responded with a sound Alison knew to be laughter.

Sitting beside him, her eyes narrowed momentarily as she wondered if Dirk had just gotten John's joke.

She let the thought go when Clay groaned and moved himself forward. He felt silly with the floatation belt wrapped around him but the less he had to move to keep afloat, the better. And under the circumstances, Clay decided pride was the least of his worries.

With gritted teeth, he eased himself into the water and immediately bobbed back up to shoulder level. His arms gently waved back and forth, providing just enough motion to keep his body upright.

Alison slipped in behind him and floated close by. Her eyes filled with empathy. Clay was not one to complain. Not surprising giving his previous life in the Navy, but it pained her heart to see him in so much agony—a suffering she could do so little about. Except for getting him here and into this water, along with whatever miraculous properties it contained.

11

It did help. Just the sensation of being back in the water helped Clay relax, allowing his face to soften as he floated effortlessly on his back.

Dirk's head abruptly rose from the water beside him. After staring at John, he spoke, and Alison rushed to get her earbuds in for the translation.

She chuckled. "He's worried about you. When humans don't move in the water, it's not a good sign."

Clay laughed. "Tell him, this time I'm not trapped underwater inside a ship."

Alison slipped her facemask over the top of her head and spoke back to Dirk through the mask's microphone. She then shook her head. "IMIS can't translate *trapped*."

"That's all right." Clay rose back up to a vertical position. "It just feels good to be back in the water again."

"As opposed to a hospital bed?"

"Exactly."

Alison reached out to pet the top of Sally's head. "How are you, Sally?"

Me good. How you Alison?

"Better."

We miss.

Alison cocked her head. Sally hadn't used that phrase before. It was a new translation. "I missed you too."

You home now. We talk.

"Yes, we can talk more."

Learn.

Alison glanced at Clay, who was listening to her muffled voice. "What would you like to learn, Sally?"

We learn people. After a pause, Sally finished the sentence. *You learn us.*

"We'd like that."

Clay turned to Dirk who was still staring curiously at him. With a wince, he raised a hand and patted Dirk's leathery gray head. "I'm fine, Dirk. I promise."

Sally was still attentively watching Alison, seeming to smile. There was something in Sally's face, in her mouth, that Alison was able to recognize. She wasn't sure what it was—perhaps a slight change in the curvature of Sally's mouth, or maybe just a *feeling*, but she could tell. Sally was smiling at her.

How you...

There was a pause in the translation—a sign that Lee Kenwood had explained as a conflict. A moment where the IMIS system was unsure of the right word given the context. When it made its decision, the word finally sounded through her earbuds.

...love?

Alison was taken aback by the question. *How do we love?* She couldn't help but glance over at Clay, floating quietly. *Did she love Clay? Yes, she did.*

She had just spent a month with him at the hospital. And he amazed her now even more than before. His injuries were extensive, but he barely complained. Instead, he was driven more by a feeling of gratefulness than anything else. Nor would he tell her everything that happened to him in China. He refused to burden her with it. With the visual images of what he must have endured. What he did reveal to her, however, was that at a certain point he was convinced that he wouldn't be coming back. And what he said then brought Alison to tears. In his darkest moments, it was thinking of her that got him through it.

Just thinking of his story caused tears to begin welling up again in her eyes. Alison quickly shook her head and focused more intently on Sally who was still waiting for an answer. There was something about the way she asked the question that left Alison doubtful of the translation. She didn't think those feelings were what Sally meant by love.

"How you love?" Alison repeated to herself. "How you...love." Love could be used in so many ways. In this case, it wasn't a noun. It sounded like Sally was using it as a verb.

Alison looked again to Clay who was looking at her

curiously. He hadn't heard the translation.

Sally repeated the question. *How you love?*

Alison opened her mouth but closed it again. Finally, she shook her head. "I...don't understand."

How love Alison? How people love?

It took Alison a full minute to eventually get it. To finally understand what Sally meant. It wasn't until she turned the question around and considered what were the most common, and perhaps most primal, questions humans asked when discovering a new species. What Sally was asking was not how humans actually love one another, but rather how humans *reproduce*.

Clay now peered at her more intently. A nervous expression crept across Alison's face inside her mask.

Under the circumstances, she wasn't about to touch Sally's question with a ten-foot pole.

4

DeeAnn Draper stood silently beneath the large netted ceiling of the habitat. Her hands on her hips, she watched as Dulce studied the object in her human-like hands. It was an old Rubik's cube, and the young gorilla was absolutely fascinated by it.

Of course, DeeAnn held no expectation of her solving the puzzle. Although from an educational standpoint, it helped Dulce better understand the concepts of three dimensions and patterns while improving her fine motor skills. Pattern recognition was a key element in gauging intelligence and overall cognitive ability. But what interested DeeAnn even more, was the small capuchin's interest in the cube.

Sitting on a large rock next to Dulce, the more reserved monkey Dexter was also studying the toy intently. When Dulce would periodically turn one side of the cube, Dexter promptly cocked his head and studied the bottom of it. It reaffirmed her belief in how intelligent the older creature really was.

DeeAnn's thoughts drifted momentarily to her old friend Luke Greenwood, the man who had discovered Dexter and the first to suspect just how special the capuchin was. A discovery that ultimately cost Greenwood his life and very nearly DeeAnn's.

But Greenwood's instincts had proved correct. So far, every test DeeAnn had administered clearly substantiated his hunch. For a capuchin, Dexter's intelligence was literally off the charts.

DeeAnn's phone suddenly chimed, and she reached down to retrieve it from her pocket. It was a message she'd been expecting. She looked back at the two primates.

"Dulce, I will be back soon. Okay?"

The young gorilla looked away from the cube and blinked happily at DeeAnn with her soft hazel eyes.

Okay.

DeeAnn smiled and looked at Dexter, who had not taken his eyes off the cube. She then glanced around the habitat, noting the dozens of high-resolution cameras surrounding them. It was peculiar. Using a wireless connection to the IMIS computer system, the vest translated everything Dulce said. At least to her.

What it wasn't translating was anything Dulce said to Dexter. Even when they were clearly communicating with one another. One of DeeAnn's former colleagues had published the first examples of instinctive gesturing between primates, and DeeAnn continued to witness it now firsthand. But the IMIS system, even as powerful as it was, was not picking up any of it.

It was *very* peculiar.

Something she would have to bring up with Lee again. When he was ready.

She let herself out through the wide glass door before reaching down and turning off the power to the vest. She had something more important to talk to Lee about right now. They all did.

Lee Kenwood looked up as Alison and Clay entered the computer lab. The large metal door swung closed behind them with a loud click, and Lee instinctively rose from his chair to get Clay a seat.

Clay crossed the room on his crutches and smiled. "Thank you, Lee. I think I'll stand for a bit."

Lee nodded and looked up to see the door open a second time, with DeeAnn stepping quietly inside. He looked back to Alison and Clay.

"What's up?"

The lab was quiet, eerily so. In the absence of their

colleagues Juan Diaz and Chris Ramirez, the entire research center didn't feel quite right. It felt...empty.

Alison smiled as she approached. "What are you working on?"

Lee turned back to his monitor with a solemn expression. "Uh, just some coding. Trying to improve the pattern recognition between multiple—" He suddenly stopped himself and shrugged. "Nothing important."

Alison put a gentle hand on his arm. "You okay?"

"Yeah. Just...kind of having a hard time with it all."

"We all are," DeeAnn replied softly.

"So, what's going on?"

"Lee," Alison said, "we need to talk to you."

"About what?"

"About Juan and Chris. About what's been happening."

Lee glanced at each of them. "What do you mean?"

"I think you know what I mean."

"Uh…"

"Lee, you've been friends with Juan and Chris for a while. So I'm sure they've told you some things, not to mention what you've already witnessed firsthand. I'm betting you know quite a lot."

Lee displayed a subtle but nervous grin. He eventually turned his attention to Clay, who was watching him intently. "Well, I know *some* things."

Clay took a deep breath. "Have a seat, Lee."

"Okay." He reached back for the arm of his chair and lowered himself down.

"Tell us what you know."

"Well, I saw what happened with Sofia. And what happened with us. Like my ribs. And how fast they healed. Chris did tell me about the plants. The ones in South America and then the ones you found in the ocean." He paused. "And...I've also been reading through IMIS's translation logs."

Clay nodded. "Then I'm guessing you know even more about what we found in Guyana."

"Some."

"That's what Juan was killed over," Clay said.

"Yeah…I know that too."

"And then we found something related. Near Trinidad."

"Where all the plants and dolphins are."

"Correct." Clay glanced at Alison before continuing. "Lee, what we're about to tell you is highly secret. It cannot be repeated to anyone. Ever."

"Including your wife," Alison added.

"Okaaay."

"It's a ship, Lee. It's an alien ship."

Lee's eyes instantly widened. "What?!"

"A spaceship, hidden beneath the coral. And what we found in Guyana *came from that ship*."

"What was it?"

Clay stopped and took a step back, leaning against the edge of a large metal table. "Embryos. Millions of embryos. In perfect hibernation. Buried inside a mountain."

"No way!"

Clay grinned. "We're pretty sure those embryos were transported on the ship we found. Brought here and intentionally hidden."

Lee blinked in fascination. "When?"

"We're not sure," Alison answered. "But we know it was a long, long time ago."

Lee sat in stunned silence. He continued staring at them, trying to grasp the meaning behind all of what they just said. His reaction felt strange. After all the years of speculation, of movies and stories about aliens, now for it to actually be real, felt…odd.

"So…what do you need from me?"

Clay rested his weight onto one of the crutches. "We need you because we don't think the place we found in Guyana is the only one."

"You think there's more?!"

Clay nodded. "One more. Hidden somewhere in Africa."

The younger Lee looked back and forth between them again. "How do you know that?"

"We're theorizing," DeeAnn answered. "The place we found in Guyana was hidden inside solid rock. But everything, even rock, eventually erodes. It eroded there. Enough to let some of what was inside trickle out and seep into the water. Which is how it reached the plants. We think it's what caused the changes in Dexter too."

"The monkey."

"Yes. He's old, Lee. Very old. Much older than he's supposed to be. And he's smarter than any primate I've ever seen before. You've witnessed some of the tests."

Lee turned and looked at his monitor at the live video feed from the habitat downstairs. "I didn't realize…" He let his voice trail off before clearing his throat. "So, what does this all mean?"

"It means there might be more of what changed him still out there. And if there is, we have to find it, before someone else does."

"It extends your age?"

"It's more than that," Alison said. "It accelerates healing and slows aging to almost nothing. In fact, it might even reverse it."

"We saw it happen," Clay nodded. "Onboard the *Bowditch*, while you and Chris were in sickbay. But the ship was attacked and the Chinese destroyed whatever was still left in Guyana. They were not about to let anyone else have it."

Lee looked intently at DeeAnn. "And that's what you and Juan went back for."

"Yes."

Lee fell silent for several minutes. His eyes grew somber as his brain worked to piece things together. When he finally looked up again, a glint of determination could be seen in his tired eyes. "So, if there's another location out there, we have to find it before the Chinese."

"Bingo."

"Do we know where it is?"

To that, Clay turned to DeeAnn.

"No," she said. "Not really. The reason we think there's a second site is because of our own genetics." She paused, then took a deep breath. "We think what we found in Guyana changed Dexter's DNA. We think the same thing may have happened to the dolphins and their DNA based on the plants we found underwater. And we think it may have happened with humans too."

Lee's eyes grew wide again. "You think it influenced *human* DNA?"

"It's possible. A discovery by a research group recently found very similar brain types existing between just a few different species on Earth. Brains that not only evolved to have very similar designs and functions but share common genes that affect brain development. So similar, in fact, that the chances of this happening independently through evolution is almost nil. Dolphins, humans, and primates all have practically identical looking brain designs. What differences there are tend to be rather slight. Things that affect size and weight. The discovery by that team was called the Trio Brain theory."

Lee was still incredulous. "Wait. If whatever it was you found is responsible for Dexter's DNA, and Sally and Dirk's, you think it could be responsible for ours too?"

"Correct. Probably a long time ago, and much earlier on our evolutionary path. And probably close to where humans first originated. In Africa."

"Wow," Lee said, shaking his head. "Just wow! If you're right, then that's huge!"

Clay continued. "And there's more. But before we go any further, you need to decide on your level of participation."

Lee leaned forward in his chair. "I'm in. I'm definitely in."

"It's not that easy, Lee. Alison, DeeAnn, and I are now part of a very small team that knows. Some, like you, now have pieces of what we've found so far, but not everything."

Alison nodded. "No one knows what is happening here, Lee. Or how big this is. Not the public, not even the military beyond our core team."

"And no one can find out," Clay finished.

Lee's expression abruptly changed. "Wait a minute. You've already told me a lot. At what point do I know too much?"

"We want you, Lee. We want you and your skills on the team."

"And what if I say no?"

Clay shrugged. "We're not going to make you disappear if that's what you're asking. The government has far more sophisticated ways of keeping people quiet. Better ways to deal with *loose ends*."

A sudden look of worry passed over Lee's face before Alison shook her head at Clay with mock displeasure. "Stop that."

Clay laughed.

"Oh my God," Lee exhaled. "I thought you were serious."

DeeAnn's eyes were also wide. "So did I."

Clay's laugh faded, and he grew serious again. "I'd be lying if I said this wasn't dangerous. The Chinese killed a lot of people, including Juan, and destroyed an entire mountain to try to hide it. Which should give you an indication of just how far people are willing to go for this."

"How many people are on this team?"

"Myself, Ali, DeeAnn, Steve Caesare, and Will Borger. Plus, Admiral Langford and Secretary of Defense Miller. A few others have some limited involvement, but they only know what they have to."

Lee sat quietly, thinking.

"This is big, Lee," Alison said softly. "Really big. Some of the biggest questions we've ever had, not just as a civilization but as a species, might just get answered."

DeeAnn shrugged. "Or they might not."

"True."

"Before you say yes," Clay added, "there are a few things you need to understand. There are caveats. Steps that will need to be taken to ensure no one finds out what we're really after. And I mean *no one*."

"What kind of caveats?"

"No contact with family or friends. At least for a while. We'd have to make an exception for your wife under strict guidance, but you'd be away from her for at least a few months. Maybe more. You would have to tell everyone else that you were off the grid, on a remote project."

Lee frowned.

"Phones would be restricted to only a few numbers, and encrypted." Clay paused and took a deep breath. The next part was something he hadn't spoken to the others about yet, not even Ali. But Langford and Miller were adamant.

"There's something else too," he said, his gaze turning to Alison. "And it's something none of you are going to like...at all."

5

Alison's expression changed at once, and she looked expectantly at Clay. As did the others.

He rose again and propped one arm under a crutch for support, keeping most of his weight off his left leg. There was no easy way to say it, so he spit the acronym out quickly.

"IMIS."

The three looked at each other with confusion before Lee responded. "IMIS?"

"Yes."

"That's the caveat?"

Clay nodded.

"I don't—" Lee stopped when he noticed the look of understanding on Alison's face. It was combined with fear stemming from years of paranoia over what the government might decide to do.

"No," she said, slowly shaking her head.

"Wait," Lee said to Clay. "You mean…"

"Your computer system has done something that no other has," Clay said grimly. "It has data that can now point back to that mountain and what may lie in Africa." He was still looking at Alison. "And that data needs to be protected."

Alison instantly hardened. "They're not taking it, John! They're not taking IMIS. If they do, it's going to be over my dead—"

"Easy, Ali," he said, interrupting her. "Langford and Miller are right on this, but that's not what they're saying. If the rest of the government can't know what we're up to, then they certainly can't have access to IMIS. No one can. But here, in this research center, it's not safe. It can't be protected here."

"So what do we do?"

Even on his crutches, Clay's blue eyes were strong and determined. "We move it."

"Move it? Where?"

"Borger is working on that. But that's not the part you're not going to like." He paused again while the others stared at him impatiently. "It's not just the data…it's also the *work*."

DeeAnn was the first to understand. And while Alison and Lee were still pondering his words, she spoke up with a smirk. "You mean our achievements."

"That's right."

Alison looked back and forth, confused. "What?"

"He means what we've done. Our achievements…and our press releases."

They still weren't following.

DeeAnn stared at them wryly. "Don't you see? They want us to *retract* everything."

They all turned to Clay, dumbstruck.

"Is that true?"

Clay had been waiting to break it to Alison at the right time. And this particular moment was clearly not it. He nodded apologetically. "Yes."

"Retract? Do you have any idea what you're saying?" Alison asked. "A retraction is like saying we're incompetent. *To the entire world.*"

Clay's voice became low. "I know."

"I don't think you do," she said, crossing her arms. "And I'm not going to do it."

He frowned. "They're going to come for IMIS, Ali. Sooner or later, someone is going to connect the dots. When they find out what IMIS is and what it can do, and what's in the data, they will descend on this place with a vengeance and a single goal."

"Not if it isn't here," offered Lee.

Clay turned to him. "We'll move it, but ultimately it won't matter where it is, Lee. Even if we hide it, once someone realizes this, they'll find it. All secrets eventually come out, and this one leads directly to IMIS."

"No," Alison said. "There's got to be another way."

But DeeAnn shook her head, thoughtfully. "No. The world already knows what IMIS can do. At least partly. The best way to avoid creating a path to IMIS…is to make people think it never worked in the first place."

"No," Alison argued. "We can do it without destroying our careers! We can do something else. We can announce that IMIS is damaged, irreparably. Or the data was lost. Or—"

"Computers can be repaired," Lee mumbled. "And data can be recreated."

"Then think of a way it can't!"

He shook his head. "There isn't a way, Ali. Even if we thought of a cover, and hid the system away, we still need a connection to it. And all connections are traceable, eventually. And if we broke that, we wouldn't be able to communicate with it either. Hiding IMIS isn't as easy as it sounds."

"The only way," DeeAnn said, "is to convince everyone that it doesn't work."

"But too many people have already seen it work!"

"I don't think that's what DeeAnn means," Lee said quietly. "We'd have to claim the translations themselves were faulty. That the results themselves were wrong. That's the only way the scientific community would dismiss it. The only way the *world* would dismiss it."

This time, Alison didn't reply. She simply stood, facing them in utter astonishment. Her sudden anger with Clay was already fading to helplessness. Her mind tried desperately to find a way that he was wrong, but she couldn't. She knew as well as they did how critical IMIS was to all of this.

It was the catalyst that had changed everything. That was *still* changing everything.

But she just couldn't do it. She couldn't throw it away.

Every bit of recognition she'd fought so hard for. Every bit of acceptance by those who had criticized her efforts and claimed it could never be done. The same people who mocked her in their own papers. She had proven them all wrong! And now she was faced with the prospect of letting them all think they were right. While simultaneously becoming a laughing stock of the entire scientific community. The very idea was simply horrifying, and it left her utterly speechless, standing before Clay and the others.

That kind of retraction would take more humility than she could even imagine.

All to protect a secret, resting on the bottom of the ocean.

6

"What do you think it is?" Caesare asked, peering intently at the screen.

Borger slowly shook his head from side to side. "I have no idea."

Together they watched the video footage again with Caesare in the foreground, next to Lightfoot, one of Captain Emerson's engineers. The two men floated almost motionlessly underwater, facing the large, smooth gray wall. In the video, Caesare continued to probe the wall's surface with his black diving glove, watching the illumination appear and linger for a moment before fading away once again. He examined the glove through his mask and rubbed his fingers together. He then turned and presented his glove to the camera. After staring into the lens for several long seconds, Caesare turned back around with an afterthought and silently withdrew a diving knife from the black sheath strapped to his calf.

The large blade glistened only briefly before Caesare held it up close to the ship. Then something happened. The blade unexpectedly sprang from his fingers and stuck itself to the wall in front of him. It was there that the video froze.

Borger turned to face Caesare. "What kind of knife is that?"

"Stainless steel."

"I thought stainless steel wasn't magnetic?"

"Most knives are. Not enough nickel in them."

"Hmm," Borger mused. "Well, I guess the thing is magnetic then. But that glow—it doesn't appear to be any kind of bioluminescence. Or film."

Caesare nodded his head in agreement. "Nothing came off on the glove."

"And we still haven't found any marks on the thing."

"None."

"Strange," Borger muttered, instinctively reaching for a sip of Jolt cola only to find a bare desk top. Disappointed, he reached instead for the keyboard and began typing. "Well, this is what we have so far."

The frame quickly zoomed out and into place among dozens of others. Combined, they presented a picture similar to a jigsaw puzzle, with most of the pieces still missing. But even without the rest, the parts they had were already intimating at the ship's overall size and shape.

"The damn thing is big."

"Very," Borger agreed, nodding. He leaned back, staring at the curvature of the alien hull. It wasn't as long and straight as they had originally thought. Instead, the edges were a bit rounded. Somewhat like a softly shaped rectangle. And even though most of it hadn't been thoroughly mapped yet due to all the underwater vegetation, the thing was undeniably *huge*.

Caesare ran a hand through his black damp hair, and then dropped it to cover his mouth, pondering. "How could it not be damaged at all?"

"Exactly. Thousands of years underwater takes a toll on everything. Especially in warm water. Cold preserves things better."

"Like the *Titanic*."

"Exactly. And we saw what kind of shape *it* was in just seventy years later. But this thing, even in warm water, doesn't look affected at all."

"Well, it's clear we have a lot more mapping to do."

Borger nodded again. "Which brings up another strange thing."

"No doors."

"No anything," Borger quipped. So far, every piece of the hull had been found to be as smooth and unblemished as the next. They hadn't found any edges anywhere. Even grooves. Nothing to indicate a door or the slightest separation.

Borger turned and looked up at Caesare. "There's something else. Another thing I've been thinking about that doesn't make any sense."

Caesare frowned. "You mean *other* than a glowing alien, magnetic ship…that looks like a giant block?"

He grinned. "Yeah. But this is more of a logical contradiction."

"Hit me."

Borger took a breath and tilted his head. "So, we talked before about efficiency and the limitations of making such a long distance trip through space."

"That's right. The reason why this was likely a one-way trip."

"Precisely. The amount of energy needed to travel fast enough becomes prohibitive at a certain speed or vehicle size."

"And that's the strange part?"

"More or less. See, if efficiency is everything, which it is in space travel, then why is the ship so *big*? The embryos we found hidden in Guyana would only have taken up a fraction of the ship's capacity. Oversizing it makes the whole propulsion issue very impractical."

Caesare nodded. "A one-way trip lets you get here faster, with less. But instead, they brought a big one."

"Not just big, a giant one. That's the contradiction. It just…doesn't make any sense."

"I'm inclined to agree." Caesare glanced away from the screen to his watch. "It's time for our call."

Borger nodded absently, eyes still fixed on the monitor's screen.

***

Upon seeing DeeAnn Draper's face appear on Borger's second monitor, Steve Caesare slid into the seat next to him. His muscular frame made the old chair look even more fragile than it was. With a loud squeak, he promptly leaned forward and smiled at DeeAnn through the computer camera.

"Hello, beautiful," he grinned with his trademark smile.

DeeAnn narrowed her eyes in response, with a trace of humor. "Hello, Grizzly Adams."

Caesare rubbed a hand over his long whiskers, some of which were already showing hints of gray.

"I hope you guys are at least taking showers," she chided.

"Well, some of us are." Caesare leaned back and motioned sarcastically toward Borger.

Will Borger glowered. "Not funny."

On the screen, an amused DeeAnn changed the subject. "How are things going with the ship?"

"We have the general dimensions but not much else yet. How about you?"

She sighed. "Well, we talked to Lee. Which turned out to include a big surprise for all us. I presume John has already told you."

"He has. I'm sorry about that. I think retracting is the last thing anyone wanted, even Admiral Langford."

DeeAnn nodded with a contemplative expression, and Caesare noted the background of her office behind her. She had decorated. After a moment, DeeAnn changed the subject again. "So, how are things going with Africa?"

Borger brought up a map on his primary screen. It was a richly colored, high-definition image of the entire African continent. "I've got everything downloaded, and the servers are ready. But searching an area this big, pixel by pixel, is going to take a while. To save time, we've started narrowing things down using some assumptions from Guyana."

"Such as?"

"High elevation, heavily obscured, and difficult to reach. We might also want to consider a similar latitude."

Caesare considered Borger's last point. "Actually, if they were going to store something for thousands of years, why wouldn't they have done it near one of the poles, like we did with the Seed Vault?"

"I think it's going to depend on the purpose. Very hot and very cold temperatures both introduce their own challenges. A higher elevation would also provide a cooler environment. But even if it is somewhere along the same latitude, it leaves a heck of a lot of land mass to search."

"Well, at least it's a start," DeeAnn sighed. "Actually, maybe I can help narrow it down a little more. After all, we're looking for something that could have affected the course of primate evolution, including Homo sapiens. Which means maybe we can find out *where* by determining *when*."

"And when would that be?" asked Caesare.

"That's the million-dollar question," she replied. "Nobody really knows…exactly. We only have guesses. The earliest fossils of recognizable Homo sapiens appeared about two hundred thousand years ago around the region known today as Ethiopia. But the *event* couldn't have taken place that long ago because our evolutionary paths still weren't that far away from the other primates. And as similar as primate and human brains are today in complexity, they are still *very* different in size. So we're probably looking at an event that happened long after the two species split, but one that still affected them both. So the real question probably isn't when did our genetic lineage split, but when did we stop being neighbors?"

Caesare and Borger both looked at each other and then back to DeeAnn on the screen. "And that would be…"

"About fifty thousand years ago. Maybe even twenty. Much closer to our present, evolutionarily speaking."

"And then what?"

DeeAnn shrugged. According to a group called the Genographic Project, our genetic and paleontological records suggest we moved out, beginning with the colonization of modern day Yemen. The migration then rippled out from there. So my guess is that whatever event might have occurred, it probably did so before that."

31

"So Ethiopia then."

"Maybe," DeeAnn answered hesitantly. "That's where some of the earliest remains have been found. Other remains have been discovered more recently, like the site near Johannesburg, but they were nonhuman."

"Okay. Anything else?"

"Not really. But I suggest we start our search in the higher elevations. Those locations will have the most in common with the Guyana site. How fast do you think your computer can sift through the data, Will?"

"Computers," Will corrected absently. "I've got a lot lined up, but when we did this before, the search algorithm was much simpler. We were looking for objects in a large area of ocean so it wasn't as hard to find things that stood out. It just took time. This time, it's different. Terrain is much more complicated. At best, I'm guessing we can process maybe a hundred square miles per hour. But we might get lucky. There were stone markers on the mountain in Guyana. If there are similar shapes in Africa, and if part of them are exposed, the servers might be able to pick that up."

"But if not?"

"Then we could be in for a long wait."

"Well, let's hope you two have better luck than I do," DeeAnn said.

"The problem," continued Borger, "is the testing."

"What do you mean?"

He looked to Caesare, then to DeeAnn, both visible on his monitor. "This is going to take a lot of tweaking. It's not just something that we flip on and wait for coordinates to be spit out. We're going to need to do some benchmarking, followed by verification on more complicated sections of the map."

"How long will that take?"

"I'm not sure. The good news is that there are a lot of companies doing some impressive things with visual imaging." A wry grin curled the corners of his mouth. "We just need to leverage some of their technology…without them knowing about it."

"Sounds right up your alley," Caesare smiled.

DeeAnn watched with amusement. "Okay, let me know when you're closer. I'm going to do a little research of my own."

***

After the video call had ended, DeeAnn stared at her screen, feeling a slight pang of guilt over something she had said. Or rather had *not* said. She hadn't exactly explained everything about the Trio Brain theory. Mostly because it wasn't relevant. Yet.

But even more than that, she was working to quell a small but growing nervousness of where this search might lead, and the terrible fear that it might somehow bring them to the last place on Earth she ever wanted to go.

7

Both Caesare and Borger were analyzing more of the video when a small window appeared, signaling another incoming call. The display indicated it was coming from the *Pathfinder* only a short distance away.

Borger accepted the call, and a window opened, framing the attractive face of Neely Lawton.

Caesare reacted with another award-winning smile, this one more genuine. "Good morning, Commander Lawton."

"Good morning," she answered. Her hair was pulled back neatly into a bun, highlighting the smooth contours of her face. She noticed Caesare's tussled wet hair. "I take it you've already been down this morning."

He grinned. "No rest even for us old guys."

She smiled. He was only in his forties. "Do you both have a few minutes? I need to talk to you about something."

"Sure, we're just going over footage. What's up?"

She frowned briefly. "This might be a little premature, but I'm beginning to worry."

"About what?"

"About the bacteria."

Both men's faces turned serious. "That doesn't sound good."

Neely blinked before continuing. "The DNA code that this bacterium is carrying was extracted from the plants found on top of the mountain. Similar to the DNA we've found here in the sea plants. But the bacteria seem to be acting differently from what I'm observing in the plants themselves."

"How so?" Caesare asked.

"As expected, the plants are repairing themselves at an

accelerated rate. And repairing parts of their biologic structure that they shouldn't normally be able to repair. But they're doing it more smoothly. As if by design. That's what was so astonishing when we saw it before. But the bacterium is different. These are replicating even faster. It's as if once the DNA was infused into the genes of the bacteria, something happened."

"I don't know if the Chinese changed something during their extraction process, even inadvertently. But if they did, it could explain the difference in cellular function. In fact, even if it wasn't something during extraction, just the transfer from one life form to another could be enough to trigger a modification. Or a mutation. Even a single base pair change could affect DNA behavior."

Caesare rubbed a finger against his chin. "That doesn't sound good."

"But wouldn't an acceleration be an *improvement?*" Borger asked.

"On the surface, yes. But the question is, at what cost? There's no free lunch in science. Or in genetics. Ultimately, everything is a tradeoff. Even if you can't measure it. What worries me most is if a modification occurred just moving this genetic code into a simple bacteria strain, what happens when that code is transferred into another environment? A much more *complex* environment."

Borger looked up from his chair as Caesare finished the thought. "More complex like an animal."

On the screen, Neely nodded. "Like a human." She let that sink in a moment before continuing. "Even if the behavior *didn't* change, even if it were exactly the same, going from something as simple as bacteria to a much more intricate genetic system would likely result in some unpredictability."

"Assuming it was even observable."

"Exactly."

Caesare remained still, thinking. "You're talking about Li Na, the Chinese girl."

"I am. She was injected with the DNA directly. And if we already see differences in a small sample, the effects could be magnified in her."

"If a modification took place."

"Correct."

Caesare was frowning, looking for a more obvious possibility. "Is there any chance what you're seeing in your sample is a fluke or some kind of anomaly?"

It was a question that Neely had pondered herself. She glanced away from the screen to the large number of Petri dishes nearby. She shook her head. "To be honest, I was hoping it was. But it's happening with all of them."

She continued staring at her samples. Her worry was escalating at the thought of what the bacteria might now be doing inside the young woman's system. It was still possible nothing would happen, even if some DNA *had* changed. Neely truly wished that was the case.

Because if her fears were correct, and given the results of what she'd already witnessed, young Li Na Wei could, in fact, be the equivalent of a genetic tinder box.

8

Both men remained silent for almost a full minute after their call with Neely ended. The implications were more than just worrisome. To make matters worse, no one knew where they could find Li Na Wei. Or whether she was even alive.

It was her father who had injected her with the bacteria, to save her. The last act of a father desperate to help his dying daughter. And he had. At least temporarily. Until a Chinese agent named Qin found her.

Now Li Na was gone, having escaped certain death from the hands of Qin. And if she *was* still alive, she was on the run.

"Well," sighed Borger, "I suppose this is as good a time as any to mention it."

Caesare stared at him, raising an eyebrow.

"They're still looking for her."

"Who is *they*?"

"The Chinese."

"You mean Qin?"

"No. I'm pretty sure Qin is dead. But their Ministry of State Security is still searching for her, using every piece of technology they have. They're the same group that found her before."

"You mean their hackers."

Borger nodded.

"How many?"

"As far as I can tell, the entire department."

Caesare grinned. "And how exactly do you know this?"

Borger folded his arms with a look of satisfaction. "I've been eavesdropping."

Eavesdropping was putting it mildly. The Chinese MSS-sponsored hackers were not a group to be trifled with. They were arguably the best in the world and part of one of the most ruthless organizations within the Chinese government. Anyone trying to worm their way into that group was either stupid or insane. Will Borger was neither. He was in a third and very small classification of potential intruders: specialized experts. The team China had amassed was extremely talented, but its members had one common flaw which not even they had considered. They were young. Each of them were born into the digital age, living and breathing technology since birth. But while some people considered that an asset, Borger knew better. Young hackers understood how the technology worked, but their knowledge would never match someone like Will Borger who was part of the technology's very *inception.* They would never understand the building blocks as thoroughly as he did. Nor the vulnerabilities of those building blocks.

And now Borger was hacking in for one reason and one reason only. *Retaliation.*

Caesare was all ears as he dropped himself into the chair next to Borger. "Okay. Spill it."

"They haven't given up," he replied, "which means they've probably figured out what happened to the vials of bacteria. That they were injected into Wei's daughter. Which is why I think Qin was killed."

Caesare savored the thought. He wished he could have been there to see the look on Qin's face when he realized John Clay had tricked him. A simple, but brilliant move that no doubt left the murderous Chinese agent in a moment of stunned disbelief. And if Qin was dumb enough to try to double-cross the wrong people on his end, Caesare had to agree that Qin was probably no longer alive.

"So what do they have?"

Borger rolled himself forward to the edge of the old tarnished metal desk, where he reached out and began typing. A window appeared, filled with unreadable—at least to Caesare—Chinese logographic characters. With another command, the Chinese text was promptly replaced with English. But the cryptic logs were still readable only to

Borger.

"These are system logs. Captured from several of their internal servers. Things like search strings, along with breaches of access into telephone and transportation systems. Including one system which is their own version of our FBI's facial tracking database. But China is way behind with their local infrastructure, so only the largest cities have enough cameras to yield anything helpful. Which means they are much more limited in trying to find Li Na in a country of a billion people. But they're trying."

"Any leads?"

"A lot. But it's truly a needle in a haystack. At least for now. However, their challenge isn't being able to identify the needle, it's finding the right haystack. Coverage is spotty, but if Li Na happens to walk through an area that is plugged in, they'll find her quickly."

Caesare peered at the screen of cryptic computer syntax. "Wonderful."

***

In a large nondescript, twelve-story building in Shanghai, a set of dark eyes were staring at another computer monitor. With strands of straight black hair hanging in front of his face, the Chinese hacker known as M0ngol was carefully studying a list of cell phone logs. His pale complexion was awash in the glow of his own monitor. Behind him, in hundreds of similar cubes, sat the rest of China's notorious group known as PLA Unit 61398. Or more specifically, *Advanced Persistent Threat 1*, the state-sanctioned hacking group identified in 2014 when a United States Federal grand jury returned an indictment for five of the group's officers.

After the allegation, the Chinese government quickly denied any existence of such an organization, only to acknowledge a year later that it had "multiple" cyber warfare personnel working within its military.

Personnel who were now trying desperately to locate the

teenage girl, Li Na Wei.

They had sifted through every piece of information they could find on the girl and each member of her family. Everything. Emails, phone calls, school records—any personal connection they could establish. Which meant every conversation they could find a record of, even handwritten correspondence.

Unfortunately, the girl's father, General Wei, had been exceedingly careful to destroy every shred of evidence he could on the whereabouts of his dying daughter. In the end, he even took his own life in an attempt to protect her. But eventually, M0ngol found her—at a remote hospital where she was being hidden.

But Li Na had escaped with the help of an American and was now either dead or on the run. The first possibility, he just didn't believe.

She was out there. He was sure of it. And so far, still hidden. She hadn't reached out to anyone that M0ngol and the others were monitoring. Nor had she returned to any familiar places in Beijing. Or withdrawn any money from the active accounts they had purposely left in place. Not a hint of a trace.

M0ngol was again at the cell phone logs, still working to identify unseen relationships among millions of calls. If he could establish enough connections, they could begin analyzing voices and keyword patterns. Anything that could suggest someone was in need of help. From there they would start whittling down leads to the most likely proximities.

It was a huge, drawn-out effort, but M0ngol forced himself to be patient. He was eager to redeem himself in the eyes of the MSS. After what had happened to Qin. He had to find the girl. Because in the end, it was either her…or him.

9

The People's Republic of China held many distinct titles. One, being the most populous nation on Earth. And another, being one of the greatest coal producers in the northern hemisphere. With production peaking at a staggering four billion metric tonnes per year, the country generated nearly seventy-five percent of its electrical energy needs from Earth's most abundant and dirtiest fuel source.

Yet, its mining industry, like many others, was now in a state of terminal decline. Once-great production areas of the country were systematically being turned into ghost towns. And it was ironic that what had once stood as one of the country's greatest strengths had now become a major weakness.

Beneath a field of stars, Li Na sat quietly in the train's last car, nestled into the corner and leaning against the freezing metal. She wore two shirts beneath a thick dark sweater and two pairs of pants now colored almost black from the coal.

The heavily loaded train rocked from side to side under the strain of its own weight, passing the switch point and causing the metal cars to screech briefly as they switched to a different track.

The swaying subsided, and the cars resumed sounding their rhythmic *clack-clack* as the train began to regain speed.

Li Na's eyes were low and dull, her arms wrapped around herself to keep warm. The large city of Chifeng passed by in eerie darkness, strangely silent considering the city's recent prominence as one of Inner Mongolia's central rail hubs. The government had used it primarily in transporting China's dwindling coal shipments from the mountains of Dornod to the hundreds of power plants spanning the country's northern territory.

It was the last place anyone would have thought to look for her. Stashed away in a train car and almost completely covered in black coal.

It was not intentional but she'd been there for almost two days now. It hadn't taken long for Li Na to realize how well the dark powder concealed her.

A sudden jolt of the car caused her large satchel to slide off, and she reached down to pull it back up and over her shoulder.

Her father hadn't just saved her. He also knew the government would be coming for her if she lived and had provided her with the means to escape. If she was lucky enough. Included in the satchel, among other things, was some emergency food, a small GPS unit, and several stacks of money.

She reached into the satchel again and withdrew a fourth item. Under the crescent moon, she could make out the faint picture of herself. By including a falsified passport, he had sent her a message that could not have been clearer: *get out of the country.*

She was now headed toward Shenyang. But first, she needed a place to stay. To hide until she could figure out how to make it to the coast. It was a place her father had once told her about and a place that most people would not believe, even with their own eyes.

It was the best plan she could think of. She was completely alone now and prayed they wouldn't find her. At least not until it was too late.

Li Na's thoughts suddenly drifted to the one person she most wished was still with her. Someone she barely knew but was the reason she was still alive. A man who had saved her from the clutches of agent Qin and allowed her to escape. A man who she was sure had lost his life in the process.

She could still see his face. With his dark hair and broad

shoulders, the American soldier pulling her through the damp tunnel, trying to escape Qin's men.

10

Surrounded by shelving units and computer hardware, John Clay eased himself into a chair in Lee's lab and moved closer to the screen. He motioned affirmatively to Lee who then accepted the incoming video call. Appearing immediately onscreen, Caesare and Borger's tired faces seemed to be further highlighted by a dirty, dusty wall behind them.

"Looks like you guys are enjoying your new digs," mused Clay.

"It's like the Hilton. Will and I are headed to the spa."

Next to him, Borger frowned with disappointment. "I'd settle for a vending machine."

"Don't mind him," Caesare chided. "That's just the caffeine withdrawal talking. Soon we'll have him on this delicious coffee." He raised a mug in front of the screen and took a sip. It was all he could do to keep from grimacing. "Okay, maybe it's not all that funny."

"Well at least you're both in good spirits," Clay offered.

"How could we not be? We're in paradise." Caesare's eyes turned to Lee's image on their screen. "Hey, kid. Welcome aboard."

"Thanks, Mr. Caesare."

"So, how you feeling, Clay?"

"Better. The water seems to be helping."

"You don't know the half of it. Wait until you're swimming around for a while out here."

Clay peered curiously at the screen. "What do you mean?"

Caesare touched his side. "No more pain."

"At all?"

"Nope. Whatever this water is absorbing from that alien ship is amazing."

Borger nodded solemnly. "Maybe too amazing."

"What do you mean?" Clay asked.

"Commander Lawton is worried that whatever's in those plants may be too good to be true. That there could be a caveat. A big one."

Clay shook his head. "Any other good news?"

Caesare grinned. "Yeah. As long as by *good* you mean troubling."

He nodded to Borger who cleared his voice. "It, uh, looks like our Chinese friends don't like to give up."

Clay's brow furrowed. "Meaning?"

"They're trying to find Li Na Wei. And this time, they're pulling out all the stops."

"How do you know?"

"Because I'm in one of their systems."

"And they don't know?"

"Not yet. When they found me last time, we were breaking into the same servers to get cell tower data. They then hacked my system but not before I tunneled back to them using their own packets to transfer a piece of my code. Which opens a secondary connection back to me with the same packet ID. Unless they're reading binary at the packet level—"

"Okay, okay. I believe you, Will," Clay interrupted.

Next to Clay, Lee whispered the word "wow" under his breath.

"The point is," Caesare said, "they want her. Bad. They must know what she's carrying."

Borger nodded. "They're looking everywhere. Electronically and visually. They're taking images of the entire area and doing a pixel search, just like I am."

"Can we find her first?"

"I doubt it. They have far more resources. Their urgency is another reason why they haven't noticed my code in their system yet. I'm only watching their results and communication. If I tried to get any real data, they'd see it."

Clay rubbed his chin. "I can't believe they haven't found

45

her yet. A teenage girl can only move so fast."

"It helps that their satellite technology is not quite up to our standards yet. But they're flying dozens of aircraft over the area, taking ultra-high-resolution pictures."

"How is she eluding that?"

"Probably some brains and a hell of a lot of luck," Caesare said.

"The problem is," Borger added, "luck doesn't last."

"No, it doesn't." After a quiet moment, Clay leaned back in his chair, thinking. "There is one more possibility."

"She's not alive."

"Correct."

"But they would have found her body by now."

"Probably so," Clay nodded. "She's more likely to be alive. And from what I saw, she may be scared but she's also very bright. And she knows that they're looking for her." Clay suddenly paused, remembering what she had with her: the metal case of vials and a leather bag she carried on her back. Both had been left by her father. Clay was starting to wonder what else the General had left his daughter.

"There's something else," Caesare said, interrupting. "Commander Lawton isn't just afraid of what this bacterium can do. She's afraid of what it may have already done. The samples you brought back are acting differently, and if any of that has been passed on to the girl, there may be side effects."

"What kind of side effects?"

"She doesn't know yet. But one thing she made very clear is that genetic mutations can be very touchy things."

Clay returned to his previous thought. "If she has enough resources, where would she go?"

Caesare thought about the question. "I'd get the hell out of Dodge. Staying in China means it's probably just a matter of time before they find her."

"So she heads east."

"I would. Unless she wants to freeze to death. East is

also the shortest way out of the country."

Clay's face showed a small ray of hope at the thought. "She *is* smart."

They all reflected for a long moment until Caesare broke the silence.

"So…how did things go with Alison?"

11

Alison.

"Yes, Sally."

You not happy.

Alison folded her arms and forced a smile through the wall of glass to where Sally was floating on the other side.

No, she wasn't happy. In fact, she was angry. Even furious. Furious at the very idea of her having to retract it all. Everything they'd done. Achievements that had literally changed the world. Forever.

Frustrated because retracting their work was the equivalent of telling thousands of peers that they were wrong. Really wrong.

That all the results of the studies were ruined by their own ignorance. And not only was their scientific reputation severely tarnished, they ran the risk of being ignored and branded a laughing stock for the rest of their career. It was the ultimate insult, and to make matters worse, Alison would have to do it herself. Ironically, in science, if one's assertions had been disproven by someone else, such as a peer, it would have been less shameful. But when you announced it yourself, it was an acknowledgment of just how incompetent you really were.

Of course, none of it was true. IMIS worked, and it worked beautifully. Too beautifully. The problem, literally, was the unforeseen extent of their success. And while Alison wanted to blame both Admiral Langford and Secretary Miller, she couldn't. Nor could she blame Clay. They all knew the truth behind the danger IMIS now posed both to the team and itself.

There had to be another way.

Even Lee was surprised. He too admitted that there was

something in their computer code, in the algorithms, that he didn't fully understand. Something that allowed the giant machine's vast array of silicon and copper to achieve more than they ever expected. Whether it was the hardware or software, or the combination, he wasn't sure. But what he did know, and what they all understood, was that the system could be replicated. The exact hardware could be reassembled, the software studied, and the data copied. IMIS could be reverse engineered until all of its secrets were eventually revealed.

They would have to do more than just make it vanish. They'd have to make the world forget it. And a retraction would be the first and most painful step.

"No, Sally," she finally replied. "I'm not happy."

What wrong Alison?

"It's hard to explain." She took a deep breath. "We can talk again, but I don't know if it's safe anymore for people to know. At least not yet."

Alison paused, expecting a reply, but Sally remained silent. She continued.

"Sally, how many dolphins are there?"

Sally's response was short.

Thousand.

A loud beep sounded, signifying a bad translation, and IMIS changed the word.

More thousand.

Another beep sounded and one more adjustment was made.

Thousands.

Alison nodded. The occasional corrections always reminded her that IMIS was still learning.

"Do dolphins fight?"

Yes, she answered. *But no like peoples.*

"What do they fight for?"

Sally's response was not immediate. As if she paused to consider the question. *Love.*

"You fight for love?"

Yes. Another pause. *Dirk fight me.* A moment later the sentence was revised. *Dirk fight for me.*

Alison smiled warmly. "I guess humans and dolphins have that in common." *Actually,* she thought, *all life had it in common.*

"How do you learn, Sally?"

From heads.

"You mean your elders."

Yes. Many heads. Many teaches.

Alison grinned. "So have we." Again she paused, considering other species. How other animals taught each other. And when they couldn't, how nature stepped in to fill the void, through environment and instinct. It brought her back to a question she and Chris had pondered many times. *What exactly was instinct?*

In almost all species, parents taught their young. But in many cases, the rearing window was simply too short. Not enough time to convey *everything.* How to survive or how to forage for food was one thing. But other things, like what *not* to eat, were just as important. Yet how could a parent teach and warn for everything—let alone how to mate or how to raise their own young? Because with or without parents, even a newly born animal still managed to figure most of it out. There were just so many tiny but critical lessons to ensure the continuation of their own species. What made it all possible, especially with some brains possessing only the tiniest capacity?

The answer was instinct.

But what exactly was that? Some miracle of innate intelligence buried deep inside our genetic code? If so, where? And what exactly did those base pairs look like? And if we all had it, why could some animals stand and walk just hours after birth while humans took months to do the same thing?

Talking to Sally, a new and fascinating thought emerged. Had humans somehow evolved out of our instincts? Perhaps as a trade-off for higher cognition? And if so, given

50

how similar dolphin brains were to human's, had the same thing happened to them?

In other words, just how much instinct did dolphins still have compared to humans? Her thoughts then drifted to Dulce, and gorillas.

"Sally," Alison said. "Do you remember your parents?"

A loud beep sounded. IMIS didn't have a translation for 'parents' yet. She tried again. "Do you remember your mother?"

There was a delay before she finally heard IMIS relay the sentence through the underwater speaker. She was a little surprised when it successfully translated *mother*.

Sally stared at Alison through the glass, considering the question.

Yes.

"Did she teach you too?"

Yes. Mother teach. Much.

Alison smiled. "Just like humans. Do you remember your father?"

Another loud beep.

Alison frowned. *IMIS could translate mother but not father?* "Sally, do you still talk to your mother?"

For some reason, it felt like an odd question to Alison. And apparently to Sally too. The dolphin stared at her through the glass with just enough change on her gray face for Alison to notice.

Yes.

It was at that moment that Alison felt something. Something completely indescribable. A connection. A link. Something in Sally's eyes as they peered through the glass at one another. The translations through IMIS were still relatively limited. Even crude by some measures. But in their communication, it felt as though there were something more between them. A reason why she had such a strong bond with Sally. She always had. Ever since rescuing her those years ago.

Yet the look in Sally's eyes now triggered a different

question in Alison. She already knew how similar the dolphin and human brains were. Even genetically, based on the Trio Brain theory as explained by DeeAnn. And for over a year, a single question had been haunting her. It was a question she'd never been sure how to ask. She was not confident that IMIS would understand, let alone relay it correctly. Or even that Sally would comprehend it.

But now, Sally's ability to understand Alison's questions was deepening.

Their brains were so similar, but there was still one glaring difference that she desperately wanted to investigate. And it was based on one of the greatest misnomers in human biology.

It was so commonly stated as fact that Alison had long ago given up trying to correct people. Because everyone either didn't understand the distinction or they simply didn't care. It was the mass belief that humans only used ten percent of their brain.

The conclusion was simply not true. What most people didn't know was that modern brain scanning techniques had proven that the vast majority of the human brain was indeed being used. Neurons and synaptic activity could now be monitored with great precision. However, the distinction that most people misunderstood was that the mystery wasn't about the percent of *utilization*; it was about the brain's collective neural capacity!

The size and activity of a brain were easily established. What was far more difficult, and frankly more exciting, was what could be done with it? Or in simpler terms, what was each brain actually *capable* of?

That was the question that had plagued Alison.

Human brains had been recorded doing things that were simply amazing. Eidetic memories, capable of memorizing any book ever read, or the ability to recall virtually every detail from any day of the person's life. Mathematical conceptualizations of the universe and physical world that made some of the greatest technological breakthroughs possible. Even works of art and music that could make generations weep.

The human brain had so much neural capacity that it was hard to imagine limits. In fact, some cognitive scientists had recently suggested that, given each brain's billions of neurons, there were no limits.

But dolphins had just as complex a synaptic network and their brain sizes were even bigger. Much bigger! In fact, studies had suggested that brain intelligence was also associated with the amount of "folding" in a brain's cerebral cortex. A theory strongly supported by the study of the unusually increased folding of Albert Einstein's brain. And it was well-established that the only species on Earth to have a cortex more folded than humans was *dolphins*.

And if human brains had achieved such remarkable feats…then by the same standard, the potential of dolphin brains could be even greater in some ways. They'd already established that dolphins were much smarter than previously thought. Their "echolocation" was vastly superior to man's best sonar technology. And Sally's ability to read Alison was becoming almost uncanny.

Alison didn't take her eyes off Sally. Instead she stepped forward, maintaining eye contact and studying Sally's expression. Alison turned her mouth only slightly toward the microphone on the desk and when she spoke it was clear and deliberate.

"So, Sally…what *else* can you do?"

12

Alison was still standing in front of the tank when she was interrupted by the sound of the double doors opening behind her. She turned to see Bruna, the center's admin assistant, standing between them. Her dark eyes searched across the expansive room before finally finding Alison.

"Miss Alison, someone is here to see you. It's Mrs. Santiago."

A look of worry briefly passed over Alison's face, and she turned to face Bruna. "Sofia?"

The short, overweight assistant shook her head. "She's alone."

Alison gently touched the tank before turning away and heading for the door. Bruna's announcement was eerily similar to the first time they'd met Lara Santiago. When she had come to talk, it was a plea for her daughter. At the age of eight, Sofia was dying of leukemia. She'd asked if her daughter could talk to their dolphins as one of her last wishes. But Alison and her team arranged more than that.

Now Alison followed Bruna back out and into the wide hallway where Lara Santiago was waiting. Her demeanor was more relaxed than Alison was expecting.

"Hello, Mrs. Santiago," she smiled. "Is everything okay?"

Lara nodded. "Yes. Thank you for seeing me."

"How is Sofia?"

The expression on Lara's face became mixed. "She is doing well," she replied. "And her blood cell counts have improved dramatically. But improvement is now slowing."

Alison immediately frowned.

"The doctors think that what Sofia experienced was a temporary change. And that her blood cells and her condition will turn down again into its final stage."

Alison and Bruna remained quiet, listening.

"My husband and I don't believe that," she said. "What Sofia experienced over the last few weeks was too…incredible. It even shocked her doctors. The same ones who now insist it is only temporary."

Lara Santiago worked to contain her emotion before lowering her voice. "But we don't want to give up."

Alison smiled and reached out, squeezing the woman's arm.

"Miss Shaw," Lara continued, "I didn't tell anyone about Sofia's experience here. Neither one of us did." She glanced through the glass into the giant tank. "The doctors think it was a temporary remission, but we think it had to do with your dolphins. We…we *have* to bring her back."

The smile on Alison's face faded, and she stared at the woman as if frozen. It was something she'd just said that struck Alison like a hammer. *They didn't tell anyone.*

Yet it wasn't the words she'd spoken—it was how she said them. Lara Santiago had not used them as a threat, but something in the tone of her voice told Alison that she might. In other words, neither she nor her husband had told anyone, but they would if they had to.

They believed the dolphins were the key to Sofia's mysterious recovery, and they wanted to get her back into the water. And keeping the secret was their leverage.

Alison glanced at Bruna, the only other witness to the exchange. Her expression gave no indication of having noticed Santiago's subtle implication, making Alison wonder if she had imagined it. But it didn't matter. Whether Lara Santiago intentionally implied it or not was almost irrelevant. The message was the same and it underscored exactly what Clay had told her. As soon as someone found out even part of what Alison's team knew, everything would change. Rumors would spread like wildfire, and attention would focus on them like a giant spotlight. Then eventually on IMIS.

And by then it would be too late.

After a long silence, Alison managed a warm smile. Her hand lay still on the mother's arm. When she spoke, it was in a quieter voice, matching Lara's.

"Bring her in."

***

She found Clay in the lab. Alison entered calmly through one of the heavy double doors, and without saying a word, held them until they closed softly.

Both Clay and Lee watched her cross the room to their workstation where she simply stopped, staring at them.

"Lee, can you give us a few minutes?" She spoke in a low voice.

"Sure," he said, promptly standing up. "I'll, uh, go talk to DeeAnn."

Alison watched him exit through a smaller door at the back of the room, leading outside. The room was momentarily awash in bright sunlight until the door swung back and closed with a loud *click*.

Alison turned to Clay, seated in front of her.

"Are you okay?" he asked.

"You're right," she said plainly. "As much as I want it not to be true, you're right."

Clay raised an eyebrow, curiously.

"IMIS. Dirk and Sally. Everything. It's not safe. When people find out about it they'll come for them, won't they?"

Clay nodded. "It's human nature."

Alison lowered herself into the chair next to him and exhaled. "There's nothing more powerful than the self-preservation of any given species. No matter what the cost."

"It's how it's always been."

She nodded solemnly. "I just spoke to Lara Santiago downstairs, the mother of Sofia, the girl we helped. She knows it was no fluke. She knows it was the dolphins. Now

Sofia's weakening again, and she wants to bring her back."

"And?"

"And I don't think she would take no for an answer."

Clay leaned back in his chair, ignoring the pain. "There is one thing more powerful than self-preservation."

Alison nodded. "A parent trying to save their child."

They both sat quietly as the room fell silent. The monitor on Lee's desk displayed a small window with a live feed of the habitat downstairs. On it, Lee could be seen approaching DeeAnn, at which point he reached down and patted Dulce's head.

On the rest of the monitor and behind the video feed, a much larger window displayed part of IMIS's vocabulary, mapping small parts of audio profiles to corresponding words. The massive system was still discovering new translations. And while most of the word choices seemed obvious, a few did not. They seemed odd, indicating IMIS still had a long way to go in understanding human context.

Alison looked at Clay's chiseled face and was continually struck at how every time she looked at this guy, he seemed to grow more handsome. She realized it wasn't merely his face or build. It was his character. He knew she was still fighting the idea of the retraction. But even now, after she finally saw the danger with her own eyes, he would never say, "I told you." He would never even imply it. He understood what IMIS meant to her. What it meant to all of them. And Alison knew the last thing Clay would ever do was make that struggle worse. Instead, he simply waited for the rest of them to see it.

"So now what?" Clay asked.

Alison didn't answer. Instead, she felt her mouth resisting to say the words. She thought of all they had done and the many young children who visited them, especially those wearing the blue T-shirts with pictures of Dirk and Sally. The children loved those dolphins. And finally, painfully, she thought of little Sofia. When the words came, it was an effort just to get them past her lips. "We undo it."

Clay said nothing. Instead, he merely nodded and reached for one of his crutches, gripping the metal poles tightly in his hand. Alison noticed the strong, almost determined muscles flex in his forearm.

She redirected her focus to Lee's lab, scanning first the shelves of books and equipment, followed by the fluorescent lighting overhead. "This is going to be harder than anything I ever could have imagined."

"I know. I'm sorry."

She tried to joke. "You know, a year ago, I would have tried to blame it all on you."

Clay smirked humorously. "I know. I'm sorry."

"And you know that after this you can never break up with me."

Clay's face spread into a smile at her attempt to break the tension. "Finally, a silver lining." He continued staring into Alison's eyes. The joke's timing was more than ironic, given his plans.

"So where do we move IMIS?"

"I don't know. We're working on a plan."

"It won't be easy. But you guys *did* steal it once before."

This time, Clay's eyes narrowed playfully. It was something she'd reminded him about many times. By "you guys" she meant the Navy. And while they had stolen the original system, he had not been part of it. Something she always seemed to leave out of the joke.

"Well, at least this time you're in on it."

She chuckled, then reached out and wrapped both hands affectionately around his. "How long do we have?"

"Not long," he replied. "What about Dirk and Sally?"

Alison exhaled, thinking. "I have an idea."

Clay glanced again at Lee's screen and the live video feed from the habitat downstairs. "What about DeeAnn and Dulce? And your new little friend?"

She peered at the screen with him and took a deep breath. "I don't have a clue...yet."

As Clay stared at the video, his thoughts quietly shifted

to another very different concern. Something he hadn't shared with the rest of the team yet. A recent and private conversation between Clay, Caesare, and Admiral Langford.

There was still something missing in all of this. A question that hadn't been answered. One last piece that had been missing since the Guyana Mountains, where the Chinese had made their great discovery.

The uncomfortable fact was that the U.S. had only stumbled onto all of this through the capture of a Russian submarine, which had evidently been watching the Chinese as they brought the plants out of the jungle. A sub found to be equipped with a highly advanced system, allowing it to travel almost undetected underwater. And oddly, that particular submarine was one of Russia's oldest.

The submarine, called the *Forel*, had ultimately escaped Guyana only to be destroyed in tandem with the Chinese warship. And that led to the question at the root of it all.

How did the Russians tie into all of this?

13

The answer to Clay's question was walking briskly down a long, brightly painted hallway in Saint Petersburg. More specifically, on the third floor of the General Staff Building in Palace Square and home to the Russian Defence Ministry's Western Military District.

The twelve-story building was situated just blocks from the famed Neva River, the route used by Nazi forces during the "Siege of Leningrad." Its legacy as the symbolic capital of the Russian Revolution came when Adolf Hitler set a goal to burn both the city and its people to the ground. The battle lasted more than two years and resulted in a devastating loss for Nazi Germany.

Dressed in a dark blue Caraceni suit, Dima Belov was tall and lean. He was covering the distance easily with long strides, at least compared to the two shorter guards walking shoulder to shoulder beside him.

Belov was no stranger to the building, having been received there several times before.

But today was different.

A dour expression painted his aged face, reflecting the seriousness of his visit, under armed guard. This time, Belov wasn't here by choice, or to engage in political brinkmanship with some of Russia's powerful military leaders. This time, Belov was here for one reason and one reason only: to save his own life.

At the end of the hall, two ebony wood doors swung outward to where two more men in modern green uniforms and berets awaited Belov. As he had with the first two, the older man detected a faint sense of disgust in the faces of his guards. Judgment for a situation Belov wondered if they knew anything about.

Still, Belov fought to remain calm in spite of the subtle shaking in both of his hands. After reaching the final door, his new guards halted with a firm stomp of their boots. Here, a fifth man stepped forward and began patting the older man down.

He raised his arms up to either side and peered through the thick glass wall to where Admiral Oleg Koskov waited in his office. From his chair, the thick brow of the admiral hung heavily over a set of dark and ruthless eyes.

Belov would have mused at how quickly the tables had turned were it not for the very real prospect of leaving this building as a dead man.

The officer in front of him stepped out of the way, forcefully pushing Belov into the large office and causing him to stumble through the doorway. Once clear, the officer quickly pulled the thick glass door closed behind him.

Once they were alone in the room, the admiral silently studied Belov with the same look of revulsion. Tables had indeed turned, in a short matter of weeks. Until just recently, Belov had been one of the Defence Ministry's most prominent insiders. A trusted ally to the country's political elite and Russian military. No, more than that. A veritable hero, with a secret capable of returning Mother Russia to its former glory, and more.

And while Belov may not have fully understood *how* his status had changed so suddenly, he certainly understood why. Russia, quite simply, was on a razor's edge of utter economic collapse.

Their nation had been hit hard by the global devastation now spreading throughout dozens of major economies around the world. Russia was the planet's second largest producer of oil, the most ubiquitous commodity on Earth and the very cornerstone of the entire Russian economy. A commodity whose recent massive oversupply glut and falling demand was now crushing the country to depths never before seen in modern history.

Now, like China, Brazil, Venezuela, and a host of others, Russia had found itself unable to stave off the unrelenting economic destruction within its own borders, where all manners of civilized life were systematically disintegrating. And nowhere was that more evident than in the Russian military.

Belov's fall from grace was not due to a calculated decision on anyone's part. It was driven by sheer desperation, within a government that was quickly splintering. Dima Belov's dire situation resulted from the conclusion of many desperate politicians that he had squandered nearly a billion Rubles on what amounted to little more than a pipe dream. Whenever governments fractured and began to collapse, the resulting behavior was desperation and blame, promptly followed by condemnation. This time, it was Belov who found himself on the receiving end.

Now, as his eyes met the admiral's, he stepped forward, moving to a dark leather chair and lowering himself into it. The irony was that Admiral Koskov was just as deeply involved in the mission as he had been. But judging by his demeanor, the man was quickly working to separate himself from the mess...by sacrificing Belov.

Behind the desk, Koskov glared through a thick air of tension. When he finally spoke, his voice was deep and grave.

"There's nothing I can do for you."

Belov showed no reaction. Instead, he kept his hands lowered, still trembling from fear. Belov had few cards, and he was determined to play them as carefully as possible. "We were in this together."

The admiral shook his head as if batting the thought away. "No. I provided you resources. Nothing more."

They both knew it was a lie. "We convinced the Ministry together. We were both there."

Belov's first card. Yet he had to be careful not to sound as though he were trying to pull Koskov down with him.

"I provided assistance."

"And we both explained the risks."

"Which did not include instigating a war."

Belov shook his head. "The Americans blame us for something we didn't do. It's something we could not have foreseen."

Koskov did not answer.

"The truth is, the American's *wanted* it to be us. They wanted a reason. But it was the Chinese who destroyed their ship. You and I are not the only ones to know this."

"What we know and what matters are two different things," Koskov responded. "It does not change the fact that a billion Rubles have been spent chasing ghosts. A billion Rubles which our country needs."

Belov cleared his voice, keeping his eyes on the admiral. The first card was useless. He moved to the next. "The money can be recovered."

Now a slight curl formed in the corner of the admiral's mouth. It was an empty promise. They both knew Belov was almost broke, having been nearly wiped out from the collapse of the economy. There were many to blame but few who could be made an example of.

Belov was one of them. And while the man was playing the victim now, Koskov knew how dirty he truly was. And how shadily his fortune had been made. Belov was no victim. He was a snake, caught in a trap of his own making.

"I cannot help you." With that, the admiral's eyes rose above the man's head, searching for one of his men.

"Wait," Belov said. "Wait!"

The admiral coldly dismissed him. "You requested a meeting, Dima. I gave it to you. It is now over."

He was out of time. Belov quickly leaned his tall frame forward and reached inside his suit jacket. It was now or never. "It's not over."

Sharply, he pulled out a large piece of paper and unrolled it. With his right hand, he slapped it down on the desk in front of Koskov.

The admiral's large eyes dropped to glance at it. "What is this?"

"A picture."

Unamused, the admiral glared across the desk. "A picture of what?"

"Of *it*."

Now the heavier man's eyes narrowed and looked more closely. "Do not play games with me, Dima."

"No games."

"All I see is an oil rig."

Belov nodded. His life would hang on his next sentence so he spoke the words carefully. "The *Forel* is gone…but the discovery remains."

The pause in the admiral's expression seemed endless, while Belov waited. Finally, the admiral exhaled slightly. The change in his demeanor was slight, but his voice was unchanged. "No. It's over." He slid the paper back toward Belov.

"It's *there*."

"On an oil rig? I think not. Your desperation has failed you."

"Not on the rig," blurted Belov. "Below it!"

This time, the admiral's dark eyes changed. They darted back to the picture, and very slowly, he reached for it again.

"You're lying."

"It's the truth."

Belov watched as the admiral studied the picture again. He raised his head dubiously. "How do you know this?"

"It's a decoy."

The admiral glanced up but said nothing.

"My source has confirmed that there is nothing wrong with that rig. The Americans have commandeered it."

"What source?"

"The SVR," Belov lied. The SVR was the modern successor to the KGB, following the dissolution of the Soviet Union. Belov's source was decidedly *not* the SVR. But it didn't matter. Convincing Koskov, however, did.

"And what is below it?" the Admiral growled, bringing the picture up to his eyes for a closer look.

"Something important."

Before the Admiral could ask another question, Belov retrieved a second picture. This one was a headshot. "This man was spotted in Georgetown shortly before the *Forel* was destroyed. Brazilian intelligence has traced him to a murder in São Paulo. They have also put him on the mountain before the thermobaric blast."

Koskov peered across the desk. Every government on the planet knew about the explosion now—one that leveled the top of an entire mountain peak. "So what," he said. "So the man is dead."

Belov shook his head. "He's not dead." He paused for effect. "He is alive and on that oil rig."

"Now?"

"Yes. Now." Belov's eyes were unblinking. His face perfectly still and composed. He could not give the slightest hint that his last comment was nothing more than a guess.

The admiral took a deeper breath and stared again at the photo. It was a dated driver's license of a much younger Steve Caesare, sporting a mustache and partial smile.

After leaning back in his chair, the admiral crossed his arms, still doubtful. "If what you say is true, then what? What do we do with this oil rig?"

He had him. At that moment, Belov's hands finally stopped trembling. He raised them to his knees and spoke forcefully.

"We take it! While it's still unprotected!"

14

The *Valant's* large and somewhat aging hull cast a wide shadow over the clear blue ocean water, the swells rolling beneath it. The warm Northeasterly breeze whistled slightly as it swirled past the massive steel columns, holding the structure upright and steady.

In the control room, situated beneath its heavily smudged glass ceiling, an anxious Will Borger was accompanied by an equally anxious Les Gorski. Together they watched a live video feed of the morning's dive with apprehension. The mapping of the alien ship's upper hull was complete, leaving the team to now venture deeper into more dangerous territory. Most of the lower hull rested below the surface layer of coral at depths beyond the reach of standard SCUBA systems, requiring the unique expertise of Les Gorski and his team.

The practice of "deep diving" was far more perilous than that experienced by even the best recreational divers. Even worse, special equipment, meticulous procedure, and relentless training were all that stood between deep water divers and a watery grave. These lower depths were so alien to the human body that men survived only by inhaling hypoxic breathing gasses to stave off the deadly effects of oxygen poisoning.

In recreational diving, any one of a dozen problems could threaten a diver's life. But in deep waters, it took only seconds for a single mistake to become fatal.

"Are we ready?"

The voice of Steve Caesare rattled over the speaker, sounding like a long-distance telephone call. His diving "hat" was a helmet invented by Gorski himself. Chrome in color and sporting a hexagon shaped faceplate, the helmet included two large hoses on either side which circulated the gasses to and from the rebreather. The diving hats were completely self-contained and still allowed for free two-way communication. But with sound quality that was notably degraded.

Borger looked behind himself and up at Gorski who had one elbow propped on an arm and a hand covering his mouth. Gorski was silently working through the numbers. Depth, pressure, time, and rate of ascent. The men should have a little over twenty minutes to explore before ascending back to a safe depth. Plenty of time before their next piece of equipment arrived.

Without taking his eyes off the monitor's video feed, Gorski nodded.

"We got a steady signal from all three of you, plus the camera. We're ready when you are."

"Roger that," Caesare replied, after a slight delay. The camera feed from one of Gorski's divers, Jake Corbin, swept between them with its bright LED light showing their obscured faces as they stared back into the camera from behind the helmet portal.

The camera caught the last of Caesare before he raised his gloved hand and motioned downward. "All right. Descending now."

Air suddenly erupted around them and surrounded the men in a curtain of rising bubbles. They were obscured for just moments before beginning to sink. It would take the men several minutes just to reach their new depth with each second being monitored carefully by Borger and Gorski. All the while, outside, several more engineers worked the feed lines to keep the thick umbilical cables moving at the same rate of descent. Too much slack could cause entanglement below the surface and too little would slow their descent, wasting precious time.

The second of Gorski's men, Alan Beene, checked his dive computer. "Eighty feet." The number matched the depth on Borger's monitor.

Gorski's new "hat" design had recently undergone a technological leap of its own. By adding an uplink to the back of the helmet, a diver's wrist-sized computer could transfer its information wirelessly, piggybacking on the audio transmission. It was a clever design, which increased the electrical draw on the tiny computer only modestly.

"Slow and steady," the older Gorski said, almost in a whisper. His concern didn't originate from anything related to the men themselves. They were skilled divers, including Caesare. Instead his worry was of the unknown. SCUBA diving was wrought with danger, below the surface where it took time to return safely to the top. Anything from equipment malfunction, to rapid air depletion, to unpredictable physiological effects could spell trouble for anyone. At deeper depths, those dangers were radically increased. Pressure, and by extension compression, caused strange things to happen to the human body. Things that provided precious little margin of error if something went wrong.

Gorski had lost two men on a rescue dive several years before. On that dive, a sudden lateral shift in a damaged sub's position caused his men to become trapped. The worry quickly turned to panic when the men were unable to move, held tight by their tethers. Turning to desperation as their heliox gas was slowly depleted, the men eventually succumbed to the inevitable. Their voices, and ultimately their final screams of helplessness, would remain in Gorski's ears forever. Along with the anguish of being able to do nothing to help them.

Sounds he prayed he would never hear again, but feared he someday would. Because in an environment humans were never meant to tread, it was little more than wishful thinking to truly escape fate.

Beene called out their depth again as they passed 150 feet. The camera remained fixed on the side of the dark hull as the faint, remaining traces of ambient sunlight began to fade. Soon the only light was from their camera's LED bulbs.

Against the hull, awash in that light, a small speck of red followed the men lower. A laser pointer tracked their every inch in three dimensions and transmitted the data above—like a high-tech equivalent of a tape measure. This one was much more sensitive, tracing the size, shape, and curvature of the hull down to a thousandth of an inch.

"Two hundred feet."

"Okay," Caesare's voice responded. "Let's slow it up."

A deep burst of noise sounded as air was redirected into their BCD's, causing the passing hull to slow before coming to a gradual stop.

"You guys still with us?" Caesare asked.

Borger nodded. "Yep, still here. Everything is reading fine."

Caesare peered at his dive computer and nodded in slow motion. "Same here." He kicked with his fins and moved out of the way of the camera, which was still focused on the hull. "No change in appearance," he noted.

He moved in closer, together with Beene, and reached forward. Brushing his hand across the surface elicited the familiar glowing trail behind it.

"No change there either."

Gorski cleared his voice. "How much farther down?"

A moment later, the camera pivoted and pointed down into the darkness. In the glow of bright light, the wall could be seen, descending until it disappeared into pitch blackness.

"Damn, this thing is big."

Beene moved in and touched the wall after Caesare.

"No indication of where it ends. Looks like at least another couple hundred feet, if not more."

Above them, still standing behind Borger, Gorski noticed something on the monitor and leaned forward. He peered at the readings from their dive computers. When his eyes returned to the video feed, the camera was panning back to the hull and caught Beene in the frame.

"Stop!" Gorski suddenly bellowed into the desk's microphone. "Beene, don't move!"

The sound of his voice crackled back over the speaker. "What? What is it?"

Gorski was quiet, still studying the screen. "Corbin, pan away and then back to him."

A moment later, the frame of the live video moved away into blackness and then back to the figure of Beene with the dark hull behind him.

"Turn off the camera's light."

"You want me to turn off the light?"

"Affirmative," nodded Gorski through his dark glasses. "But keep the camera on Beene."

Floating next to the men, Caesare watched as the bright LED lamp went off a second later, leaving only the smaller lights on their helmets. Darkness quickly closed in around them.

The helmet lights illuminated only their immediate area and left their umbilical lines moving eerily behind them.

Gorski's voice continued through their headsets. "Now, Beene, turn toward that hull again. Then back."

Beene did so, wondering what Gorski was getting at. He turned back slowly to look at the dark wall, then back at the others.

Gorski's voice came again. "Do you guys see it?"

Caesare nodded. "Yes. His helmet's light is dimming." He floated in closer. "Try it again."

Beene repeated the movement, turning his head closer to the wall and back again.

This time, Caesare spoke to Gorski. "We couldn't see it with the brighter lamp on."

"That's not all," Gorski replied. "Beene, how much battery are you seeing on your dive computer?"

He looked down at his wrist. "Ninety-two percent."

"Same here," Gorski confirmed. "Now put your hand

on the wall again."

Beene complied, reaching out and pressing against the gray metal. He kept it there for a long time, watching as thin green lines rippled out from his gloved fingertips.

"Okay, now what does your battery say?"

Beene pulled his hand back and looked at the reading. "Eighty-nine percent."

On the *Valant*, Borger watched the same number decrease on his screen and twisted around to Gorski. "Whoa."

"Let's make sure it's not a faulty unit," Gorski frowned. "Mr. Caesare, if you please."

In the video, Caesare glided forward to the wall and reached out his own hand. After several long seconds, both Borger and Gorski watched the power gauge from Caesare's battery begin decreasing.

"Same thing."

Borger nodded from his seat and said what every one of them was thinking. "That thing is sucking energy right out of your units!"

Without the slightest hesitation, Les Gorski leaned past Borger toward the microphone and spoke loud enough for everyone to hear.

"All three of you get to the surface. Right now!"

15

It took almost thirty minutes for the men to reach the surface, where they were helped out of the water onto a wide platform. It was large and made of thick stainless steel grating, creating a deep resonating echo when the men dropped their equipment. An old utility elevator ran up the inside length of one of the oil rig's giant pillars, requiring the men to take turns returning to the rig's operations level.

Waiting inside the large maintenance bay were both Gorski and Borger, along with the rest of the engineering crew. A few of them had already suited up for the second dive. Together they sat in a semicircle on standby.

Gorski stood, with arms folded, in front of two rusted double doors. Both were open and leading into the *Valant's* giant machine shop. The rest of the engineers faced Gorski, sitting on metal benches or against larger tables near the opposite wall.

Caesare, Beene, and Corbin entered through a smaller door. Upon seeing the others, Caesare grinned sarcastically at Gorski. "Well, *that* was interesting."

Gorski scoffed. "Not exactly the word I was thinking of." With arms still crossed in front of him, he raised his voice to address the group. "It seems our spaceship is full of surprises, gentlemen."

Elgin Tay, wearing wire-framed glasses and of Chinese descent, raised both eyebrows. "What happened?"

"It appears the ship doesn't just attract metal," Borger answered. "It attracts energy too."

"What?!"

"Our dive computers just experienced a sharp battery draw down."

"When we got right next to it," Beene added.

Jim Lightfoot, another of the *Pathfinder*'s engineers, frowned at Borger, then Gorski. "Is that even possible?"

"I'm not sure," Borger shrugged. "Maybe if there was a transformer or a motor involved. They have magnetic lines of flux to operate." He thought for a moment. "If this ship had an energy field, it might be possible for it to absorb some of that energy. But that's theoretical, and we're not using any motors."

"I think we're a little beyond what we consider *possible* with this thing," Gorski replied. He glanced at Borger. "There's not a hell of a lot making sense here. And this drawdown presents some serious problems. Those computers control the oxygen-helium mixture in the heliox. If something causes them to malfunction, and that mixture is off by only a fraction, then we're going to be collecting your corpses when they float to the surface. At that depth and pressure, Mother Nature is damn unforgiving."

Tay looked back and forth between his team. "So, are we still going down?"

"Not today. Not until we understand exactly what we're dealing with."

"You know," Steve Caesare thought aloud, "we could still get down to it, without being enough to need the computers or the lights. We can still get to the top of the thing using standard SCUBA equipment to get the drill on it."

The "drill" was a large two-handed unit used by underwater construction crews. It had been left onboard the *Valant,* and after undergoing some minor repairs, was now sitting on the metal floor in front of Lightfoot.

The truth was, they could only go on mapping for so long. Sooner or later, they needed to know what the damn thing was made out of. Now more than ever. And that meant a sample. The waterproof drill was old but should nevertheless be able to provide a large enough piece of the hull to study.

Gorski stared at Caesare, contemplating. The first

drilling was expected to be done quickly, down and right back up. They could still go with all mechanical gear, without the need for any electronics. The only battery would be in the drill, and it was enormous. Once against the hull, thirty seconds was likely all they would need.

"We do need a piece of it," Borger acknowledged.

"We can always go down again later to understand this energy draw," Caesare offered.

Gorski reluctantly nodded. They'd already carried out dozens of shallower dives, and only just detected the draw. Admittedly, the risk for the next dive wasn't great.

He looked to Tay. "Okay. But you're down and back up inside of thirty minutes."

"Yes, sir."

Gorski twisted his wrist and looked at his large Oris Pro dive watch. "Then let's get in the water. Time is not our friend."

***

Once in the water, it took less than seven minutes to reach the highest point of the alien hull. The broadly rounded section was exposed by only a small opening, which the team had made in the dense coral.

Tay, along with Smitty, another of the *Pathfinder* engineers, moved into position. Lightfoot continued down behind them, lowering the tip of the drill for the first two men to guide in.

The full-face rotary drill weighed over a hundred pounds out of the water, and even with the buoyancy of the ocean, they still had difficultly positioning its crystalline diamond cutter.

Once it was finally in place, a small tripod extended forward around the end of the giant drill bit until each pad touched the hull, keeping the angle straight. More ripples of green snaked out from each of the three contact points and eventually faded.

Tay nodded through his SCUBA mask, and the large unit was powered on, setting the large drill cutter spinning. Lightfoot grasped the large steel arm at the rear and slowly pulled it back, watching the cutting bit move forward inside a clear shaft.

Tay checked the small cameras atop Lightfoot and Smitty's neoprene-capped heads. Both appeared to be recording. Between the three of them, even with draining batteries, they should be able to capture some video.

He double-checked the whirling bit and gave a thumbs-up before Lightfoot pulled farther back on the lever. The spinning increased and the charcoal-colored bit became a blur, extending out farther toward the alien hull.

When the drill bit finally made contact, none of them were prepared for what happened next.

16

"Good God."

Borger couldn't believe his eyes, nor could the rest of the engineering crew standing behind him. All packed into the small room.

Behind Borger, Gorski was frowning again. It had only taken minutes to get his divers back to the surface but that was more than long enough for him. He turned around and looked at Tay, Lightfoot, and Smitty. All three were standing near the back. "You boys sure you're okay?"

They nodded almost simultaneously.

In the video, the moment the giant bit dug into the metal, a huge section of the hull burst into a bright white light. It was so intense that the normal ripple of green had all but disappeared.

The video from each of the three cameras playing simultaneously onscreen abruptly jumped around as Tay and his men scrambled to disengage the drill. Lightfoot slammed the lever back up, while both Tay and Smitty clung desperately to each side as a series of massive jolts caused the machine to buck wildly.

In all the commotion and shaking video footage, there was no sound. None of the cameras being linked to audio, the videos played in eerie silence. But the panic was evident. Each man worked desperately to get to safety without losing control of the drill, still spinning as it withdrew into its protective sheath.

But what came next was truly remarkable.

Tay, thinking quickly, ripped his tiny camera from its bracket and turned the angle of the lens back toward the illuminated hull. There the video on his camera showed a large fist-sized dimple where the diamond cutter had bored into it. A hole that was barely visible under the blinding light. And a hole that, within seconds, began to change.

Borger reached forward to zoom in on the picture and watched in fascination as the outside edges of the hole began moving. Subtly, as if it were shrinking, its outside edges began to soften and close inward, millimeter by millimeter. It appeared as if the edges were actually attempting to crawl toward one another—bit by bit, until the last edges reached each other and the hole disappeared.

The entire team stood watching in stunned silence, equally fascinated. In less than three minutes, any trace of the damage—any hint of anything—was gone.

After several more seconds the video ended, leaving the entire room in silence.

"Okaaay," Caesare breathed out slowly. "Anyone ever seen anything like *that* before?"

17

Admiral Langford sat somberly around the dark rich mahogany table while listening to another heated debate between National Security Advisor Stan Griffin and Fred Collier, the Chief of Naval Operations.

To Langford, the president's morning security meetings were growing, or rather devolving, into little more than political theater. At the same time, the geopolitical relationship with China continued to unravel. Most of the senior officers around the table remained fixated on the sinking of the *USNS Bowditch*, one of the Navy's most prominent science vessels, several weeks earlier. To them, it was a blatant act of war that deserved an immediate response, if not an all-out retaliation.

But what surprised Langford was how little those same men understood or appreciated the ramifications of what the U.S. had just done. In a last ditch effort to save John Clay, and more importantly what he held in his possession, the Central Intelligence Agency was forced to recall their entire network of undercover operatives throughout China and several other Asian countries. It was a proverbial *Hail Mary* play that by the grace of God worked, but the political vacuum it left in its wake was immense.

The problem wasn't simply the recall of U.S. operatives, but the unavoidable exposure that went with it as well. And just how deeply those operatives had penetrated various government departments in China. Espionage was rife between all major countries, but the *depth* of U.S. penetration that China was now coming to grips with was devastating. And the impact wasn't just about those who had been extracted. It was about those who were still left. Chinese officials who had been utterly deceived and would now have to face the wrath of the Chinese government for allowing their departments and their secrets to be compromised.

So the implications weren't just about a U.S. extraction. It was about the damage left behind. About people who would be killed as a result and a seething Chinese government hell-bent on revenge.

For the foreseeable future, any friendly relations with the Chinese were now merely superficial—the thinnest veneer of public relations for the world to see. China may have started the fight with the sinking of the *Bowditch*, but now after the extraction, the gloves were officially off.

Langford looked to the head of the table and into the tired eyes of President Carr. The leader's tall stature paused unmoving in his chair, slouched slightly and sharing the same look as Langford. They both knew that the price paid for getting Clay and the special DNA out was likely greater than most of the other officers in the room were admitting.

His eyes flickered briefly at Langford's stare and then back to Collier, whose voice suddenly grew louder.

"If we are to do nothing in response to this, then when will we?" he said, stabbing the table with his finger. "If they can sink a naval ship, an *unarmed* ship, in broad daylight without a response, then what else can they do?! Will they have to invade before we fight back?!"

Griffith shook his head. "What you don't understand is that what we've just done is far worse than any military strike. We've just set off a bomb in the very heart of China and attacked their pride as a sovereign nation. It's already a government barely holding itself together while its economy crumbles to the ground. Honor and reputation are everything to them—"

"Honor?!" Collier exclaimed, leaning forward again. "Honor and reputation is everything to us!"

To that, Griffith's voice lowered and he merely shook his head, exasperated. "Not like this, Admiral. Not like this."

Collier shook his head in admonishment. "You tell them then. You tell our troops that their honor isn't as great as the Chinese. You tell them and see what kind of reaction you get. Honor is the only thing that some of these men live by. They will fight to the death to defend this country. With no—"

This time Langford interrupted. "And how hard would they fight if someone exposed them as fools? For the entire world to see. How mad do you think they'd be then?"

"Take your anger over the *Bowditch*," President Carr blurted, "and start multiplying."

Collier didn't answer. His face showed his desire to but instead he forced himself back in his chair.

Merl Miller, the Secretary of Defense, frowned. "They're going to come at us hard. And it's going to be nasty."

"Meaning what?"

"Meaning something quiet. And out of the public view."

"Cyber warfare," the president said.

"Most likely. The NSA is already working to harden every system they can. So far they haven't seen plans for any concerted attack, but it's just a matter of time. God knows they've already been in our systems enough to know where our vulnerabilities are."

President Carr leaned forward onto his elbows and sighed. They couldn't wait until it was too late. They had no idea what form the retaliation would take, but they had to do something. "Raise the threat level. And tell local law enforcement to remain sharp. This could come from anywhere."

The grave irony of the situation was not lost on anyone in the room. Years ago, the NSA had embarked on a mission that would forever change the face of cyber warfare—all under direction from the White House. It started with developing the Stuxnet worm to help Israel disable Iranian centrifuges, just enough to render the uranium enrichment unusable. It was the first time in history such development had been undertaken at a state level. And when Stuxnet proved successful, it didn't stop there. The NSA pushed forward with more sophisticated forms of hacking that pushed the envelope even further. Coupled with their secret monitoring of every system they could access, the secret directive initiated a firestorm around the world, bringing their espionage tactics to the attention of other countries, including allies. The viruses or "worms" that had been created were almost something in the realm of science fiction. Spyware that could infiltrate every hard drive on the planet it came in contact with. And so malicious that it could never be removed, even when detected. The only remedy was to destroy the hardware itself.

In just a few short years, all major countries had their own state-sponsored hacking teams. Armchair soldiers now waged wars on a battlefield that few could even see.

What the NSA and its Stuxnet brain child had done was to demonstrate that it was possible to inflict real-world damage from the cover of the virtual world. The greatest irony of all was that it was the U.S. who had opened Pandora's Box. And now, years later, it was the U.S. who would bear the brunt of a full-scale cyber war as a result.

Carr stared blankly across the table in front of him. An air of dread hung heavily in the room.

"God, I hope this was worth it."

18

The city of San Juan, Puerto Rico, was founded by famed explorer Juan Ponce de León. He was a man obsessed with immortality and the search for the legendary Fountain of Youth—an ironic twist considering one of Hospital San Francisco's patients, recently transferred from a nearby island.

Outside, a row of palm trees waved in the soft morning breeze as a veil of thin white clouds passed overhead. Inside, the morning sun left the room inundated with bright light and drew attention to Alison Shaw as she sat on the edge of the soft bed, smiling warmly at Chris Ramirez.

He was raised almost into a sitting position and returned the smile to both Alison and John Clay, who was standing behind her. Chris noticed Clay's cane and gave him a tired wink.

"It looks like you're healing up well, Mr. Clay."

"We both are."

Alison placed one of her hands on top of Chris's. "How are you feeling?"

"Not bad. A little loopy from the medication, but all in all, pretty good."

She nodded and studied the gauze on his head. "Well, the bandages seem to be getting a little smaller. That's encouraging."

"I can't tell," Chris grinned. "They won't give me a mirror."

"I don't blame them. It looks worse than it is."

"Well, I'm clearly getting better. They're letting me drink coffee again."

Alison followed his nod to the side table and an empty mug, causing her to shake her head sarcastically. "You and your coffee."

"It's better than jelly donuts."

At that, her eyes narrowed playfully.

"What was that?" Clay asked.

"You don't know?" Chris's grin widened. "Ali here has a jelly donut addiction."

"No," Clay replied, amused. "Somehow that's never come up."

Alison glared at Chris before twisting around. "Addiction is a bit of a stretch."

"Oh, really? I seem to remember you eating the whole box."

Alison stopped before shrugging at Clay. "It was during our research project in Costa Rica. The family I was staying with made them for my birthday." Her eyes widened when Clay laughed. "What?! You couldn't find them anywhere down there!"

The men laughed together and watched Alison's face redden. She opened her mouth to speak but was interrupted when the large door to the room burst open, slamming against the inside wall. Alison and Chris both jumped, and all three turned to find Lee Kenwood standing in the room.

"Geez, Lee! You scared us!"

"I'm sorry," Lee replied, still panting. "I didn't mean to." He nodded at the bed. "Hey, Chris."

"I thought you were coming this afternoon?"

"I was. But something came up." Without waiting, he rounded the far side of the mattress and stopped at Chris's bedside table. "I have to show you guys something!"

In one motion, he slid off his backpack and pulled his laptop computer out. He set it carefully on the surface of the table and turned it sideways.

"What's going on?"

Lee opened the lid, and the screen came back to life. He took a deep breath and tried to slow his breathing. "Something big. Something *really* big."

"Did something happen?"

Lee nodded excitedly. "You could say that." He typed quickly on the keyboard and logged in. When his screen brightened, it had a large window open. Lee turned back to the others with hands that were almost trembling. He suddenly stopped, catching himself, and looked at Chris. "Wait, how are you feeling?!"

"I'm fine, Lee. Now spill it!"

"Right. Good. Glad to hear it." He turned back and addressed all three. "I've been doing some research. On IMIS. You know, checking errors and stuff. I wanted to go through the translations we imported from the vests. I think there may be some issues with one of the algorithms that measure context, especially given—"

"Lee!" Alison blurted.

"Right, right. Sorry." He stopped and put his hands together. "Okay. Here it is. I was looking through the translations…and found something. Something more than what I was looking for."

"Like what?"

"Like *more* translations!"

Alison and Chris looked at each other. "And that was surprising?"

"Yes, very surprising!"

"Because…"

"Because they weren't supposed to be there. None of them. And they weren't supposed to be there because *we* weren't there!"

Chris squinted at Lee. "I'm not following."

"What do you mean, because we weren't there?"

Lee shook his head with a grin. "Sorry, let me back up. I say *more* translations because IMIS only translates when we're present. Obviously. But in this case, translations were occurring *without* any of us being present!"

Alison frowned. "Okay…now I'm not sure *I'm* following."

"Don't worry about it, you will in a minute. The point is, none of us were there. But IMIS was still translating."

"What would IMIS be translating if we weren't there?"

"Exactly! But since the whole purpose of IMIS is to translate languages from and to English, the question isn't what was it translating, it's *to whom*? And that," Lee exclaimed, "is what I'm about to show you." With that he turned and hit a button on his keyboard, starting the video. He quickly hit another button, enlarging it.

The picture was a darkened image of their lab. The hundreds of blinking lights from the IMIS servers could be seen in the background, and part of the giant saltwater tank filled the left side of the frame. Centered in the frame were their work desks, one of which was facing the tank's glass wall. On the desk was a monitor and keyboard, along with a long-necked microphone standing vertically next to it.

Standing to the side, Lee watched the video with them. "Here's the lab," he said, pointing to the top of the screen. "Notice the time."

"1:34 A.M."

"Exactly."

"What happens at—"

"Shhh!" Lee said. A moment later, something moved on the screen, triggering the rest of the lights in the room to go on. The form briefly disappeared from the screen before suddenly appearing again. It was small and dark, and when it stepped fully into view, Alison gasped.

"Dulce!"

Lee nodded.

"What is she doing out? How did she—"

"Wait!" Lee said, raising a finger. "Just watch!"

The small gorilla stood quietly, examining the room. Her large hazel eyes passed over the camera and continued to the tank, where she appeared to spot the dolphins on the other side. She remained still, studying them for several long seconds before a second figure eventually neared the edge of the tank. It was Sally.

The dolphin continued gliding in slowly until her rostrum, or snout, reached the glass.

"That's incredible," Chris whispered.

Lee beamed back at him. "It gets better."

On the screen, Dulce tilted her head and slowly unfurled her long dark, lanky arm, touching her finger to the glass. Sally studied the glass curiously before twisting sideways and touching her right fin to the same area.

Then something amazing happened.

The monitor on the desk suddenly blinked to life. On the screen, a familiar image appeared: the translation application for IMIS. Visible on the left-hand side was a thin line, and on the right, a window which listed both IMIS's vocabulary and words translated.

Alison looked incredulously at Lee. "How did it do that?"

"I have no idea."

It was then that they heard Dulce speak in a low grunt.

In the hospital room, all three leaned forward to get a closer look at the screen.

The monitor in the video showed the thin line dancing briefly, indicating it had detected and captured the sound. It was promptly followed by words being listed on the right side, but the video resolution was too tiny to read them.

A moment later, the translation sounded through the water inside the tank. Sally responded and the computer screen promptly sounded a loud beep, signifying a failed translation. It was there that Lee reached down and paused the video.

Alison and Chris were both staring at him with open mouths. When Alison began to finally shake her head, her words sounded in disbelief.

"That…happened?!"

"Yes!" Lee cried. He looked between them excitedly.

Chris was just as stunned. The only word he could get out was, "*How?*"

"I have absolutely no idea!"

"Is there more?"

"Yes! A lot more."

Clay's blue eyes were still fixated on the screen. "Lee, when was this recorded?"

"That's the most amazing thing," he replied, growing even more thrilled. "This happened eight days ago. And it's happened every night since!"

Clay peered curiously at Alison, who was still trying to process it all. "How on Earth did Dulce even get out?"

"She learned the code for the door."

"She learned the code?"

"Yes. Evidently, she's been watching us."

"Holy—" Chris began, searching for the right words but failing. "That is just…so unbelievable."

Alison returned her gaze to the screen. "What did they say to each other?"

Lee reached into his backpack and pulled out several sheets of paper. "I brought the whole transcript."

19

Lee handed out copies and watched them all read through several pages without speaking. By the time they finished, Alison and Chris stared at each other with mouths open.

"Oh…my…God!"

Chris dropped the papers on his lap and raised both hands to rub his face. "Is this really happening, or am I hallucinating from my medication?"

"Oh, it's real!"

Chris blinked at Lee. "How do I know?"

Lee barely paused. "Do you want me to slap you?"

"Okay. It's real."

Alison immediately turned to Clay, who was grinning at her. "That's really something."

"Something," she said blankly. "It's…amazing!"

"I told you," Lee said with a wide smile.

Alison glanced down at the first page. "It's hard to even comprehend what this means. I mean—" She looked at Lee. "IMIS is short for Inter Mammal Interpretive System, but we never imagined the "Inter Mammal" would actually mean *inter mammal*! I mean we're talking about communication between two non-human sentient beings. I can't even begin to conceive of how profound that is."

"Neither can I," murmured Chris. "Never in our wildest dreams would we have considered this."

Alison shook her head before noticing Lee, still grinning. She eyed him suspiciously. "What?"

"There's more."

"What do you mean?"

"The communication between Sally and Dulce is incredible. But how it's happening is just as amazing."

"You mean through IMIS."

"Not just through IMIS. But how the system is actually doing it. The logic IMIS is using is something I've never seen before." Lee retrieved his own folded-up copy of the transcript from his pocket. "Look at the first page. Dulce says, *You Fish*. A simple enough translation. But then a few translations later, she says, *Me Dulce*."

Lee looked up at them. "There is no dolphin equivalent of Dulce. But there's no error message signifying a bad translation."

"Then…what did it translate?"

"I don't know," Lee answered excitedly. "But it said *something*. In a sound pattern we haven't seen before. My best guess is that IMIS translated the *meaning* of Dulce, not the word itself."

"Dulce means sweet in Spanish," Clay said.

"Exactly! But IMIS doesn't have a dolphin word for *sweet* either!" Lee said. "Which means it either made something up, or it actually figured *out* the word sweet!"

"Would it actually make something up?"

Lee shook his head. "IMIS has never made a whole new word up before. It's gotten words wrong. A lot of words. But it's never just made one up."

Clay considered Lee's explanation. "So IMIS is getting smarter."

"I think so. I think it's getting a lot smarter. So much so that it's not just deciphering their languages, it's beginning to *understand* them." Without warning, he pulled off the top piece of paper and showed them his second page, filled with marks he'd made. Then the next sheet and the next. "Look at this. Every page is littered with examples of this."

Alison looked back at her own set of papers and noticed something else. "Lee, how long was Dulce in the lab?"

"That's another thing. The first time it was about ten minutes. I'm not sure why she left, but the second time it was longer, and the next night longer still."

"But…" Alison flipped back and forth between pages.

"The translations for each night get shorter and shorter."

"That's right," Lee affirmed. "And to be honest, that's where this really gets a little strange. "Dulce is in front of the tank longer and longer, but IMIS is translating *less and less*!"

Alison's eyes grew wider, and she urgently looked at Chris.

Neither one of them needed to speak. Their eyes said it all.

20

Onboard the *Pathfinder*, the look on Neely Lawton's face could not have been more different.

Four small wire cages rested before her on the cold metal table, each with a small mouse inside. Neely studied them closely while each mouse sniffed at the metal wires and ran around inside excitedly.

But in all four mice, something was notably wrong. They were all twitching uncontrollably, in spite of each one being in perfect biological health.

Neely's fears were quickly becoming a reality. She was now sure of it. The Chinese-extracted DNA was flawed. Not because it didn't work but because it worked too well.

Each mouse had been subjected to a small contusive jolt, resulting in a bruise to the rodent's spinal column. A common, nonpermanent injury, resulting in a temporary but significant loss of motor skills.

After then injecting the mice, Neely observed in fascination as the DNA deposited by the infused bacteria began to take hold. Within hours, it began infiltrating the mouse's existing genetic code. The changes were extraordinary as the DNA began a systematic repair of the damaged spinal area.

In less than a day, the hind legs on each mouse recovered their full range of motion. The experiment worked perfectly. All of it.

That was until the mice stopped sleeping.

Neely had been afraid that the sample the team had gone to such great lengths to recover might be too good to be true. And early signs indicated that *it was*.

The modifications had supercharged the body's own ability to regenerate, preventing cells from dying while also replicating at an accelerated rate. The problem was that it wasn't just the damaged cells that were infused, it was *all* the cells. The rodents' entire genetic structures were being *fixed*, which meant every cell was being enhanced. Including brain cells.

And that was a problem.

For millions of years, nearly all living things on the planet had evolved with a circadian clock—a deep biological coordination with the Earth's natural cycles. At the center of this metabolic hourglass was something so deeply ingrained in all Earth's organisms that without it every mammal, bird, and reptile would die within weeks. It was called sleep.

One of the most critical and fundamental needs for survival, sleep cycles gave organisms the time needed to regularly repair themselves, both mentally and physically.

When sleep cycles were interrupted, the entire system began to suffer. Permanent deprivation created serious problems in all animals, including mental functions. If the deprivation continued, the problems quickly spread down the nervous system to the cells that regulated the body and its critical organs.

But the DNA extracted in Guyana was not just healing the cells in the mice—it was doing so much too quickly. The repair normally achieved during an entire sleep cycle was now happening in a fraction of the time, causing a ripple effect throughout the rest of the body's cells. The end result was hyperactive neurons that now refused to sleep.

And the evidence was not just in their motor skills. Clipped hair on the mice now grew back within hours. A pricked ear healed almost fast enough for Neely to watch. All of this was putting their brains into overdrive, since they were now unable to sleep, destroying themselves and the rest of their nervous systems from within.

The small satellite phone rang on the table behind her, and Neely spun around in her chair. She picked it up and studied the screen, recognizing Alison's number.

At Will Borger's direction, none of their phones had names assigned to the numbers, requiring them to memorize each team member's satellite phone number. It made her feel like they were back in the 80s.

Neely picked up the handset and answered it, waiting for the small icon to appear on the screen verifying the encryption was successful. Finally, she held it to her ear. "Hi, Ali."

"Hi, Neely. How are things?"

Neely leaned back in her chair and glanced over her right shoulder at the mice. "That's debatable. How about with you?"

"I'm not sure either," Alison answered. "That might depend on you."

Neely raised her eyebrows. "I sense a surprise coming."

"You could say that."

On the other end, Alison lowered her phone and pushed another button. "You're on speakerphone now, and I'm here with John, Chris, and Lee."

"Hello, gentlemen," Neely said aloud. "How are you feeling, Chris?"

"Well, I *was* feeling—"

Alison interrupted him by slapping his leg through the thin blanket.

"Good!" Chris finished. "I'm really good!"

"Glad to hear it. To what do I owe the honor of a group call?"

"You might want to sit down for this," Alison warned.

The corner of Neely's mouth curled. "Already taken care of."

"Good. We need to talk to you about something. Something Lee discovered with the IMIS system."

"Shoot."

Alison took a deep breath. "Neely, do you remember how we talked about genetics, when you were here? And how it was possible that two species might be able to communicate?"

"I do."

"Would you mind explaining that theory to the guys here?"

Neely absently tucked a strand of brown hair behind her ear. "The discussion was based on the fact that much of our genetic code is shared with virtually all other animals on the planet. Even with plants, though to a lesser extent. As I told Alison, this is all covered in genetics 101. So we know that the amount of genetic differences between species can be surprisingly small, making the idea of common abilities more than possible."

"Like communication."

"Like communication. Assuming that specific DNA still remains common in both. My point was that if there were commonalities that once allowed a different form of communication between humans and dolphins, we may very well have evolved out of it. Or if not, the base pairs responsible for it may have been deactivated through centuries of evolution. We already know that the vast majority of DNA in our systems is inactive. Left over from a time and a world our bodies likely wouldn't even recognize anymore."

In the hospital room, Alison stared at the others, listening intently. She looked straight at Lee as she asked her next question. "Neely, if that were true, if a different ability for communication did exist in us at one time, how likely might it be to exist in another species as well?"

"Well, how likely would be impossible to say. We're only talking about plausibility here. But considering how similar primates are to humans, it stands to reason that a fair amount of our junk DNA, that which has been deactivated, could also be in another species too. It would depend on where our evolution split and when."

"And whether what was deactivated in us also got deactivated in them."

"Exactly. Of course, communication is pretty complex, and includes areas of the brain too."

"Meaning?"

"Meaning that if a common communication method was even possible, the likelihood would be strongest in brains that were most similar."

"You mean the tri-brain theory that DeeAnn told us about."

"Yes. Although I believe she called it the *big brain trio*." This time, Neely smiled. "So, is that enough to let me in on Lee's big new discovery?"

Alison almost laughed. "Yes. More than enough." She paused for a moment before explaining. "We think IMIS has been translating directly between Sally and Dulce. Dolphin to gorilla."

"Really?" Neely stood up. She stared absently out the starboard side window. The *Valant* oil rig could be seen clearly in the distance, towering above the blue water of the Caribbean. "Are you sure?"

"Lee's pretty sure."

"When did this happen?"

"It's been going on for the last week. But it gets better. Dulce has been sneaking into the lab for longer and longer periods, yet the translations from IMIS are happening less and less."

Neely's interest became piqued. "Are they still talking?"

Alison watched Lee nod his head in response. "We think so."

"Alison," Neely said carefully. "You need to find out. And make sure. Because if they are..."

"I know," Alison replied with a smile. "This communication-related DNA may still be alive and well in *both of them.*"

21

Alison hung up the phone and looked at the others.

"Well?"

"Unbelievable," Lee breathed.

"Guys," Chris added. "If we're right, this...may be the greatest discovery in human history."

She thought about Chris's words and looked at him with amusement. "I know what you're thinking."

"This could be it, Ali. This could be the key to it all."

"The key to what?" John questioned.

Alison answered him without taking her eyes off of Chris. "*Instinct*. It was part of Chris's thesis."

Chris nodded. "The theory I posited was about where instinct left off and cognition began."

"And what was missing," Alison added.

"And what was missing," concurred Chris.

Clay looked at them both curiously. "Care to give us an introduction?"

"When it comes to biology," Chris replied, "what's referred to as *instinct* is still a giant unknown. The ability for animals to learn through observation is one thing. But it's widely accepted that something else is at play, which we don't understand. The sheer speed at which animals learn, coupled with the limited time some species spend with their parents, suggests something more. What to eat and what not to eat. How to fight, how to prey. There is a myriad of environmental variables that they cannot possibly observe in their upbringing, yet they still know what to do. It's especially evident when animals are separated from their parents at a very young age. Somehow they still know. As if there is *genetic knowledge* hardwired into their genes. It's what humans clumsily classify as instinct."

"And you think there is something else?"

Chris nodded. "I do. The vast majority of animals have very limited cognitive abilities. Their brains are simply too small. And yet the communication between them is surprisingly sophisticated. More than the cognitive capacity of their brains should be capable of. Not to mention how they *sense* things in each other, or even in another species. Animals, for example, that can read us. That seem to know what we're feeling. Fear. Grief. Love. How do they know that? It can't simply be through scent. Most animals don't have the olfactory receptors of dogs. Nor can it simply be through instinct. The most logical explanation is that there's something missing. A level of communication that lies between instinct and cognition. Something that we're not aware of." Chris ended with his eyes directed at Alison. "At least not yet."

Clay smiled when the room fell silent. "That sounds like a hell of a paper."

"I thought it was," Chris grinned. "Especially now. Because if we're actually seeing what we think we are between Dulce and Sally, it could be one of the greatest biological discoveries ever made. And as much as I hate to say it," Chris said to Lee, "given how little I understand all the tech stuff, IMIS is at the center of it all."

Alison cleared her voice. "I guess we have some checking to do." She flipped through the sheets of Lee's transcript. "Beginning with what is missing from these pages."

22

Inside the habitat, DeeAnn Draper raised an arm and, using a sleeve, dabbed a bead of perspiration from her forehead. The morning sun was hotter than usual, blazing through the thin netting above her. Coupled with the absence of any breeze, it left the habitat warmer than even the African continent it was supposed to emulate.

Dulce and Dexter seemed unperturbed, sitting calmly beneath the broad cover of a rosewood tree. Dulce was attempting to show the smaller capuchin how to match colored blocks on top of a short wooden table. The smaller monkey watched intently but made no effort to participate.

He was highly intelligent, but his desire to communicate did not match his aptitude. His only communication was through Dulce and in short spurts. Sounds that DeeAnn's vest could not seem to detect. It had puzzled Lee to no end.

DeeAnn ignored the heat, instead reading through the sheets of paper and shaking her head. When she finished, she looked back up to Alison and Lee with a look of incredulity.

"Is this for real?"

Lee nodded.

"It's…incredible. I mean this is a breakthrough beyond anything we were expecting." She flipped back to the first page and reviewed with amusement one of the first lines that Dulce had asked Sally—how she *got in there*. From an anthropological standpoint, what IMIS had just done was simply off the charts.

"How did she get out?" DeeAnn asked.

"She learned the code to the door."

DeeAnn rolled her eyes and looked back at Dulce, sitting

on the ground. "Of course she did."

"I guess we should have thought of that," Alison said.

Lee nodded at the papers in her hand. "Did you notice there're fewer translations on the subsequent pages?"

"I did," DeeAnn looked again. "I presume these midnight visits were shorter."

"Actually," Lee mused, "they were longer."

"Wait. What?"

"They were longer," he repeated.

"So they spoke less?"

Alison grinned. "Maybe. Maybe not."

"What does that mean? Either they were talking, or they—" DeeAnn's face froze before she could finish her sentence. The implications had just caught up to her question. The possibility hit her like a freight train.

"Are you kidding me?!"

Alison and Lee both shook their heads.

"That's impossible!"

"Is it?" Alison shrugged. "We've already seen this between Dulce and Dexter. IMIS can't hear them speaking."

"That's because it's more innate. Species-specific. This is different."

"It might not be as different as we think, Dee. There's a possibility that they both have genes that we don't. Or at least genes that are still working."

"That allow them to *talk*? With Dirk and Sally?!"

"We don't know. Not for sure anyway. But it's a possibility."

"And it may not be talking," added Lee, "as much as another form of communication."

DeeAnn raised a hand and covered her mouth. "My God. If that's true, I can't even begin to imagine what it could mean."

"Yeah. Neither can we."

23

Hello Alison.

"Hello, Sally."

You want talk.

"Yes, I'd like to talk."

I want talk.

"Good. Sally, where's Dirk?"

Dirk gone. Come back soon.

Alison nodded. Dirk was developing a habit of disappearing for short periods of time. And she had no idea where to, or why.

You question Alison.

"I do," she mused. "I have a lot of questions." She paused in front of Sally, who was studying her through the glass wall. Before, she had marveled at how Sally was able to read her so well. She now wondered if they were beginning to finally understand.

"Sally," Alison said, "I understand that you've met Dulce."

The speaker on the desk beeped with a bad translation, but Sally's response showed she had gotten enough of it.

Yes. Dulce. Little person.

Alison frowned thoughtfully. *Little person is what Sally had called Dulce in the transcripts, which was clearly a generic term, given that dolphins would have no word for gorilla.*

"You've been talking to Dulce?" she asked.

When the translation sounded through the underwater speakers, Sally swished her thick tail with interest.

Yes. Talk Dulce. New friend.

Alison grinned. "What did you talk about?"

She already knew most of the answer based on the transcripts. But what Alison really wanted to know was what had IMIS *not* picked up?

The answer surprised her.

She want swim.

***

Barely a hundred yards away in the habitat, DeeAnn peered curiously down at Dulce.

"You want what?"

Dulce clapped her black hands together and rocked from side to side.

Me want swim fish.

DeeAnn's brow lowered. "You want to swim with the fish."

Yes. Swim Sally.

DeeAnn looked up at Lee, standing beside her, for his reaction.

He smiled. DeeAnn hadn't caught the relevance of Sally's name being translated, but he had. He blinked but said nothing.

"Dulce," she replied. "It's not that simple. Swimming with Sally is…complicated."

A quick tone sounded on her vest.

She corrected herself. "Swimming is hard."

Dulce's grin faded and changed to a look of confusion. She thought for a moment before replying.

Me like swim.

DeeAnn opened her mouth to speak but stopped, considering what it had taken to make diving gear for little Sofia. That was one thing. But trying to explain it to Dulce suddenly left her at a loss.

"Um…Lee?"

He snapped out of his thought and looked at DeeAnn. "Huh?"

"Is it even possible that we could get her into the water? I mean the gear and everything? Is that even feasible?"

A new smile slowly spread across Lee's face, and he glanced down to Dulce. "Hell yes, it is."

Another tone sounded on the vest. As soon as the small gorilla had heard enough, she began hopping and clapping.

It was an exciting concept. Yet even as they both mulled the possibility over, neither noticed what Dexter, the small capuchin, was doing in the background.

It wasn't until DeeAnn straightened that she finally noticed. Several yards away, beneath the mixture of green and yellow leaves of a banana tree, Dexter was rearranging Dulce's blocks. Instead of the matching game, he had carefully stacked them. Into the crude, but very recognizable, shape of a pyramid.

24

It was strange.

To see young Sofia Santiago standing next to the top of the giant tank was surreal. Heartwarming but surreal. The last time they had seen her, Sofia's bare head was hidden under a colorful scarf, her body so weak she had to be lifted into the water.

Now, she stood upright on her own two feet. In spite of the crutches, her balance was steady and she remained steadfast, staring down into the shimmering water where Dirk and Sally waited.

No longer wearing a scarf, the girl's beautiful head was budding with dark stubble. Her warm brown eyes appeared even more enthralled than they had been the last time.

"Are you ready, Sofia?"

Grinning widely, she nodded and handed the crutches to her mother. Sofia placed her tiny hands inside Alison's and stepped shakily onto the top step.

Behind Alison, Lee and Clay waited a couple steps below with her dive gear. DeeAnn remained standing behind the girl, on the edge of the tank, ready to catch her with a hand out. But she didn't need it. After a second step, Sofia lowered herself down onto the step and sat upright.

As weak as she was, the improvement was simply astonishing. Her energy and strength were like…that of a different child.

But Sofia barely seemed to notice. Instead, she held up her arms while Clay wrapped a small weight belt around her. Then came her custom-made face mask followed by the waterproof ear buds.

Alison gently tested the seals with her fingertips before lightly touching the face mask to ensure it stayed in place.

"Can you hear me?"

"Yes," Sofia answered, nodding. "I hear you fine."

"Good."

Alison raised a hand and motioned for Dirk and Sally to approach. They did so immediately, reaching the side of the tank and making sounds at Sofia.

"Hold on," Alison smiled. "We're not plugged in yet."

She inserted her own ear plugs and reached down to power her vest back on.

"Dirk? Sally?"

Both dolphins turned their heads to her.

Alison. We ready. Now swim.

"Okay, okay. Just a minute." She continued adjusting her own equipment while Sofia reached out and patted their noses. Both dolphins laughed.

It wasn't about the swim. Last time Sofia had spent less than twenty minutes in the water and yet the changes were profound. It was a surprise to everyone, which led to a string of other discoveries including unexpected healing properties within the water. Properties that had seemingly been stored in the dolphin's thin layer of blubber. Alison and Neely Lawton had found it.

Of course, whatever *it* was had yet to be defined. All they knew so far was that whatever was in those plants near Trinidad had made its way into the water, in addition to Dirk and Sally's fat cells, where they were absorbed. Now those same properties were circulating throughout the water of the research center's tank, where they were absorbed by anyone else in the tank, including Sofia.

Still, even if they hadn't yet identified *it* precisely, they knew enough to know that a longer exposure of Sofia to the water would undoubtedly improve the potency affecting her own cells. And this time her swim wouldn't be minutes, it would last for hours.

And it wouldn't just be for Sofia.

When it was over and Sofia had left in the care of her parents, DeeAnn gazed at Alison from a chair in the observation area. Clay and Lee both sat nearby.

"How long should we wait?"

Alison exhaled, with both arms leaning back on the edge of a table. "I don't know. A couple of days. Then we do it again. For her and for Juan's sister, Angelina."

"And by then it will almost be time to leave?"

Alison lowered her head and nodded.

John Clay watched her expression silently.

It was killing her. First the retraction and now the abandonment of their research center. The first place in her career where she had truly felt at home. And a series of accomplishments that were beyond meaningful. They were life changing. For everyone.

She raised her head but kept her eyes on the floor. "I never thought it would come to this—not even in my worst nightmares—to denounce everything we've done and abandon this place. It just feels…so wrong."

"Like we're running," Lee added.

"Exactly."

"You've changed the world, Alison," Clay said. "Even if the world doesn't know it yet."

She stared at him, softly but still with a look of bewilderment. "Will they *ever*?" She didn't wait for an answer. "I used to think that all the world needed was truth. And even if it were shocking, we would all still manage to come away better off. We'd be better people. Enlightened. Or something. Instead, we're having to hide, and run. So that everything we've discovered can't be exploited."

Alison shook her head. "My God, what's wrong with us? Why are humans so self-serving?"

Clay smiled warmly from his chair. "Not everyone is."

"Maybe not," DeeAnn said. "But decent people are *not* the ones in power. It's the power hungry that run the world. And our governments and our militaries." She turned to Clay. "No offense."

"None taken."

"It's the same ones who talk about how great the future can be," DeeAnn continued. "They're always promising a better tomorrow, but when there's a chance to really change the future, they fight over it like children. I mean, look what the Chinese did. They murdered their own people to keep it secret. Then when they couldn't have it, they destroyed it all. God, what kind of mentality is that?"

Clay frowned. "It's not unique, unfortunately. When survival is on the line, especially for an entire nation, values change quickly."

Lee peered at Clay. "We'd do the same thing, wouldn't we?"

"Sadly, yes."

"So what are we doing this for then?" asked Alison. "We can't possibly win. It's just us and our tiny group. Against everyone else. What difference can we possibly make?"

Clay thought about the question. "Under the right circumstances, even the most unexpected person can make a difference."

"Not always," quipped DeeAnn.

"No. Not always," Clay agreed, looking past them into the empty tank. "But we're in a unique position. *We* have nothing to lose."

"Nothing to lose?"

"We can't force the world to change, Ali. All we can do is give it a chance."

Clay knew the odds were against them. But he also knew that one day each of them would be gone. Laid to rest just like everyone else. And it would be forever. On the grand evolutionary timeline, their lives were little more than the blink of an eye. Everyone would be gone eventually, and all that would matter then would be what they had *stood* for. A truth he had just recently become acutely aware of.

He paused stoically, thinking. "Have any of you ever read the Declaration of Independence?"

The other three looked at each other, surprised at his

question.

"Uh…no."

"In it, it says that whoever has the ability to do something…has the *responsibility* to do something."

"Really?"

Clay nodded. "I'm paraphrasing. My father was obsessed with U.S. history, and that was his favorite part of the Declaration. The fifty-six men who signed it risked it all and changed the world." He looked at them. "And now we have a chance…not just to change the world, but maybe humanity itself. Either we fight and lose, or we fight and win," he said simply. "If we lose, the world is no different. But if we win…"

His words hung in the air, causing Lee to grin. "If we win, it will be epic!"

Clay nodded at Alison. "Epic."

Alison gradually smiled at Clay. "Well then, I guess we'd better win."

"We'd better win," repeated DeeAnn. "No matter what."

One by one they stood up. Clay last, now only barely using his crutches.

DeeAnn then straightened her clothes. "Well, *we* are headed to Africa. What are you going to do with Dirk and Sally?"

"Take them home," Alison replied.

"And where is that?"

She stared at her reflection in the tank's glass wall. Her answer was short and solemn. "Trinidad."

25

At over eighteen hundred square miles, Trinidad was the fifth largest island in the West Indies: known as the region shared by the Caribbean Basin and North Atlantic Ocean. Named "Island of the Trinity" by Christopher Columbus in 1498, the large island was also one of the most industrialized.

Trinidad also laid claim to several facts of cultural significance, including both the inspiration for the famed character Robinson Crusoe and host to one of the largest carnivals on the planet. In the present day, the island was a beacon of progress and economic stability derived largely from its vast natural gas reserves.

On the large screen, the pipe-shaped neighboring island of Tobago moved out of view and the frame quickly panned across miles of blue water where it stopped again, on the image of the *Valant* oil rig. From the top, the vessel resembled a large flat structure, its deep shadow hovering above the water.

The screen briefly zoomed out, revealing the crystal-clear image of the large, white *Pathfinder* ship anchored nearby.

The rest of the room was dark, illuminated only by the giant screen on the wall. Around a table sat several high-ranking Russian officers, one of whom was Admiral Koskov. A junior officer stood at the head of the table, presenting with a remote mouse in his hand. Now waiting patiently for the first question.

"And this is where Belov thinks it is," a voice stated flatly. It belonged to Russia's Minister of Defence. The head of the country's armed forces and second in command only to the President of the Russian Federation.

"Yes, sir."

"And he says the Americans are hiding it."

"Yes." The junior officer turned to face the table and put his hands behind his back. "The oil rig is made by Transocean Limited in Geneva. The SVR has verified that it had no reported problems before it was decommissioned. Ahead of schedule. And one day after three senior U.S. government officials arrived at Transocean headquarters in the middle of the night. Chairman Admiral Langford, Defense Secretary Miller, and CIA Director Andrew Hayes."

"They're sure of this?"

"Yes, sir. They have also confirmed the Americans were on the premises for less than three hours before flying back to Washington D.C. The next day Transocean issued the order to decommission the *Valant* rig."

"So there's nothing wrong with it."

"We don't believe so."

The defence minister suddenly raised his voice into a growl. "I don't want to hear what you *believe*. I want to hear what you know."

The junior officer glanced briefly at Koskov's frame in the darkness, but the older man offered nothing. When the junior officer replied, his voice wavered slightly. "It would be extremely unlikely, sir."

The minister was silent. Russian intelligence was second to no one, not even the CIA. And Belov was no fool. He wasn't about to go down without a fight, but he wouldn't risk being wrong either. Not this time. He of all people knew that there were worse punishments a man could face than death.

Now it seemed the billionaire Dima Belov had seen through the Americans' deception. Which meant they would now have to keep Belov alive, at least for the time being. The man was ruthless beyond all measure, and yet he alone appeared to know what the Americans were truly hiding. But how?

Not long ago, Belov had convinced the Russian government of the magnitude of what the Chinese had first discovered in Guyana. But his intelligence tactics had also failed miserably when the *Forel* submarine was later destroyed.

But what if it was true? If the prize remained in play, they would be stupid to ignore it. If the prize was as powerful as Belov claimed.

And of course, the Americans had initially blamed Russia for the sinking of their research ship, until fragments proved the Chinese were behind it. The Americans quickly backed down from their accusations, but the situation underscored just how easily they would be prepared to blame Russia again.

"How many people did you say were on the rig?"

"Twelve at any given time. Several regularly travel back and forth to the ship."

"Twelve men on an oil rig that isn't broken," the minister said. "Doing what?"

This time no one answered.

He stared at the image on the screen. "Trying to take the oil rig from the Americans will not be easy."

This time a silhouette sitting next to the minister spoke up. "We see no signs of armaments or weapons."

"Then they know they're being watched," the minister replied dryly. "They have to."

Koskov nodded in the darkness. "If they claim the rig is simply undergoing repairs, it is doubtful they would send fighting ships, for fear of discovery."

No one could see the minister's lips press tightly together in bemusement. "They have already been discovered."

"They don't know that."

The minister leaned closer, studying the screen carefully. "They accused us of destroying their ship, yet they did nothing. Now they know it was the Chinese, and still they do nothing. Perhaps," he said, "they are more vulnerable than we know."

"Sir?"

The minister remained quiet, thinking. *Why hadn't the Americans retaliated? Why no word out of NATO?* It was more than a little odd. Especially given that governments routinely obscured facts to justify their actions in the public eye. But this felt different. This didn't feel like it was part of the normal political playbook. There was something unique about this oil rig, and the fact it was unguarded. It reminded him of something the Americans had done in WWII to throw off the enemy. And if he was right, if they were doing it again, then the oil rig was little more than a prop. A facade allowing them to hide something in plain sight.

He spoke to Koskov without taking his eyes off the image. "How soon?"

"We can reach it in three days without being detected."

"Until the rig is taken."

"Yes. Once we take the vessel, by force, we will have two hours before American reinforcements arrive. Maybe less."

"We can't get enough ships there in time to hold it."

"Correct."

The minister pursed his lips, contemplating. "Perhaps we don't need to hold it." He leaned back and inhaled. "Perhaps...we just need leverage."

"Sir?"

"It's not just us the Americans don't want to know about it. They likely do not want *anyone* to know about it."

Koskov smiled. "Extortion."

The defence minister frowned. "Such an ugly word. But, yes. We need enough information to prevent a counterattack."

"Or enough hostages."

"True," he nodded. "Assuming that enough survive."

With that, the minister sighed and turned his attention to one of the other details of the report: the visit by the

Americans to Transocean. One of the names listed earlier had caught his attention. The name of *Langford*.

It was a name the Russians knew well.

26

Unlike the Russian defence minister, Admiral Langford's eyes bore a look of grave worry. Without a word, he closed the large white door behind him and looked across the table at U.S. Secretary of Defense Merl Miller, wearing an expression very much the same.

Neither spoke as Langford made his way to the table and sat down in a dark leather chair across from the secretary. A silent Miller watched as Langford reached into his pocket and withdrew a small round disc, resembling a miniature hockey puck. On the top was a single button along with several small holes.

He calmly depressed the button and waited a moment before settling back in his chair. The small device was something Will Borger called a voice jammer. Inside, a set of integrated speakers emitted competing noises in the same spectrums as both Langford and Miller's voices. Enough to make their conversations unrecognizable to any listening devices.

The Pentagon was one of the most thoroughly swept buildings in the country for bugs and other spying devices, but that was still no guarantee. Borger's device allowed both men to talk freely without the risk of being recorded. Or more accurately, if they were recorded, the result would be digitally undecipherable. At least that's what he'd claimed. To them, it was hard to know if the unit was even working, save for the small green light on top.

Across from him, Miller stared at the small unit absently. When he spoke, his face was long. "I hope he's right." His eyes moved to Langford. "The President. I hope this was all worth it."

"So do I."

"The Chinese have to know that we have the bacteria."

Langford nodded. "We must assume so."

"Which means they're going to want it back."

"Presumably."

Miller managed a wry grin. "I don't think we need to presume. If they'd taken it from us, we'd be working on a barrage of retaliations."

"Yes. We would."

Both men fell silent, sinking deeply into their thoughts. The implications were expanding rapidly. The President's National Security Council knew about the bacteria as well as the plants found underwater near Trinidad.

But there were also things they did not know. Things that Langford and Miller were keeping secret. If the President and his staff felt the implications were extensive now, they'd be absolutely stunned to learn the whole story. Or at least the parts that had been uncovered thus far.

"Eventually," Miller said, shaking his head, "this thing is going to blow up on us. And when it does, it will be impossible to contain without the mother of all diversions. I mean a multilateral effort of the biggest kind."

Langford's tired eyes stared back at him. What Miller meant by *multilateral* was an international effort. Something beyond a single government. The U.S. government had learned many years ago both the importance of and the best ways to suppress information in an internationally coordinated effort with other friendly countries. And they had become extraordinarily effective at it. But the real question was what happened when friendly governments became competitors for the same prize? There was a point where even allies knew too much.

Bad things, Langford thought to himself. *Bad things were going to happen that would eventually end up in war. Because this discovery by the Chinese had everything it needed to set the world on fire.*

However, as bad as the situation was, Langford was also mulling over another possibility. A much more radical idea that he'd thought long and hard about before he'd been ready to mention it to Miller.

Langford cleared his throat and spoke carefully. "What if there's another way?"

"Another way for what?"

"To avoid war."

Miller stared curiously across the table. "I am all ears."

Langford reached up and ran his finger back and forth over his bottom lip. "We let it loose."

"We what?"

"We let it loose."

Miller squinted at him dubiously. "What do you mean by *loose?*"

"We give it to everyone."

Miller frowned. "Are you on some sort of medication?"

Langford smiled at the joke. "As a matter of fact, I am. My blood pressure and cholesterol are both too high. And this isn't helping." When his amusement faded, he continued. "When you boil it right down, there are only two real options here. Keeping the whole thing secret, or exposing it."

"And you think exposing it would be better?"

"I honestly don't know. But one thing it *would* do is destroy anyone else's leverage over us. And it would almost completely eliminate the Chinese's reason to attack."

Miller leaned back. "Jesus, Jim. If I didn't know better, I'd think you'd gone off the deep end."

"Maybe I have," Langford shrugged. "But if I haven't…"

"If you haven't, it's an intriguing idea. But a scary one. Beginning with one hell of a population problem."

"Eventually," Langford acknowledged, "there's clearly some downside. But there could be a hell of a lot of upside."

"There could be a hell of a lot of *downside* too. There would be no way to know. No way to anticipate just how things would unravel."

115

"True. But ask yourself this: What would happen if every country had more than enough food? More than enough energy? What would it mean if we only needed healthcare for accidents? All of us."

"Now you're sounding crazy. That's just a liberal's dream. It would never happen like that, and you know it. Not with human nature being what it is."

"No," Langford said. "It's *everyone's* dream. Even us conservatives." He leaned forward, staring intently at Miller. "We're both pushing seventy, Merl."

"God dammit, don't remind me."

"Tell me something. What's the biggest cause of your problems today? Personally." He watched Miller's expression tighten. "What causes you the most grief every day?"

Miller replied, reluctantly. "Health."

"Health," Langford nodded. "Same for me. It's the same for everyone, sooner or later. And *later* ain't that far away. For any of us. And that's just getting old. What about *diseases*?"

Miller shook his head. "We're not just talking about a court-martial, Jim. We're talking about *treason*. Giving this secret up isn't some token of goodwill by a couple of old farts who've seen enough war. I mean, this is actual treason, to our own country. And you know as well as I do the type of people who run this place. The same that run every country. So let's not be naive."

At that, Langford stopped and considered Miller's words. He knew it wasn't that easy. But at some point, someone needed to stand up for what was right. For humanity.

Miller could read his face. "Doing what's right is one thing. Knowing who *decides* what's right is another."

Langford nodded. Twenty years ago he would have given up the idea without another thought. Hell, ten years ago. But being within view of the end of one's life had a habit of changing most men.

Eventually, Langford looked back across the table. "This bacteria...this *miracle* is going to take us to war. It's going to take the whole world to war. Millions of people, Merl. Millions are going to die, over the very thing that can save them."

***

Unfortunately, Langford's idea was short lived. Less than an hour later, onboard the research ship *Pathfinder*, Neely Lawton sank slowly down into her chair.

Her eyes moved across the table in front of her, from cage to cage, with a look of pure horror. Every last one of her mice were dead. And her nagging fear was now fully realized.

Their miracle bacteria came with the worst possible vengeance. Anyone carrying the DNA extracted by the Chinese would be completely healed, physically, just before their minds were literally worked to death.

27

With weary eyes, Li Na Wei peered out over the distant cityscape, studying a blanket of gray clouds as they filled the sky above seemingly endless rows of towering high-rise buildings.

She could feel the faint mist on her face, causing what was left of the coal dust to begin to dot and streak down her cheeks. From the hillside, her dark almond-shaped eyes studied the span of buildings which spread out even further than she had realized.

Li Na blinked and continued staring, mentally exhausted. She hadn't slept in two days, and though her mind wasn't feeling the familiar dullness of sleep deprivation, her thoughts still felt impaired. Some were beginning to feel scattered.

However, as strange as her head was feeling, her body had never felt better. With only a faint twinge in her heart from her degenerative disease, the rest of her felt strong. As though she could walk forever.

Of course, she already had. It had been almost twelve hours since she'd leaped from the train as it began slowing into its last stop, a giant refinery now roughly eighty kilometers away.

A small pond had helped to remove most of the grime from her face and hands, leaving the remnants to now be finished off by the heavy mist.

Without a sound, she held her gaze and felt both a sense of awe and foreboding. The city standing before her was one that few had seen and yet everyone knew about. Fabled. Talked about only in rumors and stories among the working class, yet denied or ignored by the government. This brand new city was one of dozens like it scattered throughout the country, and one that Li Na's father had mentioned specifically. Mysterious cities known to many people outside of China as "Ghost Cities."

No one knew why they were built, or for whom, but they knew who had it done. The government. And yet the most remarkable thing about the city in front of her was that it was *empty*.

All of them were. Standing solemnly in the middle of nowhere, waiting to be populated and used. Row after row of high-rise towers stretching for kilometers.

And it wasn't just the towers. Included in the landscape were city buildings, parking lots, and shopping centers. All empty. Sitting idle, littered with weeds stretching waist-high and growing out of what appeared to be thousands of fresh cracks in the concrete. Already eroding given their poor quality and several years of inattention.

The image was nothing short of apocalyptic, as if a neutron bomb had detonated, killing everyone but leaving the buildings intact.

After descending from the hills, the first sign of life Li Na encountered was a moose, grazing on a bush near the base of a still-functioning traffic light. Rows and rows of green lights stretched down the multilane boulevard, managing traffic for cars that were nowhere to be seen.

It took an hour before she saw her first human. Several people, in fact, as they moved between buildings in the large downtown square. None of them noticed Li Na or, if they had, none had paid her any attention. Instead they moved casually, but with purpose, disappearing into another building or around a street corner.

Still more appeared a few blocks further in, but far less inhabitants than a city that size should have. It felt eerie, leaving Li Na with a feeling of…despondence. A look of despair seemed plainly visible on their faces and in their eyes. Li Na had never felt anything like it. It was as if the people were planted there solely to prove the city was viable.

She watched them all for several minutes before

following a man as he walked along a row of empty storefronts. Each displayed wide expansive windows with advertisements pasted to the glass, faded and peeling.

The man paid her no attention. He moved deliberately across another empty intersection and past more buildings until he reached two dirty glass doors. He pulled one open and promptly disappeared inside.

Li Na followed, guardedly. She looked cautiously through the glass doors before reaching to open one.

It was a shopping mall.

She stepped inside and remained near the door. It was a mall unlike any she'd ever seen. One as empty as the streets and buildings outside. She moved further down the wide hallway until she could see further in each direction. Some stores were open—a few at least—with bright neon signs over their entrances. One was a small convenience store. Another looked to be an electronics outlet with no one inside. The walls and shelves were sparsely stocked, and she could see neither customer nor employee.

It wasn't until she turned to face the other direction that her heart nearly stopped. A feeling of excitement ran through her body, followed immediately by relief. At the end of the expansive walkway was a giant food court. Dozens of counters ringed the area, but only two were open. One served an array of soups and noodles and the other a selection of Korean dishes.

Having nearly depleted the food in her bag, Li Na allowed herself a grin and watched as the man she'd followed approached the counter and ordered a bowl of noodles.

Dozens of people were scattered around the large court, sitting randomly at different tables. Most were alone, with only a few small groups talking quietly to each other.

Even now, no one was watching her.

Li Na decided to let her apprehension go. Hunger was absolutely her first priority. Thirty minutes and two bowls of noodles later, she rested in a red plastic chair, feeling full and watching two people sitting nearby. They were too far away to hear. Too far to bother anyone. Still, they whispered as good Chinese did.

Li Na tried again to listen but couldn't. Instead she waited, bringing her bag in close and preparing to follow them when they left. Her thoughts had already moved from food to shelter, and she wondered where the people lived. She doubted that finding a place to hide in an empty city would be difficult. And she was right.

What she didn't know about, however — what she failed to even consider — were the cameras positioned around the storefronts, buried subtly in the ceilings and overhangs.

The vast majority of cities in China still had little to no surveillance built out. It was a herculean job given the vast majority of the country was agrarian just three decades earlier. But some of the larger and newer areas *were* online, collecting and storing video images around the clock. Collected by giant data centers around the country, they were stored in immense databases. A practice replicated from the American FBI's *NGI* system. And ironically, the ghost city of *Yuhong* was one of them.

But Li Na's primary objective was survival. She did not have the years of experience to comprehend just how sophisticated a modern surveillance state could be. Or how pervasive. Even if she had seen the cameras, she would never have dreamed how quickly computers could search through millions of pictures. Or how accurate they could be in matching even the subtlest of facial features.

It would take mere hours.

28

Much like Li Na Wei, the older and much more calculating Dima Belov was also fighting for his life. Banking it, in fact, on the set of satellite pictures he'd given to Admiral Koskov—a political gamble on a man as unscrupulous as any he'd ever met. But by then it was all he had.

And so far, he'd been told exactly nothing.

Instead, he'd been taken from his cell in the middle of the night and led in handcuffs to a waiting, unmarked van. The black doors at the rear were already open when Belov was pushed forcefully inside, landing hard on his chin before rolling onto his right side. Belov was thankful there was no gag, so clearly someone knew that he was not stupid enough to try to call for help.

There were only two possibilities now. Either he was being taken to be executed, or he still held some speck of value for someone. Belov prayed it was the latter. And that the allure of immortality was still alive in the minds of Koskov and his superiors. Because the higher the secret went, the higher the chances were that someone would want to keep Belov alive.

The billionaire twisted himself against the cold metal into a slightly more comfortable position. He would know soon enough whether or not his gamble had paid off. A bet that human greed would once again prevail.

***

Belov estimated the trip at three hours in when he felt the van slow considerably and finally pull to a stop.

The most torturous three hours of his life.

Each passing minute left him clinging increasingly to the

hope that this wouldn't be his last day on Earth. A truly surreal thought. Intellectually, every person knew their last day would come eventually. As certain as night became day, and yet still unexpectedly. But even the acceptance that one day would eventually be their last never stopped them from praying it would be a different day.

Any day but today.

It had been Belov's only thought for three long hours. Until the rear doors of the van were suddenly yanked open, and the bright sunlight washed over him, lying there helpless and afraid.

Large hands grabbed each arm and pulled him out of the vehicle. The old man tried to stand but only made it onto a knee before he toppled forward, hitting the hard cold ground. The same hands hauled him, stumbling, to his feet where the dizziness faded, and he caught a glimpse of his location.

The low-lying hills were heavily developed in every direction. Trees and other vegetation gave way to wide swaths of industrialized sections of land, all along the coast and facing outward over the waters of the Black Sea. A huge mass filled with dozens of large naval ships and submarines, most of which were resting idly in the cool gray-blue waters of the most strategic peninsula in the world.

Considered by many to have been wrested from the hands of Ukraine, the Crimean Peninsula was the single most important naval hub for all of modern-day Russia. A country whose majority of native shores and naval bases were located along Earth's most northern oceans, and locked in by ice most of the year. A warm water base like Sevastopol in Crimea was of critical importance for the former superpower to have faster access to the greater Atlantic Ocean and the rest of the "political" world.

Belov recognized the base immediately.

The moment he recognized the area of Sevastopol, he was yanked again, stumbling forward.

He shuffled quickly and glanced at the men on either side. Large and strong, he recognized neither. They looked relatively young with faces that were hard and chiseled, and unquestionably military.

Neither of the two men paid him any attention. Instead, they headed for a door on one side of a nearby building. A warehouse surrounded by a dozen more just like it. All old and worn. Though clearly still operational.

One of the men flung the door open, and without missing a stride, stormed up a narrow set of stairs.

Belov was sandwiched between the two hulking frames and tried desperately to get a foot on each stair as they ascended. It wasn't until they pushed through a doorway at the top that the older man finally lost his balance. After being shoved forward into the large room, Belov hit the ground and remained sprawled in front of a wide wooden desk.

When the first words were spoken, he recognized the voice immediately.

Behind the desk sat Admiral Koskov, joined by another younger man.

"Get up," he commanded flatly.

The admiral watched Belov struggle with some amusement before adding, "You're not *that* old."

Belov remained silent and at last managed to stand only to find Koskov smirking at him. The second man, dressed in a captain's uniform, bore no expression at all.

The old office surrounding them looked to be completely abandoned except for the desk and chairs. But what really unnerved Belov was the material he was standing on.

Only then did he raise his head and notice the gun sitting on the desk in front of Koskov, with the admiral's hand resting only centimeters away. When his eyes rose to meet the admiral's eyes, all signs of humor had disappeared from the man's face.

"If you're surprised to still be alive, so too am I," the

larger man said. "It seems some important people also want to know what the Americans are doing."

Belov did not answer. His eyes flickered to the captain then back to Koskov.

"But one thing we all agree on," he continued, "is that you know more than you're telling us." Koskov glanced past Belov to ensure the other two had left. "So, you will tell me everything. Now. Or when my men return it will be to wrap you in the plastic you are standing on."

Belov swallowed. "Of course."

"Beginning with the *Forel*."

Nodding his head, Belov thought for a moment. Most of what he'd told them about the *Forel* was accurate. The retrofit, the skeleton crew, and what they found. Everything except the final piece. He paused, contemplating where it had all gone wrong. Why he was now standing where he was.

"The Chinese warship," he said slowly, "was to transfer its cargo to the *Forel* before."

"Before what?"

"Before our *Forel* sank it."

Koskov's eyes narrowed. "Who was your agent?"

"A man named Wang Chao. A lieutenant charged with the excavation of the find. Working under General Wei of the People's Liberation Army."

"And how did you discover him?"

"We were introduced by a mutual friend in Pakistan. The two needed funding."

None of this had surprised Koskov. He'd known Belov for years and was well aware of the other things he'd been involved in. But it was the next question that Koskov was most interested in.

"Who did you bribe on the *Forel*?"

Belov didn't react physically. He had been waiting for this. His next word was spoken calmly.

"Ivchenko."

Koskov's eyes suddenly widened, and his mouth opened

before he quickly shut it. There was no hiding his surprise. Ivchenko was one of the best captains in the Russian fleet. He was one of *Koskov's* finest. Losing him had been devastating. But now, to find out he'd been bought, by Belov of all people, was almost beyond belief.

Koskov simply stared at the man, dumbfounded. When he finally spoke, it was with anger.

"You lie."

Belov gently shook his head. There was nothing else to say.

It was the ultimate miscalculation. In any military around the world, the highest officers simply couldn't fathom one of their most loyal turning on them. Even completely and utterly corrupt generals and admirals. Those who had sacrificed everything and everyone to reach their position of power.

Yet when finally faced with the facts, those same leaders were left in a state of absolute confusion. Stunned and trying to understand where and when the treachery began. It rarely dawned on them that the loyalty they had come to depend on so dearly had never been real.

Belov watched the changes in Koskov's face as he went through the same process. Denial, then anger. He saw Koskov look at the gun, badly wanting to lift it off the table and to pull the trigger.

It was in that endless, excruciating moment that Belov finally realized his fate. And it wasn't death. At that moment, Koskov would have killed him. Unquestionably. If he could have. But it was now clear that Koskov was not in charge. Someone else was. Someone else had decided Belov's sentencing.

The fight in Koskov's eyes was evident. "You have no idea what you've done. You have no idea of the war that has been waged. All as a result of your empty promises."

The words were icy. But Belov did understand. He knew that the fights staged by Russia, like that over Syria, were little more than political theater. A diversion to ensure no one was paying attention to what was happening in South America. A diversion that had now spiraled dangerously out of control.

Koskov stared at him for several minutes in silence. Wishing he could end it right there. Right then. But he also knew that if he did, *he* would be the next one standing on plastic.

With a seething tone, he motioned toward the captain next to him. "You know Captain Zhirov."

Belov's eyes moved to the younger man before nodding. He was another of their navy's top men. Less experienced than Ivchenko but considered by many to be smarter and defter at naval strategy.

"Good," Koskov stated. Then his eyes abruptly changed, taking on a more sardonic expression. "Because you will be accompanying him. And his crew."

"What?"

"You are the expert," Koskov grinned. "What could be better than to have you join the attack for your precious find?"

Any trace of confidence quickly evaporated from Belov's face. He was no soldier. He had never been in physical combat in his life. And now, given his age, he would be of little use to Zhirov or his crew, with or without a rifle in his hands.

Across the dilapidated desk, Koskov was still grinning. It was the only satisfaction he would get from their exchange. Knowing that if they lost, if the fight for the oil rig failed, Belov would never return.

And if they succeeded in securing the platform until reinforcements could arrive, Belov would still be dead. Once they verified the find, Captain Zhirov would carry out his orders to execute the traitor. He wished he could be there to see Belov take his last breath, but knowing it would come regardless of the outcome was almost as good.

And when he got the news, he would toast the end of this son of a bitch who had not just betrayed their country but damn near taken Koskov down with him.

29

Less than an hour later, Belov sat silently in his seat aboard the Antonov AN-148 Russian aircraft. The 100E was one of several variants of the original 148 design, modified specifically for maximum range in a smaller transport plane. Its overhead wing design allowed it to takeoff and land on all but the shortest of commercial runways—a key requirement for their destination in Northern Africa.

Belov turned and peered out the side window into the drizzling rain and out over the slick runways of the airport in Belbek, Crimea. It was Russia's closest airbase to Sevastopol, which was still under turmoil following its turbulent return to Mother Russia.

Beyond the rain-soaked runways, Belov noted the airport's tower. A sea of dull green hills stretched behind the towers until they disappeared into the thick grayness and beyond.

His attention was interrupted as he twisted and felt the bite of the steel handcuffs into his wrists. He looked down again and tried to gently rotate them into a more comfortable position, but nothing alleviated the sensation of losing feeling in both his hands.

The outer door at the front of the plane suddenly slammed shut, and a lone female crew member secured it from the inside. Moments later the AN-148 began to move, and Zhirov reappeared behind Belov from the back of the plane.

The captain sat down and watched the woman move past them. His eyes fell back onto Belov. "Koskov doesn't like you much."

The older man shrugged. "I'll live."

A brief bump caused the men to bounce in their seats as

the plane taxied onto its designated runway. Outside, the intensifying airflow caused the drops of water running down the windows to begin streaking at an angle.

After another bump, Belov raised both hands and his eyebrows.

Zhirov stared at the handcuffs with amusement. He took his time, reached into his pocket, and withdrew a small key. After unlocking the handcuffs, he tossed them onto the empty seat next to Belov and watched him rub his wrists with relief.

If he were there, the gesture would have struck Koskov as strange. But he wasn't. It would have taken several more seconds before the mistake would finally begin to dawn on the admiral. More than a mistake, another colossal miscalculation.

Belov knew something that Koskov didn't about Zhirov. He knew the younger man was an extraordinary captain, as did everyone. One of the shrewdest and calculating men he'd ever met.

But what the Russian Navy did not know was that their captain had a secret. One that threatened to steal the young officer's legacy before it was fully written. A secret that Belov had found out.

The older man watched as the captain returned the key. Even with the movement of the aircraft, he noted the slight shaking of the captain's hand before Zhirov quickly made a fist and shoved it back into his pocket.

Belov returned his gaze to the window, where the view spun slightly as the pilots slowed and turned the plane. After they came to a stop, there was only a brief pause before the whine of the engines turned into a thunderous roar and they surged forward.

The last thing Belov expected was to be assigned to the submarine crew ordered to take control of the oil rig, but it was far better than the alternative.

And yet, if Koskov was angry at Belov for "turning" the captain of the *Forel*, he was going to be absolutely livid when he found out about Zhirov. Even worse, when the ministry learned that Belov had, in fact, bribed *several* other Russian captains, Koskov would likely be executed. A fate the corrupt admiral most assuredly did not see coming.

Of course at the time, Belov hadn't bribed the men to aid him as much as to prevent them from blowing the *Forel* out of the water once it became evident that the plan had gone awry. Something Belov fought hard to avoid…only to see the Chinese do it instead.

It wasn't Belov's first choice, although given the circumstances, being sentenced to Zhirov's submarine was not the worst punishment. In fact, the more he considered it, the more beneficial it was. Not only did he have one of the best captains in the Russian fleet, but unlike the older *Forel* sub, which had been abruptly retrofitted, Zhirov's boat was very modern and a very deadly weapon, virtually impervious to enemy sonar.

And yet the one thing he was certain of, more than anything else, was that *nothing* would ultimately go according to plan.

30

It was a plan that already felt as if it were coming apart at the seams. At least for Alison. Every surprise, at least in her mind, had been followed by a gut-wrenching consequence.

She sat motionlessly in her chair, staring at the phone on her desk. The small red light was still blinking. And it would continue to blink until she went through all the messages. Which she wouldn't.

She lowered her face into her hands just as the phone rang again. Without looking, she lowered a finger and pressed the large button with a message icon on it, sending it to voicemail along with the others.

The retraction had finally been published. In a crushing blow, her reputation was permanently tarnished. And the calls flooding in now were little more than scandalous probes from scientific publications veiled as inquiries. Cynics hungry for condemnation.

As the echo of the last ring faded away, she heard a knock on the open door of her office. When she looked up, she saw John Clay watching her from the doorway, keeping himself up steadily now with only a cane.

"Are you okay?" he asked in a low voice.

"No. Not really."

Clay stepped in and quietly crossed the room until he was beside her, where he dropped a hand gently around her shoulders. "I'm sorry."

Alison closed her eyes. "It's like I've got a giant knot in my stomach—that feels like nothing I've done even matters anymore."

"It does," Clay said. "People just aren't ready."

"What if they just don't *want* to be ready?"

Clay frowned and reached out to pull a second chair closer. He then sat down and faced Alison somberly. "I know how you feel."

She glared at him sarcastically. "No, you don't. You're perfect."

He laughed at her joke. "I'm far from perfect, Ali."

"Uh huh."

Clay watched her, with a smile. "I don't like broccoli."

"What?"

"I don't like broccoli," he repeated. "I hate it."

She folded her arms and tilted her head. "Oh, please."

"I hate beets too. And I'm not a huge fan of heights."

Alison's eyes widened. "You're afraid of heights?!"

Clay nodded.

"*You*...afraid of heights!"

He shrugged. "I said I wasn't a fan."

"Now *that*, I don't believe. I've seen you—"

"It doesn't mean I liked it," he grinned.

"But, you didn't..."

"Panic? No, I didn't. I had to talk myself through it. My point is, I'm not perfect, Ali. Not by a long shot. None of us are. And the frustration you're feeling is the same frustration I felt when I was a SEAL. Like a feeling of purpose wrapped inside a blanket of thanklessness. No one outside of a very small department ever knew what we did. And to make it worse, those times that the public did find out, the government lied about it or twisted the story until it was almost unrecognizable. In the beginning, I considered it a necessary evil, required to protect our great country. But after enough years, I began to realize that's not true. That instead we are nothing more than a political pawn. Fighting over things that really only matter to some very powerful people." He paused before continuing. "A lot of men have died for this country. Good men. Men of integrity and loyalty. And men that didn't deserve to die for a lie."

Clay stared into Alison's reddened eyes. "But this is

133

different. People may not know about it, yet, but it doesn't change the fact that the entire world has just evolved into *more* than it was. How long it takes the planet to know and accept it is another story. And as much as we might not want to admit it, that part is not really up to us. The painful truth is that real change always takes longer than we expect. But you *are* making a difference in the world. A huge difference. I know it, our team knows it, and most importantly, you know it. So who cares what the rest of the world thinks?"

Alison's face softened as she listened to his words. He was right. As painful as it was, some things were simply not under their control. "That may be true, but God, when do our own sacrifices end?"

Clay took her hand and kissed it. "The greater the struggle, the greater the life."

She looked down at her hand, still inside his. She took a deep breath. Her eyes followed his muscular arms up and over his shoulders, then back into his eyes. She ended at his dark, wavy hair.

"What do you worry about, John?"

His lip curled at the question. It was an easy one. "I worry about you," he said.

"About me? Why?"

Clay squeezed her hand. "My greatest fear is for us not to be able to grow old together."

She melted. Alison leaned forward and placed her head gently against his chest. She'd never felt safer with anyone else in her life.

Still resting against him, Alison had a thought and suddenly smiled. "You know...Steve would say you guys are *already* old."

***

When they emerged from her office, they found Lee Kenwood climbing the wide set of stairs.

He stopped and looked up at them. "We're ready."

Alison, still holding Clay's hand, looked down at the room below them. The desks and tables sitting solemnly, near the glass wall of the giant saltwater tank. Their area seemed eerily quiet as if waiting for them.

***

Inside the tank, Sally and Dirk watched Alison on the second level. Her face was still and eyes filled with sorrow. They had never seen her quite like this: struggling to let go…to move on.

They felt her pain and both dolphins floated side by side in the water, wondering if they'd ever be back. Judging from Alison's appearance, they wouldn't.

Sally drifted forward, nosing up to the glass, and watched Alison as she descended the stairs. After crossing the carpeted floor, Alison flattened her hand against the tank. She left it there for a long time before Sally spoke.

We ready Alison. We go now. Beautiful.

On the other side, Alison listened to the translation and merely nodded her head. She then let her hand fall from the glass and turned around to face Clay and Lee. Her eyes scanned the room before stopping on IMIS. The giant computer loomed large against the far wall, made up of racks filled with servers from top to bottom. Their fans created a gentle hum, with hundreds of green lights blinking on and off. A reminder that it was forever churning through its data, searching for ever more complex relationships between the languages.

The rest of the room was surprisingly nondescript: blank white walls and dark, two-tone carpet. The simplicity of not just the room but their entire research center seemed odd now. Almost surreal.

With that, she blinked and followed the men out through a door on the other side of the tank and up a set of stairs. While they climbed, Dirk and Sally darted up and through the deep concrete channel extending out to the shallow beach and the open ocean beyond.

At the shore, a long dock extended much farther over the water. It served as a lingering reminder of the old cannery that had once occupied the site. Most of the dock had been repaired and now held a large Teknicraft aluminum-hulled catamaran, tied securely to the dock's cleats from both bow and stern.

Alison mused at the sight of their latest boat. They'd been going through boats faster than…well, almost as fast as Dirk went through fish.

They reached the dock to find DeeAnn and Dulce already waiting. Their friend was wearing her dark gray translation vest.

"You okay?" DeeAnn asked.

"Yeah. It's just sobering, that's all."

"I completely understand. It just hasn't been the same since Juan."

"No, it hasn't." Alison turned and looked back at their research center. The paint was already beginning to fade under the punishment of an unrelenting Puerto Rican sun. The windows seemed older and a little dirtier than she remembered. Or was it just her mind trying to help her let go?

Dirk and Sally appeared next to them in the water.

No sad Alison. We journey.

She smiled at Sally. "No sad."

They all turned when Dulce rocked from side to side excitedly, then promptly squatted down on the edge of the wooden planks. Alison reached out next to her and patted Dirk on the nose.

DeeAnn tried to smile. "Don't worry. We're going to see you soon."

"I know," Alison nodded. She looked back at the center briefly. "Funny. Doing the right thing doesn't make it feel any better."

"You're starting to sound like me."

Alison chuckled and hugged her, then Dulce, who instinctively rose up to embrace Alison with her long fur-covered arms. With an affectionate pat on the gorilla's head, she turned and approached the short ladder to the boat.

On the side, black hand-painted letters read *U.S.S. Dubois* and following those was a brightly-colored addition: *and Juan.* Once under the shade, she sat quietly down in the cockpit. And hoped it was all worth it.

Less than ten minutes later they cast off, with dual engines rumbling aft, churning the water and pulling the craft backward in a slight arcing motion.

The distance between them and the dock continued to grow until Clay finally pushed both throttle levers forward and unleashed the roar of the engines.

31

Two hours later, Dulce burst out from a group of dense bushes, her heart pounding and small black chest heaving. The gorilla's wide eyes darted back and forth. Searching but finding nothing, she turned around and looked behind her.

She wrinkled her large nostrils and breathed heavily in and out. The smell was all around her. After several seconds, she took a small step and eased forward, now listening carefully.

She never heard it coming.

Just above her head, from the bottom branch of a tree, his small gray head appeared. Without making a sound, Dexter lowered himself down, first by his legs then by his strong tail wrapped firmly around the branch.

Dulce stopped breathing and kept pivoting around, then jumped in the air unexpectedly when Dexter reached down and gave her a playful thump on the head.

She let loose a flurry of shrieks and grunts, smiling and then laughing. Dexter was very good at playing hide. And very sneaky.

The smaller capuchin fell from the tree to the ground and howled. He pointed his tiny hand at Dulce.

You. You.

Dulce laughed so hard she rolled over, continuing all the way back onto her feet.

***

From the lab upstairs, DeeAnn sat in Lee's chair, leaning onto the desk and watching from his monitor. The habitat was fully illuminated beneath the darkness of the night sky. Inside, a gentle flow of air-conditioning washed over her from above, drying the last of her perspiration.

Playtime between the two was amazing. Not just from a maternal standpoint but from an analytical one as well. The comradery between the two primates was simply fascinating. And she could clearly see the communication between them taking place, even if IMIS couldn't translate it.

It still didn't make complete sense to her. If IMIS could translate between Dulce and Sally, then why wasn't it deciphering between Dulce and Dexter? Lee had explained it was because IMIS hadn't recorded enough of Dexter's sounds and mannerisms to begin decrypting them. But if Dulce understood it, why couldn't IMIS when it already understood her communication patterns? Lee's answer to that was because the limited amount that IMIS had already decrypted of the gorilla's language was still very superficial. The tip of the iceberg really.

She followed Dexter on the screen from camera to camera as he searched for Dulce. He was fascinating to watch. He moved differently. To anyone else, there was little difference between him and the monkey they might see in a zoo. But to DeeAnn's trained eye, the distinctions could not be more obvious. Dexter moved differently and much more like a human. Not anatomically, but cognitively. The way he watched and observed. Not just the way he saw the environment but the way he understood it. When the wind blew, he would search for the direction of it. And he would study the water funneling through the small artificial stream for hours.

The hair samples she'd taken from him, and the resulting DNA tests, confirmed that he was very old for a capuchin: almost one hundred, which was unheard of. And it suggested that his enhanced cognitive ability was not only due to brain-related genetic changes but also due to his longer life. That enhanced intelligence wasn't only possible through physiological changes. It was also developed through experience and time. Or in other words, wisdom.

She was watching it before her eyes. Dexter was measurably smarter, which called into question a very big and very controversial theory.

Lucy was the name of the hominin remains discovered in Ethiopia, Africa, and believed by most of the scientific world to be the missing link between apes and humans. It was the crux from where a significant leap forward took place to get humans to where they were today. And while some of that catalyst was related to physiology, DeeAnn now believed that some of it may have also been related to a longer life span. After all, the smarter the species became, the longer they lived. And the more time they had to learn from their mistakes and successes. Something hardly considered before, but Dexter was a living example of that potential. He was the modern equivalent. A second missing link.

***

There was a knock on the door, and she turned to see Bruna peek inside. "I'm sorry, Misses DeeAnn."

DeeAnn smiled. "Come in, Bruna." She still thought it funny that Bruna called her "Misses DeeAnn," especially since they were nearly the same age.

Bruna stepped inside and crossed the large room. "I'm sorry to bother you."

"Not at all. What can I do for you?"

The shorter Puerto Rican woman noted the video feed on the monitor and smiled. "I just wanted to talk more before your trip. You want me to keep all machines on, yes?"

"Yes. Just like last time. At least for a while." Bruna had been a godsend over the last year, keeping on top of all the daily needs of the center. Bruna handled the food and provisions, internal and external maintenance of the old building, and the coordination of the children and their field trips. She was amazing and multitasked like an expert.

When asked, she claimed it came from being a mother. And DeeAnn believed it, given that Bruna had six children.

She also had a sixth sense about her, an intuition, which often allowed her to pick up on things others missed.

Now was one of those times.

"Can I help you please, or the monkeys?"

"No, I think we're all ready. Thank you. Just a ride to the airport would be great."

"Yes, yes." She nodded. "I will take you. Early."

"Thank you, Bruna. I really appreciate it."

The woman smiled broadly and nodded. She backed up and returned to the large double doors where she slipped out with barely a sound.

DeeAnn continued staring after her long after both doors had closed. She hated the feeling of keeping something from them, even from Dulce and Dexter. But she had no choice. The smaller Dexter was already skittish, and understandably so, given what he'd been through. Unfortunately, that meant she couldn't take any chances.

Her goal was to keep her two charges as calm and comfortable as possible. For the next three days.

More than that, DeeAnn knew something the rest of her team didn't. Something she had been reluctant to accept. Even though, down deep, she knew it was true. A sickening dread that told her she could not pretend any longer.

There were simply too many signs to be ignored.

She reached into a breast pocket and withdrew her phone. She then sat it down on Lee's desk and stared at it for a long time. Because once she made the call and let the information out, there would be no putting it back into the bottle.

DeeAnn closed her eyes for a moment before slowly opening them again, and began dialing.

When his phone rang, Will Borger was gripping a section of railing and trying to steady himself over the violent rocking of their small boat. It was a supply craft, used for transferring items back and forth to the rig, and kept secured beneath the platform during the day to avoid being picked up by aerial photos.

But it was no match for the incoming storm. A small tropical storm building from the southeast had changed the conditions drastically. It caused their boat to pitch wildly as they motored through the steep swells. With every up and down motion, Borger gripped the rail tighter and prayed that he wouldn't get sick before they reached the *Pathfinder*.

Upon hearing the ringing from his phone, he switched hands and attempted to steady himself by widening his stance. With his free hand, he pulled the phone out and studied the screen before answering.

"Hello?"

"Will, it's DeeAnn."

He looked curiously at Caesare who was watching from several feet away, though seemingly much less affected by the boat's pitching. "Hey, Dee. What's up?"

"I need to talk to you. About the search."

"Uh, can we talk later? This isn't the best time."

"It's important," she replied firmly.

"Okay." Stepping inside the boat's large pilothouse, Will pressed himself firmly against an interior wall for support. "Shoot."

"Do you have any results yet?"

"Not yet," Borger said. "The servers are making good progress, but they haven't found anything yet." He frowned. "Why, is everything okay?"

"I have a place for you to search."

Borger glanced forward and out through the window at the bright lights of the *Pathfinder*'s stern. Outside from the bow of their own boat, two members of their team were yelling to each other over the powerful wind. Borger turned away and covered one ear with his hand. "Say again?"

DeeAnn raised her voice. "I said, I have a place for you to search."

"Where's that?"

As she spoke, DeeAnn felt the name roll off her tongue like poison. "Rwanda."

Borger thought a moment. "I think we've scanned that area of the map. Everything above fifteen-degrees latitude. We didn't pick up anything there."

On the other end of the phone, DeeAnn's response was blunt.

"Then scan it more carefully!"

With the phone still in his hand, a puzzled Will Borger stared at Caesare and abruptly swayed sideways in response to their boat's first bounce against the stern of the *U.S.N.S Pathfinder*.

32

"Hello, beautiful."

Neely Lawton recognized the voice immediately and turned to spot Steve Caesare standing in the doorway of her lab.

"Commander."

Caesare rolled his eyes. "We've been over this before. It's Steve."

She let out only a trace of amusement. "Right, Steve."

He stepped into the brightly lit room. Behind him, the door began to close before it was caught and pushed back open.

"And good evening to you, Mr. Borger."

Caesare squinted at her upon hearing the change in her voice to Will. "Really?"

She let the grin spread across the rest of her face and reached out to secure a mug on the table as the *Pathfinder* rolled over a large wave. "And to what do I owe the pleasure tonight?"

"Langford wanted us on the call. And we have some parts to pick up."

The "parts" that Caesare was referring to were more than just normal supplies for restocking the *Valant*.

The most important was a piece of hardware procured from the International Ocean Discovery Program or IODP. Established in the mid-20th century, the global project constituted the longest running collaboration of international scientists to study the Earth's history by drilling beneath the seafloor.

And true to Langford and Miller's word, they managed to procure one of the IODP's most sophisticated underwater mobile drilling units with few questions asked.

Of course, what the IODP did not know was that the *Pathfinder's* engineering team was about to replace the giant drill bit with one designed to chew through some of the hardest substances on Earth. What was singularly unique about the IODP's Mobile Undersea Platform (MUP) was its design as a self-contained environment, allowing "dry drilling" even while completely submerged below the ocean surface. A perfect solution when drilling through substances that one did not want to simultaneously flood.

Neely nodded and looked at her watch calmly. "The call's in about a half hour."

"Perfect," Caesare replied. "Just enough time to get some grub. Care to join me?"

She paused, considering it. Then shrugged with a smile. "Sure."

While Neely turned and opened a drawer to put some things away, Caesare looked at Borger and lowered his voice. "You're not invited."

Borger feigned a hurt look. "Fine. I'll try to find some more Bonine."

"Try ginger tablets."

When Neely stood up, Caesare noticed the several cages secured atop the table behind her but said nothing. Instead he smiled and extended his arm for her.

Neely glanced at his muscular arm but made no movement toward it. Without a word, she grinned and moved quickly toward the door, opening it before he could and promptly stepping out.

An amused Caesare raised his eyebrow at Borger. "Feisty."

***

In the galley, surrounded by stainless steel counters and partitions, rows of long blue tables filled the dining area as several of the *Pathfinder's* crew sat together conversing.

At a smaller table against the wall, Neely sipped a cup

of tea while Caesare took a bite from a corned beef sandwich.

"So how's it going over here?" he asked.

"Mmm…not so good."

Caesare paused in mid-bite before continuing. "That doesn't sound like good news."

"How about you?"

"Pretty much the same. This thing sitting under us is pretty damn big. I honestly don't know how long we're going to be able to keep it quiet."

"And there's probably been about a hundred satellite flyovers by now."

"Exactly. If anyone's paying attention, it won't be long before they get just a little curious."

"How much longer do you think we have?"

"A lot less than we need," Caesare frowned. "Maybe weeks. Or less if someone figures it out."

"Then what do we do?"

"Then we all start speaking Spanish and act like we're lost." Caesare winked at her. "You'd be surprised how well that works."

Neely smiled and raised her cup toward her mouth. "I get the impression you're speaking from experience."

"It's gotten us out of more than one tight spot."

She watched him, his wide frame completely relaxed, as he finished the first sandwich and then picked up a second. It was interesting because in some ways he and John Clay were very different, yet they were fairly similar in others. Clay had a slightly more serious or quiet personality, and Steve Caesare was more jovial. Not in an immature way, just more…unrestrained. Caesare was also a few inches shorter and more muscular than Clay.

"So how are *you* doing here?" he asked.

"I'm okay." She smiled appreciatively, then glanced nervously around the small room. "I could sure use my team though."

"Where are they now?"

"Reassigned to another ship. Continuing the project we were working on."

"The sonar array project?"

"Mmm hmm," she nodded, and took another sip of tea. "I know it's safer that way, but I wish I had their full brain power with me on this. Occasional phone calls just aren't the same."

"I think we can all relate. Frankly, I think the admiral made this plan sound *a lot* easier than it was."

This time Neely laughed. "He did, didn't he?"

"Almost like a recruitment commercial. Join the Navy! Save the world! But don't screw it up." Caesare watched as each laugh seemed to soften Neely's shell. Between the loss of her father and the stress of their mission, she needed it. Grief was the worst kind of penance. Something he'd already experienced more than his share of. And to see that pain in eyes as beautiful as hers was just another reminder of how ruthless life could be.

He watched as Neely stared pensively at her cup. "So, do you think there's going to be any good news on this call?"

She looked back up. Her smile had completely disappeared. "I don't think so."

"Does it have to do with those cages in the lab?"

Their eyes met across the table and she nodded without a word.

33

Admiral Langford stared at the monitor, his face drawn with a look of disbelief.

"Come again, Commander?"

On the screen, Neely Lawton blinked and repeated herself. "My test subjects are dead. All of them."

"So it doesn't work?"

"No, sir. If anything, it works too well."

"What exactly does that mean?" Miller asked.

On Neely's larger screen, she could see both video feeds—one for Langford and one for Miller. She remained seated at a small round table, flanked on either side by Caesare and Borger.

"Sir, this kind of hyper regeneration is one thing for the body, but it's quite another for the brain. All cells are not created equal. Regenerating things like muscle tissue and organs don't present many problems. But for brain cells, the effect is much different. When brain cells are improved, so are their synaptic responses. The more they regenerate, the more active they become."

"And why is that a bad thing?"

"Because, sir, the human brain can only take so much. When we sleep, we dream. And those dreams are the manifestation of an overloaded system. Whether we remember them or not, dreams are the by-product of a cognitive system's need to dump excess stimuli."

His expression grew more intent. "And this is what the bacteria is doing?"

"No, Admiral. It's doing the opposite. Instead of allowing the brain to slow down, rest, and resume, the synaptic activity is causing the cells to work harder. So much harder that they *can't* rest. Again, the body's repair cycle works differently than the mind. Everything below the neck slows down and is in a state of disuse. There may be an increase in *some* signaling, but not like the brain, which is all signaling. The bottom line is that the DNA, hidden within the bacterium cells, simultaneously gives us two sides of the same coin. One side will heal you in ways we previously could only dream about. The other side causes the brain to literally burn itself out."

When Neely finished, there was not a sound to be heard until Langford finally exhaled. "Christ."

"Just when I was beginning to think nothing would surprise me anymore," mumbled Caesare.

"Sir," Neely quickly added. "Before we start talking about what this means, it's important that you understand…what I just said is only my assertion. I've only done a limited amount of testing. There is far more left to verify here. Weeks of study. I *could* be wrong."

Langford stared quizzically at her. "Are you?"

Surprised by the question, she stopped and looked at each of them before finally shaking her head. "I don't believe so."

"And as of this moment, how sure are you?"

Neely shrugged. "Ninety percent."

With a sigh, Langford took a step back and sat down. His dark polo shirt highlighted his thick gray hair, combed neatly back atop a rugged face. A face that thankfully gave away none of what he was thinking.

Because what he was thinking was not good.

From his own monitor, Miller watched Langford raise a hand and rub his chin.

"Commander Lawton," Langford said. "Could this effect be changed? So it didn't destroy the brain?"

"Conceivably, yes."

"And how long would that take?"

She didn't reply immediately. But when she did it was not the answer Langford was hoping for.

"Years. Maybe decades."

Langford fell silent again. It was a devastating setback. The Chinese were going to attack. As retribution for the United States having taken something of theirs that, for all intents and purposes, may not even work. At least not as the Chinese believed.

"Okay," Miller countered, leaning forward. "If not this bacteria, then what about those damn plants or that monkey from South America we brought back? They have this DNA too. Don't they? Why didn't it destroy them?"

"I don't know." Neely shook her head. "The plants do have it, but I'm not sure about the capuchin. We've been running tests on his DNA but haven't found any of the base markers yet that we see in the bacteria. But that's not altogether surprising. Even common genome markers don't always work the same way. Now why the plants have survived, I don't know. They have very different structures than we do. Their cells are rectangular with protective cellulose walls. They have chloroplasts. It could be any number of differences. And their absorption of minerals is also much slower through their roots. Which means their exposure, even directly, would likely be much more gradual. In evolution the more gradually a life form is exposed to something, the easier and more moderate its adoption, generally speaking."

"So the plants haven't been destroyed by this because their DNA changes more slowly over time?" Caesare asked.

Neely turned and nodded. "Probably."

"And in South America, the absorption was slower because the monkey was eating the same plants."

"Possibly." Neely turned back to the screen. "Nothing happens quickly in evolution. Only through direct intervention. And that is often where we experience side effects."

"Like we're seeing with the bacteria."

"Correct."

"So the bacteria itself is no good to us."

"Well, I'm sure it could be altered. Through testing and

experimentation, but there will always be some tradeoff. Everything in life is balanced, even physics. For every give, there is a take. Even in common pharmaceutical medications. Every new drug treats something but negatively affects something else."

"What are you saying?"

"I'm saying that tweaking this bacterium in an attempt to avoid overworking the host's brain may ultimately be possible. But there *will* always be another tradeoff. Regardless of what it might be. For now, something *may* have happened during the Chinese extraction for the bacterium. Something that made it unstable. Therefore, the plants are likely more valuable."

This time Miller leaned back, throwing out a sarcastic retort, "Wonderful."

"And that's just regarding the plants," Borger spoke up. "Not the source itself, which is the liquid we found. *That's* the real catalyst."

"You're talking about Africa."

"Yes, sir. If there really is another vault, it's the liquid inside that everyone will eventually be after."

Langford frowned. "This just keeps getting better and better."

"If it's something that really did affect our evolution," Neely said, "the implications may only get bigger."

"So, now what?"

"Sir, I think we need to step back and think about this," Caesare said. "This bacteria, now that we know it's not perfect, could still lead to some frightening scenarios if other people got a hold of it."

"Or other governments," added Borger.

"Or other governments. And even if it's flawed, I'm guessing there's still a hell of a lot someone else could do with it."

"That's true." Neely nodded.

"Admiral," Caesare said, peering at the screen, "unless I'm mistaken, this DNA-infused bacterium is the only sample in existence. It was the only stuff extracted by the Chinese, before—"

He suddenly stopped, not wanting to finish the sentence in front of Neely.

"What's your point, Steve?"

"My point, sir, is that if this stuff *is* as dangerous as Commander Lawton suggests…*maybe we don't want it.*"

"Whoa! Whoa!" started Miller. "Let's not get ahead of ourselves here. It is the only sample on the planet, which means we need to be very careful here. Let's not do anything irrational."

"I'm not, sir. I'm merely pointing out that this thing is already a weapon. Even if it's not altered, what would happen if this got into the general population? What if someone managed to dump it into a public water supply? Or found some other way to infect a large group. Remember it was that liquid that was in the water in Guyana, which caused the plants to mutate in the first place. So it's not a huge stretch for the bacteria to get out in the same way. And as Commander Lawton explained, this stuff is potent."

Langford and Miller were now both looking at each other through their screens.

"Commander Lawton," Langford said. "Once infected, how long of a gestation period are we looking at?"

"Absorbed is probably a better word," she replied absently. "And I'm not sure. My mice took only a few days. A human…could take…weeks maybe. But I'm only speculating. Once that DNA takes hold, and their cells stop dying, the rest could come on very quickly."

"And what do we think a person infected with this DNA would experience?"

"Rejuvenation, mostly. A level of healing within their bodies that would probably seem…magical. Their senses, their strength, even their minds would all probably feel stronger. Much stronger. At least until their brains could no longer shut themselves off. That would be the first sign." Neely stopped for a moment before adding one more thought. "And maybe one of the last."

34

In Beijing, a blaring musical chime awoke M0ngol from a fitful sleep. With his long dark hair plastered to his head and still dressed in the previous night's clothes, the hacker instinctively rolled over and retrieved his phone from a side table. He then found his glasses and slipped them on to study the phone's bright screen.

It wasn't a person calling him but rather one of his computers. And instead of a call, it was actually a notification generated by one of the computer scripts he'd written. Known as a *bot*, the program was constantly churning through thousands of pages of communication logs from other agencies, looking for anything that could be related to their search for Li Na Wei.

It wasn't until M0ngol clicked through a series of links that the information that triggered his script was revealed, and he practically slid off the side of his bed. The source was an image, from one the Ministry's public surveillance databases. And even though they had been scouring for any possible trace of the teenage girl, when he finally saw the digitized image of her face, he couldn't believe it.

The photo appeared to be taken from an angle and under less than ideal lighting, but it was her. There was no question. She was alive.

And she was still in the country.

***

It took only minutes to find the number and make the call. To his surprise, the call was routed several times before someone finally answered. The voice was slow and deliberate and not one he recognized. But it was clear that whoever it was had not been sleeping either. And they knew exactly who M0ngol was.

"What is it?" the voice asked.

"I have a positive identification!" M0ngol nearly shouted.

"Where?"

He dropped his phone from his ear and studied the data again. "I'm not sure yet. The Heilongjiang province, I think. From a surveillance camera. I only have coordinates."

"What are they?" the voice asked.

M0ngol read them off, and the person on the other end repeated them, slowly.

"Is that correct?"

"Yes."

"Who else knows?"

M0ngol suddenly paused. It seemed an odd question given the entire department was working on the search. "I don't...I don't know." A sense of fear suddenly welled up in his chest. It was his bot script that had found it. Sure it was already on the Ministry's servers, but they obviously hadn't made the connection yet. His script had done it first. And it was a script that no one else knew about. In fact, it was running on a different system even fewer people knew about, and its results wouldn't be in the rest of the logs. So anyone monitoring his progress wouldn't see it.

M0ngol grew increasingly nervous. He wasn't trying to keep anything secret. A lot of hackers had their own systems. Systems that avoided having to worry about someone else changing something, or screwing it up.

But now he realized how it might look from the other side.

"I wasn't..." he fumbled. "I just...wrote some of my own code. Something easier and faster. I just wanted—"

The voice cut him off. "How long ago?"

"Uh..." M0ngol looked back to the small screen. "Twelve minutes."

"Disable your program."

"Okay."

"Speak to no one else about this until we can verify. Is that clear?"

M0ngol nodded. "Yes. Perfectly."

"Delete the record of this call from your phone. We will call you back if needed."

"Okay."

The voice promptly hung up, leaving M0ngol sitting in the dark, still in his wrinkled clothes. And praying that he hadn't just signed his own death warrant.

35

With a start, Li Na Wei woke up in the darkness. She looked around the room listening for it again. The sound of movement. But it never came.

She remained motionless, propped onto her side, before she allowed her breathing to normalize.

To her surprise, she found a few of the apartments in the ghost buildings to be unlocked. With locks either picked or mistakenly left open by someone. Maybe a facilities person or a security guard assigned the arduous task of checking hundreds of apartments in each building. Eventually, anyone was bound to miss locking one or two. At least that's what Li Na hoped.

There were over thirty floors, and from what she could guess, a couple dozen apartments on each level. The people she tried to follow had to be hiding in some of them. And like her, without any electricity or water.

But the empty, one-bedroom apartment she'd found near the top floor still had a working door. The lock appeared to be broken, but a few scattered pieces of furniture gave her something to prop up against the other side. And a dirty stripped-down mattress provided a softer place to lie than the floor.

The windows were all still intact, and even in the darkness, the walls and counters showed little signs of damage. Even after years of sitting idle, the apartments and the towers were in surprisingly sound condition. At least for now, until the rest of the homeless eventually discovered them and made the long trek inland. In the meantime, Yuhong, along with the other ghost cities, were left without a soul.

Li Na pushed herself up and continued listening. The

silence or lack of any appreciable sound was…eerie.

She strode across the room and approached the bedroom's large window. Never had her ears been so devoid of any noise whatsoever. With the sealed windows and a nearly empty city far below, it left her almost wondering whether the world outside still existed.

Li Na stood behind the window, trying to think of a plan. She was getting less and less sleep, yet each time waking up just as alert, although struggling more and more on a plan to survive. And how to get out of China. But she was safe for the moment. Hiding in a city that everyone seemed to have forgotten.

She could relax and take her time trying to piece together a strategy that entailed more than just surviving. As long as she could manage to stay hidden and still find food, she could finally relax.

Li Na breathed a silent sigh of relief.

She had no idea that a Chinese military helicopter had just lifted off and was headed straight for her, a mere two hours away.

36

The voice on the other end of M0ngol's call belonged to a man named Lam. Who, unlike his predecessor Qin, was largely immune from the political and professional greed affecting so many of his compatriots.

All politicians had it—all "infected" with the dream, whether they were willing to admit it or not. Leaders, ambassadors, statesmen, or whatever they chose to call themselves, it was always the same. Attain as much position and prestige as possible, no matter what the cost.

Kings of old and ancient pharaohs did the same—insisting on being buried with all of their earthly possessions, and in many cases the very slaves who served them too—in hopes of living again, and more importantly, ruling again.

It was the ultimate human desire, whether most admitted it or not. To rule. To be worshiped. To live in the hearts and minds of the masses *forever*.

And yet, one man who did *not* have it, at least this particular *infection*, was Lam himself. No, his motivation was far simpler, even if just as self-serving.

He didn't know who had gotten him released from prison. Or what they ultimately wanted with the girl. He didn't know, and he didn't care. What he wanted was *revenge*.

General Zhang Wei was the man responsible for his imprisonment. After a particularly nasty battle several years ago, Wei settled on him as the army officer who had to be made an example of to the rest of the People's Liberation Army.

But the general should have known. If anyone understood what hell war really was, it was Wei. He should have understood that in the heat of battle soldiers had to do things that civilians on the sidelines would not approve of. Things that might seem barbaric on the surface but served a very important role in flushing out the enemy. An enemy that was trying to kill Lam and his unit.

Wei had seen enough war in his own life to know the difference. There was a huge difference between a war on paper and a war in person—that when it came down to a choice between you and your enemy, you did whatever you had to do. No matter how offensive or how grotesque.

But instead, the general turned his back on Lam, having him and his men brought up on charges. Charges that landed Lam in prison for most of the remainder of his life.

It was there, sitting in his cell these past few years, that Lam finally grasped what Wei had become. He had become one of *them*. One of the political elite hell-bent on nothing more than his own personal power. No matter whom he had to use or step on to get it. And Lam was one of the casualties.

But the tides had turned. And he would have his revenge. He would strike back at the man who had destroyed his life. With Wei now dead, the next best thing was the man's offspring: a daughter who Lam had even met briefly when she was a young child.

He had dreamed about it for years, sitting alone behind the bars of his prison cell. An almost feral yearning to strike back at the great general. An opportunity he never thought would come.

But it had.

Almost as if by miracle, his opportunity had finally arrived—out of a failed mission, leaving Wei a traitor to his country. And his daughter a prize of extreme importance to the state.

Wei's daughter was now the instrument of this revenge.

With dark, unmoving eyes, Lam sat on the Russian-built, Mi-17 transport helicopter without saying a word. Next to him were four soldiers of the PLA Special Operations Forces. Dressed in black fatigues, their assault rifles hung over their shoulders and pointed down at the black metal floor. The men's hands never traveled far from their triggers. Emblazoned upon their shoulders was the familiar red insignia bearing a sword and lightning bolt.

The helicopter's cabin was eerily silent except for the whirling blades overhead, beating the air into submission. The glowing city lights of Jinzhou passed slowly beneath them.

Lam kept his eyes low. His mind was fixated on one thing and one thing only.

What he didn't know was that the four soldiers sitting next to him were not there entirely for the reason he'd been told. They would help find her, but in the end, they were there to keep Wei's daughter alive. Or put more simply, to protect her…from Sheng Lam.

37

Li Na sat quietly in the nearly empty living room of the abandoned apartment. With knees pulled up to her chest and arms wrapped around them, she waited patiently for sunrise.

Her stomach growled, reminding her the previous night's food had not lasted long enough. She tried to eat as much as she could, but her stomach wasn't used to holding so much food. Which left her counting the hours until she could return downstairs for more.

She tried to distract herself by examining the apartment for the hundredth time. Even without lights or a working door, she had to admit it felt nice. The mattress alone had been worth the loneliness, for a while. But eventually the gravity of her situation crept back in. Soon her mind returned to the priorities of food and a way to reach the coast.

She had actually grown optimistic that it might not be too hard. Some people in the city had to have cars. She just needed to find them and bribe one of the owners to take her as far east as possible. It would be worth losing even a large chunk of her money as long as it got her there quickly.

If she couldn't find a car, there were always the trucks. Even a mostly empty city required some things brought in. Equipment, maintenance supplies, and especially food for what few shops existed. And if a truck didn't bring it then something had to. She just needed to find out what.

Li Na instinctively looked up at the door, putting a foot on the cold floor at the same time. There was a sound outside. Something barely detectable, but there. She lowered her other foot without a sound and leaned forward, listening.

It sounded like scratching. After several long seconds, it became louder. It wasn't scratching though. It was the sound of skittering.

She breathed a sigh of relief. Rats were much better than something bigger. Li Na lifted both feet off the floor again and wrapped her arms back around her legs, gently easing her head against the wall.

She closed her eyes in the darkness, trying to relax, and reminded herself that she had plenty of time.

38

Sheng Lam pushed a button on the side of his watch to read the illuminated face. It was similar to what he'd worn before prison, including his fatigues and boots, but better quality. His only weapon was a P19 semiautomatic pistol, holstered on his left side. And it gave him a sense of carnal pleasure each time his elbow brushed back against it.

He'd snuck a look at the magazine before they lifted off to make sure they hadn't given him an empty gun. Years ago he would have been able to tell just from the weight, but not anymore. Some of his skills were nowhere near as sharp after years of being unused. But others, the more innate abilities, were still intact. Especially his tracking abilities.

His call with the hacker M0ngol was just another example. The kid was clearly frightened, but several slight pauses in his speech told Lam he was also hiding something. A hunch further confirmed by some of the subtle fluctuations in his voice. The hacker was beginning to worry more about covering for himself than finding the girl—which meant he needed to be watched very carefully.

Lam could also sense the mood amongst the five men sitting around him. Something…deceptive. A second agenda he clearly didn't know about.

But it didn't bother him. He'd had more than his share of secrets when serving in the army. Lam's only concern now was whether those men would get in the way of his objective. Because if they did, he was ready to kill every single one of them.

Impatiently, Lam glanced again at his watch.

Less than two hours.

39

Li Na was moving before dawn broke. Once there was enough ambient light to navigate the stairwells, she began quietly descending, pausing briefly at each floor to listen before continuing.

She stopped at a floor where she thought she'd seen one of the others disappear, but there was no sound. No talking, no movement, nothing. Li Na abruptly gripped one of the handrails when it occurred to her that perhaps the others might be listening for *her*.

She looked up the stairs behind her, then down below, listening harder. She placed each step toe to heel to eliminate any pounding, no matter how subtle. On each stair, she moved down the gray metal steps with only a slight reverberation.

When she finally reached the bottom, she pushed open one of the beige double doors and checked the exit at the end of the hall. She eased the door closed behind her and bounded lightly down the hallway.

There was no one outside yet. Still half dark, the streets were both easily visible and very empty. From a nearby corner, Li Na scanned up and down her street, spotting the entrance to the mall she'd found the night before. She spotted movement further down the street on the far side. A man with his head down, dressed in gray pants and a white shirt.

She inhaled and stepped out onto the sidewalk.

***

The team's Mi-17 helicopter landed several kilometers outside of the city, where the thumping of its rotors would not be heard. The men climbed out to see the towers of Yuhong rising solemnly into the air, silhouetted by the first rays of sunrise.

From that distance, there was little indication that the metropolitan area was empty. Instead, the cityscape looked calm, almost peaceful, in the morning air.

The leader of the five soldiers, a man named Peng, stopped almost two hundred meters beyond the chopper's spinning blades and withdrew a small handheld device. The flat screen came to life, promptly displaying an aerial map. It was quickly followed by the appearance of a red dot, indicating their location. The others, including Lam, closed in around him as the leader zoomed in on the mall where the video images had been recorded.

"Eight, maybe nine kilometers," he instructed in Mandarin. He looked up to observe the tip of the morning sun peeking over the distant mountain range. "It'll be too light when we get there. Leave the rifles and change clothes. Take only weapons you can conceal."

"We should split up," one of his men offered.

"When we get a few streets in. Our target is here," he replied gruffly, pointing at the screen. "We see if she comes back first." The leader then turned to Lam. "You stay with me."

Lam didn't reply.

Peng ignored him and nodded to the rest of his men, a nod they promptly returned before running back to the helicopter.

40

The first sign of hope Li Na found was in the form of a large parking garage. It was several stories tall, attached by a glass bridge to a very large and expensive building, towering high overhead. Mirrored glass covered all sides. The spacious entrance to the building was visible in the far corner and looked as deserted as the rest. Once-tall Gingko trees planted on either side now stood wilting and neglected.

Inside the garage, Li Na found the first two levels empty. However, on the third level, where the skyway connected the two buildings, she was surprised to find several cars. They were all parked together in a small group, leaving the rest of the level as barren as the first two.

She recognized the symbols on each of three Mercedes and one Jaguar. But the last two she hadn't seen before. All of them were expensive.

Li Na turned to check behind her, then eased behind a concrete pillar, watching for movement. There was no motion at all. Just the row of automobiles parked in silence.

Across the bridge, she could make out a large heavy glass door. Opaque and still.

She moved cautiously. Walking forward in a wide arc allowed her to keep her eyes fixed on the glass bridge. Without a sound, she reached the group of cars and moved in close enough to look inside the windows. It wasn't their opulent interiors or upholstery that surprised her. Or even the wide television screens embedded in the thick leather of the backseats. What surprised her was that two out of the three cars she examined did not have their doors locked.

Searching the other levels confirmed the rest of the garage was empty. Her growling stomach kept interrupting her thoughts. If she was going to find another option, it was going to take time.

From the top level of the garage, she peered out over the early-morning city. Even with the sun's light casting long shadows, she could see much more now than she had the night before, including a larger city center. And a park that stretched almost a half kilometer on the other side. Both locations, to her surprise, showed signs of movement.

This revelation caused a brief wave of optimism to course through her veins. There were more people here than she thought, which could mean an opportunity for making a friend—someone who might be able to help her get out of the city.

And now with the hope of a new day, the most logical place to start was back at the food court.

***

Even dressed in normal clothes, the emergence of all six men from the tall grasses outside of Yuhong appeared ominous. With the squad leader in front, followed closely by Lam, they quickly covered the open distance of grass and dirt. They then crossed the first major, yet empty, road. Upon reaching the other side, the men split up. Each one moved separately through various side streets and alleys, toward the city center just two kilometers away.

Peng and one of the leader's men remained close to Lam, keeping him within eyesight—half for the man's tracking ability and the other half a result of their second priority. If they found the girl, they were to keep her alive, no matter what the cost.

This also meant that once the girl was secured, they were to kill Lam immediately.

41

Four of the six men were already in position by the time Li Na returned to the mall entrance, including Lam. They waited by the door nearest the cameras that had spotted her.

They hid in the waning shadows or behind objects, eyes fixed on the entrance. When Li Na appeared, Lam recognized her immediately.

Through a small handheld scope, he could see her father's characteristics in her. The shape of her eyes and nose were the same. Even the way she moved.

"Wait," the leader breathed, standing several meters away. "Until she's inside." He raised a small hidden microphone closer to his mouth and whispered for the last two men to continue around the building to the opposite side.

The rest of the team continued watching until the teenage girl reached the set of double doors and pulled one open.

As soon as it closed again behind her, Lam was in motion.

***

The line for food this time was longer, now with over a dozen others waiting in front of the same kitchen. The seating area also had more people, few of them speaking, and the same eerie feeling she'd had the night before.

But there was something else. As Li Na approached the line, something felt very odd. More than just eeriness. More than the city's dark mood. This was stronger.

It was a feeling…or a smell. A strangely putrid sense that quickly grew into something even worse: *fear*.

Suddenly, the hair on Li Na's neck and arms stood up, and the very air around her seemed to stop. It was her last thought before she saw the flash of yellow and felt the air flutter past her face. She turned instinctively to see something large stuck into the shoulder of the man standing in front of her. The man staggered and turned, before abruptly collapsing onto his knees.

Time slowed, and Li Na watched with confusion as the man fell forward, hitting the marble tiles like a sack of meal, folding at the waist and pushing himself onto his side—his last movement before his frightened eyes went blank.

The next sensation followed immediately: *panic.*

Li Na whirled to see another yellow blur just before it hit her above the clavicle. She stumbled back, squinting at the group of men running toward her.

She reached down and felt the fibrous yellow tuft. It was a dart. The end was soft, and she plucked it from her skin, unable to feel the sting.

The momentum of the dart's tiny steel ball had already pushed the entire dose of vecuronium into her bloodstream, where it immediately began to spread. The first traces instantly reached the closest skeletal muscles.

The men drew nearer as the teenager's arms and legs began to tremble and slow. The neuromuscular agent was now binding itself to receptors on the motor nerve cells to block the conduction between cells, rendering Li Na's muscular functions inoperable.

***

A manic Lam was now almost to the girl with the larger Peng only steps behind. But realizing he wouldn't reach Lam in time, he immediately reached under his shirt to withdraw his pistol.

Once firmly gripping the weapon in his hand, Peng slid to a stop and raised his arm, aiming squarely at Lam's back. "STOP!"

Lam slowed and looked back at the very moment Li Na collapsed to the floor in front of him. The dark barrel of Peng's QSW-06 semiautomatic trained directly upon Lam, who glanced at him and then down to the girl.

"Get away from her."

Lam watched Peng intently, inching to within a meter of his target before the soldier's finger snaked through the trigger guard.

"Don't touch her."

The shorter man's eyes narrowed, moving yet again toward the girl. *No. He was so close! He had to have her.* He tried to step closer. *It was so easy. His dream was within reach. Literally within reach!*

"Get…away," Peng repeated.

Lam didn't move. He couldn't step back. Not now. Instead, he angled himself away, hiding his own gun on the other side of his body, and slowly raised his hand toward his hip.

In a flash, Lam whipped the gun from his holster and fired three rounds at Peng, who remained motionless. Screams erupted around them with the deafening cracks of the gun, leaving the two men motionless and staring into each other's eyes.

But Peng did not fire back. He swayed slightly before finally surprising Lam—by smiling.

"Get down, or I will kill you."

Over the screams, Lam's face grew nervous, and he stared at the gun in his hand. *Blanks.* His eyes returned to Peng's finger now beginning to tighten around his own trigger.

Without a word, Lam complied and lowered himself onto his knees.

***

Li Na lay still on the floor, the paralytic agent having reached over eighty percent of the teenager's muscle receptors.

But something was different.

The synaptic conduction between Li Na's muscle cells was in overdrive. And the binding strength of the agent was already beginning to weaken far more quickly than its normal twenty minutes. Moreover, as the bindings decreased, the stalled conduction between the cells began to *re-accelerate*. The result was that the girl's muscles were already beginning to respond again. Catching up to her brain cells, which never slowed and were now fully processing what had just happened.

They had found her.

***

Motionless in front of her, Lam was turned away, facing Peng. His eyes seethed at the officer behind the pistol, who was now flanked by two more of his men.

"Stay down."

Lam did as he was told, not moving. When he finally opened his mouth to speak, he was interrupted by a sudden commotion behind him.

***

Before anyone could reach her, Li Na was back on her feet. She glanced at the men, and seeing one aiming a strange gun, she sprang forward and ran hard for the far exit. Hearing another dart blow past her, she accelerated, driven by two legs surging with renewed strength.

Another dart caught the corner of her shirt, but the needle found nothing except air on the other side.

Li Na was now running at full speed, headed for a short hallway ending with double doors. And then she felt it. Again. The same tingling under her skin that had given her the first warning.

Someone was on the other side of the doors.

Instead of slowing, Li Na raced even harder and lowered her head. She hit the horizontal release with all of her might, sending one of the doors slamming open and squarely into the face of Peng's man.

The impact was a complete surprise, knocking his head against the wall behind him then crashing to the floor.

Through a short corridor and another set of doors, she reached the cool air outside with only a singular thought.

Run!

42

The most surprising realization upon reaching the garage was how strong she felt. Li Na's legs carried her with a speed she'd never experienced before. And it wasn't just the speed. It was the endurance—in her lungs, and more importantly, in her heart.

It was all driven by sheer panic. The adrenaline releases she had read about in fight or flight situations. *But how did they find her? And how did they manage it so fast?*

Li Na was barely winded when she reached the third level of the garage and spotted the cars again. This time she ran straight for them, without hesitation, and opened the first one she found unlocked. She prayed desperately that if the owners worried so little about locking their cars, then perhaps at least one also left the keys behind.

And they had. In the second to last car, Li Na found a set of keys under the center console. She grabbed them and looked for an ignition but found nothing. No key slot like she'd always seen before. Instead, there was only a round, gray button.

She pressed it.

Nothing.

She pressed it again. Multiple times. Still nothing.

Li Na turned to scan the garage behind her. They had to have seen where she'd run to. She slammed her hands desperately against the steering wheel and tried again. There was no response.

She grabbed the keys and began pushing buttons on the remote. The doors locked and the horn immediately began blaring.

Oh God!

With frightened eyes, she looked through the windshield

across the glass bridge. She fumbled for the remote and pushed the button again to silence it. But it was too late. The echoing through the garage had to have been loud enough for everyone to hear, including the men chasing her.

She had to find something else. Li Na grabbed the wheel with one hand and opened the door with the other. She slid sideways to leave and had just pushed against the brake pedal on her way out when something happened.

Several lights lit up on the car's dashboard. She froze and stared, dumbfounded. With her foot still firmly against the brake, she reached forward and pushed the round button again. The engine came to life.

With insurmountable relief, Li Na reached out and slammed the heavy door shut again. She then found the gearshift and pulled it back into reverse before punching the gas pedal.

The gray Jaguar XJ lurched into motion, throwing Li Na hard against the steering wheel. She struggled for control before screeching to a stop. She looked across the glass bridge, which was miraculously still empty.

She took a deep breath and gripped the wheel tightly. Her father had taught her how to drive…once.

Li Na carefully pulled the gearshift back further into drive, this time pressing lighter against the gas pedal. The car surged forward, causing her to quickly steer away, barely missing the other cars.

With a wide, almost uncontrollable turn, she was gone.

43

The plunge into the bright blue waters was a refreshing change from the stifling sun overhead. Even the Bimini top of the aluminum-hulled boat could not protect them from the hot breeze blowing across the ocean's glimmering surface.

For Alison, getting into the water was a no-brainer.

Hello Alison.

"Hello, Sally," she replied, breathing calmly through her face mask.

You swim.

She nodded. "I swim."

Before she could continue, Dirk darted playfully past her, leaving her reaching out too late to touch him. Several more dolphins appeared and followed him, diving down and around a large outcropping of coral.

Who she? One of them whistled, which Alison was surprised to hear from the vest. Lee's improvements appeared to be working better at separating out different threads of language.

She turned to capture another approaching dolphin with her camera as it sounded off in reply. But *She* was all Alison heard before IMIS's familiar error tone returned through her earbuds.

She name Alison, Sally replied, as she circled in tightly around her human friend. *Come Alison. Play.*

Alison smiled. "Okay, Sally. I'll play." She kicked her own fins hard to catch up and grabbed hold of Sally's powerful dorsal fin. Sally accelerated, causing Alison to quickly grab hold with her other hand as she felt her face mask press harder against her face. Their sleek shape allowed the dolphins to move surprisingly fast through the water, unlike the human figure which added a significant drag to Sally's effort. Something she hardly ever mentioned. Dirk, on the other hand, always did with a joking tone, calling Alison *heavy*. It was ironic given Alison's rather petite frame.

Still, their abilities seemed almost effortless, even with Alison in tow. Sally had carried her to safety once on her back, leaving Alison stunned and appreciative of the amount of innate strength dolphins possessed.

She smiled and gripped her hands tighter around the fin, turning side to side to see other dolphins swimming with them—dozens, all darting back and forth.

"Whoa!" Sally suddenly dove, leaving Alison laughing and clamoring to hang on.

***

On the surface, Lee Kenwood raised his eyebrows and glanced at John Clay. He leaned forward toward his standing microphone. "You okay, Ali?"

Alison's voice responded over the speakers as clear as a bell and still chuckling. "Yes! I'm fine!" After a pause, she added, "We're playing. Wow, you should see this coral. It's *beautiful*."

Clay peered at the speaker curiously and leaned in. "You don't mean beautiful like Trinidad?"

***

"No," Alison shook her head and watched another pod of dolphins skim below them. Like small hills, the coral dipped and rose for as far as she could see. And with life teeming everywhere. "Not like Trinidad. Just...beautiful. Like Costa Rica." She squealed again as Sally made a sudden turn, rolling up and over above Dirk.

You fun Alison?

"Yes, Sally." She smiled inside her mask. "Very fun.

And beautiful."

Waves of fish zipped by as the dolphins simultaneously dipped into a large depression. They skimmed along the bottom next, before turning to rocket up over the next rise.

Hold hard Alison.

Alison widened her arms and wrapped herself tighter around the base of Sally's head. "What are you going to do?"

More hard Alison.

The clicks of the other dolphins echoed in her ear, sounding like laughter. Alison's eyes grew larger as she saw the bright water of the surface approaching.

"What are you going to do, Sally?!"

More hard.

She gripped Sally with all of her strength just moments before they broke the surface. One after the other, dozens of dolphins all leaped into the air together with Alison, who was hanging on for dear life.

She gasped inside her mask as they became airborne. And just for a moment, time seemed to stand still. At the apex of their leap, everything grew quiet, suspended momentarily over the water before gravity reasserted itself and they plunged smoothly back into the waves.

Alison finally lost her grip and tumbled backward into the turbulence behind them. She allowed herself to relax, twisting with the water before regaining her bearings and floating back to the surface. With her head bobbing above the water, she spun around until she could see the gleaming aluminum boat behind her.

She reached up and pulled off her mask, allowing her to see Clay and Lee watching from the starboard side of the craft. Alison raised her fist and yelled at the top of her lungs, "WHOO HOO!"

***

Both laughed and Clay clasped Lee's shoulder zealously.

"Yep. She's definitely okay."

Lee smiled and waved, then watched Alison wave back. "Good. I think if anyone needs this right now, she does."

"Agreed." Clay's gaze moved to the water and the horizon behind them, where he noted that the island of Saint Lucia had disappeared from sight.

Steadying himself with one hand, he moved closer to the stern of the boat and breathed in deeply. There was something extraordinarily peaceful about seeing nothing but water around him. Something inexplicable. Just the breeze and the lapping of the waves against the hull reminded him there was a certain peace in the world that humans seemed to forget too easily. Nature provided its own pace as a means for nurturing the human soul.

"You seem to be healing up pretty well," Lee said.

Clay turned around. "I am. Thanks to them."

"Things are sure different."

"Yes, they are."

"I just hope we haven't given up too much."

Clay considered the question. "So do I." He looked out over the water at Alison, still playing with Sally, head also bobbing above the water.

He was still staring out over the water when, all of a sudden, both he and Lee heard a loud screech, quickly spinning around. Inside the door, the boat's VHF radio burst into noise—static, laced with words being shouted through the unit's small speakers.

Clay was already halfway to the radio when the shouting stopped, only to quickly resume again. The yelling was now beginning to sound more like screams and was almost unintelligible.

"What the hell is that?"

Clay reached inside and checked the channel while snatching up the handheld microphone. He glanced briefly at Lee.

"It's a distress call."

From under the water, Alison jumped when she heard the sound of the boat's diesel engine roar to life. She stared up through the blue water with a look of confusion and kicked her fins hard to reach the surface.

Once above the water, she pulled her mask off and watched, puzzled, as their aluminum craft turned and charged directly for her with John Clay at the helm. She cleared water from her eyes to see Lee hanging over the starboard hull, his hands cupped over his mouth.

It took less than half a minute for them to cover the distance. Clay immediately forced the engine into reverse, slowing the boat and swinging its gleaming stern toward Alison.

"ALISON!" Lee called. "You have to get aboard! Now!"

"What is it?!"

"It's an emergency!"

Still confused, Alison watched as Clay left the wheel and ran back to Lee. Once there, both leaned out over the rear ladder with their hands extended.

Alison kicked forward and reached up. The men grabbed and pulled hard, lifting her out of the water like a rocket.

"What's happening?"

"Distress call," Clay yelled, running back toward the pilot house. "Hold on to something!" he called, just before jamming the throttle forward again.

Lee and Alison both caught themselves in mid-slide, keeping firm handholds on each railing.

With a grave expression, Clay checked their bearing and pushed hard against the throttle. He did the math in his head and frowned.

They were likely too far away. And listening to the details over the radio…probably too late.

44

It was known as the Terra Firma Fleet. Composed of seven Spanish galleons, the flotilla was the most successful of the *extraction* efforts of Spain during the early 1600's. They were charged with the extraction of valuables from the new world, including gold from Peru and Colombia, which were wildly more productive than Europe's older mines.

Yet what historians did not know of the Terra Firma Fleet was that as the ferocity of the Spanish government's war with the Dutch continued, the more desperate their need became to replenish its dwindling coffers. And ultimately the more fearful the Spanish became of losing their critical, ill-gotten treasure galleons.

They even went so far as to create falsified sailing logs showing those very galleons to be sailing Caribbean waters much farther to the north than was actually true. And it was an essential detail that would be missed by nearly every historian since, until it was realized centuries later and hundreds of miles away by a Greek treasure hunter.

Forty-seven-year-old Dimitris Demos was that man. And his years of painstaking research and personal loss to locate the Spanish galleons now paled in comparison to the sacrifice he was about to endure.

All of the dreams, of fame and riches, of being the first to find what no one else in history could—it all meant nothing as Demos stared into the eyes of his seventeen-year-old son and felt utterly horrified at what he had done.

Demos knew the look. He had seen it before. His son was now moving beyond fear, and into the early stages that would soon become uncontrollable panic.

And yet Demos was still struggling to understand where

things had gone wrong. He'd taken the precautions: the equipment, the unexpected changes in pressure, and the guideline back to the exit. *He had been careful.*

But somehow they'd still gotten lost. And Demos was about to pay the ultimate price: to watch his son die before his very eyes, only minutes before he himself succumbed to the infernal darkness.

The guilt and shame were simply indescribable and were already being overtaken by the worry for his son. They'd managed to find a small pocket of air at one end of a tunnel but what little oxygen existed was quickly being replaced by carbon dioxide, spewed forth by their hyperventilating lungs.

In fact, Demos could already feel the remaining oxygen growing thinner, due to the rapid depletion of their last breathable air.

Not knowing what else to do, Demos checked his regulator again, depressing the large valve. Nothing. His dive light desperately searched the cave, shining upon the dark ceiling less than a meter from their heads, with scattered minerals sparkling in the bright white beam.

"Dad."

Demos turned to face his son, who stared back at him with a listless terror in his eyes. There was no way out without drowning. No way to make it back to the boat. *My God*, Demos's thoughts turned back to the boat. *His wife and daughter. They were going to lose them both!*

The guilt returned in a flood of emotion. And the realization was like a stab directly into his heart. *He had killed himself and his son and left his wife and daughter alone. And for what? A shallow, superficial quest of adventure. And for something that might not even really exist!*

Demos now felt the panic overtaking him, just as it was his son. And it was the terror alone that kept him from crying, knowing what was about to happen and that his last memories alive would be of shame.

Helplessly, Demos reached out and grabbed his son,

pulling him in close. A fleeting thought came to him as he searched the tunnel in vain. At least their lights had not failed them. At least his son's last memory would be the face of his father, who loved him more than anything.

At least they would go together.

45

It was the same bright dive lights in their hands that prevented them from seeing anything else, above or below the water. All they could see were themselves. Not even the reflection of a slightly dimmer light, or for that matter, the faint shadow approaching.

And when it finally arrived, the first thought for both Demos and his son was that they were hallucinating.

After all, what would a dolphin be doing in a place like that?

Their second reaction was bewilderment…when the dolphin poked its gray head out of the water, less than a few feet away.

In fact, both Demos and his son were so surprised at the appearance of the dolphin that they failed to notice the eruption of bubbles all around them as John Clay, still ascending from below, held out a regulator and began flooding the small cavity with fresh air.

***

It took several seconds longer before his head slowly emerged, covered with dark dripping hair. He raised the regulator above the water and kept the button depressed. Talking over the loud hissing sound made by the escaping air, he smiled with a calm expression. "Good morning."

Demos was stunned. There were simply no other words. His son, floating nearby, looked utterly frozen in shock.

Another light appeared beneath Clay and slowly rose from the darkness. Two more figures, human and dolphin, breached the surface together. The second diver peered at them through a fully enclosed face mask with large attractive eyes.

"How—" Demos fumbled his words. "How...did you find us?"

"We didn't. *They* did," Clay replied, with his eyes fixed on the teenage boy. He let go of the button, plunging the small cavern into near silence. He then approached Demos's son. Sounds of splashing echoed off the overhead rock.

"What's your name?" he asked.

The teenager didn't respond. Instead, he remained fixated on Clay with large dilated pupils.

"His name is Angelo."

"Angelo," Clay said, peering into the young man's face. "Angelo? Can you hear me?" He held a hand up out of the water and snapped his fingers.

Nothing.

Clay reached beneath the warm water and found the boy's arm. He followed it quickly to the wrist where he lightly pressed the tips of his fingers, feeling for a pulse. After several seconds he let go. The kid was in shock and barely breathing.

"Dirk. Here!" He said the words over his shoulder, and Dirk quickly moved closer. Clay grabbed the teenager's hands and pulled them out of the water, placing both on Dirk's gray head. Dirk squealed and clicked loudly.

The noise, along with the tactile connection from Dirk's rubbery skin, caused Angelo to blink several times. He studied the dolphin with a look of confusion.

"Angelo!" Clay repeated, louder this time.

When the boy abruptly turned, Clay smiled and looked through the teenager's goggles. "Can you hear me?"

To his relief, Angelo nodded.

"What's your name?"

"Angelo," he murmured. "Angelo Demos."

"How old are you?"

The teenager blinked again. "Seventeen."

"Are you a senior?"

Angelo stared at him, puzzled, but eventually answered.

"Yes."

"What school do you go to?"

"Leonidas."

"Nice. You play any sports?"

"Yes."

With his eyes focused on Clay, Angelo failed to notice Alison behind him, helping another regulator into his father's mouth. After several long breaths, the older Demos began to relax.

"Yes, I play rugby."

"Is that right? You any good?"

Angelo smiled unexpectedly. "Yes."

Without missing a beat, Clay raised the second regulator in his own hand and placed it into Angelo's mouth, before inhaling more from his own.

"You know, I have a friend who played for Texas Tech. You follow college ball?"

The boy nodded.

"He was pretty good and had a chance to play pro. But he gave it up to join the Navy. Now he's stuck working with me. Crazy, huh?"

Angelo grinned and nodded again.

"Ah well, to each his own." Clay glanced back over his shoulder before continuing. "Angelo, I want you to listen to me. You're going to be fine. Looks like you two just got a little lost. Luckily our friends here managed to find you."

Angelo looked back at Dirk, and then to Sally.

"What I need you to do," Clay said, "is to listen to me very carefully. We've got some extra air for you, and these dolphins here are going to lead us back out. A piece of cake. Do you understand?"

"Yes."

"Good," Clay smiled. "Now tell me what I just said."

Clay helped the boy wrap one of his hands over the regulator. Angelo then pulled it out briefly to repeat what Clay had said.

"Excellent. It's just going to take me a minute to secure

this second tank, okay? It's going to feel a little light for a minute while I remove your old one."

"Okay."

Behind them, the father studied the dolphins and looked at Alison. "How did they find us?"

Alison had to lift her mask to answer. "Believe me, it's a long story." She kept her mask open, waiting for Clay, who had just finished securing the boy's tank. He quickly moved to the boy's father and did the same. The truth was that although he'd managed to calm them down, they were far from being out of danger. At this depth, they could still go through the air in those extra tanks too quickly. And if that happened, they were all going to be in a world of hurt.

When he finished, Clay looked at Dirk. "Dirk, lead us out, as fast as you can."

Alison heard the translation in her waterproof earbuds, including one of the words that didn't convert properly. But the message got through, and Dirk responded with a series of clicks and whistles.

"He's ready," Alison nodded.

Clay reached below the surface, pulled up a thick white rope, and held it out. In one fluid motion, Dirk seized the rope and gripped it between his powerful teeth.

Clay grabbed for the other end, which had multiple knots tied into it. After wrapping Angelo's hands tightly around the first loop, he clamped his own around a second one further up. "Remember, slow down where it gets tight."

After only a brief delay, Dirk clicked again.

The older Demos watched the exchange in fascination. "Are you...talking with them?"

"Yes," Alison winked. "But don't let *that* one think you have any food."

The man didn't understand the joke, but it didn't matter. She was busy handing the end of her own rope to Sally. "Here," she told Demos, "hold onto this and don't let go. They can get us out a lot faster. If you have a problem, tap me hard on the shoulder."

Clay looked back and forth between all of them. "Ready?"

"Ready," Demos replied. His son stared back nervously but nodded in agreement.

Alison pulled her mask into place.

With that, Clay gripped the rope tight with one hand and the teenager's vest with the other.

"Go, Dirk!"

46

They traveled less than a hundred feet before Dirk stopped. He remained still for several seconds, moving his head back and forth and emitting a long series of pulses resembling loud clicks.

Clay, just behind Dirk, felt a curious feeling in his arms and hands and turned back to Alison in surprise. She smiled inside her mask. What Clay was experiencing was the "buzz" that most humans felt in the presence of a dolphin using its echolocation, causing powerful sound waves to bounce off everything around them. Dirk's melon, a mass in his forehead, picked up the waves he emitted upon their return. Genetically speaking, a much more advanced form of naval sonar.

But Alison's smile at Clay was brief. At that moment, something else occurred to her. Echolocation, as it was understood by humans, was an evolutionary ability allowing dolphins to gauge objects and distance in little to no visibility. Yet when Alison twisted around with her bright flashlight, she found they were surrounded by rock and coral. With only three passages visible.

When Dirk continued emitting his loud clicks, Alison finally turned to Sally.

"Sally, what is Dirk doing?"

Sally's peered back at Alison through the dark water. *He look Alison.*

"For what?"

Sally paused as if confused by her question.

He look for out Alison. More fast.

"A faster way out."

Yes.

It was exactly what she had hoped Sally would say.

Finding a faster way out was critical given their dwindling air supply. But at that moment, it wasn't what Dirk was doing that perplexed her. It was *how* he was doing it.

If echolocation were really just a more sophisticated form of human radar or sonar, then it wouldn't travel very far in their current surroundings. Some distance down the tunnels perhaps, but given the winding of their paths, it wouldn't be far at all before the bouncing of Dirk's pulses would stop returning to him.

Or would they?

In those few seconds, a sudden realization hit Alison like a brick over the head. *Dirk and Sally's melon or "sound lens" must be far more sensitive than they thought.*

Which returned her to a question she'd pondered several days before. With the larger size and folding of a dolphin brain over a human's, just what *else* were Dirk and Sally truly capable of that they didn't yet know about?

It was an exhilarating thought—one that was promptly interrupted when Dirk began moving again, pulling Clay and Angelo along with him.

***

Unfortunately, several sections of Dirk's new path were too tight to pass through smoothly. Twice, Clay had to fade back and briefly unsecure their tanks, allowing them to float behind each person to reduce their girth. Only then were they able to squeeze through and continue forward.

To make matters worse, there was no way for Clay or Alison to communicate with Demos or his son, except by hand signals. Of which they didn't seem too familiar. And each minute of delay meant more air their frightened lungs were consuming.

Once they were out, the ascent would help reduce the pressure and expand the air in their lungs. But until then, it was a race that left Clay hoping desperately that Dirk knew what he was doing.

The last thing he wanted to do was to end up returning two lifeless bodies to the surface.

So when they finally burst out of the caves and into the rays of shimmering light from above, an excited Clay turned and smiled at Alison.

She grinned and pulled hard on her rope to bring Dimitris into view and ensure he was still lucid. He was. And grateful beyond words.

Angelo, his son, was grinning widely despite the bulky regulator between his lips. And as he ascended slowly, he reached out his hand and swept it through a small school of silver fish, all of which darted quickly away.

**

When they all finally breached the surface, both Dimitris and Angelo Demos wasted no time removing their mouthpieces and breathing in a lungful of fresh, cool air.

Dimitris kicked forward and immediately wrapped his arms around his son, weeping as small, ocean swells gently washed over them.

"I thought I would lose you!" he sobbed. "Please forgive your father and know that I am so very sorry!"

Angelo embraced his father just as hard and cried into his neck.

Clay raised his head, squinting at the bright sun as he scanned the horizon. Less than seventy yards away, their gleaming aluminum boat was clearly visible and lashed to the side of a chartered catamaran. And peering desperately over one of its hulls was a mother and a young girl.

Dimitris's wife, clearly at her wit's end, clung tightly to her daughter and, upon seeing both her son and husband, she began to weep.

"Alina!" her husband called out in a trembling voice. "We are all right!"

At that, his wife simply collapsed, falling backwards onto one of the boat's fiberglass benches, dazed and covering her face with her hands. Standing next to them, Lee Kenwood smiled and watched the young daughter wrap her tiny arms around her mother.

Both Clay and Alison followed as the father and son swam breathlessly to their boat. Dirk and Sally remained nearby with heads still bobbing out of the water.

Them happy.

Alison turned to Dirk. "Yes, they are happy. Thanks to you."

Them want metal Alison.

She smiled. "You could say that."

Metal close.

Alison nodded and turned back to the boat. "Yes, it is. Thank goodness."

Old metal. No far.

Dirk stared at her for a long moment. Soon dozens of dolphins appeared above the waves.

Clay smiled warmly at Alison. "Well, I guess you were wrong."

"About what?"

He nodded toward the boats, where Lee was reaching down and awaiting the teenager. "About everything you've done. All your work, all the achievements. And IMIS. You were beginning to feel that none of it made a difference."

"And?"

Clay was still smiling. "It sure made a difference to them."

47

Less than an hour later, the chartered sailboat was visible only as a tiny shape over their wake, perched atop the brilliant blue water of the Caribbean.

The hum of the Teknicraft's engines was unable to drown out the sound of the splashing swells against their own aluminum hulls as the boat motored forward at full speed.

Trinidad Island and the *Pathfinder* were now less than a day away.

Alison sat resting in the shade at the stern of the boat, watching the sailboat behind them. It grew still smaller until it was eventually indiscernible from the sun's sparkles upon the water. An amazing scene that was also teaming with dozens of dolphins, all swimming excitedly behind them.

With a look of contentment, she breathed deeply and looked down at her feet extended out in front of her. *Clay was right. It wasn't all for nothing. And it didn't have to happen all at once. Changing the world took time. Years. Sometimes decades or even longer.*

She knew it wasn't up to her. How things changed, and how quickly, would be driven by events and circumstances beyond her control.

For her own sanity, she just had to remember her part in all they had achieved.

48

But the changes would not take decades. Nor would they happen in a way anyone could possibly foresee, or even imagine.

It was how all human history occurred. Important events creating ripple effects through an unfathomably complex minefield of social and political consequences. Ending with what could only be described as unexpected and unpredictable results. Only to be recorded later, by thoughtful but biased individuals, as "history."

And the events unfolding now would be no different. For the Americans *or* the Russians.

***

Dubbed as "Black Holes" for their ability to virtually disappear from sonar, the Kilo-class submarines were a leap forward in modern Russian stealth technology. And while considered one of the quietest diesel-electric submarines on the planet, they *paled* in comparison to Russia's newest Lada-class sub. Utilizing a next-generation, anti-reflective acoustical coating and lower profile, the newest *Sea Ghost* prototype was all but *invisible* to even the most modern sonar systems. It was another leap that left Western militaries scrambling.

Onboard the *Sea Ghost*, billionaire Dima Belov uncomfortably sat three decks below in a gray metal chair. He rested quietly, massaging his wrists which were still sore from the handcuffs. It had now been more than twenty-four hours since they had departed Dakar, the nearest and largest city on the West African coast. It was also the one by which the brief presence of a Russian submarine would draw the least attention. The remainder of the trip would be made beneath the surface to avoid detection, putting them in range of the *Valant* oil rig in less than three days.

Belov actually relished the peace of being submerged. There were, of course, the sounds from the rest of the crew going about their business, planning for their offensive. Nonetheless, there were also many long periods of near-silence in which he heard practically nothing. He even thought he could feel the barely perceptible motion of the submarine as it slid noiselessly through the cool waters of the mid-Atlantic.

Belov looked down at his watch to remind himself what time it was. The rest of the crew knew instinctively, given how much they'd spent underwater, but not Belov. Between the stale overhead light and simple isolation, he struggled to keep his internal clock in sync.

Although "isolation" was probably too strong a word. He wasn't banned from leaving, in truth. He had gone out a number of times, for food or just for simple exercise. But while he was technically free, there was an *atmosphere* on the boat—a mood he could see in the eyes of the crew. It was a look that resembled ambivalence, at best. And in other cases, derision.

It seemed that while Captain Zhirov knew the true circumstances surrounding the older Belov, the message hadn't made it to the rest of the crew. To them, he was clearly a prisoner aboard their boat.

When the door to Belov's quarters opened next, it was Zhirov who stepped through, followed by his first officer. A tall and lean man with dark eyes, Zhirov carried himself with a pronounced air of authority.

After closing the door behind them, both sat down—the first officer remaining noticeably more erect in his seat.

"The two GRU teams are nearly ready," Zhirov started. "It will be a subsurface attack, with one team taking the oil rig and the other the American science vessel."

"What do they plan to do with the ship?"

"Hold it until our air support arrives. Once we find what we're after, the priority is to exit both vessels and the area as quickly as possible. Before the Americans can mount a counterattack."

"That will leave only a few hours."

"That's correct," the first officer replied curtly. "The first priority is to assume control of their communications system. That will give us the longest possible window. When we have the information, GRU will evacuate immediately. The rest will be airlifted out."

"Helicopters are the only thing that can land on the *Valant* or the American ship," Belov said.

"Or a Yak," Zhirov replied, referring to the subsonic jet trainers. "They can't make it onto the ship, but there's enough space to set one down on the oil rig. And it can make it back to Dakar."

"At low altitude?"

Zhirov smiled at Belov's comment. "Yes, at low altitude." Evading radar was going to be key. Flying below radar at night would reduce what the Americans could track, but it wouldn't eliminate it completely. There were still satellite images and the thermal signatures of the Yak's jet engines. To conceal that, they would need another, albeit less exotic, cover. "A larger Ilyushin transport will be positioned to fly the exact same route and speed at a higher altitude. Above the Yak. Its larger profile and exhaust stream is perfectly designed to help obscure anything the American satellites can pick up."

Belov raised an eyebrow at both men before him. It was a clever ruse. "They'll know it's connected, somehow."

"Yes," the first officer replied. "But they won't know how. And by the time they figure it out, our cargo will be in Dakar."

Belov's expression changed to curiosity at the mention of "cargo." There were only two types in his mind: things and people. "What kind of cargo are we talking about?"

Zhirov half-grinned. "That depends."

196

"On what?"

"On you," the captain said. "You are the only one who knows what they've been doing. And you know more than anyone else what it is we're after, so *you* tell us what our cargo will consist of."

Zhirov was right. It was the single-most reason why Belov was still alive. And it was finally time to play his cards. All of them.

"Samples," he said. "Biological samples." After a moment, he let himself grin along with Zhirov. "And some key personnel."

"They must be captured alive?" the first officer said.

"If possible." Belov was not officially part of the Russian military or government, but he'd seen enough skirmishes and battles to know how rarely these things ended well. There was simply no avoiding it. Once the battle began, the outcome was unpredictable.

"If they survive, it gives us a huge advantage," he said. "If they don't, it will at least make things that much harder for the Americans."

49

The faint outline of Tobago was visible soon after dawn. The rippling waters had returned, along with a warm morning breeze, stripping the distant island of its thin white cloud cover.

Down below, Alison awoke to the gentle rolling of the boat and the soft clinking of something outside.

She rose curiously, leaving an empty bed, and made her way up the four steps into the main cockpit, where she peered out through the window in the metal door.

John Clay looked up when the door opened. A large compartment was open with Clay standing inside, waist-high. His shirtless, lightly tanned chest and back were first to catch her eye.

"Morning."

Alison stared for a moment before looking out over the water. Small, scattered whitecaps dotted the water as far as she could see. "Good morning," she answered cheerfully, while squinting briefly at the morning sun. "What are you doing?"

"Just making a small repair. The fuel line to the port engine is clogged."

"Is that serious?"

He smiled. "Only if you want to use the port engine." He then motioned to the water beyond the boat. "I've been going slow. Trying to keep quiet until most of our friends wake up."

She smiled. "That's very thoughtful."

"Noise travels easier underwater," Clay said, searching through the toolbox and picking up a different wrench. "How'd you sleep?"

"I'm guessing pretty well since I didn't hear you get up."

It was a joke. They both knew Clay generally didn't make a lot of noise—another trait, or remnant, from the training of his past. She wondered if he even thought about it anymore.

"There's some hot water on the stove for your tea."

She turned around and looked at the small, stainless steel tea kettle. "How'd you do that without making noise?"

Clay grinned. "It's a secret."

She gave him a sarcastic grin and disappeared inside, returning a minute later with a mug in her hand, complete with bobbing tea bag.

"How much longer until it's fixed?"

"Ten or fifteen minutes. Just putting things back together."

Lee Kenwood emerged behind her in shorts and a T-shirt, his glasses propped atop a slightly sunburned nose.

"Morning, Lee."

"Good morning," he nodded, looking down at Clay. "I hope we're not sinking."

Clay laughed and continued working. "If we are, then I did something very wrong." He winked at Alison. "And if I did, don't tell Steve."

She sipped and held up three fingers with her other hand. "Scout's honor."

Clay stopped and frowned. "Actually, I think that's the Girl Scout pledge."

"Oh, right."

Lee laughed and stepped back inside. "I'm going to make some coffee. You want any, Clay? I know better than to ask Ali."

"I'm fine. Thanks."

Alison cocked her head playfully. "He's an orange juice man."

She turned when she heard clicks and whistles from the water. Several dolphins were awake, including Dirk. But still no sign of Sally.

Without a word, Lee's arm extended out through the

open door to Alison, holding out her vest. She took it and turned on the power switch. Without putting it on, Alison turned the vest around so that the camera was facing the water.

"Good morning, Dirk."

Hello Alison. You ready now.

"Not yet. But soon. We're fixing the metal." She immediately made a funny face. "John big strong man!"

The translation sounded an error, but she didn't care. The joke was still worth it.

"Oh, you're funny."

Alison turned back to Dirk with a wide grin. "Where's Sally?"

Dirk's reply was short.

She sleep. Sally tired.

With a nod, she replied. "Okay. We'll leave when she's ready."

***

The previous night's visit left Neely Lawton thinking about Steve Caesare. She looked out pensively through the largest window in her lab and across the water to the *Valant*, rising mightily from the shimmering blue water.

Every time she talked to him, he became less stereotypical for a Navy man. After a long minute or two, Neely sighed and peered at her watch. If the rest of the group were on time, she'd probably only get to see Steve one more time. She was more than a little surprised to find herself secretly hoping for a delay.

***

Aboard the *Valant*, and inside the oil rig's large machine room, Steve Caesare stood in a precarious position. He was holding one of the heavier pieces of the drill bit while Tay wriggled the rest of the assembly beneath it, trying to secure

200

everything into place. When it was set, Caesare released the drill bit and took a step back to wipe the beads of sweat from his forehead. The morning temperature was warming up quickly, and the lack of ventilation on the lower level of the *Valant* had him wondering whether the rig's original engineers had ever been outside, let alone in the tropics.

On the other side of Tay, Lightfoot was quickly bolting the two pieces together. When finished, he called up through an opening in the middle.

"Next!"

Caesare faithfully lowered another piece down to meet Tay's guiding hand. One of the several heavy titanium blades lined the bit's outer edge. Unlike older designs, these blades were much less jagged, able to grind through even the strongest materials with minimal vibration.

"Hey, Steve," Borger entered the room behind them. "You got a sec?"

"Sure, Will. Not in the middle of anything at all here."

"Sorry." He hurried across the marred metal floor and helped to hold the blade in place.

"Try again," Lightfoot called up.

They pulled the piece out and lowered it again, even slower this time. The alignment had to be perfect.

"Nope. Again."

It took several tries before the blade finally slid correctly into place. Lightfoot began tightening while Caesare and Borger stepped back. Borger's brightly colored shirt already looked damp with perspiration.

"Can I talk to you for a sec?" Together they walked to the wide exit and out of earshot.

"What's up?"

"Clay and Alison should reach Trinidad in a few hours," Borger said. "So your ride will be here just after nineteen hundred. As soon as it's dark enough."

"Thanks. I'll be ready."

"There's also something else I wanted to talk to you about. A couple things actually."

"Okay."

Borger glanced around apprehensively. "It's probably better if I show you."

***

"Where is this?" Caesare asked, straightening back up behind Borger. On the screen in front of them was a detailed aerial picture of a lush green forest. In the center of the frame were several patches of open space, scattered with large boulders.

"Rwanda." Borger tapped on the keyboard and zoomed the image out, bringing part of Lake Kivu—one of Africa's Great Lakes—into view.

"Where DeeAnn told us to look again."

Borger nodded. "Correct."

"And?"

Borger swiveled around in his chair. "And I think she was right." He promptly turned back around and zoomed back in. Closer this time, advancing down to one of the rock-strewn areas in the picture. "Anything look familiar?"

Studying the screen, Caesare shook his head. "No."

"Don't feel bad. I didn't catch it at first either." With his mouse, Borger pulled a menu down from the top and selected a rotate option. The screen turned at a 90-degree angle. He then dragged the corner of the frame down, rotating it a little more before finally dragging a square over one section with his mouse.

When the square was enlarged, a recognizable shape emerged.

"Now that looks familiar."

Borger nodded. "It's very similar to one of the outcroppings we saw in Guyana. One of the four."

"How many are here?"

"Just the one so far. But this is right against the forest, so the rest could be obscured if they are indeed there."

"You can't penetrate through that?"

202

"Actually, I can." He enlarged the shape of the rocks further. "These are multispectral images. The problem isn't composition, it's depth. And for that, we would need some ground-based Lidar scans to overlay—"

Caesare frowned and interrupted Borger. "So is this it or not?"

"I can't say for sure. It looks like what we're looking for, but the human brain can play tricks on things like this. Finding visual patterns in what often are random or natural shapes."

Caesare suddenly eyed Borger with a faint look of both surprise and amusement.

"Hey, just because I'm paranoid doesn't mean I'm not objective."

Caesare grinned. "Evidently."

"Besides. You know how I hate to be wrong."

This time Caesare laughed. "Yes. I do."

They both turned back to the screen. "Without being able to see more, we can't be sure."

"Agreed."

"But if this is it," Borger began, pressing his hands together, "why wouldn't DeeAnn have told us sooner?"

Caesare folded his arms in front of him, pensively. "I think she's battling more than we know."

"Hmm, maybe." After a brief pause, Borger turned around again to face Caesare. "Well, changing subjects, there's more I need to tell you."

"Go ahead."

"It's about our *friends* in China."

"Which ones?" Caesare grinned. "We've made so many."

Borger smiled. "Well, do you remember that hacker kid I told you about? The one that helped that Chinese MSS agent find Li Na Wei?"

"Yeah. You said his name was Mongol or something?"

"That's his handle, actually. M0ngol, M-0-n-g-o-l. All serious hackers have one."

"So what's our friend up to?"

"I wish I knew. He's gone," Borger said simply.

"Gone where?"

"I have no idea. But all information on him has vanished. Wiped from every source or system I was monitoring. No driver's license. No birth certificate. No picture or bank account. Nada."

"Just like that?"

"Just like that," Borger acknowledged.

Caesare brushed a hand against his jaw, pondering. "Why would they delete him from all their systems?"

"Well, the most obvious explanation isn't good."

"No, it's not."

"I can't find anything on him, even internally—which I'm presuming means it's the government's doing, or perhaps the Ministry of State Security itself. Eliminating one of their own."

Caesare still had his hand under his chin when he frowned. "Well, they would certainly have the resources to erase any trace of him."

"They sure would." Borger hesitated a moment before adding, "There's one other thing."

Caesare rolled his eyes. "You're killing me, Will."

"Sorry, but it's important. Especially this last piece, about our alien ship."

"Let me have it."

Borger lowered his voice. "Okay, so we both know what we saw on that video."

"A ship that repairs itself."

"Exactly. I was shocked when I saw that video footage from Tay and his men."

"I think we all were, Will."

"Right, right. But here's the thing. *It makes sense.* That it does that. Listen, if you're traveling through space on a ship, the distances are huge. Almost unimaginable."

"Agreed. Including the energy required. Which is a big part of why it was a one-way trip."

"That's right," Borger said. "But it's not just the energy. It's also the distance. Most people don't understand what kind of distances we're talking about. We're talking vast. *Really vast!*"

Caesare listened and took a step backward, lowering himself into the second chair with a loud creak. "Go on."

"The distances are *so* great, that you'd have to be traveling at speeds most people cannot really comprehend."

"Close to the speed of light."

"Yeah, but these days the speed of light is just a term thrown around by everyone. I don't think most people really appreciate what that means. Even at a fraction of the speed of light, you're talking about moving so fast that you start affecting time itself."

"Einstein's Theory of Relativity," Caesare replied.

"Precisely. But here's something that even fewer people understand. When you're moving that fast, again even at a fraction of light speed, the energy translates in two ways. One is kinetic energy but the second is *force.*"

Caesare thought for a moment. "Like an impact?"

"Exactly. Like an impact," Borger nodded. "As in something *hitting* the ship. And here's the thing. Force equals mass times acceleration, so at that kind of speed, the object wouldn't have to be very big. In fact, it could be very small. Space is mostly empty but not completely."

"When you say it could be small, how small are we talking?"

"*Really* small. Like the size of a pebble, or less. Even at a tenth of the speed of light, you would be moving so fast that even a speck of dust could create one hell of an impact and rip an enormous hole in your ship."

"Geez."

"Yeah. And let me tell you, there is a LOT of dust floating around in space."

Caesare folded his arms. "Well, that could ruin your trip in a hurry."

"Exactly. Which is why you would need to be able to

repair your ship, and quickly. So, either you'd have to be ready at all times, or you would need a ship that could do it by *itself.*"

Caesare leaned back. "Which is exactly what we saw."

"Exactly what we saw!" Borger repeated excitedly.

Caesare sat silently, contemplating. He watched a familiar expression form on Borger's face.

"That's not all of it."

Borger smiled and slowly shook his head.

"Keep going."

"We know the ship can repair itself. We all saw it. But I didn't know how, until this morning. In the shower."

Borger pulled up his sleeve and exposed a small scrape on his arm. It was red but already beginning to heal. "I got this last night when we were bringing the stuff over from the *Pathfinder.*"

Caesare glanced at Borger's arm. "A scrape? Okay."

"What I'm trying to say is that this is all tied to the green liquid. The solution we saw in those containers before they were destroyed. Do you remember when we found them inside the mountain?"

"How could I forget?"

"Then you'll remember that when we were inside, there was no system or power source to keep all those embryos in suspension like that."

Caesare peered curiously at Borger. "Something needed to provide that energy."

At that, Borger's expression grew even more excited. "Exactly what I was thinking! What we saw was amazing, but it wasn't magic. It all still has to work within the same laws of physics, regardless of whether we understand it."

Now Caesare grinned, seeing where Borger was headed. "It did have a power source."

"It *had* to have had one! We just didn't realize what it was."

"Until now."

Borger smiled. "Exactly! It's the liquid, Steve! The

solution is more than just the nutrient; it's *also* the power source!"

"Wow," Caesare replied slowly.

"And that's how the ship can repair itself! Because it's not just surrounded by that green solution, it's *infused* with it!" Borger leaned forward in his chair. "And that ship isn't merely making its own repairs, it's HEALING itself!"

50

Steve Caesare stared silently at his friend for a long time. What they had already witnessed was incredible, but what Borger had just suggested could only be described as astounding. Simply off the charts.

"Are you saying that ship is alive?"

Borger shook his head. "No. Not like that. But what I am suggesting is that whatever it's made of...is *organic*." He sat back up in his chair. "And infused with a solution that may be even more incredible than we thought."

Caesare nodded, digesting. "We've already started research with organics — OLEDs and semiconductors."

"And those are just baby steps. What we're talking about here is an element, or something, that could be both a super-nutrient and a power source, and still be *part* of an inorganic structure. I can't even begin to fathom the implications of that."

"That makes two of us."

"We have to protect this ship, Steve. We've got to protect it no matter what."

Caesare nodded his head. "We have to do more than that. We also need to find the second vault. In a hurry."

"That's true. If it has more of those containers, it's not just about what might be floating in that solution, it's about the solution itself."

Caesare twisted his arm and peered at his watch. "Nineteen hundred you said?"

51

The old diesel engines were put into reverse, roaring as their propellers churned through the dark water and bringing the large fishing trawler to a slow next to the much larger *Pathfinder.*

Captain Tomas Lopez, a young Venezuelan not more than thirty, stood at the helm. His one hand calmly held the wheel with the other babying the throttle. Behind him, the outlines of the boat's towing warps and net drums were easily visible along with several large hand-crank winches.

With dark piercing eyes and a mind as sharp as anyone John Clay had ever met, Lopez was the epitome of a modern-day entrepreneur, with a dry sense of humor and thick Spanish accent.

Raised in near poverty, the Lopez family had managed to migrate to Trinidad Island before the real suffering began in Venezuela. Brought on first by the dreams of Hugo Chaves, his idealistic revolution would later set the stage for an utter failure of government by his successor Nicolás Maduro.

Even at a young age, Lopez had witnessed both the emotional and financial helplessness around him and swore not to fall victim to the same fate. Instead, he became a fisherman by day and a smuggler by night.

The wiry young captain brought his boat to a full stop next to the Navy's research ship, long enough for the crew to tie the large lines off and secure themselves to the port side of the ship's stern. Something they had now done many times over the last several weeks.

Lopez and his three-man crew had seen it all. Everything a person could want to smuggle, they had. Done normally for gain, they more recently began doing it for those needing help, oppressed beneath the tyrannical clutches of Maduro and his corrupted government.

It began with smuggling in food past government checkpoints and was now escalating to smuggling families themselves out of the country, to some of the nearby islands.

Lopez had smiled when he told Clay he was an equal-opportunity smuggler. But the sad truth was that he couldn't save them all. And both Lopez and his crew knew it.

For Clay and his team, Lopez had been the perfect man to transport their shipments back and forth between Trinidad.

Two days a week, without fail, Lopez and his men delivered the supplies needed by Clay and his team. All untraceable and purposefully mislabeled.

When the last line was tied and a gangplank extended between both boats, supplies quickly began to appear from hidden holds and move efficiently across to the *Pathfinder*'s waiting crew.

As the supplies were delivered, John Clay stood up from his wooden bench, along with Alison and Lee. Clay approached the ramp and immediately spotted Steve Caesare and Neely Lawton arriving on the other side.

When the exchange was all but finished, Caesare marched down the gangplank in heavy boots. He clasped Lopez on the shoulder as he passed. "Right on time, Tomás. Gracias por traer a nuestos amigos!"

"Es mi honor," the young captain replied.

He turned to examine Clay, standing on his own, no longer needing even a cane. "You're looking downright spry, Clay."

"I was shooting for snappy." Clay grinned and peered at him more closely. "Are you dying your hair?"

Caesare laughed and turned to Alison. "Nice to see you again, Ali. And Mr. Kenwood. Welcome to our humble abode."

"You know we've actually been onboard before," Lee said.

Caesare grinned. "Oh, I'm not talking about the *Pathfinder*. You ever vacation on a forty-year-old oil rig?"

When Lee's smile disappeared, Caesare laughed again. "I'm just kidding, kid. You get to stay shipside. Lucky for you."

Alison shook her head, rolling her eyes before reaching down to pick up her bag. She turned to Clay wistfully. "I guess this is it."

He nodded and wrapped his arms warmly around Alison, kissing her. "I'm afraid so. But you'll be safe here until we get back."

"You're going to call me, right?"

"I will. Whenever I can."

Alison nodded and pulled him down for another, longer kiss. When she pulled back, Alison turned to Caesare. "Don't let anything happen to him."

He frowned. "Why doesn't anyone ever worry about me?"

In response, Borger piped up from the edge of the *Pathfinder*, cupping his hands around his mouth. "Clay, don't let anything happen to Steve!"

Clay laughed. "I'll do my best." He took Alison's hand and helped her up and over the short plank, letting go once she stepped firmly aboard the *Pathfinder*. He then stood by as Lee crossed over with his own bag.

"Good luck, Mr. Clay."

"Thanks, Lee. I look forward to hearing what else you've learned from our friends when I get back."

"You got it."

With that, the plank was removed. The lines of the trawler were then untied and thrown back aboard. As the swells gently pushed the unlit fishing boat away from them, Alison watched as John and Steve's figures grew dimmer, quickly fading into the night.

It was only after she heard the trawler's diesel engines

211

roar back to life and the boat's outline disappeared entirely, that she approached Neely and Borger, giving them a proper greeting.

"It's great to see you guys," Alison exclaimed, hugging them both.

Neely's lips spread into a wide grin. "Welcome back."

"Thanks," Alison replied, her own grin matching Neely's. She looked her friend straight in the eyes with an abrupt change in demeanor. "We need to talk."

52

Neely stared at both Alison and Lee as they all sat beneath her lab's bright fluorescent lights. With arms folded, she pondered what she had just been told. After a long pause, Alison spoke again.

"Is it possible?"

Neely nodded her head, slowly. "It's possible. Yes. But what you're talking about is bigger than just a form of communication between a few species. Which is already a big deal. What you're talking about is much bigger. You're talking about something that could effect dozens of species. Maybe more."

"So, genetically speaking," Lee asked, "how deep could this go?"

"I have no idea. As much as we currently know about genetics, it's only the tip of the iceberg. We're truly only scratching the surface at this point. But the idea of a communicative ability, connecting cognition and instinct is intriguing. And if it's true, it might go even deeper than you think."

"What do you mean?"

Neely thought for a moment. "You all know what gastric bypass surgery is, right?"

Alison, Lee, and Borger all nodded.

"Then you know that it's a weight-loss surgery that changes the shape of the stomach, severely limiting the consumption of food, and usually a last resort for those who are truly obese. You might also know that the vast majority of patients who undergo that surgery are also diabetic. Diabetes and obesity are very closely correlated."

Alison wrinkled her brow. "How is this related?"

"This may sound a little technical, but stay with me.

What's interesting about the gastric surgery is that while most patients undergoing the procedure are diabetic, the majority of those same patients lose their diabetes after the surgery."

This time Lee frowned. "Why would that be surprising if they're correlated?"

"What's surprising is not that their diabetes disappears…it's *when* it disappears." Leaning forward in her chair, Neely continued. "It takes most patients weeks or even months for the weight to start coming off. But in many cases, the diabetes disappears almost immediately. *Before* they lose the weight."

Alison studied her curiously. "Before they lose the weight?"

"Yes."

"How is that possible?"

"That's just it," Neely shrugged perplexedly. "No one knows."

"That's…kind of bizarre."

Neely turned to Lee. "Isn't it? Now you're probably wondering why this is relevant. The answer is that scientists and doctors don't know why this happens to the gastric bypass patients, but they *do* have a theory, which is rooted within obesity itself."

Neely then explained the theory to the group. "Obesity, as I'm sure you know, results in all sorts of health problems. From processing insulin to circulatory problems, heart disease, stress, even things like gout. An overabundance of fat cells can be downright insidious to our health. Which is why researchers are wondering if something else may be happening at a deeper level. At a cellular level."

"You mean genetically?"

"No," Neely shook her head. "More like chemically. Researchers now believe that there is some kind of chemical communication happening at a cellular level—in this case, among fat cells. And this communication may be how so many patients lose their diabetes much sooner than the

214

weight that helped to cause it."

"Oh my gosh. Is that true?!" Alison exclaimed.

"Yes, it is."

All three stared at Neely in fascination. "You're saying," Alison began, "that there is communication happening within our cells?"

Neely smiled. "No. We've always known that. At least to some degree. I'm saying that there may be a lot more happening than we expect, which makes Chris's idea of a new form of communication a real possibility. Perhaps one that has yet to be discovered."

"And what if we evolved out of some of this cellular communication?"

"Also possible."

"And the DNA that was extracted from those plants turns it back on!"

At that, Neely's smile disappeared. "Well…there's a larger problem there, I'm afraid."

"Like what?

"Remember when I said there's no such thing as a free lunch?"

"Yes."

Neely glanced worriedly over their shoulders at Will Borger. "It seems our super bacteria has some problems."

"What kind of problems?"

"Terminal ones."

Alison replied. "For *who*?"

"We were exposed to it," Lee added nervously.

"Not for you, as far as I know. I mean for someone *injected* with it."

53

The gray Jaguar XJ got Li Na out of town with the help of its GPS, but the car's gas tank was more empty than full, leaving her far less than needed to reach the next city.

It was a miracle she hadn't crashed it trying to get out of the parking garage. Yet once outside, the wide empty lanes provided enough room to gradually improve her steering. Now on the highway's two empty lanes, she tried to study the inboard GPS screen without swerving. At least enough to get her bearings.

Fortunately, she was still headed east.

She raised herself up and peered through the rearview mirror, looking for other vehicles but saw none.

The men had to have transportation. Why weren't they chasing her?

Li Na noticed the turn signal blinking in the dashboard display and tried to remember how to turn it off. She finally found it, pressing her foot down harder on the gas pedal while her eyes returned to the mirror. Still no one.

***

She was several miles out of the city before the helicopter appeared and circled the top level of the parking garage. All six men watched impatiently as it completed the circle and closed in, hovering less than ten meters above the thick concrete. Finally, it dropped all the way down and bounced gently onto the top level of the parking garage.

Once aboard, Sheng Lam did not speak. He sat silently, pushed into one of the middle seats, and watched the men around him carefully.

Now he knew. Now he knew what they were hiding.

They were to dispose of him. And not let him touch the girl. Someone in the chain of command knew more about Lam than he had realized.

The chopper lifted into the air and tilted toward the east. The pilot had spotted the car on the road before landing and was now headed to see if it was still traveling in the same direction.

A few minutes later, the last of the city passed below them and disappeared through the side windows, replaced by fields of grass and vegetation, then trees.

***

Li Na heard the deep thundering sounds of the helicopter's rotors long before she could see it. She pulled back an interior cover revealing the Jaguar's sunroof and searched the sky. As the sounds grew louder, she finally spotted it behind her, steadily closing the distance between them.

She mashed the pedal down and clung tightly to the steering wheel, trying to keep it straight. While the numbers on the digital speedometer increased, the bushes and trees on the side of the road sped past in a blur.

Her heart felt like it was in her throat, and she was scared to death.

***

Next to the right-side window, Peng could see the car now. It was just a few hundred meters or so below.

The lone black car was moving at an impressive rate of speed, swaying slightly between lanes. The girl appeared to be struggling to keep it straight. And stretching out in front of her lay a highway that disappeared far into the distance.

She had nowhere to hide.

Behind the wheel, Li Na was thinking the same thing. Her mind was racing faster, trying to find a way out. There was no one else on the empty highway, no one at all. *How was that possible?*

She glanced again at the GPS screen, this time closer, and studied the colors. She found that some of the screen was displaying a darker area, and she fumbled with the controls until she zoomed out.

Li Na looked out through the front window to check the landscape around her. *The dark patches were trees!* Not quite a forest, but some areas dense enough to help.

Suddenly startled by the bumps on the road, she looked up to straighten the car again with both hands. She needed a place to exit the road. From the screen, the nearest exit appeared to be several kilometers away. She searched for the helicopter again and found it. This time, it was closer but not any lower.

They weren't trying to stop her, she thought. *They were simply following.*

54

After what felt like forever, the off-ramp finally appeared ahead of her. But as she drew nearer, the distinct images of orange and yellow barriers emerged, indicating it was not yet finished.

Li Na braked hard, overcompensating before easing down on the gas again to continue forward. Given her limited experience behind a wheel, she was surprised she'd made it this far.

Now with the barriers directly in front of her, she pulled the car to a stop and looked for a way through. They didn't seem to be affixed to anything, so she eased forward and ran into one. The colored plastic frame was knocked backward, and she rolled over it with a jolt. Once the back tires rolled over, her eyes returned to the ramp in front of the car. It was littered with debris, covered mostly by scattered pieces of asphalt and concrete. But the ramp continued downhill to a wide-open dirt area, where hundreds of large concrete blocks were stacked.

Dozens of the heavy road barriers had fallen over and some had broken into pieces. Then she saw it. Beyond them appeared to be a roughly strewn dirt road, snaking through the fields of weeds and grass toward one of the distant group of trees.

***

The pilot of the Mi-17 helicopter watched with bemusement as the car below navigated off the main highway and onto a small dirt road. It bounced and weaved through the fields toward an outcropping of nearby trees.

The girl clearly knew they were behind her. And enough

to know that her only chance was the trees that she was speeding towards. Leaving a very visible trail of dust swirling behind her.

The girl would have had a better chance had she'd stayed in the city. Where it could take hours, or even days, to find her.

But now, once Peng and his men were on the ground, it would take only minutes.

***

Li Na barely made it beneath the trees before what little of the road that remained became blocked by a fallen tree. Old and uprooted from a past windstorm, the tree lay there deteriorating in several large sections. Long dead branches coming from the last piece reached over and down a steep embankment.

This was as far as the car was going.

With her satchel in one hand, Li Na pushed the driver's door open and jumped out. She quickly approached and had begun to scale a section of the fallen tree's trunk when she abruptly stopped.

She emptied her hands and hurriedly ran back to the car, which was still running. She climbed inside and peered back at the GPS screen. Reaching forward, she zoomed out on the screen. First once, then several times, until she could see far beyond her location to the city of Shenyang and the ocean beyond. She looked back out through the car's rear window and located the distant highway to get her bearings.

With that, she backed out again and ran back to the tree trunk. But when she reached down to pick up her satchel, something stopped her. Even with the approaching sound of the helicopter's rotors, she lingered.

Li Na breathed in deeply, remaining as quiet as she could. Unmoving.

55

The Mi-17 pilot reduced power on his cyclic and gradually eased back on the stick in front of him, slowing his approach. Using his pedals, he rotated slightly to his right, giving him a better view of the car as it rested just under the edge of the trees.

He smiled to himself. The girl wasn't even smart enough to get completely under the protection of the canopy, where he wouldn't be able to use his infrared.

Her dumb luck had clearly run out.

***

With the thumping of the helicopter drawing closer behind her, Li Na remained still, almost hovering, and staring strangely at the area around her.

Covered in brown decaying leaves and needles, the ground felt soft underfoot. The tall green trees overhead shaded most of the area, providing not only cover but a cool crispness in the air. But something felt different.

The branches, still covered in leaves, fluttered in the light breeze, moving slowly—a rhythmic back and forth. The grasses, bushes, and even the rocks felt strangely dissimilar. Even the sound of the helicopter seemed to have changed. Reverberating with a pitch that made them sound slower, or heavier.

Li Na began to waver and reached forward to steady herself against the fallen tree. Yet when her hand touched the deteriorating bark, even *it* felt different.

But far more difficult to understand was that the billions of tiny bacteria inside her body were slowly and very methodically changing tiny areas of her DNA. And in the process reawakening genes that had been dormant in the human body...for thousands of years.

56

It was called "crate training." A task left to DeeAnn Draper who was standing under her own tree with a completely different set of problems. Keeping her eyes on Dulce and Dexter, she adjusted the small computer on her chest and approached the primates—both of whom were playing under a stream of water from a garden hose.

Crate training was the way most zoo animals were transported. Weeks of conditioning were involved to train the animals to feel comfortable inside a special shipping crate built for the trip.

But DeeAnn's goal was not to train her animals to like it. Her challenge was just to train them not to *hate* it. Dulce's first trip aboard a plane had been to South America to help search for someone. The second was to return to the same area in search of Dexter. And neither of those trips had ended well. In fact, it was a miracle that one of them didn't have a nervous breakdown during either trip. And Dexter hadn't fared much better.

The result was a reaction to cages that was nothing short of terrifying. And it was DeeAnn's job to coax them in, yet again.

She had already started the discussions with Dulce, but each time she broached the subject, it left her with an uneasy feeling as to just how exactly the gorilla would do. It also brought to light Dulce's growing hunger for the *out*, as she called it—which was gorilla-speak for the "outside," a simple transliteration, but one that left DeeAnn with a twinge of guilt. Dulce wanted to be with her, there was no doubt about that. But the gorilla was still decidedly and undeniably captive.

Crate training to date had not been nearly as successful

as she had hoped, which left her now hoping for a small miracle.

As she approached the two, she pushed the thought from her head and smiled at Dulce. The gorilla was snorting and playing happily beneath the flow of water from a garden hose. She had become fascinated with the emergence of clear water from such a small thing. But after DeeAnn sprayed her for the first time, she became absolutely obsessed—even learning how to turn it on and off by herself.

Yet after several uses, it was DeeAnn who was captivated when Dulce moved from merely playing in the water to actually *cleaning* herself with it. This was fascinating because Dulce had never seen another human shower themselves.

Now DeeAnn stood still, amused, watching as the small gorilla used her free hand to splash Dexter. The smaller primate returned the interaction with an expression similar to disdain. He reached up and rubbed the top of his small head dry, leering at his playmate.

"Dulce," said DeeAnn though the vest.

The translation was lost to a sudden, loud snort from Dulce.

DeeAnn repeated. "Dulce."

"Mommy," she responded with a smile, lowering the hose. She was nearly waist-high and peered innocently upward with her bright hazel eyes.

"Turn the water off, Dulce."

After a long a pause that had DeeAnn wondering if Dulce had heard her, the gorilla dropped the hose and waddled several feet to the faucet. She then carefully twisted it closed with her oversized hands.

Once the water was off, Dulce turned and smiled pleasingly at DeeAnn. *Water off.*

"Good girl." She stepped forward and retrieved a hand towel from a tree where it was drying. DeeAnn then bent down and used it to rub the top of Dulce's head, leaving a dry tuft of fur sticking up. "It's time to go, honey."

Dulce's smile immediately returned. *We go. We happy.*

She peered over Dulce's head at Dexter, who was gnawing on a green stem, watching them. "And Dexter?"

Yes. Dexter. We happy go. We help.

"Thank you, Dulce." She swallowed, wishing she could leave them there. "But…we have to fly. Again."

On metal?

"Yes. On the metal."

Dulce stared at her as if contemplating. *Fly like bird.*

"Yes," she grinned. "Fly like a bird."

Dulce turned and motioned to Dexter. He didn't reply.

No cage.

DeeAnn nodded in agreement. "No cage."

Her reply was troubling. Because DeeAnn knew eventually they would both have to be in a container again, at least for a short time—which left her words insincere, at best.

***

The Luiz Muñoz Marín was the largest airport on the island. As the Airbus A300 thundered from out of the gray cloud cover over the airfield, its glowing landing lights were the first to be seen. They were immediately followed by the plane's landing gear, and seconds later, a long and dark purple-painted underbelly. The rest of the Airbus appeared white with large block lettering displayed prominently on the side of its fuselage.

Five of the world's most famous and unmistakable letters: FEDEX.

It was the company best known for the delivery of many of the world's most important packages. And less known was that the company was also used by many researchers and zoologists to ship crate-trained animals worldwide.

On the ground, waiting on the tarmac under a light drizzle and fading daylight, Steve Caesare glanced at his watch. He then looked to John Clay, standing next to him. "Right on time."

Clay nodded and scanned their surroundings. They were at the far end of the airport, near the shipping terminal, where there would be significantly less activity. The fewer eyes the better.

They watched the FedEx airliner disappear behind the top of a small building. Clay then scanned the paved roads again. "Hmm."

"Don't worry. She'll be here," Caesare reassured. "This ain't gonna to be easy for any of them, especially DeeAnn. I think she's struggling with some things."

"I know."

***

Several minutes later, the aircraft appeared again, rolling toward the terminal, where several of the airport's ground crew guided it to a stop. A tall, motorized stairway followed and was pushed into place. Then the aircraft's passenger door was swung open by someone inside.

A man in a dark blue and purple uniform stepped out, peering down at Clay and Caesare. The man then descended the stairs, crossing the asphalt.

"John Clay?" he asked aloud, over the whining engines.

"Right here." Clay walked forward slowly and reached up to shake hands. "This is Steve Caesare."

"Gentlemen," the man nodded, speaking in a distinctly South African accent. "I'm James Murphy. I understand we're here to give you a lift."

"Much obliged," Caesare said, shaking hands. "How long will it take you to unload?"

Murphy smiled. "We've got nothing to unload here. We've been diverted for you and your cargo only."

Caesare grinned at Clay. "I feel important."

"I'd say so," Murphy nodded. "First time I've seen that.

226

I'm guessing someone called in one hell of a favor." He paused, looking around. "Where is your cargo?"

**

After being waved through a security gate, Bruna handed the papers back to DeeAnn, who was sitting behind her on the first bench seat. A sudden bounce sent her higher in the rearview mirror along with Dulce and Dexter, both of whom were sitting awkwardly next to her. Neither one looked comfortable on the vinyl surface. Behind them, the rest of the van was filled with supplies, including two large boxes of food.

Bruna navigated slowly behind two rows of tall hangars before reaching the end of the row, easing to a stop. She studied the area briefly before turning the wheel and continuing forward. Darkness was descending as they reached the end of the terminal and spotted the giant plane with three figures standing below it.

Two of the figures walked briskly toward the van as Bruna came to a gradual stop. She unfastened her seatbelt and turned over her shoulder to DeeAnn.

"You are okay, missus?"

DeeAnn stared silently out through the front window at the terminal's lights around them and inhaled. "I'm fine." She looked down at Dulce and winked. The gorilla smiled back.

Seconds later, the side door of the van was opened from the outside and pulled back, revealing the figures of Caesare and Clay.

Caesare's grin found DeeAnn, pausing for a moment before smiling at Dulce. "There's my girl!"

With no hesitation, Dulce's giant smile returned and she immediately jumped from the seat into Caesare's muscular arms—an exchange that Dexter watched with interest.

Caesare winked. "Nice to see you, Dee."

She frowned at him sarcastically. She hated being called

227

Dee, much to Caesare's enjoyment.

Caesare extended his hand, which she ignored as she grasped the handle above the door, lowering herself onto the ground.

"Was it something I said?" he grinned.

She smirked at him, humorously. "It's always something you said."

"Aw, come on, Dee. That's just my Texas charm."

Caesare was still wearing his grin when he turned back to the van and noticed Dexter carefully observing them. He reached out his free hand and watched the monkey take a tiny step back.

***

The monkey studied him cautiously then looked to Dulce, who was hanging on the large human's left shoulder. Dexter remained still for a long time before finally taking a step forward. His small, dark eyes glanced at the others before returning to Dulce.

***

Patiently, Caesare waited, his hand still out. When Dexter finally moved forward again, the primate reached out and sniffed Caesare's hand before climbing onto his forearm. He paused again…and nervously crawled higher onto the other shoulder.

When Caesare turned back, DeeAnn was surprised. And more than a little relieved.

Clay chuckled. "Okay, Doctor Doolittle."

Caesare winked at DeeAnn. "See, Dee? Charm."

Her expression softened. Their playfulness remained the cornerstone of their love-hate relationship. But it was the trust that Caesare seemed to instill in both the animals that she was absolutely counting on.

With her own grin, she shook her head jokingly. "Maybe you could put that *charm* to more constructive use."

"If I had a nickel…" Caesare replied.

With that, DeeAnn turned to Bruna, who had joined them and was now standing next to Clay. She stepped forward and wrapped her arms around the shorter woman. "Thank you, Bruna."

"You are welcome, missus."

DeeAnn straightened. "I'll call you when we're getting ready to come back."

Bruna nodded warmly, her eyes reassuring DeeAnn. They both knew it was a call that would likely never come.

Murphy approached from behind, now with another man dressed in the same uniform. DeeAnn thanked them and motioned to the back of the van. From there, the men quickly unloaded the boxes and began carrying them back to the plane.

After waiting until they were out of earshot, Caesare glanced briefly at Clay again and spoke for the two of them. "So, DeeAnn. Care to fill us in here?"

Her face grew serious. She watched as Bruna instinctively turned around, stepping back toward the van and giving them privacy.

DeeAnn cleared her throat. "I think it's in Rwanda."

"That's not what we mean."

When she didn't answer, Caesare continued, "Borger thinks he found fragments of the markers we were looking for pretty close to where you had him scanning. How did you know where to look?"

"I wasn't sure. Exactly."

"Well, then that was one hell of a guess."

DeeAnn finally took a deep breath and reached down to turn off her vest, causing Dulce to twist her head curiously from Caesare's shoulder.

"It was a hunch," she sighed. "One that I actually hoped would be wrong."

"And why is that?" Clay asked.

"Because it was not a place I wanted to go. Any of us."

"Rwanda?"

She nodded. "It's a bad place—a country run by thugs and warlords, claiming to be militia. Ruthless men that have no compassion for anyone or anything. Where people are kidnapped or killed on a regular basis."

Both men's expressions grew serious.

"There are a lot of places like that in Africa."

DeeAnn shook her head. "Rwanda is worse. Years ago, a colleague of mine was murdered, and I swore I'd never set foot in that place."

"What happened?"

"She was a well-known researcher, world-renowned actually, studying gorillas in their natural environment. She was one of the *Trimates*."

"What's a Trimate?"

"It's a term for the three researchers originally sent by Louis Leakey to Africa, to expand upon his original work into primates and their biological history. DeeAnn paused, grimly. "My friend was one of them, and she was killed as a result."

Clay's brows furrowed. "What was her name?"

"Someone you've probably heard of. Dian Fossey."

Clay recognized the name. "I remember reading about her."

"You should. They made a movie based on her work."

"Dian Fossey, the anthropologist."

"And primatologist. Dian studied gorillas, Jane Goodall studied chimpanzees, and Birute Galdikas researched orangutans. All three of whom continued the work originally started by Leakey and his wife in Olduvai, where they uncovered the first true origins of human evolution."

"You mean the actual place from where we all originated?"

She nodded. "Evolved. Yes."

"And she was murdered?"

DeeAnn continued. "Some of us at the Gorilla

Foundation had followed Dian and her work for years. It all started when Leakey helped secure the funding for a long-term study of gorillas in the Congo and hired Dian. She traveled to meet Jane Goodall and observe her work before heading to the Congo. But not before she was caught in a country-wide revolution, causing her to move to the other side of the Virungas Mountains. That was where she spent the next twenty years doing research in the rain forests of Rwanda. Studying gorillas, who until then, knew humans only as predators."

DeeAnn reached up and gently stroked the fur atop Dulce's head.

"It took her a long time to gain the trust of the native gorillas. And when she finally did, she fell in love with them." A faint smile appeared briefly on DeeAnn's face. "The locals called her 'the woman who lives alone on the mountain.' And it was there that she died trying to protect them."

"From what, poachers?"

"Yes," she nodded. "It was a grizzly scene when they found her. And there were a lot of unanswered questions. But it was clear who had done it and why. She had exposed them with the help of others who were trying to fight back. Dian was creating havoc for the poachers, and they had to shut her up for good."

DeeAnn's voice trailed off leaving only silence behind. The men looked at each other.

"We're sorry, DeeAnn. Truly. But how is Dian Fossey's death related to us?"

"Because I think there may have been more to her death than we know. Than anyone knows. She lived in the most densely populated area in the world for gorillas. An area that we know was integral in the journey of human evolution. With gorillas, who are also one of the *tri-brain* animals." She let those words sink in before continuing. "What if Dian wasn't killed just for harassing the poachers? What if during her time in the mountains, she discovered more than just anthropological secrets of those gorillas? What if she discovered clues to what *we're* looking for?"

Caesare's eyes opened wide with surprise. "Whoa."

"Exactly. Which could also explain why she was murdered so suddenly after being up there for so many years."

Clay listened quietly, pondering. "If that's true, then it also means that others knew too. About whatever she found."

"Probably. And then killed her to keep it quiet. Like I said, they're ruthless. Rwanda is an extremely dangerous place, with no regard for the law or their fellow man. Everything around them is nothing more than a means." DeeAnn stared at the two men. "It's a country that's as corrupt as any I've ever seen."

Caesare folded his arms across his chest and looked at Clay. "Well, that sounds lovely."

Clay frowned. "And we thought Brazil was bad."

DeeAnn shrugged. "You can see why I never wanted to go."

"Now that makes three of us."

57

Sheng Lam was still fuming. In China, he stood silently, visually constraining his anger, studying the ground at his feet. The Jaguar kept idling behind them until one of Peng's men leaned in and switched off the ignition. The sudden disappearance of the running engine plunged them into silence for several seconds. Then the more subtle sounds of the forest gradually filled the void.

A soft swaying of the trees overhead and scampering of an animal in the bushes could be heard as Lam bent down to examine the tracks in the dirt.

A few prints left behind included a partial design from what appeared to be a sneaker or athletic shoe. He touched one of the prints gently, testing the firmness of the soil.

Lam then stood and walked back toward the car, studying the ground. The "shinings" from the bent grass and leaf depressions were clear, displaying more partials of the forefoot flipped in opposite directions.

She had run back to the car for something.

Behind Lam, their squad leader held a compact two-way radio to his ear. Peng then spoke into it, in a lowered tone. She couldn't be far.

One of Peng's men stood nearby, staring up at the chopper as he watched it slowly spin through a full 360-degree turn, scanning thoroughly without changing its position.

Hiding on the ground from helicopters was easier than most people thought. Anything from logs to small holes or caves could keep you hidden long enough for eyes above to pass over your location. It was why most helicopters hunted in packs and used thermal imaging to detect body heat.

Lam returned, and in one smooth motion, jumped over

the fallen tree trunk, landing on the other side. He squatted down and examined the ground again, looking for small broken twigs or matted grass.

He continued forward, methodically sweeping the area back and forth until he found a pattern. The indentations were more than a meter from each other and heading further into the trees.

"Well?" asked the leader.

Lam turned to find Peng's eyes nearly boring through him, waiting for an answer. He spoke reluctantly. "That way."

"How fast?"

"She's running."

***

Running was an understatement. Li Na was sprinting.

Her heart and legs felt stronger than ever. Hitting the ground like coiled springs, they sent her bounding over rocks and scattered tree limbs. But while her body felt strong, her mind was continuing to falter. Her thoughts, increasingly scattered, barely pushed through as she ran between the tree trunks that towered over her.

She had to make it to Shenyang, the largest city in the province. According to the car's GPS, it was not more than thirty kilometers away. But she also had to eat. *And who was following her?* They had to be the same men who caught her before, when she was in the hospital. Although her legs felt strong, she didn't know how long they would hold up. Without food, they had to run out of fuel eventually. In school, she'd learned about the muscles and their use of carbohydrates and proteins. When those ran out, her energy would be gone. Then they would have her.

The teenager noticed something and came to a sudden stop. Her lungs were still heaving and her legs pounding. It was still there. The weird feeling.

It was different…not a smell and not a sound. It was

234

more of an awareness of the trees and foliage around her. As though it was buzzing—not just in her head but throughout her entire body.

Li Na turned back and held her breath, listening. She became still and closed her eyes, trying to concentrate. She could hear the faint sound of the helicopter easily as it moved in a wide arc, now passing somewhere in front of her.

But more than the thumping of the distant blades…was a stream of unfamiliar noise all around her— like background noise that was only growing louder.

And yet there, in the middle of all that noise, was something else. Something deeper. A sound or a feeling that seemed to resonate much further down. A reverberation that felt oddly like an *echo*.

***

Lam, along with Peng and another of his men, jumped down from the chopper. Their boots hit the ground firmly with a thud while the blur of the aircraft's blades still whirled overhead. The downdraft plastered their straight, black hair against their heads and they marched forward. The men eventually stopped to watch the aircraft lift back into the air.

They were now in front of Li Na, while Peng's other three men remained behind as the *beaters*, spreading out and making noise to drive her forward.

Humans, just like animals, used patterns in their line of travel. Even without realizing it. Instinctively following the easier path, they sought out the flattest land with the least amount of vegetation to obstruct or slow them. Subtle differences that often guided the animal as much as the animal guided itself.

Providing Li Na made no sharp turns, her path was easy to predict. And given the maximum speed of a human through this terrain, Lam estimated there couldn't be more

than a kilometer between them.
Now they just had to wait.

58

Lam was more right than he knew. It was less than a kilometer. And in only a few minutes, Li Na heard Peng's three *beaters* behind her.

They were moving louder than she expected. Detectable in three different directions, sounding as though they had spread out. The men were clearly unaware of how much of their noise was carrying through the trees, or even the thumping of their feet upon the damp soil. They were either unaware or much closer than she thought.

Li Na rose to her feet and continued forward for a few steps before she stopped again in her tracks. The breeze, flowing gently from the front...smelled. Traces of an odor not belonging to the plants or wildlife around her.

It was very subtle and more akin to body odor. Human body odor.

Li Na suddenly stiffened. *They were in front of her too!*

Her body flushed with a fresh dose of adrenaline, and she instinctively cowered lower to the ground. Turning her head and ears told her the men in front of her had also spread out, leaving few options.

She could hear them clearly now. They were so close! The adrenaline surged powerfully through her veins and heightened her senses even more.

And there it was.

Listening carefully to the sounds both in front and behind her, an opening between two of the outermost men revealed itself. A sliver of space just big enough that would take them too long to close in. A sliver that Li Na could use if she moved quickly.

Her movement was almost instantaneous. She leaped,

with her head still down, and moved through the tall grass as quickly as she could, scrambling down a small embankment and through a grouping of large granite rocks.

59

Cruising at three hundred feet below the ocean, the large Russian submarine pushed slowly and silently through the dark water. Deep enough to remain immune from surface currents, the sub's gentle rocking was virtually undetectable to all but the most sensitive of its crew.

In front of the control room in the sub's forward hatch, the ten-man Russian team surveyed and inventoried their equipment one final time. Like U.S. forces, the Russian Special Forces, referred to as *Spetsnaz*, were meticulous to the point of obsession. Everything had been planned. Every essential system and piece of equipment checked and rechecked. Repeatedly.

They had rehearsed the plan dozens of times, looking for anything that might go wrong and building contingencies. Every variable the men could think to eliminate from chance, they had.

The Western nations first became aware of the Russian Spetsnaz group in the 1970s, at the height of the Cold War. Also known as troops of "special purpose," the teams numbered nearly 30,000 men, providing one regiment for each Soviet theater of operation.

However, with individual companies numbering at just over a hundred, most teams operated on a smaller scale consisting of eight to ten specialists. The teams were trained and used for a variety of covert missions, some of which included seeking out and killing enemy political or military leaders. Spetsnaz soldiers, whose existence was a closely guarded secret under the Warsaw Pact, were forbidden to even admit their membership, even conducting operations while wearing standard army and naval uniforms to avoid detection.

Most Spetsnaz missions were designed and carried out as reconnaissance and sabotage actions. This was including the destruction of foreign command posts and communications systems for foreign nuclear guidance programs. And much like the U.S. Special Forces, the Spetsnaz underwent exhaustive psychological and physical training, eventually being left to operate autonomously for days or weeks at a time. As they were now.

Sergeant Alexander Popov, the mission lead and a man who couldn't fit the Russian stereotype any better, stared pensively ahead. His bald head, dour expression, and wide frame stood before the hatch as if made of stone.

Due to the nature of their designs, research ships were easier to board than most others. Low sterns for their equipment and instruments left them vulnerable to attack––the reason why those that were deemed important were usually escorted by warships.

The oil platform was a different story. It would be harder. Much more defensible, although not by intention. It was merely a fortunate benefit of having the bottom platform designed to be much higher off the surface of the water. Getting to that first level without detection would be tough and would need to be carefully timed with the team that would overtake the *Pathfinder* ship. The element of surprise was the greatest advantage in any fight, and this time Popov's men would need as much as they could get.

Fortunately, the submarine would provide most of it.

But it was still a big boat, meaning they could only get so close while submerged. The final hour would be spent gliding in slowly with only a wisp of propulsion until the men were ready to exit the sub, still submerged—something that every sub crewmember in the Navy was trained to do.

Once they broke the surface, both Spetsnaz teams would have to move quickly. Because even at a thousand meters, detection prior to reaching the vessels was a huge risk.

If they were spotted in the water, the advantage would be lost and the attack would quickly turn into a firefight on the water. And that meant shooting to kill every person they saw, as quickly as possible.

It was the worst scenario for both Popov's team as well as the unsuspecting Americans.

60

DeeAnn awoke to the bounce on the runway and sudden reversal of jet engines outside, followed immediately by intense shuddering as the plane's brakes began to slow the powerful aircraft.

The shaking subsided, and she cleared her eyes to find Dulce at one of the small windows, peering out excitedly. Twisting around on the padded bench seat, she turned as far as her five-point seatbelt would allow her.

The small gorilla was talking and moving her hands quickly, leaving DeeAnn scrambling to turn her vest on.

-bird. Home now. We home. Down.

DeeAnn glanced at the smaller Dexter, wearing his own makeshift harness, then to Clay and Caesare. Both men were sitting directly across from her. "How long was I out?"

"Just through the scary part," Caesare grinned.

"Very funny." She looked to Clay for a serious answer.

"A couple hours."

"Wow." She straightened up and adjusted her own belt. "Doesn't feel like it."

We fly mommy. We fly.

"Yes, we did," she replied, simultaneously ruffling the tuft of fur on Dulce's dark head. She gave Caesare a sidelong glance and covered the vest's microphone with one hand. "And this time, we didn't almost die. Or have to jump out of it."

"The day's still young, Dee."

"All right, *that's* not funny."

DeeAnn turned back and studied Dexter, who was once again watching them all carefully. It had taken hours, and a lot of back and forth with Dulce, before the monkey allowed her to put him into the harness. And only after Dulce was already in hers. But that was the hardest part of the flight, which was to say the whole thing went much smoother than she'd feared. Traveling with Clay, and especially Caesare, tended to introduce surprises, and the trend had left her constantly on guard.

Across from her, Steve Caesare was enjoying the playful exchange. The truth was he cared a great deal for DeeAnn, and like it or not, they were becoming fast friends. Not the least of which was due to the turmoil they'd been through together. But while it had obviously been a harrowing experience for her and the others, to Clay and Caesare it was just another day at the office.

Still covering the vest's microphone, DeeAnn looked softly at both men. "Listen, I'd like to apologize to both of you. I should have told you about Rwanda sooner. I'm sorry."

"That's okay, Dee," Caesare winked. "We know what it's like to be scared."

She smiled and nodded, appreciatively. "There's a bit more to it, I'm afraid. Rwanda terrifies me. That much is true. But there's something else too." She sighed and glanced at Dulce, who was still peering out the window. "I'm not sure if this is something you realized, but I, uh…can't have children."

She watched both men's expressions soften.

"I've always wanted to, but I can't." She paused. "I tried to adopt when I was younger. A little girl, from Indonesia. But at the last minute, things fell through." DeeAnn tried to force a smile. "I was…kind of devastated."

Clay and Caesare remained quiet.

"I know it probably sounds a little silly, but when I found Dulce, when I rescued her, I think it helped me. It helped heal part of that wound."

Clay shook his head. "Doesn't sound silly at all."

DeeAnn smiled again and actually laughed. "But I didn't expect to completely fall in love with her." She turned back to both the men. "You know, young gorillas are similar to young children. Developmentally. And…I think Dulce not only helped heal me, but I think she actually filled that void––the longing I've had to be a mother."

Caesare smiled warmly. "You are her mother, Dee."

"I know." She nodded again and blinked small tears away. "Which is the biggest reason why I didn't want to come to Rwanda."

Clay frowned. "You're afraid that once back in the open, Dulce will want to stay."

"Yes," DeeAnn replied. She was struggling to speak. "Or worse. But yes, what if she doesn't want to come back? What if she doesn't want to stay with me?" Tears returned to her eyes. "I was afraid of the same thing when we went to South America, and there are no gorillas there. But this is Africa."

The men searched for something to say, but they had no words. All Caesare could think to do was to lean forward and place a hand gently on her knee.

***

As the aircraft slowed and turned off the runway, the two crewmembers returned from the rear of the plane, through an aisle running between two sides of secured cargo. Each man held on to an overhead rail.

"Everyone okay?" Murphy asked, raising his voice over the engines.

DeeAnn shot the men an anxious glance but said nothing.

"Peachy," Caesare replied. "Where's the continental breakfast?"

Murphy smiled. "I'll see if I can find you some pretzels." He glanced at his colleague behind him and continued. "As I'm sure you might guess, this is a rather unusual delivery. All the other animals we transport are usually crated. We do have several cages in the back, but it's up to you on how you'd like to deplane."

Clay and Caesare both turned to DeeAnn. This was the

hard part. Their "cover" in Africa was that they were a group of researchers transporting their primates to a research center in the Gishwati National Park. Which meant it would look out of place if both animals were *not* caged. And the last thing they wanted here was undue attention. But getting them into the cages willingly was not going to be easy.

"We're probably going to need a little time on this one," DeeAnn said to Murphy, quickly pulling herself together.

"Understood," he nodded. "Would you like us to bring the cages forward or leave them in the back?"

"Best to leave them, I think. This will need to be done gently."

"Very well. We'll give you some space then and check in with customs. If there is anything we can do to help, just shout."

"Thank you."

Clay and Caesare stood up, shaking hands with both men. "Thanks, fellas. Really appreciate the help."

"Any time," Murphy said, with a wink. "It's always fun to do a little clandestine work. Good luck with whatever you're working on."

They watched both crewmen continue to the front and open the door to the cockpit before Caesare leaned closer to Clay.

"Well, I guess we've got to kill them now."

Clay shrugged, then deadpanned, "It's a shame."

From the seat across the aisle, DeeAnn rolled her eyes. "Do you two ever stop?"

"She's starting to sound like Langford."

With a playful grin, Clay stepped forward to help DeeAnn unbuckle Dulce and Dexter. The former jumped into her lap and wrapped her lanky arms around DeeAnn's shoulders.

Dexter climbed up and quietly peered out Dulce's window, studying the objects moving past.

"What's the plan for getting them into the cages, Dee?" She grinned at Caesare. "I'm going to need your help."

61

DeeAnn's plan was simple, and so far, effective. Trusting Caesare, and taking it slow, both Dulce and Dexter reluctantly agreed to be placed inside for a short time—as long as their cages were not locked.

Now, lifted out of the plane and placed on the back of a waiting open-top Jeep, the chrome-colored bars of both cages reflected brightly under Rwanda's bright morning sun.

Located just a few degrees below the equator, the Rwandan climate was surprisingly comfortable, given the country's high elevation. With green, lush mountains and plenty of rainfall, the natural beauty of the small country presented a stark contrast to the incredible atrocities it sheltered.

Kigali, the capital, was the epicenter of the country's civil war, erupting in the 1990s. Even more horrifying was the "Rwandan Genocide" that witnessed the mass slaughter of nearly one million Rwandan Tutsis in only 100 days, by the Hutu majority government. The event, following the Burundian president's airplane being shot down, resulted in the extermination of seventy percent of native Tutsi.

The damage to Kigali was repaired, but the sheer barbarism and enormity of the event was a stunning reflection for the rest of the world. And perhaps the greatest historical disparagement considering that the travesty took place in the very birthplace of humankind.

For decades, anthropologists and scholars around the world would question just how far the nature of mankind had truly come.

And while Rwanda had grown somewhat from the horror of it all, the structure of the government, the bias in the political and racial divisions, and the power of the country's individualized militias were as prominent as ever.

Deep rifts within a tiny, violent country was still largely hidden from public view.

For the moment, Dulce stared anxiously from her cage, studying the bars with an unmistakable look of doubt. Her big eyes blinked and slowly peered back up at DeeAnn, standing beside the vehicle.

Me no like.

Next to her, in a second smaller cage, Dexter said nothing. Instead, he merely fingered the door, pushing it open and closed again—testing it over and over, making sure it didn't lock.

"I'm sorry," DeeAnn said. "But it's very important you stay in the cage. For a little while."

Something in her reply didn't translate correctly, but Dulce seemed to understand, though she remained unhappy. She turned and motioned to Dexter, communication which the vest could not pick up.

Steve Caesare stood on the other side of the Jeep, lifting their bags onto the extended rear carriage rack.

"It shouldn't be long. We should be out of the city within an hour." He hefted the last bag into place and looked at DeeAnn while snaking a rope over the top. "After that, we'll be remote enough that having them out won't seem all that odd."

"Are you sure?"

Caesare grinned. "Trust me, people in Africa are used to seeing some strange things. A couple primates in a Jeep will look less odd than you think."

"Have you been to Rwanda before?"

He shook his head. "No, but I've been to a lot of other places in Africa. Places a lot like this."

They turned to see Clay approaching from the old and faded terminal building. Outside, a long line of passengers waited along the building's outer wall, clutching their bags and suitcases. All were waiting to board a smaller turboprop airplane belonging to RwandAir, the country's solitary airline.

"Everything go okay?"

"Well, *okay* might be a little relative, but yes." Clay returned their passports, then folded several forms and tucked them into a pocket. "Fortunately for us, the protocol's a bit light here."

"Good." DeeAnn withdrew two bundles of vegetables from the box, handing one to each of her furry friends. "The rest of this food isn't going to last long here. We'll have to find a new supply."

Caesare nodded. "We'll need more than that." He finished lashing down the bags and stepped back to open the rear door for her. "Everyone ready for the field trip?"

Clay nodded, scanning the area one last time before climbing into the front passenger seat.

DeeAnn checked the cords securing the cages before reaching inside to rearrange a pillow for Dulce. "I guess so."

***

A few miles outside Kigali, they stopped at a dingy, run-down gas station to fill up the Jeep. The station had two pumps, both looking older than anyone using them, and only one appeared operational.

A short line formed at the single pump and several patrons waited patiently, all dressed in ill-fitting dirty clothing. Some sat on plastic containers or jerry cans, seemingly unaffected by the wait.

Clay and Caesare both climbed out, then stood in front of the vehicle. The air was damp with a soft breeze flowing past. Beneath the Jeep's thick canopied top, DeeAnn watched the primates finish off a second helping of kale.

Caesare unfolded a map and placed an aerial picture over it, given to him by Will Borger.

"Well, it shouldn't take long to get there."

"Good. The sooner, the better," Clay replied. He

studied several Rwandans who were watching them from a distance. "Even with these clothes, I don't think we're exactly fitting in."

Caesare didn't look up. "What we need is a guide."

"Hallo," a voice said from behind them.

Clay and Caesare turned together to see a boy standing near the Jeep, wearing a friendly smile. He was dressed in a colorful but dusty shirt, his hair cropped short. A pair of baggy shorts were held up by a faded belt, all perched atop a pair of dark skinny legs and sandals.

"Are you English?" the boy asked.

Clay and Caesare looked at each other before turning back to the boy.

"American."

He smiled wider and came closer. "I like America!" The boy's accent was strong with traces of South African English.

Caesare raised an eyebrow. "Is that right?"

"Yes," he nodded excitedly. "Justin Bieber and football!"

With a sad expression, Caesare peered back at Clay. "This is what we've become?"

Clay grinned. "Something tells me they don't have a lot of channels out here." He stepped forward as the boy turned and scanned the Jeep, paying special attention to Dulce and Dexter. "What's your name?"

"Jimmy."

Clay frowned. "What's your real name?"

At that, the boy paused. "Yves."

"You live around here, Yves?"

"Yes. Over there." He pointed at a distant hill, dotted with small houses. "Are you going to the mountains?"

"What makes you think that?" Caesare asked.

Yves shrugged and pointed at Dulce and Dexter.

"How old are you?"

"Ten."

"And what are you doing around here?"

"I work here."

"You work here? Doing what?"

The boy smiled. "I help people. With everything."

Caesare straightened up and looked at DeeAnn, still in the Jeep, who had quietly turned off her vest.

"Do you know someone who can show us the way to the mountains?"

"Yes! My mukuru!"

***

Yves's *mukuru* was his older brother. He was in his mid-teens with a strikingly similar appearance to Yves. Most of the difference between the two was in the extra foot of height.

The teenager was brought back to the station by his younger brother while Clay and Caesare remained, waiting for gas. The older brother was just as friendly and twice as eager.

"I'm Janvier," he said quickly. "You want to go to the mountains? I can take you."

Clay and Caesare studied the young man and motioned him behind the vehicle. They spoke in a lower volume.

"How well do you know the way?"

"Very well. I have been many times!"

"How many?"

He paused, thinking. When he answered, Clay couldn't tell if it was a statement or a question. "Fifty?"

"Fifty times?"

"Yes!"

Caesare motioned to DeeAnn who climbed out of the Jeep. Janvier noticed her vest, but promptly met her eyes and smiled.

"We need to go quietly," Caesare said.

Janvier nodded repeatedly. "Yes. No problem. Everyone goes to mountains quietly."

"What for?"

251

"For gorillas."

"Everyone wants to study the gorillas?"

"No," DeeAnn replied dryly. "He's talking about the poachers."

She peered hard at Janvier. "They go to capture the gorillas. Don't they?"

The teenager's expression grew nervous. He shrugged innocently but continued smiling. "I...do not know. I just show the way."

From where he was standing, Janvier glanced over DeeAnn's shoulder at the small gorilla in the Jeep. Dulce had left her cage and was crawling curiously onto the backseat. When DeeAnn followed his eyes, she walked back and picked Dulce up, returning her gently to the cage while whispering something.

Janvier continued watching DeeAnn until she returned to them, studying her face and disposition. "You are researcher?"

"Yes. I'm a researcher. But I'm not here to trap anything."

Janvier either didn't hear the remark or ignored it. Instead, he looked down at his younger brother Yves and spoke in Kinyarwandan.

The older brother looked back and forth between all three now, lowering his own voice. "You come for the researcher?"

"What do you mean?"

"The woman researcher." Janvier glanced at DeeAnn. "Like you. The one that died."

62

"You know about the woman who died? That was thirty years ago."

Janvier nodded. "Everyone knows about her. She is famous."

"What else?"

He looked down at his younger brother and made a shooing sound. The smaller Yves nodded and promptly ran back the way they had come.

"She is killed. In the mountains. With the gorillas."

"You know where?"

"Yes. Her cabin is there. The real one."

Suddenly, DeeAnn's expression turned from surprise to astonishment. With wide eyes, she stared at Clay and Caesare.

"Janvier, you're saying Dian Fossey's original cabin is still there?"

He nodded again. "Yes. It is blocked. But there is still a way. I can take you."

DeeAnn took a deep breath and put a hand over her chest. "Oh my God."

Clay stepped forward. "Are you all right?"

"No." She shook her head and took several more breaths. "I'm not sure if I want to see that."

"Janvier, how long does it take to get there? Just *near* the cabin?"

"If I take you now, we are there in this afternoon."

"Quietly."

"Yes. Very quiet."

"How much?" Caesare asked.

"Two hundred American dollars."

Caesare smiled. He liked this kid. "*Three* hundred...and

you help us get some things."

Janvier grinned. "Of course."

"Beginning with some petrol, rapido."

***

Not surprisingly, there was another, much faster place to get gasoline. For an additional cost. Two more boxes of food were also secured with little trouble. By the time they made it beyond the outskirts of Kigali, it was still barely ten o'clock.

The road was in better shape than expected, allowing them to make it to the base of the mountain in less than an hour. The climb up, however, was very different. Plagued by ruts and deep potholes from the heavy rainfall, the road was missing many sections. This required the trio to slow to a stop before carefully inching forward onto the dirt.

And Caesare was right. Once they'd made it far enough out, they passed few people, none of whom paid the slightest attention to the gorilla or the monkey. Both animals had now moved forward and were sitting on the backseat between DeeAnn and Clay.

They'd be able to reach the mountain within hours. And while it would take time to find the coordinates Will Borger had identified, if the current road was any indication, they might be able to do it before anyone even knew they were there.

From the driver's seat, Caesare was beginning to feel downright enthusiastic, which worried him. Because if there was one thing Clay and Caesare had learned from previous missions, it was that when things seemed to be going well...that was just about the time the bottom usually fell out.

63

The horror of the Rwandan Genocide finally ended in 1994, on the 4th of July. The armed wing of the Tutsis, known as the Rwandan Patriotic Front was the responsible party. Originally backed by Belgium and France, the RPF fought back against the Hutu-driven attacks, cutting off government supply routes and taking advantage of the rapidly deteriorating social order.

And yet, while the Tutsis had since reclaimed the Rwandan government, and driven most of the Hutus back across the Congo border, not all who had been responsible for the genocide had fled.

Amir Ngeze was one of those men. Powerful, and now into his late sixties with short white hair, his dark face and eyes resembled anything but a killer.

But inwardly Ngeze was, in fact, the very embodiment of corruption and death. He was a man well-known for his unforgiving ruthlessness and feared by everyone who knew him.

However, to Ngeze, the "genocide" was nothing of the sort. To him, it was the cleansing of a virulent pest. One responsible for the infestation and downfall of their once great country. A country that was now overrun with them.

But as dark as Ngeze was, he was also a man of extreme patience. The day would come when the tide would turn once more—when the Hutu would reclaim their country and their birthright, and God willing, Amir Ngeze might become their next president.

Ngeze was certain of the resurgence. Because unlike the Tutsi, he had something that no one else did.

Now dressed in ornate, embroidered clothing of red and gold, Amir Ngeze stood in a large, beautifully decorated courtyard with hands placed calmly behind his back—staring down at a man on his knees, sobbing.

The elitist watched while the man begged for his life, and he shook his head with a look of pity. He inhaled and let his eyes rise to scan the walls of his complex, peering out over the five-meter-high walls at the lush green mountains beyond.

"What did you see?" he asked in a low voice.

But the man on the ground did not hear him over his own pleas.

"I said," Ngeze repeated impatiently, "what did you see?"

Now the man stopped and squinted upwards. His eyes filled with tears and a trace of spittle dripped from his lips. "Nothing! I saw nothing! I swear it!"

Ngeze's cold eyes darted to one of his own men, standing next to him. He was dressed in red crimson fatigues. The color of blood.

Ngeze's soldier shook his head silently.

Why were the lower class so extraordinarily stupid? he thought to himself. *Why was it always the same? Saying anything to try to turn their lies into truth.*

"You saw nothing?"

"No!" cried the man. "I swear to you! Nothing!"

Now Ngeze nodded to both soldiers. They reached down and pushed the man flat against the cold stone. One soldier pressed his boot hard against the man's neck, keeping him in place, while the other pulled an arm free, nearly dislocating it at the shoulder.

The man screamed in pain, echoing eerily against the thick walls.

The soldier moved down the man's arm until he held it like a vice at the wrist.

"Listen to me," Ngeze said, raising his voice over the man's wailing. "Are you listening?"

The man struggled to speak with his face and lips pressed against the floor. "Y-yes."

256

"You have lied to me four times. And now you will lose four." Ngeze bent down closer to him. "But I will have the truth. And you will only have six fingers left to tell it."

***

Less than an hour later, Ngeze sat in a plush chair, shaded by a broad overhead umbrella. The terrace, adorned with statues and handcrafted chairs, provided a cool breeze as Ngeze sipped and savored a cup of Columbian coffee. It was considered an imported delicacy after Rwanda's own coffee and tea industries had been utterly devastated.

He set the cup down and had just reached for a pastry when one of his soldiers appeared, waiting at a distance. Beside him was a young boy.

Taking a bite, Ngeze chewed slowly and deliberately. He then leaned back against the cushion before motioning them forward. He peered contemptuously at the boy who he'd seen before.

"Yves. What do you want now?"

The ten-year-old stepped closer and spoke in native Kinyarwandan. "My Eminence, you told me if I had information to bring it to you."

"What is it now?"

"Some Americans are here."

He shrugged. "So what?"

"They are scientist people."

Ngeze took another bite of his pastry and waved them both away. "I don't care."

The soldier was already reaching for Yves when he quickly stammered, "They come to learn about the one that died. The Mountain Lady."

Ngeze stopped chewing and held up a hand. The soldier froze with a hand on the boy's arm.

"What did you say?"

"They came to learn of the Mountain Lady."

"What did they say?"

"They wanted to go to the mountains."

"For her?"

"Yes," Yves nodded.

"Are you sure?"

"Yes."

Ngeze glanced at his man before letting his eyes fall back on Yves. "When?"

"This morning."

This morning? Ngeze's eyes became more intent. "Have they already left?"

"Yes." Even at ten, Yves was smart enough not to mention who took them.

"What do they look like?"

"Two men and a woman. And two monkeys."

"And you're sure they're Americans?"

"Yes."

Ngeze stared at the boy for a long time. "You can go."

The boy nodded and stepped back away from the hand of the soldier. But he wasn't done. "Is this enough? To help my father?"

Ngeze squinted at the boy. "We'll see. Maybe."

Yves smiled. The man had never told him *maybe* before. He promptly turned and left, reaching the stairs and descending out of sight.

Amir Ngeze watched his man disappear behind Yves. He let himself chuckle at the boy's naïveté. He wanted so badly to have his father set free, he would continue to do anything. It was too bad the kid hadn't figured out yet that his father was already long dead.

Ngeze pushed his chair back and stood up. He looked out toward the top of the distant mountain. *It had been a long time. What exactly did the Americans want to know about the Fossey woman now?*

64

The Jeep's engine roared loudly as it crawled up a steep embankment and around another washed-out section of road. Overhead, the towering mahogany and kapok trees shrouded the area under dense canopy for as far as they could see. Rich green plants leaned out from the edge of the dirt road, their leaves slapping the sides of the vehicle as they passed.

Now on DeeAnn's lap, Dulce eagerly leaned out the side window laughing when brushed by a passing leaf or small branch. Her eyes caught sight of a cluster of bright pink bromeliad flowers, before they disappeared again behind another wave of green flora.

But to Dulce, the excitement was not just in what she saw. It was in what she *smelled*—a symphony of scents and odors that seemed to reawaken her senses. Sensations that her olfactory system remembered, even if the young gorilla's memory did not.

Even Dexter seemed mesmerized by their surroundings. He sat, cautiously, half perched on John Clay's shoulder with his thin gray arms resting on the window strip.

It had taken two hours to reach the first crest of the Volcanoes National Park and nearly another to spot the first glimpse of the snowcapped peak of Mount Karisimbi.

Mommy. Dulce hooted, turning back and motioning with her hands in front of her. *We home. We home.*

Clay leaned in closer. "Did you ever meet Dian Fossey?"

DeeAnn nodded. "Once. In college. She was giving a talk, and a friend invited me. To be honest, I'd never even considered this kind of work until then." A deep pothole shook the Jeep from side to side before she continued. "I remember thinking that I'd never seen anyone so passionate about what they were doing before. I even got to talk to her for a few minutes. But she wouldn't have remembered me. It was after that when my friend and I started following her work. Fascinating woman."

Clay smiled. "Like you and Ali, I think."

DeeAnn let out a small chuckle and turned away, looking out the window with Dulce.

***

Several minutes later, Janvier leaned forward in the front seat, peering through the dirt-splattered windshield. When they came around another tight bend, he bolted upright. "Stop! Stop here!" he shouted over the engine.

Caesare slowed and pulled to a stop against the inside embankment, leaving just enough space for Janvier and Clay to open their doors.

"Is this it?"

"No. The cabin is far ahead, but this is where we can get in."

All four climbed out. Dulce, rather than reaching for DeeAnn, readily climbed down onto the dirt road and touched it gingerly with her fingers. She sniffed several times and scampered across the road to the opposite side, looking down the mountainside through the trees.

"What docs it smell like, Dulce?"

After the translation, she grinned up at Caesare. *Smell happy.*

The exchange was the first time Janvier had realized what was happening, and he was immediately taken aback. "Y-you can talk to them?"

"To her. Yes," DeeAnn replied.

The teenager stepped forward in amazement and studied the strange vest. "How?"

"It's a computer," Caesare explained. It was a tremendous simplification, yet it seemed to satisfy the youth who nodded and continued watching.

Behind them, Dexter also crossed the road and approached Caesare. He lowered his arm and the monkey promptly climbed up onto his shoulder.

"He's really beginning to trust you," DeeAnn declared.

"I wouldn't hold it against him," Clay joked over his shoulder. "I've made the same mistake multiple times."

Caesare squinted at him. "Aren't you supposed to be the strong *silent* type?"

"I forgot." Clay noticed an odd look on DeeAnn's face. "Everything okay?"

She moved several steps back and motioned both men toward her. When they stepped forward, she lowered her voice. "I think I should remind you of the other reason I didn't want to come back here."

"Which reason was that?"

"The poaching. We talked about it, but I need to re-emphasize just how serious things are here. In Rwanda, gorilla poaching isn't just bad, it's *really* bad. Probably as bad as any place on the planet."

"What exactly does that mean?"

DeeAnn took a deep breath. "We're talking about a very bad place, where poaching ends and outright murder begins."

"I thought poaching was for capture?" Caesare asked.

"Some of it is."

"Then what would be the purpose of just killing them outright?"

DeeAnn shook her head. "Primarily for their meat. But as bad as that is, it brings certain…consequences. That we all need to stay aware of."

"Such as?" Clay questioned.

"The other reason I didn't want to come here is that if we see other gorillas in the wild, things may not go well."

"And *not well* means what exactly?"

DeeAnn glanced past them at Dulce, who was playing with the branches of a small kapok tree. "Dulce has not experienced other gorillas before, at least not that she can remember. And certainly not in the wild. I don't know how she's going to react. But that's not the part I'm worried about. It's what happens when *they* see her. It's one thing to run into a female adult out here. Even a mother with her young. But it's very different if we see a silverback."

"A male?"

"Exactly. The males are the protectors. And they're not stupid. They are intimately aware of what's happening to them up here. They understand who's doing the killing. Which means that if a silverback spots us with Dulce, he will most likely conclude that she has been kidnapped. And he'll try to recover her."

"So he might attack?"

DeeAnn shook her head. "Not might. Gorillas fight to the death to protect their young. If he thinks Dulce has been kidnapped, there's no question that he'll attack."

Caesare frowned. "Crap."

"And believe me, a silverback is the last thing you want to fight. They are not just strong, they're Superman strong. Strong enough to literally rip arms off if they get angry enough. And they can run much faster than you think."

"How fast?"

"Let's put it this way. Unless there's a significant distance between us, we won't have a chance."

Caesare folded his arms and glared at Clay. "Okay, I don't want to sound negative, but this trip is really losing its allure for me."

Clay turned to DeeAnn. "Remind me exactly why we bought Dulce?"

"Because I had to," she replied. "Once we leave, I don't plan on coming back here. Ever again. And although Dulce is young, this is still her first home. This is where she came from. As difficult as it is for me, the choice ultimately belongs to her."

"Plus," DeeAnn added, "there is a chance Dulce and Dexter can help us. And we'll need all the help we can get."

After a thoughtful pause, Clay nodded and turned back

to the teen. "Where to from here, Janvier?"

"That way. A path in the trees. We get in from the other side."

***

The path was about a half mile through dense rain forest. Brushing through broad, hanging leaves that were still wet, everyone's clothes gradually becoming soaked as they pushed through. It wasn't long before they heard the sound of a waterfall.

It was small. Whitewater cascaded down several sections of rock before rolling over a larger boulder and disappearing from sight. A cool mist floated outward, lightly coating their arms and faces as they stepped closer.

Janvier raised his voice and climbed carefully toward the wet, slippery rocks. "Up there." He pointed up to where the others could see a very tall chain link fence strewn across the embankment. It passed over the small waterfall, continuing through the jungle on either side.

Where the fence billowed out over the water was a small opening large enough to climb through.

"What?! Up there?"

Janvier smiled proudly. "Yes. I can lead you."

DeeAnn scanned the incline and turned to look worriedly at her companions. Caesare winked. "At least we're not jumping out of a plane."

"Some consolation."

Fortunately, what little path there was up the embankment was not steep. Instead, it narrowly zigzagged its way to a larger and wider boulder, which jutted out close to the fencing. When they reached it, DeeAnn watched the others' technique before rotating one arm underneath and wrapping her fingers through the fence for support. She then turned to reach for Dulce only to have the gorilla scamper up effortlessly from behind, passing DeeAnn and waiting for her on the next group of rocks.

Bringing up the rear, Caesare ducked below the fence, careful, like Clay, to keep his pack from getting caught. Dexter watched with interest before suddenly jumping onto the chain link and climbing effortlessly over the top.

After nearly another hundred feet of climbing, the group made it to a wider open area, where they stopped to catch their breath.

"How much further, Janvier?"

He studied the way above them. "Not far. We are close now."

"Thank God," DeeAnn muttered.

After a short rest, they continued, veering away from the cascading stream. They found an area where the dense foliage was easier to climb, and gave them more to hang onto.

When they reached the final ledge, what they were looking for was almost completely obscured inside thick vegetation. Dozens of trees and tall bushes were slowly reclaiming the area, including what was left of the old cabin.

On either side of a deteriorating foundation were signs of a once larger, flatter open area—all being methodically restored by Mother Nature.

"This is it?"

Janvier smiled with pride. "Yes."

Clay and Caesare approached slowly and rounded both sides of the structure. The walls were missing most of their planks. The entirety of the original roof had caved in, filling the inside of the structure with a mix of debris and vegetation.

"I'm guessing it cleaned up a little better thirty years ago?"

DeeAnn anxiously studied the scene, taking it all in. "I'm sure," she replied absentmindedly.

Caesare nodded and raised his leg, pushing over a broken beam. It fell away, along with a span of old shingles, onto what was left of the wooden floorboards indicating two or three original rooms. In the corner stood a small iron stove, covered with a thick layer of dirt and mud.

In the ruins of a second room were remnants of tattered bedding, where a bed had been. Just a few feet away remained pieces of a small table, strewn with unrecognizable items completely caked in dirt.

Clay studied the remains of several empty shelves, most in pieces on the floor except for one still dangling precariously from the wall.

"Why would they keep this?" he asked quietly. "Why fence the whole area off rather than just tear the structure down?"

"I don't know," DeeAnn said. She peered up at the trees above them. "There was an investigation and the only person who was ever charged was one of Dian's friends, in absentia. He had already returned to the U.S. A lot of people felt it was merely a formality by Rwandan officials. Bribery and corruption run deep here. Especially in these parts with the Rwandan National Park guards."

Caesare frowned. "Then why not get rid of what's left of the evidence? They've had plenty of time to do it."

"It doesn't make any sense."

The three were interrupted by Janvier, still standing outside. "It was for purpose."

They all turned toward their guide.

"The man who rules this area, he is very powerful. He rules the mountains. He leaves this place as a reason. As a message to everyone."

"A message?"

"I think he means a *warning*," Clay answered.

DeeAnn rolled her eyes. "My God. What is wrong with people?" She shook her head and dropped down onto a tree stump, staring at the remains. "What is wrong with everyone? Why does everything have to turn into a damn fight?! She did not deserve this! She was just trying to help the gorillas from getting slaughtered. Innocent animals that did nothing to anyone. And for that, they kill her? For trying to help? For trying to be kind?" DeeAnn gritted her teeth. "It's exactly what *we're* trying to do!"

Young Janvier watched DeeAnn as she began to cry through tears of frustration.

"You know'd this lady?"

She nodded through her hands. "Yes. I did."

He continued watching her. "My mother says the Mountain Lady was a good woman."

"She was. A very good woman. And this is what happens when you try to help!"

Janvier nodded, sympathetically. He had brought others into the mountains before, but not like these. He stepped closer to DeeAnn. "Then for this, you cannot tell anyone. I can maybe show you something else."

"Something else?"

The teen nodded. "Books."

"What kind of books?"

"Books belonged to the Mountain Lady."

Her heart skipped a beat and DeeAnn looked up at Janvier. "Books that belonged to Dian Fossey?"

"Yes."

"Which books?"

The young man looked back and forth between them. "Secret books."

Staring at Janvier, her hands almost began to tremble. When Dian Fossey was killed, not all her belongings had been accounted for. Including some of her journals.

"You're saying you have secret books of hers?"

Janvier shook his head. "Not me. Someone I know. A man who lives up here. For a long time."

DeeAnn remained still. Dumbfounded. *It couldn't be. It was impossible.*

Seeing her face, Caesare stepped closer. "How far away is this man, Janvier?"

"One hour, maybe. He lives deep in the forest."

"And how much to see the books?"

The boy thought. "Maybe one hundred dollars. But not for me."

65

True to his word, the trek was little more than an hour. Through increasingly dense forest, the group pushed forward, navigating a narrow one-foot-wide path through thickets of trees and bushes—which rose over their heads, blotting out most of the midday sun.

Caesare, whose wide frame seemed to brush every possible plant, was completely soaked from the runoff. And he now was carrying Dulce as well as Dexter.

Just behind Janvier, John Clay pushed branches out of the way for DeeAnn and Caesare behind him. In many places, the path was barely visible, leaving Clay wondering if the obscurity was intentional. Yet more than that, Clay and Caesare were silently beginning to exchange looks of skepticism. Things felt too easy. From their arrival, to finding Janvier, and now the Fossey cabin. So far it was all too smooth. Which left them both wondering what surprises were still waiting for them.

But for DeeAnn, the trip seemed excruciatingly long. The mere possibility that some of Fossey's things had survived this many years was beyond astonishing—new things that may not have been cataloged during the old investigation. And just maybe, things that would shed more light on the circumstances around her death. Like who exactly was behind it.

She remembered that the official records had shown that Fossey was clearly being harassed for months before it happened. But there was no evidence of who it was.

Now if there *was* evidence uncovered pointing to who, the case could possibly be reopened. And perhaps the killers brought to justice.

However as they continued pushing forward through

the forest, DeeAnn completely forgot in her excitement just how little political will there really was in Rwanda in seeing Dian Fossey's case finally solved.

66

Finally, the path widened in front of them, revealing an area large enough for an old garden and even older dwelling behind it. Though not much bigger than the remains of the Fossey structure, this one was at least still standing. For the moment. The outside was composed of numerous different materials, from mismatched boards to sections of rusted sheet metal, all attached to form a large shanty.

No sooner had they emerged from the dense forest, when a pair of dark eyes appeared from a crooked doorway and shouted something in Kinyarwandan.

Everyone stopped and Janvier called back, with the only recognizable word being his name.

The loud male voice replied with a single syllable and the teenager turned around anxiously. "Please for you. Wait here. I will return very soon."

All eyes watched Janvier as he approached the house. With hands raised, he spoke slowly and loudly. When he reached the door, it opened wide but not enough to let him in.

"I hope this guy actually knows something," Caesare said.

"So do I," Clay nodded. He looked at the forest surrounding them on all sides. "He may be in a world all his own here, in more ways than one."

DeeAnn didn't reply. Instead she and both primates watched in rapt attention as Janvier continued talking to the man. Several hand gestures motioned toward them followed by the boy shaking his head. Finally, the conversation ended and Janvier returned.

He smiled but didn't say anything at first, leaving Caesare to lean forward with raised eyebrows.

"Annnd?"

"He doesn't want to show you the books. But I tell him you are good people. He says five hundred dollars."

"Five hundred?!" Caesare turned to Clay. "That's some pretty serious inflation."

Clay nodded. "Five hundred dollars, Janvier. And we see everything he has."

***

The inside of the cabin looked even worse than the outside. Small gaps between wallboards left dozens of holes with the sun shining through. Along with the lack of insulation, there ironically seemed to be little air flow either. Providing a rather stuffy interior, the room was literally packed from corner to corner with discarded odds and ends. Surprisingly though, what looked to the three of them to be junk was relatively well organized.

The thin man had dark skin and appeared to be in his eighties. He eyed them cautiously while DeeAnn paged through one of the books. His face not hiding his irritation, he re-counted the bills in his hand several more times, making a few angry sounds while shuffling about the cabin.

Two other leather-bound books in front of DeeAnn were old textbooks, which she immediately pushed aside when she spotted the two she was looking for.

They were journals. Handwritten and faded, they were actual journals written in Dian Fossey's own hand. And one, to DeeAnn's stunned amazement, was the very journal she kept just before her death. Here. In possession of a recluse whom few probably even knew existed.

She looked up at John Clay, who was standing nearby, and barely managed to get the words out.

"This…is incredible."

She dropped her eyes and continued reading while Clay held his breath in anticipation. "Is there anything useful?"

After several moments, DeeAnn nodded, squinting at a

section of the faded script. "Yes. God, yes." After finishing the page, she looked up again at him. "She knew exactly who was harassing her."

"Enough to name them?"

DeeAnn smiled and continued nodding. After another page of reading, she stopped again, pushing a few loose pages back into place. "And there's more."

"More?"

DeeAnn glanced past Clay to the boy, and he took the hint.

"Janvier," Clay said. "Would you mind leaving us for a moment? We'd like to speak privately."

"Yes." He spoke briefly to the old man again in Kinyarwandan and pushed through the door to where Caesare and the two primates played outside, waiting.

"John, it wasn't just about the poaching," DeeAnn said while reading. "That's where it started…but it was only the beginning." She flipped through more pages and remained quiet for several minutes. "She'd been fighting back against them for years, destroying their gorilla traps, which is when the harassment first began. Things in the middle of the night. Like her water supply being drained or rocks thrown through her windows."

DeeAnn continued reading a couple more pages before she stopped and suddenly looked at Clay. "Over the years, things continued to escalate. But toward the end, less than a week before she died…she found something."

"What?"

She flipped through more, scanning. "She doesn't say specifically. Just that it was something odd, in the forest. But it looks like she told two people. A researcher back home, via letter. And a friend…in Kigali. Days before she died."

"Did she say where this discovery was?"

DeeAnn's lip curled, and she nodded. "Yes…she…did."

Clay glanced up at the old man, who momentarily had

271

his back turned. He quickly reached into his pocket and slipped something silently into DeeAnn's hand.

"Hurry."

Clay then turned around and walked to the door. The boy was standing under the structure's flimsy overhang, watching Caesare and the primates. Dulce was halfway up a tree, and Dexter was quietly studying the forest behind them.

"Janvier," Clay pushed the door out and stepped onto the porch. "How much to buy these books?"

Janvier looked surprised. He called to the old man who appeared in the doorway. When asked, the man's eyes and face grew angry, and he snapped at Janvier in Kinyarwandan. He pointed at both Clay and Caesare, raising his voice even further.

Janvier was unprepared for the reaction. He spoke quickly to calm the man down but to little effect. He turned to Clay, nervously. "He say the books are not for sale. And we must leave now."

The old man disappeared from the door and could be heard yelling toward DeeAnn.

"Easy," Clay said. "Tell him we're not trying to cause trouble."

Janvier called into the cabin but the shouting only got louder.

"He is not listening. He thinks you are trying to take his things. We must go!"

DeeAnn suddenly pushed through the door. "Hey, take it easy! It was just a question!"

Caesare approached with Dulce. "It sounds like we've outstayed our welcome."

"You could say that," Clay retorted.

"Okay, Janvier. I guess it's time to head out."

The youth nodded and moved quickly past the garden, followed by Caesare, Dulce, and Dexter.

Before falling in behind them, Clay stepped from the porch with DeeAnn and pulled her in close. With their backs to the cabin, she passed the small camera back to him.

"Did you get it?"

She nodded. "I think so."

67

The trip back went faster. After returning to the Jeep, they wasted no time in retrieving a map from one of their packs and unfolding it across the hood of the vehicle.

DeeAnn sifted through the pictures on the camera and stopped when she found the image she was looking for. She enlarged it on the screen and studied the faint handwriting. She held the camera over the map and traced up the paper with her finger.

"She said it was along the Albertine Rift. Just southeast of Mount Bisoke. Which would put it...about here."

Caesare peered across the hood to Clay. "Same area as Borger's images."

After a palpable silence, all three turned to find Janvier staring wide-eyed at the map. And more specifically, the location of DeeAnn's finger. He slowly shook his head, horrified. "We cannot go there. It is forbidden." He looked at them. "We will be killed."

"By who?"

"By Ngeze. He is very fierce. He will kill us all." When Clay and Caesare straightened, Janvier took several steps back. "No. From here I must leave. I cannot help you anymore."

Caesare frowned. "All right, kid. We don't want to put you in danger." He approached and extended a folded wad of bills.

Janvier glanced briefly before taking them.

"None of us were here. Do you understand?"

"Yes. But I warn, you should not go there. It is dangerous." With that, the teenager turned and began running back down the dirt road.

Both men turned back around to DeeAnn who was still

leaning over the front of the Jeep. "Okay, I don't know about you, but that sounded pretty ominous to me."

They were suddenly interrupted by the vest on DeeAnn's chest.

He scare.

Dulce was watching the teenager as he ran.

DeeAnn pursed her lips in frustration. She had forgotten to turn off the vest.

"Yes. He is," was all she could say.

Why scare?

"He doesn't want to go any further."

Why scare? Dulce repeated.

She thought about how best to explain it. "There are bad people here."

Why bad people here?

Her next reply was hesitant. "Bad people hurt other people…and gorillas."

Why?

To this, DeeAnn had no answer. "I…don't know."

Danger?

"Yes. There is some danger here."

Dulce studied the forest in front of them. She then backed up until she bumped against Caesare's leg, where she wrapped an arm around it.

"But we will be safe."

The young gorilla nodded but did not reply.

What no one noticed was the smaller Dexter, nearby and still staring into the deep brush—seemingly oblivious to the others.

There was someone else in the forest.

68

Alison listened pensively to each successive ring on the other end. When Clay finally answered, she smiled with relief.

"Hello?"

"Hi," she said softly. "It's me."

Clay smiled and walked away from the Jeep. "Well, hello there." He then frowned as he looked at his watch. "Aren't you up a bit early?"

On the other end, Alison peered out over the side of the *Pathfinder* ship and into the darkness of the ocean. "I couldn't sleep."

"Are you okay?"

"I'm fine." She nodded, absently tapping the metal railing with her finger. "Just a lot on my mind, I guess. How are things over there?"

"Interesting might be a good word."

"Are *you* okay?"

"Yeah, we're all fine. Just some surprises we hadn't expected."

Alison frowned to herself, wishing she could ask more questions over the phone. The call was encrypted, but she could hear Will Borger's voice going on about how all encryption could be broken, eventually.

"I wish you were still here."

She couldn't see Clay's smile on the other end. "So do I. I'd trade the jungle for the tropics any day."

"Oh, I see," Alison teased. "So it's not a matter of who. Just where."

"Well, let's just say that if you were here, I'd have to change my answer."

"Good. I like that better."

"What do you have planned for today?"

She shrugged. "I thought I'd get in the water."

"I could have guessed that," Clay said. "Hey, look up."

Alison tilted her head back. "What?"

"Can you see the moon?"

"Yes."

"So can I."

Alison's expression softened. "We're looking at the same moon."

"Yep. Almost like I'm there with you."

"I really wish you were."

"So do I. And not because of the weather."

Alison laughed. "Well, I should probably let you go. I just wanted to check in on you guys."

"I'm glad you did. Tell Dirk and Sally I said hi."

"I will. Any messages for Will? He's following your signal from satellite."

Clay looked toward the Jeep. "Any message for Borger?"

"Yeah," Caesare said. "Tell him next time he's coming with us."

Clay turned back to the phone. "Tell Will that Steve sends his love."

"I will," Alison chuckled. "Be careful."

"Always."

"I love you."

"I love you too, Ali. Enjoy your swim," he responded tenderly.

"Bye."

Alison ended the call and inhaled, still smiling. She looked back up at the moon, wondering where Clay was standing at that exact moment.

She had no idea that in barely twelve hours she would be wondering whether that would be the last time she ever spoke with John Clay.

69

The moon was only partially visible through the thin cloud layer sliding ominously across northeast China. Barely illuminating the ground for Peng and the rest of his squad, a glow now shone lightly on Sheng Lam. The man had not spoken a word to them for hours.

They were all irritated.

It shouldn't have taken this long to find the girl. She was still a kid for Christ's sake. But somehow she had managed to evade both them and their helicopter pilot. And while only a teenager, the girl was proving to be an exceedingly smart one. She knew enough to stay under the cover of the trees, blocking the view from above. She also seemed to know where to walk over objects such as logs and rocks when possible, causing them to stop more often to reestablish her tracks.

In front of Peng, Sheng Lam studied the ground under his dim red flashlight. Still silent. *They should have had her by now. They should have had her hours ago!* But Peng and his men were slowing him down, moving methodically through the brush when they didn't need to. The girl was moving much too fast to suddenly stop and hide. So fast, in fact, that Lam was coming to an unlikely conclusion.

She was moving as fast as she had been earlier in the day, if not faster. But that was impossible. No one's endurance could last that long. Even the best, most highly trained soldiers began to show signs of exhaustion after just a few hours of heavy exertion. It was impossible that the young girl wouldn't.

And it wasn't only how fast she was moving, but where. She was headed directly toward Shenyang, the next large metropolitan area, now less than a day away. There, the streets and walkways would leave no prints—no traces at all to help him find her. And fewer cameras. They had to find her quickly, before even Lam's skills would become irrelevant.

As he stood up and turned off the light, Peng and his men watched Lam suspiciously in the darkness. His pale skin highlighted his dark eyes.

It was their fault, he thought. *He'd had the girl within his grasp. It was their fault she'd gotten away.* And now their opportunity was rapidly diminishing—and with it, Lam's growing certainty that he was needed only to track the girl and nothing more. They were using him…like a dog. And would soon simply dispose of him.

But Lam had plans of his own. He was not going back to prison. He would get the girl, and he would have his revenge. No matter what it took.

Even if he had to kill Peng and every single one of his men to do it.

***

Li Na fell hard onto her knees in the wet mud, eagerly lunging down to the small running stream in front of her. With cupped hands, she repeatedly brought the cool water up to her mouth and gulped it down. She paused with her eyes closed, savoring the liquid before seeking more again and again.

She hadn't passed water in hours and was beginning to feel like she was overheating. Barely able to concentrate, she couldn't tell how fast she was moving or whether she was still headed in the right direction. Instinctually, it felt like she was, but the forest was becoming harder to navigate. Increasingly dense trees all around her acted more like walls, blotting out any visibility of her desired direction ahead. And the smells were getting stronger.

The wind had also picked up considerably, bringing more smells from every direction. As if she'd walked through a cloud of odorants. Some were pleasant, reminding her of flowers or pollen. Yet others were disgusting, smelling of decay. Then there were a few she didn't even recognize.

Even through her fragmented thoughts, one that kept coming back was that something was wrong. Very, very wrong. Everything seemed to be malfunctioning. Her nose, her ears, and even her sense of touch was becoming so sensitive. Now, it was almost painful to touch things with her fingers.

Another splash of cold water on her face seemed to briefly bring her out of it. Familiar and refreshing. Revitalizing.

She held her breath and tried to listen through the rustling leaves behind her. Even the thicker pine needles seemed to flitter noisily through the air before hitting the ground.

To make matters worse, she was out of food. She searched her satchel again, praying she'd missed something. But she hadn't.

Her mind switched again and she peered up, trying to locate the sun. Then she looked forward, trying to guess how much further Shenyang was. Her eyes darted to her hands, dirty and worn. She rubbed her fingers together tenderly when it finally hit her.

She wasn't delirious. She was getting sick. It explained why she couldn't concentrate, why her head felt tired and hot. She must have caught something. *But what? What could she have caught out here? God, why her?!*

Li Na began to cry and slumped helplessly to one side, resting in a cold patch of mud.

In some moments like this, she couldn't even remember why she was headed to Shenyang, or why she was running at all. It was those thoughts that left her feeling the worst. An utterly helpless dread, crashing each time like a wave over her tired body.

She couldn't do it. She couldn't go on anymore. They

were still behind her, and they wouldn't give up. Her father had warned her about them in his letter. They would keep coming for her as long as she was alive. So, all she was doing was delaying the inevitable.

Li Na broke down and sobbed uncontrollably. They would *never* give up, and she would never be safe. She was going to die, just like her parents had. Alone, in the middle of nowhere.

Then it happened.

A sound so soft and so deep that it didn't even feel like noise. It was a profound and deep-seated reverberation.

She raised her head and peered past a set of thick tree trunks, through teary eyes. A beam of sunlight managed to penetrate the canopy above and reach the forest floor. It left the spot engulfed, even if only for a moment, in a broad golden beam.

Tiny insects were temporarily silhouetted as they flittered back and forth in front of the light. But it wasn't seeing them that caused Li Na's jaw to slowly open. It was that she could *hear* them.

She could hear their clicking and buzzing. Not just from those she could see but from all around her. The girl was completely enveloped within the life of the forest.

It was the teenager's last lucid thought before she lost consciousness.

70

"Still?"

"Yep. They're still looking for her."

Neely Lawton leaned in closer behind Will Borger, studying the screen on his laptop. It was filled with windows of cryptic text. "How can you tell?"

"I can see it. Through the activity in these logs. Search strings and pieces of text within their results. They're still searching. If they'd found her, we'd know it."

"Any sign of your hacker friend?"

Borger grimaced slightly and shook his head. "I don't think anyone wants a friend like that. But no. Nothing. It's very strange. And there's just so much we don't know."

"I was thinking the same thing," Neely straightened. "If that teenage girl is going through what I think she is…none of them have very much time."

The room fell silent while they remained staring at the screen, both thinking. It felt like things were continuing to unravel with so many events and relationships that they had no control over. And every new person affected only caused the ripple to grow larger.

The silence was interrupted by a loud chime on Lawton's computer. She rolled her chair back to the other table and tapped her own keyboard. She studied it for several long seconds.

"Hmm."

"What is it?"

"A message from my team. The ones I was working with onboard the *Bowditch*." She looked at Borger. "We were in the middle of a large project when we'd gotten the orders from Admiral Langford."

"Some kind of sonar array, right?"

"Yes," she said. "A new full-spectrum system. Interlinked and much more sensitive than anything a sub or ship could do."

"Is there a problem?"

She shook her head. "No, they're still working on it and picking up some false positives, probably from the *Pathfinder*. It's not unusual since we're still fine-tuning some of the interferometer coding, allowing us to combine different wavelengths and magnifying the sensitivity to—"

Borger grinned. "Oh, I'm familiar with interferometry. That's how we first found that giant ring underwater."

"Then you know how touchy it can be."

At this, Borger chuckled. "I would say *touchy* is putting it mildly."

Neely nodded, her eyes sharing in the humor, and turned back to her screen. They still had a long way to go before the sonar project would be complete. And it would take at least a year or two after that to get it tuned properly. But when it was done, what they would be able to detect underwater was going to be one of the biggest achievements in naval history. Somewhat equivalent, from a military standpoint, to what Alison and her team had done with IMIS.

If they could only eliminate the false alarms.

71

"Well, Mister Borger, any more news on our missing hacker?"

Borger shook his head. "No, Admiral. Not that I can find. Everything has been scrubbed. I've never seen anything like it."

Langford and Miller remained quiet. Unfortunately, they *had* seen things like it. It didn't happen often, but when it did, it meant someone had been very deliberately erased. Almost always because they knew too much. The modern world wanted to believe things were different now. That the world was less…barbaric. But it wasn't true. For all of today's political correctness, the sad truth was that it was only a veneer. Terrible things were still happening. Everywhere.

"Commander Lawton," Langford said, changing the subject. Neely became slightly more erect in her chair next to Will and Alison, the latter still with wet hair pulled back into a ponytail.

"Just as expected, sir. The plants have the same replication characteristics and suspension of telomere growth. And unlike the Chinese bacterium, it is proving more stable."

"So the plants are more valuable than the bacteria?" Miller asked.

"Correct." Neely glanced at Borger next to her, then to Alison sitting to his left. Both nodded subtly at Neely. "And, sir," she said slowly, "there's something else."

"Of course there is," replied Langford, with tired eyes. "We obviously don't have enough problems."

Neely shrugged. "Well, I'm not sure I would characterize this as a problem. I would say it's more of a development."

Langford grinned at her tact. "Okay, Commander. What is our *development?*"

"It's the engineering team, sir. They've been spending quite a bit of time in the water. Beneath the surface. Studying the alien ship."

"I should hope so."

Neely glanced at the others again. "Sir, the men are displaying measurable signs of physical…alteration."

"Alteration?"

"Changes, sir."

"What kind of changes?"

"Subtle changes. The elements we found in South America are also present here. In the water. The dive teams are being exposed to it. And even a much smaller dosage appears to be affecting them."

"For example?"

"Some of their gray hair is turning back to its original color. Eyesight is improving, plus a few other things."

"You're kidding me?"

Neely shook her head onscreen. "No, sir. This is what I meant about a more organic effect. It's slower than what we saw with the Chinese bacteria."

"Are you telling me," Langford said. "That those guys are getting *younger*?!"

"I'm not sure about younger, but certainly stronger," Neely acknowledged.

"And what about this overheating brain problem?"

"So far the team is showing no symptoms indicating that. Though to be honest, if they were, I'm not sure we would be able to detect it yet. Not until the problem is much more acute. But I don't think it's happening."

"How do we know?" Miller pressed.

"For starters, the men's sleep cycles are getting longer, not shorter."

Langford considered her words, thoughtfully. "Okay. So how many of these plants do we have underwater?"

Neely paused, slightly unsure of his question. It was Borger who answered.

"Too many to hide, Admiral."

"Naturally," the admiral nodded. "And how about our ship?"

"The new drill is ready, sir. We should be able to have it in the water in a few hours."

"Good. Let's hope it tells us something new. I should probably also tell you that we're running out of time, sooner than we hoped. Our story about the *Valant's* mechanical problems is beginning to garner a lot of attention from construction companies offering to 'help' the government out."

Borger grinned. "For a very high hourly rate, I would guess."

"You'd be right. Unfortunately, the more attention we get, the more cracks begin to appear in our story. We need to figure out what we're going to do about both those plants and the ship."

The three grimaced almost in unison. Coming up with a solution was going to be a Herculean task. It wasn't as though either could simply be hidden, or moved. And if they couldn't hide it, it was simply a matter of time before someone else figured it out. And came looking.

72

Captain Zhirov stood motionlessly in the control room with his legs apart and both hands behind his back. Moderately lit, the room was lined by monitors and manned by some of the finest men Russia had to offer. Overhead, a mechanical ceiling of countless gray piping and instruments snaked above them.

They were now only fifteen kilometers away, and Zhirov had just given the order to slow the *Russian Ghost* sub down to a crawl.

The American science vessel still had sonar so if their captain was worth anything at all, he'd be constantly monitoring for anyone or anything trying to get close. And the Russian sub was quietest under five knots.

According to the information given to Zhirov, the American captain's name was Emerson—a man who had served most of his career skippering larger Navy warships, no doubt honing his skills and intuition. The fact that he chose to spend his sunset command on the open sea told Zhirov everything he needed to know about where Emerson felt most comfortable.

This captain was a man who lived and breathed the ocean, *and* the military. There was little doubt in Zhirov's mind that he was seasoned. And given what Emerson was now hiding on behalf of his country, he would likely be ready for anything.

The battle instinct in Zhirov caused his lips to part into a thin grin. He relished the thrill of combat in any form but none more than warfare at sea. The entire journey gave him an intense sense of satisfaction—from the slow, quiet stalking through the dark and cold foreboding waters, to the uncertainty of the victor until the final moments.

Zhirov's grin promptly faded when he felt the trembling in his hand again, still hidden behind his back. If the older Belov was right about what was aboard that science ship, it could save him from a future that would be as inevitable as it was torturous.

If he was right.

Yet one thing that still puzzled Zhirov was Belov himself. The man was already in control of a vast fortune and now, thanks to Zhirov, free from the tyrannical clutches of their ruthless government.

He could have found any one of a dozen ways out of Russia long ago. It made no sense for him to stay. Unless he was hoping to position himself inside what was left of the Russian government when it finally collapsed.

To Zhirov, it was a foolish gamble. The risks were far too great, as Belov himself had found out rather abruptly. No, there was something else in the man's pursuit of the American's discovery. Something even more than what he had confessed to Zhirov. A hidden agenda that the Russian captain could sense but not yet discern.

Deep down, Dima Belov was an enigma.

Zhirov reached around with his other hand and checked his watch, fighting to keep his excitement in check.

Just a few hours left.

***

Sergeant Popov looked at the four men on his left. Each one exhibited a muscular build and wore the same look of grim determination.

"Go."

Junior Sergeant Levin spoke up without the slightest inflection in his voice. "Reach and secure the first platform. Wait for mark at nineteen-thirty. Ascend and secure each level to control room. Disable communications. Any signs of aggression to be eliminated. Beginning on your mark from the ship, we take all levels, including the pad."

Popov nodded. Levin's summary sounded almost trite. But the truth was that it wouldn't be easy. Once Levin and his men located and confined all members of the oil rig, each would then have to secure a level, ensuring a clear path to the top. There, the aircraft would land to receive their cargo. Given how little time Popov and his own men would have to take the science ship itself and make it back, their path to the top of the rig had to be clear—because the backup plan for both of their teams had a much lower chance of success and survivability.

At least they knew what they were dealing with aboard the *Valant* oil rig. All they needed was a very small team, few munitions or weapons expected, and passageways that were easy to use as bottlenecks.

The *Pathfinder* ship was a different story.

They knew about the transfers back and forth from the rig to the science vessel, although Belov himself confirmed that the ship was where their prize still lay. Or prizes. And military ships, even science vessels, carried munitions with well-trained crewmembers. Most U.S. Navy science ships had a round-the-clock security detail of three to four men, likely armed with M-16s.

Taking them out would be hard enough, but if the Spetsnaz team was forced to turn to one of their backup plans, things were going to get messy. For everyone.

73

"Easy!"

Elgin Tay pulled hard on one of the stabilizing lines, helping to slow the drill after a large swell rocked the *Pathfinder* from side to side. The roll caused the giant piece of machinery to sway, its tip missing the edge of the ship's stern by less than a foot. Tay and his men desperately shuffled their feet, trying to maintain their footing as the steel deck was splashed by wave after wave of warm saltwater.

Tay shouted, hands gripping the line like a vice, and arched his short frame away for leverage. "Wait 'til it steadies and be ready to drop!"

Smitty nodded from several feet away with one hand on the winch controls. Lightfoot was on the other side, near the edge, trying to control the thick black power cable attached to the top of the drill.

It wasn't the waves they were worried about. They had dropped their remote vehicles in far worse conditions. It was the drill itself. If the tip hit anything on the ship, the damage could be irreparable. And with their custom designed bit, there were no spare parts.

Fully assembled, the thing was monstrous, almost six feet across at the back where the powerful electric motor resided. A motor so powerful that if they were to unleash its full potential, it would literally rip the rest of the drill into pieces.

If this couldn't open a hole in the alien hull, nothing would.

Tay's men waited for a break in the swells. When the ship was level enough, Smitty used the controls to extend the winch's hydraulic arm further out over the water, where the steel arm strained under the excessive weight of the drill.

Tay raised his hand over his head, watching the approaching swells. After another, more mild, rock of the ship, they reached the trough and Tay dropped his hand. Smitty instantly lowered the drill, sending it splashing into the beginning of the next crest.

Tay nodded and extended his thumb, signaling Smitty to begin rolling out the line. Lightfoot joined in by stepping beneath the winch and feeding the power cable out at the same speed.

Waiting in the water were Gorski's men, Corbin and Beene, both of whom moved into place on opposite sides of the drill and began guiding it away from the ship.

***

A short distance away, Alison provided another set of eyes on the surface, looking for any noticeable warning flags. When the heavy drill dipped below the waves, she ducked below as well and swam closer.

The bright beam from her helmet illuminated one side of the drill as it continued a gradual descent into the dark waters below.

"Everything looks fine from here," Alison called into her microphone. After Tay replied, she turned and was amused to find dozens of dolphins surrounding her, watching the operation in fascination. One of whom was Dirk.

Alison. What do?

"We're studying the metal below, Dirk."

She could hear the wild chatter around her from the other dolphins, conversations IMIS still had trouble following unless Alison had her vest facing them. Instead of allowing fragmented exchanges through, they had elected not to have IMIS attempt to translate them at all. Rather, they simply allowed the clicks and whistles through as background noise. It would at least make them aware of external conversations without overloading the system.

Floating in front of her, Dirk's eyes were still following the drill.

How metal do?

Alison frowned at the question, again left struggling to find a way to make things clear with their limited vocabulary.

"It's hard to explain, Dirk."

When the drill dropped beyond the bright wash of Alison's lamp, Dirk twisted his head back toward her.

Alison. You come now.

"Come where?"

We show now.

She smiled inside her mask. "Show me what, Dirk?"

He repeated. *You come now.*

Dirk turned and moved away, parting through the rest of the dolphins. Alison was left floating behind.

Lee's voice cut in over her earbuds. "What is he saying?"

"I'm not sure. I guess there's only one way to find out."

***

Dirk slowed, allowing Alison to catch up, where she then extended a hand and wrapped it gently around his dorsal fin. He accelerated, pulling her behind.

Illuminated by her lamp, tiny specs in the water appeared from the darkness and zipped past as Dirk continued forward. After several minutes, she could feel Dirk begin to slow. Alison looked at her dive computer and found that they were still less than twenty feet below the surface.

Together they rose over a wide reef, covered in glowing green vegetation, and descended the other side into a large circular area, protected from much of the swaying of the ocean's soft current.

***

From aboard the *Pathfinder*, Lee could hear Alison stop breathing suddenly through his headphones. "Ali, you okay?"

There was no answer.

"Alison? Are you there?!"

Still nothing. After several seconds, he opened his mouth to try again when Alison's voice replied in a whisper.

"Yes."

"Are you okay?"

Lee couldn't see Alison nodding absently, almost frozen. "I'm okay."

Her wide eyes stared out through the glass face mask, mesmerized at what she was seeing.

"Ali?"

Again, she failed to answer. Lee began typing and brought up the video feed from her vest. When the image appeared on his screen, he was just as stunned.

The picture was dark, but Alison's LED lamp and the soft glow from the plants below was enough for him to see the scene before her.

Lee was almost afraid to speak. "Is that what I think it is?"

Alison smiled. "I think so."

Below her, around the reef, were hundreds of dolphins. All swam around in the same direction, forming a veritable wall around the circular depression in the reef. But what had truly taken Alison's breath away was what she saw in the middle. Dozens of dolphins were all moving slowly, in short and tight motions—each one accompanied by another dolphin trailing cautiously just behind the first.

It was the dolphins in front, moving back and forth, that Alison watched in anticipation. Because below each one was a short tail protruding out from their belly. Or more specifically, from their birth canal.

"Wow," Alison whispered. "Can you see that, Lee? *They're birthing!*"

Lee nodded. "I can. That's amazing."

"It's more than amazing. It's never been seen before in

the wild. Only in captivity. God, there must be fifty of them! Maybe more."

Together, with Alison floating in place and Lee on the monitor, they continued watching in silence as the mothers moved back and forth, helping their calves to emerge, tail first. Until they were finally out, whereby the mother would guide the new child to the surface for its first breath.

Lee reached for his mouse. "I'm going to record this."

"NO!" shouted Alison. She shook her face mask back and forth. "Don't. This is private, Lee. Something deeply personal. It's a miracle they're letting me see it."

"Right." He retracted his hand and instead leaned forward onto the metal table in front of himself, continuing to watch in awe. "Why are all the others swimming around the reef like that?"

"For protection," Alison answered. "The males are protecting the females during the birth. From predators."

"Ah," Lee nodded. He stared closer at the dark video. "It looks like there are some adult dolphins swimming behind the mothers. Can you see that?"

Alison grinned and nodded. "They're midwives."

"Are you kidding?"

"Nope. You'd be surprised how similar their birthing process is to ours. If you take out the water."

"Wow. I can't believe they showed you this."

Alison's smile suddenly vanished upon hearing Lee's comment. *Yes, why had they shown her?* Alison wasn't the only marine biologist to grow close to dolphins. Yet to her knowledge, no other researcher had ever been allowed to see a birth in the wild.

So why did they pick her?

74

Hello Alison.

Alison peered up from the spectacle in front of her to find Sally appearing from out of the darkness, above the slew of creatures passing below her.

Dirk moved effortlessly into place beside her.

We show.

Alison blinked before looking back down to the center of the reef. "Yes," she remarked. "And it's beautiful."

Sally did not answer. Instead, she merely continued peering at Alison with her dark eyes and perpetual cetacean grin.

"Are you okay, Sally?"

Yes Alison.

She looked around through her mask. More pods of dolphins were swirling about. It was then that she saw another group of dolphins emerge, three of which she had met before. She recognized them immediately, not by their shape or sizes, but by their age. Their faded and marred skin appeared to be a slightly lighter gray than the others.

We want talk Alison, Sally said.

Alison stared carefully at the elders before eyeing Dirk and Sally suspiciously. That's why. That's why they showed her their birthing ground. *To establish trust.*

"Yes, Sally. I would like to talk too."

When another one of the elders came closer and into better view, Alison was surprised at what she saw. From the patches and wrinkles on its skin, this one was not just old. This dolphin was really old.

When it spoke, it sounded exactly like Dirk and Sally, using IMIS's computer-generated voice.

You come far. For metal.

Alison nodded. "Yes, we have."

Why for metal?

She chose her words carefully. "The metal is important."

Why important you?

"Because it's not from here."

Where from?

Alison looked at the other elders. "From the stars."

The beep of a translation error sounded in her ear.

"Really?!"

Another error.

"Come on!"

Then a third error.

"Uh!" A flustered Alison shook her head, trying to start over.

"They don't have a word for stars, Ali," Lee's voice broke in.

"No kidding." She closed her eyes for a moment, thinking. "The metal," she said, "is not made by us."

At this, the elder came even closer, studying Alison. The others closed in tightly behind. The oldest made a slight movement with its head that was akin to humans tilting theirs.

You makes metals.

"Yes. We make metals. As tools."

This time there was no error. And another of the elders spoke.

How you make metal?

At this, Alison stopped. *How do we make metal? Were they asking how to build things?*

"I…I don't know how to answer that."

No. No make. The oldest interrupted. *We talk this metal.* The strength of the dolphin's speech suggested an exclamation.

"What?"

You come this metal.

"Yes," Alison repeated. "We came for this metal."

What you do?

She wasn't following. "What do we do? About what?"

What you do metal?

Alison still wasn't sure what it meant until the elder rephrased.

What now you do metal?

This time the message was clear. So clear she felt as though she'd been hit over the head. They wanted to know what the humans were planning to do with the alien ship.

75

The door burst open, and the young Janvier was pushed forcefully ahead, stumbling into the front room of his own house. The room, though clean, was barely furnished. Most of their belongings had already been sold over the last year to pay for electricity and food.

After their father had disappeared, the family had been abandoned by most of their friends, fearful of being subjected to the same fate.

Sitting on their one remaining piece of furniture in the front room, Janvier was not surprised to find his mother and younger brother. However, the person sitting next to them scared him to death.

The teenager tried to control his fear as he looked to his mother, trembling next to Amir Ngeze, the man who controlled much of Northern Rwanda. The same man who was responsible for their father's disappearance.

One of Ngeze's men stepped forward behind Janvier, forcing the young man further into the center of the room and closer to the couch. Janvier looked away as a sadistic smile began to spread across Ngeze's face. Sadistic, broad, and dark.

He stood up and stepped toward the boy. "Well, look what we have here. Janvier Sentwali." He moved his large hands behind his back, glowering.

Ngeze then looked at his man, standing behind the teenager. "Where?"

"We found him coming back down the mountain."

"Is that right?" He stepped closer again, now just inches from Janvier, who had his head down. "With your new friends?"

The boy didn't answer. Instead, his eyes rolled up

slightly to his mother and brother still on the couch.

"You can answer," Ngeze said. "Your little brother told me all about them. The two men and the woman. And the monkeys."

Janvier kept his eyes on his mother, saying nothing.

Ngeze smiled deeper and followed the boy's eyes to the couch. His mother, still in her work uniform with hair pinned up and arms around his brother, stole a glance at Ngeze before lowering them again—the terror clearly evident in her eyes.

Ngeze could see much of the boy's father in him. Defiant. Even courageous. But his father eventually broke once he was alone and without his guards.

Hired by their new president to find a way to bring Ngeze down, Gael Sentwali and his team damn near succeeded. It was only by taking extreme measures, by killing first his bodyguards and then Sentwali himself, that Ngeze effectively broke the back of the president's mission.

Of course, Sentwali's family, now before him in what was left of their house and their lives, never knew the ultimate fate of the man they called father and husband. They only knew Ngeze had him, and each continued to believe he was still alive. That they could somehow bargain for his life. But his life had long since been stamped out.

Their collective naïveté almost made Ngeze laugh. But he held his lips tightly together, waiting for Janvier to answer.

After a long silence, Ngeze lowered his mouth and breathed sickly into the boy's ear. "Look at your mother," he whispered.

Janvier's eyes remained fixed on his mother, visibly shaking.

"Tell me where your friends are, or this is the last you will remember of her."

76

Under the glow of the full moon, John Clay tugged and tested the strength of the small nylon tent. Thick white straps traveled to the ground on either side, secured to the damp Earth. The ground, covered in grass, was surrounded by dense forest, but left a large enough clearing to provide room to camp for the night.

DeeAnn turned from the primates, busily eating in the darkness, and grinned. "For us?"

Clay nodded. "It's not the Ritz, but it should keep you dry. Assuming none of you get claustrophobic."

He then moved away and knelt next to a small propane burner heating a single pan. A wrinkled strip of foil was wrapped around the bottom to block the light from the flame.

She frowned. "That actually smells pretty good. What is it?"

"Shepherd's pie."

"Really?"

Clay smiled back at her. "MREs have come a long way."

"I thought you guys ate trail mix or something," DeeAnn teased. "Or grubs."

"We used to, but a man can only carry so much salt and pepper."

DeeAnn laughed. "That, I believe." She turned to find Dulce approaching the tent, studying it carefully. The gorilla gently pushed at the opening flap and looked inside, fascinated.

What this?

"It's called a tent."

The vest on DeeAnn's chest beeped. "A place to sleep," she corrected.

Dulce seemed to grow more excited and stepped inside. She remained still for a long time, with her head under the flap.

Clay laughed. "It's not that big." After a moment of watching, he asked, "Is she still all right?"

"Yes. She's in her element. Somehow she remembers. The smells and the sounds. She knows what this place is."

There was a nervousness in DeeAnn's voice—something she was clearly worried about and something Clay had a suspicion about. He didn't push.

Instead they both watched with amusement as Dulce climbed into the tent and moved around. Her head created a round bump in the fabric that followed her.

Dexter remained nearby on top of a fallen tree, laying in two pieces and broken near the base. Ignoring Dulce's exploration of the tent, he continued chewing through a large green leaf while still watching the trees.

An unexpected noise from the forest caused Clay to rise quickly to his feet where he unslung the Beretta M12 from his shoulder in a smooth motion. He lowered it quickly when Steve Caesare emerged from the tree line with his own gun crossed in front of him.

He approached, nodding at Clay. "Nothing around for a good fifty yards. A bit further is a stream with fresh water. We can fill up in the morning." Caesare noticed the movement inside the tent and quickly scanned the area. Finding Dulce missing, he looked to the tent again and shook his head.

"I guess she's never seen a tent before."

"Nope."

Caesare turned to Clay, who remained silent. He followed his gaze over to the smaller monkey, still quietly chewing. "Something wrong?"

Clay squinted. "Have you guys noticed Dexter?"

"What do you mean?"

"He hasn't been talking much. Even to Dulce."

"That's not too uncommon."

"And he keeps watching the forest," Clay added.

They all stared at the monkey for a long moment. DeeAnn abruptly turned and walked to the tent where she held up the front flap and faced her vest at Dulce.

"Come here, Dulce."

The bump in the fabric stopped and turned. After moving slowly toward the exit, the little gorilla abruptly poked her head out.

"Dulce. What's wrong with Dexter?"

After the translation sounded, the gorilla looked at her friend. She then carefully stepped back out of the tent and onto the moist ground.

Wrong?

"Is Dexter okay?"

Still staring at him, Dulce tilted her head. Without a word, she bolted across the grass and back toward the fallen log. She stopped next to him and stared at the trees, then turned and grunted, followed by several gestures.

His high-pitched response was short.

Dulce turned and spoke to DeeAnn. But her vest didn't catch it.

She moved closer to the gorilla. "Repeat, Dulce."

The gorilla's response was as short as Dexter's. And when it was translated through the vest, the reply caused Clay and Caesare to stiffen.

Someone follow.

77

Both men instinctively raised their guns. "What?!"

Someone follow, Dulce repeated. *In trees.*

Clay and Caesare were immediately in motion. Raising their guns higher, they swept back and forth in opposing directions.

"Get them away from the trees!" Clay barked. "Behind the tent!"

DeeAnn immediately grabbed Dulce's hand and wrapped an arm around Dexter, pulling him from his perch with a loud squeal.

"Quiet!" Caesare exclaimed in a loud whisper. He knelt down next to the tree and continued scanning.

"You hear anything?" Clay asked.

"No."

Clay turned and searched for cover. If they were in the trees in front of them, then they were likely in the trees behind them too. He backed up and reached behind himself to turn off the small burner, extinguishing the flame and its faint glow.

Clay then grabbed both of their packs and dragged them backward toward the tent, dropping them in front of DeeAnn. He pushed her lower. "Lay down. And get them down."

Out in front, Caesare suddenly held up a hand and pointed two fingers in front of him toward two o'clock. Something, or someone, was moving.

He glanced over his shoulder at Clay, then pointed to himself, making a circling motion around the target.

Clay nodded.

With that, Caesare quickly rose to his feet and moved to the left, in the direction he had just emerged from. Trotting heel to toe over the ground, he moved smoothly and disappeared back into the trees.

DeeAnn watched Clay pull the packs in closer to her and the primates. Her heart was pounding with her chin touching the ground and one protective arm over Dulce. Dexter seemed to sense the danger, and even after squeezing free, remained low.

Above them, Clay hovered on one knee and scanned the darkness behind them. Listening.

***

Caesare was moving low and fast. Swerving in and out of narrow trees trunks and patches of bamboo. He ducked under a wide sprawling fern and stopped beneath it.

Nothing.

He waited. Controlling his breathing. Listening between breaths. If there was someone out there, it was best to reach them first and use the element of surprise. If it were a bigger group pursuing them, the last thing they would expect would be an attack.

Caesare calmed his breathing further, forcing the cool air in through his nose. He held his breath for a few seconds before gently exhaling.

And then he heard it.

It was slight. Barely loud enough to reach him. But it was there—a soft scrape against one of the trees. A scrape that an animal with fur would not make.

Caesare studied the ground in front of him, using what little moonlight he had, and surged forward.

After another twenty feet, he stopped again and waited.

Nothing.

He continued pushing forward, slowly.

***

Not far away a dark shadow moved between the trees,

stopping behind a thicker trunk. He could see parts of the tent in the distance, sitting quietly in the small clearing.

The figure crept closer to see more of the area. There was no longer any movement. Or sound.

Their voices had stopped. They must have detected something.

The dark figure reached behind his back and began to withdraw an object when he promptly felt the cool sensation of a gun barrel press firmly into his right cheek.

Steve Caesare's deep voice whispered behind him, "Nice night for a walk." When the figure began to gently turn, Caesare pressed harder. "Nope. You move again, and you're going to need a whole new set of dentures, capisce?"

The stranger nodded.

"How many others?" Caesare asked, looking over the man's shoulder.

"None."

He raised an eyebrow. "Just you?"

"Yes."

Caesare finished scanning and looked down. "Drop your hands."

The man complied.

Caesare stepped back and pulled the gun away from his cheek, silhouetted in the moonlight. "Now raise them up on top of your head."

When the figure complied, Caesare next instructed him to turn around slowly. Watching as the figure turned towards him, the intruder's face became only partially visible in the shadows.

Caesare glanced behind himself and stepped back further. "Walk towards me."

The stranger stepped forward, led by Caesare, and eventually emerged into the light.

Once he saw the man's face, Steve Caesare's expression changed beyond surprise to a look of shock. He shook his head in disbelief. "You have got to be kidding."

78

Almost ten minutes later, two dark figures stepped out and into the clearing, walking one in front of the other.

Clay rose slowly as they approached with his rifle trained on both shadows. Only when Steve Caesare spoke did he relax.

"I hope you're in the mood for some amusement."

Clay lowered his weapon and peered intently into the darkness.

The man in front of Caesare was shorter, with a pale white face, and dressed in dark clothing. But it was in the unique shape of his face and bald head that Clay immediately recognized. He looked very much like Palin, the man he met who had not been from Earth.

"You've got to be kidding."

"That's what I said." Caesare gave a push forward, sending him stumbling to within a few steps of Clay. "And guess what. He ain't."

The figure flashed a brief gaze at DeeAnn as she rose from behind the bags.

"Who are you?"

His reply held only the slightest hint of defiance. "My name is Ronin."

Clay studied the man's clothing, then the pack he carried on his back. All the material appeared slightly reflective, resembling some kind of trace fibers or a soft alloy.

"What the hell are you doing here?"

The man turned carefully to find Caesare still behind him, and the gun still pointed directly at his back.

"I was following you."

"No kidding," Caesare replied sarcastically.

He didn't answer.

"You're one of Palin's men," Clay said.

The man named Ronin nodded.

"How long have you been following us?"

"Since Kigali."

"What for?"

"To see what you find," he answered.

Clay looked past him to Caesare, then to DeeAnn who was now on her feet. "What do you mean, what we find?"

Ronin's expression softened a bit. "We know what you found on the other side of your planet. In your South America. Before it was destroyed." He glanced again at Caesare behind him. "And we know what it can do."

"The vault."

Ronin nodded.

Clay stepped back and motioned to a nearby rock. "Have a seat."

The smaller man approached the rock and turned before sitting. "May I remove my pack?"

"Slowly."

He pulled one arm through and swung the load off, around his other shoulder, before easing it onto the ground. Clay and Caesare both glanced down and studied it briefly. It was a dark metallic blue. Uniform in size, the pack first appeared stiff but seemed to move slightly as it hit the ground.

Caesare stepped in next to Clay. "I hope you're feeling talkative."

For a moment, the man looked bemused. "My mission is not a secret."

"Well, it sure as hell is to us."

Ronin blinked and then placed his hands on his knees. "We need the fluid, the solution."

"What for?"

"To save ourselves."

Clay and Caesare looked at each other.

"You've been there," Ronin continued, "to our world. You know the devastation we have suffered. You know we are struggling to survive. And how little time we have left."

"We saw that you were rebuilding."

"What you saw is one of our only remaining footholds. We are trying to establish others, but the situation is dire."

The men turned when DeeAnn edged closer, and Clay looked back to check on the primates. Both were next to the tent. Dexter was no longer watching the forest.

"How dire?"

Ronin's mannerism was calm but firm. "You might say we no longer have rope."

Caesare frowned. "At the end of your rope."

"Yes. At the end of our rope." The man nodded. "I am not as good with your language. I am not an academic."

"What does that mean?"

"Like you, we have certain classes. Those that we excel at, and are born for. Academics. Engineering. Science. Things like that."

"And what class are you?" Clay asked.

"I am a fighter class. Like you. Of sorts." Ronin shrugged. "It is more complicated than that."

"I bet," replied Caesare.

"So you're following us to see what we find here," Clay said.

"Yes. As I said, we know what you search for."

"Assuming we find it, how is it supposed to save your planet?"

"We know of its attributes. Its genetic influence. It could help us restore our own environment. Before it's too late."

"How?"

Ronin looked back and forth between them. "I am not a scientist, so my knowledge is not as thorough. But I do know some. Most of our life forms have been destroyed or are on the brink of extinction. The event destroyed millions of species, and for years we continued losing hundreds of thousands more every year. We were unable to stop it, and they were not able to adapt quickly enough. We barely survived ourselves. We have managed to slow the loss, but our ecology is barely functional."

"What exactly was the event?" Clay asked.

"An asteroid impact. More than eighty of your years ago. The destruction was enormous. Cities destroyed, forests wiped clean, and most of our oceans lost."

DeeAnn stared incredulously. "How in the world could you lose your oceans?"

"The impact vaporized much of our largest ocean, but we hadn't lost it entirely. The moisture was still in our atmosphere, completely surrounding the planet and blocking out the sun. For the first year, it rained without stop—flooding and destroying areas that were not already damaged by the first impact."

Clay raised his eyebrows. "The *first* impact?"

"Yes," Ronin paused. "Two years later a second asteroid struck. We saw the first but could not stop it in time. The second was never seen. Our defense systems were all gone. The second was smaller but traveling much faster. The impact nearly breached our planet's crust. Its damage was far worse and destroyed most of the remaining life on our planet within days."

"Jesus!"

Ronin looked up at Caesare, solemnly. "Billions died. Only a few cities, situated in fortunate locations, were spared. And the second blast was so powerful it ejected most of the remaining vapor up and out of our atmosphere."

Caesare shook his head. "Good God."

"Our scientists say our gravity will eventually recapture much of what was lost. But it will take many years. Thousands. We cannot wait."

After a long silence, Clay's voice was low. "How many of you survived?"

"Less than five thousand. But over these years, we have nearly doubled that."

"Five thousand in eighty years," Caesare murmured.

"That's not a lot."

Ronin replied with a brief sound of indignation. "For us, it was nothing short of miraculous."

Caesare nodded. "I'm sorry. That's not what I meant."

The smaller man continued. "We were not without *some* luck, I was told."

"You were told?" Clay asked.

"I was only an infant when it happened. I have no memory of our world before the event."

At that, DeeAnn looked soulfully at both men next to her before replying. "We're very sorry for what has happened to you."

"Extremely," Clay added and extended his hand forward. Ronin grabbed it, and Clay pulled him back onto his feet. "So you're after the same thing we are."

"Yes. Restoring our ecosystem has been difficult. Even we are finding it much more complex than previously thought. Restoring life, even plant life, takes time. Generations. Which leaves our own existence hanging in the balance. The water we have brought from your planet has given us a foothold. But that is all."

"So you think this *solution*, if it still exists, can turn the tide."

"Yes. Our scientists believe it can dramatically increase the progress of our existing ecosystem. This is what we are in most desperate need of. The oxygen levels in our atmosphere are nearly depleted. If we cannot change that quickly, it will be over."

"What did you mean when you said you did have some luck?"

"One of our cities that was spared also acted as one of our technology centers. For research. This meant it had a larger than usual population of scientists. Those are the ones that are now trying to save the planet."

"Jesus," Caesare said, crossing his arms. "You have to terraform your own planet."

All three stood before Ronin, completely dumbfounded.

But there was still one more incredibly important piece to the story. What they didn't know, and what Ronin didn't think to mention, was that the two asteroids that devastated his world had each struck on exactly opposite sides of the planet.

79

Alison.

The voices echoed in her ears almost simultaneously—both the computerized words from Sally in front of her and Lee Kenwood's radio transmission from his location above her on the *Pathfinder* ship.

"Alison?" they each said again.

She shook her head and blinked. Still floating in the dark water, she could see Dirk and Sally, as well as the elder dolphins, illuminated in the glow of her mask's beaming light. All waiting and watching her.

Alison reached down and muted her vest. "Lee. Can you hear me?"

"I can."

"Did you hear that?"

"Yes," Lee nodded, staring numbly at the translated words on the screen.

Not only did the dolphins want to know what humans intended to do with the alien ship, they wanted something else too. Something that no one ever expected.

You make metal for us.

IMIS's translations and the words displayed on Lee's screen could not be clearer. They were both simple and shocking.

By metal, they meant tool. Tools that they were incapable of making. Lacking the dexterity of human hands and fingers, they simply could not do what humans had done. But it was not for lack of desire. The researchers already knew that dolphins had a larger, more folded brain as well as more cognitive capacity.

Their brains would not have simply wasted that cognitive potential. Without the hands they needed, that potential would have manifested elsewhere. Possibly in cognitive abilities that humans were still not aware of. But what they had lacked for so long might now be possible with the help of human dexterity.

These intelligent creatures now wanted *us* to make something for *them*.

"Now what the hell am I supposed to say?"

Lee stammered. "Uh...I don't know."

"I can't simply lie to them." Alison turned her mask, looking back to the hundreds of dolphins and their secret breeding ground. "They showed us this for a reason, Lee. As an exchange of trust."

"I know," Lee replied. "But we don't know what they mean by tool. And we sure don't know what we're going to do with that ship, Ali. Even if we did, I'm sure it won't be up to us."

After silence from Lee, Alison reached back down and unmuted. She opened her mouth to speak, but nothing came out. She didn't know what to say. *How could she explain that it was out of her hands? How could she explain that, in the end, governments did what they wanted?* All she, Lee, and the rest of their team could really do was to try to influence the outcome. Because when governments got involved, all bets were off.

Alison swallowed hard and said the only thing she could think to say, the only thing that was still the truth.

"I'm not sure."

The oldest dolphin studied her for a long time with its dark gray eyes. None of them made a sound.

"Did they hear me?"

Lee examined the translation on his computer. "Yes, they should have."

We hear. The elder finally replied, still floating in front of her.

But before Alison could respond to their second question, something happened. Without warning, several of the nearby dolphins began speaking rapidly. Very rapidly.

Dozens more turned to face the same direction. Their rapid *clicking* joined together and became a barrage of noise, far too much to be deciphered by Alison or her vest.

The elders in front of her had already turned their attention, as still more dolphins emerged from out of the darkness. In a burst of movement, the elders shot quickly past Alison, leaving her floating in the water with arms extended and a look of confusion on her face.

She looked at Sally who remained alongside her, watching. She muted her vest and called to Lee.

"Lee, can you still hear me?"

"Right here, Ali."

"I can't hear anything! Whatever's happening is blocking everything out! Can you give me just Sally?"

Lee fumbled for a minute on his keyboard, trying to pull up another program. "Yeah, I think so. Hold on."

After a flurry of typing, Lee finished and studied the flow of text on his screen. "Okay, try it again."

Below the surface, Alison re-engaged the vest and faced Sally. "Sally!"

There was no answer.

"Sally! Can you hear me?"

It took several seconds, but Sally eventually turned back to her. *Yes Alison. I hear.*

"What is it?! What's going on?"

Sally remained quiet, listening. *Some thing come Alison. Some thing bad.*

80

The massive Russian *Ghost* sub coasted to a gradual stop against the gentle resistance of the Caribbean's currents. Maintaining its buoyancy at thirty meters above the beginning of an enormous coral ridge, the sub's sail and foreplanes were left just ten meters below the surface.

In the control room, the navigation officer turned and nodded to the captain, prompting Zhirov to calmly reach out and pluck a handset from the wall next to him.

In the submarine's forward hatch, Sergeant Popov was waiting and answered immediately.

"We are in position. You are clear."

***

Popov nodded. With a simple "affirmative," he replaced the handset on the wall and turned to his men. Wearing thin black wetsuits and SCUBA gear, each man stood side by side, packing the small gray metal room.

Each of the Russians raised their face mask, pulled it over the top of their neoprene hoodie, and breathed in the cool air coming from the short aluminum tank on their back.

With a nod from Popov, two men stepped forward where they unlocked and pulled the hatch open, allowing a flood of seawater to begin bubbling up into the chamber.

Submarine escape training, or more specifically, a controlled submarine escape, was something all sailors were ready for. But to American SEALS and Russian Spetsnaz soldiers, who both trained relentlessly on land and sea, it was routine. The men waited patiently while the bubbling seawater swirled around the room, rising rapidly above their knees and then their lower legs.

The water promptly engulfed the heavy waterproof bags standing before each of the Spetsnaz troops, in addition to several black cone-shaped objects. Larger than civilian models, the Dive Propulsion Vehicles, more commonly known as DPVs, were heavier and more powerful. They made for a huge advantage, being able to deliver Spetsnaz Special Forces teams to their targets faster and with virtually no expended energy.

Once the room had filled, the outer hatch was fully opened, allowing the men to push their gear out ahead of themselves. They exited in rapid single-file fashion. After leaving the sub's outer hull, each floated silently outside.

In less than two minutes, both teams were out. Popov motioned to Junior Sergeant Levin, who remained close enough to see. In near-perfect synchronization, the men grouped into their two teams and powered up their vehicles. With each of their bags dangling behind them and the electric motors on their DPVs spinning silently, the men all disappeared into the darkness.

81

Neely Lawton had a mug to her lips when the younger Lee Kenwood burst through the door of the lab, out of breath. Next to her sat Will Borger, also frozen at the interruption.

"We have trouble! Come on!"

They each looked at the other, and then jumped from their seats, running for the door—already swinging closed.

When they made it to the small room where Lee was working, they hastily crowded behind him and his monitor. Lee tapped a button on his keyboard and spoke into the mike.

"They're here, Ali!"

"What's going on?"

"I don't know," said Alison's voice through the speakers. "But it doesn't seem good. All the dolphins down here are freaking out about something!"

"Freaking out? What does that mean?"

"It means," she answered, "that they're going ballistic. Something bad is happening."

On the ship, Lee Kenwood reached down and pressed another button, bringing up a window displaying all the sounds that IMIS was hearing. A black spectrogram presented the information on red and green graphs. The red one was pegged to the upper edge of the window.

"IMIS is completely overwhelmed," Lee said. "And it's not stopping."

"Jesus," Neely breathed. "Alison, what the hell is going on?! What is it that's so bad?"

***

"I don't know!"

317

In front of her, the wall of dolphins was steadily growing larger, intensifying the communication to a fevered pitch that was now only noise to the translation system.

"Lee had to stop all the translations, except Sally's. And she says that something is here. But she can't explain any more than that."

"Something is here?" Neely asked. "What?"

"I don't—" Alison paused, studying the massive group of dolphins. All moved slowly, facing primarily in one direction. She then peered up through the dark water to see part of the *Pathfinder's* bottom above her.

"I think…" she said, tracing from what she believed was the stern forward to the bow, "they are facing in the direction of the *Valant*."

***

Neely frowned, looking at Borger and Kenwood. "The oil rig?"

"I think so," Alison repeated. "And they are really excited about something!"

"Alison, I think you'd better get back to the surface."

***

Alison glanced at the dive computer on her wrist before shaking her head. "Not yet. I have more time."

"I'm not worried about how much more time you have," Neely's voice shot back. "I'm worried about what the hell is happening."

She nodded. "So am I. But I think I'm at a safe distance."

Neely gritted her teeth in frustration. *How could she know if she was at a safe distance when she didn't even know what it was?* She turned to Borger. "Could there be something wrong with the *Valant*?"

318

He shrugged. "Sure it's possible. But what would cause this kind of reaction?"

"Something dangerous?"

Borger squinted. "But what from the *Valant* could pose a danger to them?"

"You tell me?"

Borger continued thinking. *The vessel suddenly becoming unmoored? Or maybe a leak?* He looked at Neely. "What if there's still oil left in the rigging and it's leaking?"

Neely's eyes grew worried. "It wouldn't take much to pollute this whole area!" She leaned toward the microphone and raised her voice. "Alison, could it be an oil leak from the *Valant*?"

"I don't know, maybe. I'd have to get closer."

"How much more time do you have left?" Neely asked.

Alison glanced at the dive computer again. "About twenty minutes."

Neely's voice grew even louder. "Twenty minutes or *about* twenty minutes?!"

"Twenty-two minutes," Alison snapped back.

Neely looked at Borger, who was now shaking his head. "The *Valant* is a quarter of a mile away. She can't make it there and back."

***

In her earbuds, Alison could hear Borger. She immediately turned to Sally and found her still watching the others.

"Sally, what is happening?"

No know Alison.

"I need to get to the other metal. Can you take me? Important."

Sally twisted her slick gray body and peered back.

"Important!" repeated Alison.

The words were translated, and she waited for a response from Sally. When it came, it was only one word.

Okay.

"You'll take me?"

Sally paused again, as if considering.

Yes. Fast.

"Yes, Sally. Very fast!"

***

Neely straightened up, leaving a hand on the back of Lee's chair.

"Where are Tay and Lightfoot?"

"They're descending with the drill. With Gorski's men."

"Can we talk to them?"

He nodded. "From my machine, we can."

With that, Neely put a reassuring hand on Lee's shoulder and told him they'd be right back. Together, she and Borger raced out of the room and back to the lab, their feet pounding hard against the ship's loud metal flooring.

82

Tay and Lightfoot were less than a hundred feet away from the alien ship when they heard Borger's hurried voice over their headsets.

"Elgin! Are you there?"

Gorski's men, Corbin and Beene, were on the other side of the drill. All four slowed their descent when they heard Borger.

"I'm here, Will. What's up?"

"We may have a situation."

Tay looked curiously at Lightfoot and then at Beene, who was rounding one side of the giant drill in slow motion. "What kind of situation?"

"We're not sure yet," Borger said. "But Alison says all the dolphins down there are freaking out about something in your area."

Underwater, the four men turned in all directions and followed the bright light of their helmets into the darkness as far as they could.

Tay listened for a moment. "I don't see or hear anything." He looked at the other three, all shaking their heads in unison.

"Nope."

"Me either."

"Okay," Borger's voice said. "Something's alerted the dolphins where she is, and we're not sure what it's all about yet. But we're worried it might have something to do with the *Valant*. Maybe a leak or something that the dolphins can detect and we can't."

"What kind of leak?"

"Beats me. Maybe some lingering oil from somewhere?"

The men looked up, now staring through the dark water

above them, unable to see anything.

"It's right over us, but we haven't noticed anything in the water. If it was a leak, it would have to be pretty small."

"Yeah, but it might not take much to signal danger to *them*."

"We can come back down again when we're done and test the water."

"Okay," Borger replied. "Just keep us posted if you notice anything. We'll keep looking into it from up here."

"Roger."

With that, the men resumed and continued toward the alien ship.

***

When they reached the upper section of the gray wall, they turned the drill around and extended four legs out. Each leg ended with a massive silicone suction cup around the base, designed to assist in keeping the drill securely in place.

"All right. Let's ease it in," Tay said. While he and Lightfoot held onto either side, Corbin and Beene guided gently from the legs—all in slow motion that resembled astronauts working in space.

The huge drill kept drifting gradually closer, smoothly and without incident, when suddenly things changed. Now just several feet away, the drill began to accelerate toward the wall, subtly at first but then faster.

"Whoa! Whoa! Slow it down!" Tay yelled into his mike.

Both Corbin and Beene immediately sensed the change in speed. The giant machine nearly broke free of their grip, causing the men to pull backward, only to have it begin to pull them along with it.

"It's taking us too!"

"SLOW IT DOWN!" Tay yelled again.

"I can't!"

All four men quickly began kicking their feet and pointed

away from the ship. First hard, then almost desperately, all in an attempt to slow the drill's approach.

"It's the damn magnetism!"

"Pull harder!"

Each man kicked violently now. They gave it everything they had, desperate to keep the tool from slamming into the metal wall.

Suddenly with four powerful *thunks*, the drill hit the gray surface, sending brief shoots of glowing green lights outward from the contact point of each leg.

No one spoke until the glow had faded.

"Stronger than we thought." Lightfoot swam forward, withdrew a large piece of steel from the drill's outer housing, and edged it in under the nose of the drill as a lever. "Let's hope it's not as hard to get back off."

Simultaneously, each man tested the placement of one of the feet against the wall before pressing its thick silicone cup into place.

"Okay. We're secure." Tay pushed himself backward, running along the length of the drill to the small instrument panel. "Double-check the bit."

Lightfoot and Corbin examined the three-inch-wide bit from either side. It rested solidly in the middle, tightly packed in the shape of a spiral. The one long continuous ridge would allow it to carefully expand the hole after breaking through the first layer of wall.

"Looks good," Lightfoot nodded. "I think we're ready!"

Both men faded back as Tay flipped the safety switch out of the way and pressed the power button. In an instant, the drill's electric motor began to spin, and the powerful bit spiraled outward.

Next to the spinning bit, a red laser illuminated brightly against the metal, measuring its impact depth to a millionth of an inch.

With one last nod from the other men, Tay pressed a second button to engage the drive, and the tip of the drill abruptly began inching forward.

83

Approaching the oil rig just below the surface of the water, Junior Sergeant Levin was the first to notice it.

With both hands wrapped firmly around the handle of his underwater scooter, he and the remainder of his Russian team could all see the bright glow beneath them—four distinct glimmering points, actually.

Perhaps seventy feet below, near the coral, four tiny lights moved independently around what appeared to be a larger object. Although too far away to be seen clearly, even from a distance, it was clear to Levin and his men what the lights were.

Four of the American divers were working on something. In secrecy.

Belov had been right.

84

The Russian Spetsnaz troops were not the only ones who could see Tay and the others working the drill. Alison could see them too, from a different direction.

But to Alison's surprise, Sally was not swimming toward the oil rig. At least not that she could see. Instead, they seemed to be heading north of both the rig *and* the *Pathfinder* to an area between the two vessels, illuminated only by the fluorescent green glow of the coral below.

After several minutes, Alison could feel Sally begin to slow. She raised her head, peering forward into the darkness. Her headlamp lit up Sally's gray body directly in front of her, but little else. Even with the exceptional visibility of the Caribbean, she could not make out anything before them in the darkness, except for the specks of particles and sediment flowing past.

But Sally did not stop. Still moving slowly and rhythmically through the water, an object finally began to take shape in front of them.

Alison stared harder, trying to filter out the wash of her light, straining to see what its furthest and faintest rays were now reaching.

She patted Sally's side with her free hand. "Are we there, Sally?"

She answered with a series of clicks that Alison's vest could not capture. But Sally pressed on, still moving forward.

And then Alison saw it.

Revealed by both her own lamp and the faint rays of the full moon penetrating the water from above, Alison saw the dark outline of what was simply unmistakable.

"LEE!" she screamed into her microphone.

"Ali?"

"Oh my God, Lee! It's a submarine! It's a SUBMARINE!"

"Are you sure?"

"Yes, I'm sure! And it's HUGE!"

"Oh geez!" A panicked Lee Kenwood ran to the door and flung it open, looking down the hallway for Neely or Borger. For anyone!

He then ran back to his desk. "Okay. Wait here! I'll be right back!"

When he threw open the door to the lab, it slammed hard enough against the inside wall to put a dent on the other side. Lee almost yelled the news to Neely and Borger. "We've got company!"

***

Neely was running at full speed, pounding the metal below her feet, until she reached the ladder and sprinted up two steps at a time. She left behind a winded Borger, huffing and puffing to keep up.

She reached the next level easily and continued forward as fast as she could, heading for the side door to the *Pathfinder's* bridge. She pulled it open and scanned the room with her eyes, first seeing First Officer Harris. Captain Emerson was standing beside him.

The echoes of Borger's laboring steps could be heard as she stepped inside, a sound of panic in her voice.

"Captain!" she panted. "There's a submarine! In the water! Just over there!" She pointed out the large window, not far from the red lights of the oil rig.

"What?!"

"A submarine, sir! Right out there. Submerged."

With wide eyes, both Emerson and Harris looked forward at their sonar officer who immediately turned back around to his instruments.

"I want a full scan right now!"

"Yes, sir!"

The others turned to see a hyperventilating Will Borger open the door and step inside behind Neely.

"How do you know, Commander?"

Neely motioned back the way she came. "The dolphins…all of them began freaking out. We didn't know why. So Alison went to investigate. She just saw it…the submarine. Just now!"

"How sure is she?"

"Very!"

Emerson looked to Borger who nodded in agreement, while still sucking in air.

"Sir," Emerson's sonar officer said aloud. "I'm not picking up anything. Nothing at all."

"Then do an active scan! If there's someone out there, they damn sure already know where *we* are!"

"Yes, sir!"

Neely suddenly gasped. "Oh my God!" she said with her hands over her mouth.

"What, Commander?"

"*The sonar array!* Earlier today it detected something, and we thought it was a false alarm. But it wasn't! Oh God!"

"Sir! Nothing on active either." The sonar officer turned around in his chair. "We're not seeing anything."

Emerson turned to Neely. "Commander, get your team on the line right now! If this system of yours detected something, then find out what."

"Yes, sir!" Neely and Borger nodded before immediately running back out the door.

"Mister Harris, sound general quarters. Prepare to repel boarders!"

"Yes, sir."

Emerson raced to the tall windows and looked down upon the bow of the ship. On the front, sitting quietly, was a *Sea King* attack helicopter.

Emerson raised his voice loud for Harris to hear. "And

get that chopper in the air right now. And I mean RIGHT NOW!"

"Yes, sir!"

Emerson kept his eyes focused on the *Sea King*. It was the same anti-submarine helicopter that was aboard the *Bowditch*, stationed intentionally as a defensive tactic only to be destroyed along with the rest of the ship.   If there *was* a sub out there, they were sure as hell not going to make the same mistake twice!

85

Captain Zhirov was watching from the sub's camera, perched just above the waterline. Suddenly, the *Pathfinder* turned on all its exterior lights, bathing the entire area in an almost painful sphere of bright white. Seconds later, came the siren.

"Shit!" He turned to his own first officer. "Are we making noise?"

"No, sir. Nothing."

Zhirov motioned to the monitor. "Then explain that!"

His first officer could only shake his head. "I don't know, sir. We came in quiet."

"Well, obviously not quiet enough. They know we're here. How?!"

The first officer stammered. He had no answer.

"Go! Stop anything that's moving, NOW!"

"Aye, sir!"

"And stand by to open torpedo bay doors. On my mark."

"Aye!"

With that, his first officer disappeared, leaving Zhirov standing in the control room before the monitor. He crossed his arms and continued watching the ship. God only knew how, but the mission had just been compromised.

***

It was the same conclusion Sergeant Popov had just come to, now less than a hundred meters from the stern of the *Pathfinder*. Taking a ship was fraught with problems, but now the bright lights from the vessel would leave them virtually no cover at all. Of all the scenarios they had planned for, this was the one they could do the least about.

There was no turning back. The best the Spetsnaz team could do now would be to re-submerge and surface at the last possible moment. The *Pathfinder's* greatest weakness to attack was its abnormally low stern, designed specifically for its research hardware—a known weakness that the Americans would no doubt be ready to defend.

Which meant that all Popov and his men could do was to board as quickly as possible and immediately open fire.

86

Neely reached her lab first and ran to the far corner. There, she pulled a large satellite phone off a shelf and placed it heavily onto the metal table in front of her.

Borger arrived to see her remove the handset from the cradle and start thumbing through the numbers in the phone's memory.

In less than ten seconds, the signal bounced off a low orbiting satellite and rang on the other end, aboard a ship positioned only a few hundred miles away.

"Hello?"

"Jeff! It's Neely. I need your help! It's urgent!"

"Neely? Yeah, sure. What do you need?"

"It's the sonar array. It picked something up earlier today—a false positive in our area. But it wasn't a false positive. It was real!"

"Jesus! Are you serious?"

"Jeff, listen to me. I need a full signature scan. I need to know exactly what it picked up on. Immediately."

"Right. Okay, you got it. I'll send you a copy, right now!"

"Thanks. Next, bring everyone in. Everyone. We need every set of eyes we can get, looking for anything that may have been missed. And more importantly, turn on a full-spectrum scan. Every frequency and every database. And don't stop."

"You got it, Neely. Anything else?"

"Yes. *Hurry*!"

Neely hung up and looked at Borger. "What else?"

"We need to warn Tay and his men."

***

Neither Tay, nor any of the others, needed another warning. Like everyone else, they saw the lights of the *Pathfinder* the moment they were lit. Even from a distance.

But they had yet to understand what was wrong.

"Tay. Are you there?" called Borger's voice.

"Yes. What the hell is going on?"

"There's a sub in the water. Not far from where you are."

"Holy shit!"

Borger continued. "We're on full alert. I recommend you guys stay where you are."

"Are you nuts?"

"Probably. But you're safer down there. For the moment."

"But how long of a moment?"

Borger checked his watch. "You're not that deep. You should be good for at least another thirty minutes."

Listening quietly, both Corbin and Beene looked at each other. Their expressions were easily visible through their face masks. This was no precaution. The captain would not have lit the ship up like a Roman candle unless he believed a threat was imminent. And if correct, remaining on the bottom for thirty minutes was not a viable option.

But Tay conceded, still floating on the other side of the drill. "We'll wait."

"Okay," Borger's voice was clearly nervous. "I'll come back as soon as I can." Just when Borger was about to let go of the mike, all four men heard something in the background.

Gunfire.

87

Bullets bounced off the steel deck and ripped through several of the large equipment bins on the stern. Others ricocheted, hitting cables and piercing some of the thick rubberized hoses wrapped around giant feeding wheels.

Sergeant Popov was the first out of the water and onto the back of the *Pathfinder*, immediately drawing fire from two sailors on the upper deck. Working together, one kept firing while the other moved. They pressed in closer to cut the attackers off from both the port and starboard sides of the ship.

Popov rolled with everything he had, miraculously making it behind one of the equipment bins. Moments later, the head of one of his men bobbed up over the edge, throwing a bag up and over. It slid to within a few feet of Popov.

Under more fire, he reached out and pulled the bag closer to him. From there, he ripped it open and removed a Russian PPD-40 machine pistol. Without looking, he fired several rounds over the top of the bin, less in an effort to hit anything than to signal his men in the water.

He waited only a few seconds before raising it again and opening fire, this time holding down the trigger and running through the entire magazine—long enough to provide cover for the next man to make it out of the water and onto the deck.

His man moved into position behind the base of one of the ship's winches, cornered by M4 fire from the sailors. Popov instantly replaced his magazine and unloaded another barrage.

Popov slid one of the PPDs to his second and lowered his head, peering around the edge of the bin.

No clear line of sight. He moved further, trying to see beneath another winch in front of him. He couldn't see the sailors, but he could see the legs of two more men running along the upper deck.

***

"Bridge contact! Contact!"

Captain Emerson ignored the radio and yelled at Harris. "Get every man armed! Send half to the stern and put the others on the main deck! They could be coming up anywhere!"

Harris nodded and took several men from the bridge, leaving only enough behind to run the ship.

"Sir!" yelled the sonar officer. "I still have nothing on that sub!"

Emerson ran forward and looked down through the window again. The blades of the *Sea King* helicopter were turning.

He pushed a button and picked up another handset. "Lawton. Are you there?"

"Yes, sir."

"I need to know where that sub is NOW!"

"Yes, sir." Neely dropped the phone and ran back down the hall. "Lee!" she burst in, screaming over the gunfire. "Where the hell is she?!"

She leaned forward and yelled into Lee's microphone. "Alison, can you hear me?! Alison!"

"Yes. I can hear you. What's happening?"

"We're under attack. We need to know where that sub is, exactly!"

***

Deep below, Alison stammered, still holding tightly onto Sally. "I don't know exactly. I'm not sure what *my* position is, and it'll take me five to ten minutes to reach the surface."

"Dammit!" Neely cried and pounded the table. She stood up, trying to think, then pulled the fat satellite phone from her pocket and dialed again. When she heard the line pick up, she didn't wait for an answer.

"Jeff! What are you seeing?!"

"Nothing yet. We're scanning but don't see anything. If there's a sub there, we can't see it at all!"

"How is that possible?!"

"I don't know."

Neely Lawton growled and hung up the phone. The gunfire was growing fiercer, and a bullet suddenly ricocheted loudly outside the exterior hatch.

She looked grimly at Lee and then at Borger who was in the doorway. "We're totally blind."

***

Alison. What wrong?

Alison was desperate. "We're being attacked." She turned and pointed at the dark outline of the sub. "By *that!* Our metals cannot see it."

Sally studied the outline. *It bad, Alison.*

"Yes, *very* bad!"

Sally thrashed her tail, pulling Alison around with her. Facing the other direction, she opened her mouth and emitted a powerful call of clicks and whistles. After finishing the long sequence, Sally repeated it again and again, just as loudly.

When she was done, a calm fell over them again, like a blanket of silence. No sound came from either of them, or from Lee and the ship. Nothing at all.

Instead, Alison remained in that same spot, motionless, floating in eerie silence next to Sally.

And when the response finally came, it was not the sound that she heard—it was the sensation she felt. Right through the fabric of her dive suit, and all along her arms

335

and legs. Next her hands sensed it. A buzzing was building from a subtle tingle through her skin to something stronger. Something *much* stronger. Until it hit her like a wave.

The buzzing became so strong that it was no longer just through her skin, but went deeper into her very organs and bones.

Alison gasped as the feeling grew stronger still. Almost electrifying her. Her eyes began to glaze when she saw figures emerging out of the darkness. First just a few, then more coming behind. Until the water was filled with them.

Dolphins. Nothing but dolphins. All of them using their powerful echolocation together, creating a *wall of sound* that was simply overwhelming.

A wall that was directed precisely at the Russian submarine.

***

Neely's phone rang immediately. She answered hurriedly, pressing it against her ear.

"We've got something!" shouted Jeff. "We see it!"

Neely eyes shot open. "You see it?!"

"Holy shit, do we see it! God, Neely, *you've got to see this*!!"

***

"Captain!"

Still on the bridge, Emerson whirled around to face his sonar officer. "What?"

"I've got something!

"Are you sure?"

"Yes!" The officer nodded excitedly, watching the lines of signals running down his green monitor. "I'm not sure how, but I've got it!"

Emerson looked down through the window again to see the giant helicopter finally lifting off the bow. With its commanding rotors beating the air into submission, the aircraft rose, directly in front of the bridge deck. Like a beast rising from the depths.

"Where?" Emerson commanded. "Where is it?!"

88

Popov heard the thundering of the *Sea King's* rotors over the gunfire and cursed. Miraculously, he'd gotten all but one of his team aboard the ship, but a prime objective had been to keep the chopper grounded.

He called to his men and they raised their guns, unleashing a hail of fire at the helicopter. Nevertheless, it rose over the bridge deck, tilting forward. Their PPDs were no match for the chopper's armor, but the open door still gave them a large enough target.

Three of the American sailors were dead. But more were still coming. Popov and his men were now advancing toward the upper deck. One of the Russian team had taken a shot through his left arm, but continued to surge forward with Popov and the others.

Another barrage of coordinated fire brought down a fourth sailor. The body fell onto the overhead grating and slumped sideways, sending his M4 rattling down onto the level below.

In and out, the Russians moved systematically, with short bursts to cover each man as they moved forward.

***

On the upper deck, men were running outside, past the lab where Neely stood facing Borger and Lee. They could no longer reach Alison, and the gunfire was continuing to draw nearer.

They were suddenly interrupted by the speaker next to Borger's laptop. It was Tay.

"Will! Are you there?"

Borger grabbed the mike and held it to his mouth.

"Yeah, I'm here."

"Are you guys okay?"

Borger shook his head. "It's not good. But the captain's orders are for you to stay down there and keep on that drill. We may not get another shot at this!"

When was no reply, Neely looked at them

"You know whoever they are, they're coming *here*."

Borger and Lee both nodded.

She turned and looked back at the test tubes stacked neatly in the refrigerator behind her.

"We need to hide them," Borger said.

Neely shook her head. "There's no time." Instead she moved to her desk and pulled one of the drawers open. She reached inside and withdrew her 1911 nickel-plated 9mm Sig Sauer handgun.

She looked solemnly at the gun, given to her by her father, then to Borger and Lee. "You two better get out of here. Get to the lower deck. They're only after what's in this room."

"You can't be serious."

Neely reached down and pulled the slide back, chambering a round.

"Neely," Lee pleaded. "Let's all go. Let them have it. We've got the rest—the plants, and Africa."

She stared at him in a moment of listlessness and nodded. "Africa." She blinked and shook her head. "We can't give this up. Not like this. What's in these tubes is more important than any of us."

Borger stepped forward. "Neely. If they reach this lab, they're going to get it. That's a fact. One handgun is not going to stop them. All its going to do is get you killed."

"We can't just let them have it."

"This is not a chess match. This is you and us, being dead if we don't leave right now."

"My father died protecting this," Neely replied.

"No, he didn't!" Borger said, raising his voice. They were getting closer. "He died protecting *us*! All of us. To

339

fight another day. And you need to do the same thing!"

There was a short lapse in gunfire outside, and she stared hard into Borger's eyes. Then it hit her. She had an idea.

***

Elgin Tay was staring at the giant drill in front of him and Lightfoot. The new bit had just made contact with the alien hull, sending waves of bright light rippling outward as the drill slowly dug into the gray wall.

"Okay. Roger that," he finally answered. "We're not going anywhere for the moment," he said into his helmet. "But you should know that we're two men down."

"What?"

"I said it's just two of us down here now. Me and Lightfoot."

"What about Corbin and Beene?"

"They're gone."

"What do you mean, they're gone?"

"When they heard all the commotion they dropped their weights and headed back to the surface."

***

On the *Pathfinder*, Borger shook his head. "Why in God's name would they do that?"

All three suddenly jumped at the sound of one of the lab's doors opening behind them. Neely instinctively raised her gun and pointed it at the figure in the doorway. First Officer Harris was holding an M4 carbine in his hands, looking at them with fierce blue eyes. "We have to get you out of here."

89

Admiral Langford picked up his phone on the first ring and heard Defense Secretary Merl Miller's voice cut in immediately.

"The *Pathfinder* is under attack."

"What?"

"Right now, as we speak."

"Son of a bitch!" Langford gritted his teeth in frustration and forced himself not to smash something. "We need to get the president."

"Already done," Miller said. "We've got a call in one minute."

"What do we know?"

"Not much. We're capturing from satellite right now. Likely a small precision strike since no sign of an accompanying ship or aircraft."

"They came in on a sub."

"Most likely."

"What about the oil rig?"

"Nothing we can see yet. But they're aboard the *Pathfinder*."

"They're going after the bacteria."

"Exactly."

Langford leaned back into his chair and closed his eyes. "Son of a bitch."

***

The president leaned into his speakerphone. "This is Carr. Who's on?"

"Miller."

"Griffith here."

"And Langford."

"Mason, are you there?"

Carr's Chief of Staff answered. "Yes, Mr. President."

"All right. What are we looking at here?"

Miller spoke up. "The *Pathfinder* is under attack. We've got a live feed, but we can't contact them. Something is cutting off our communication with the ship."

"How many?"

"It's most likely a small force. Maybe eight to twelve. We're guessing Russian. Chinese subs aren't quiet enough, which means we're probably looking at a Spetsnaz team."

"Admiral? Options?"

"I just spoke with the Navy and Army chiefs. We have a team of rangers in Panama and a SEAL team in the Dominican Republic. Either of which can be there inside of two hours. As we all know, the *Pathfinder's* location is not ideal." Langford paused. "The alternative is an air strike."

No one spoke after the admiral's last comment. An airstrike on the *Pathfinder* was a desperate measure, and they all knew it. There was nothing surgical about it. Instead of retaking the ship, it would instead be an effort to destroy the entire vessel and its cargo. Something not altogether different from what the Chinese had done to their own ship off the coast of South America. And for the same reason.

National Security Advisor Stan Griffin cleared his throat. "Just how the hell did they get on our ship?"

"We're not sure," Miller said. "Our best guess is by submarine."

"Right under our noses," Griffith said.

"It appears so."

"What are the ship's chances?" asked President Carr.

"Hard to say. There *is* one thing in their favor," Langford replied dryly.

"What's that?"

"We didn't leave it completely defenseless," Langford said. "We have the dive team we brought in, under a man named Gorski."

"Who is Gorski?"

"Gorski is a world expert in diving and underwater recovery operations. He's worked with the Navy for twenty years, almost exclusively with our Special Forces teams. Including Navy SEALS. Two of whom are working with him right now on that oil rig."

"Wait a minute," the President said. "Are you telling me we have two *active* SEALS in the middle of all this?"

"That's exactly what we're saying. Their names are Corbin and Beene."

90

Les Gorksi was staring over the water toward the *Pathfinder* with a look of utter horror. Even at a distance, he could easily hear the gunfire from the oil rig, where he remained the only one aboard. The rest of the team had been ferried to the ship only hours before to assist with the drilling effort.

Now Gorksi watched helplessly as the attack ensued near the ship's stern.

And if not for the reflection on the water from the *Pathfinder's* glaring lights, he would never have noticed several figures moving in the water below him, toward one of the rig's four giant pillars.

***

On the far side of the *Pathfinder's* stern, another light appeared in the water and slowly grew larger. Then joined by a second, until two silver dive helmets breached the surface, one after the other. Both divers glided closer without a sound, illuminating the lower portion of the ship's metal hull with their bright lamps.

In unison, Corbin and Beene turned off their lights and leaned back, peering up and over the edge of the ship. They spotted the massive black cord coming over the side and powering the drill below them. Without a word, each soldier removed his diving helmet and let it sink back into the water, where the headgear promptly disappeared below the waves.

The loud gunfire could still be heard on deck, leaving Corbin to cautiously pull himself up the fat cord just enough to peek over the side. Then in one fell swoop, he pulled the rest of his body out of the water and disappeared.

91

No.

Captain Zhirov fixated on his screen and the live feed. He could see the flashes of the guns aboard the *Pathfinder* and watched as two figures dressed in black scrambled up a portside ladder. Two of Popov's men.

But that's not what worried him. It was that the Navy helicopter had successfully lifted off from the bow of the ship and was now in the air.

The American captain would soon conclude, if he hadn't already, that the Russian attack team came from a submarine. And from somewhere close. If they weren't scanning with sonar before, they certainly were now. Luckily, their systems would not be able to see Zhirov's sub.

Which explained why his concern grew exponentially at the sight of not just the helicopter but its *direction*. Aircraft that did not know the location of its target typically hovered or circled the area, trying to find the enemy. But that's not what this helicopter was doing.

After a brief pause, the giant chopper had turned…and headed straight in Zhirov's direction.

It was impossible. They couldn't have found him that quickly. There was simply no way their sonar systems were that effective.

However, one thing Zhirov knew, what all military commanders knew, was just how quickly a mission's luck could change. One variable, one miscalculation, or one simple mistake could produce a string of events impacting everything following that moment. An unseen ripple effect that could change the fate of even the most well-planned mission.

A moment that Zhirov's instincts told him had just occurred.

Without looking back, Zhirov barked two commands over his shoulder.

"Prepare to dive. And load torpedoes!"

"Aye, Captain." The helmsman, a young man sporting only stubble for hair, nodded in response. Moments later the ballast tanks began to flood, increasing the weight of the boat, while the helmsman looked curiously at his screen. He studied it for several seconds.

"Sir. We appear to be drifting."

"What?"

"We…are drifting, sir."

"Drifting? Why?"

The helmsman shook his head and rechecked his instruments. "I'm not sure. All propulsion systems are off."

"Is it a current?"

"No, sir. It's steady."

Zhirov's heartbeat accelerated. Something was wrong. If they were moving, even drifting, it would eventually affect the direction of the boat. And more importantly, the aim of their torpedoes. Worse, if the drift was too great, it would require the use of their engines to correct. And engines, even those of a *Ghost Sub*, made some noise. As did opening torpedo tube doors.

Zhirov could now actually feel the drift. "Why? Why are we moving?!" he yelled.

His crew around him had no answer. When the helmsman spoke again, it was in a nervous tone. "It's increasing."

Zhirov's eyes turned back around to the periscope feed. The U.S. helicopter was still approaching. Slowly. Intentionally. Now silhouetted by the bright glow of the *Pathfinder* behind it.

He had no choice. Noise be damned.

"Full power. Now! Emergency dive and open torpedo doors."

***

Alison still floating a visible distance away and watching hundreds of swarming dolphins, nearly jumped when the submarine abruptly began to descend. And only moments later a deep whirring sound was heard, coupled with a large circular opening appearing on the sub's nose.

Oh my God, they're preparing to fire! She called into her microphone. "Lee!"

There was no answer.

"Lee!"

Still nothing.

"LEE!" she screamed.

Something had cut off her radio communication to the ship, leaving Alison floating helplessly in the dark.

92

The bridge's starboard side door opened. Neely, Lee, and Will Borger were ushered into the room, followed by First Officer Harris. Both sides of the room were guarded by sailors, armed with similar-looking rifles.

"Sir, the sub has opened its torpedo doors!"

Captain Emerson glanced only briefly at the three before turning back to his sonar officer. They were preparing to fire.

Emerson then turned to his communications officer. "Are we ready?"

The younger man nodded. "Yes, sir. The helicopter has a fix on the sub. They're waiting for the order to launch."

Lee Kenwood's expression suddenly changed. "Wait, what?"

"Quiet."

Lee looked back and forth between Borger and Neely, then returned his focus to the captain. "Wait, you're going to fire on the sub?"

"I said *quiet!*" Emerson snapped.

"You can't fire. That's where Alison is!"

This time Emerson paused. He looked at Lee as well as the others. He'd forgotten about Alison. She was the only one close enough to have seen the sub. An attack against the sub could easily kill her.

Dammit! Emerson thought to himself. *Why was she still there? She should have moved!*

Regrettably, it didn't matter. He had only seconds to make the call and losing one life versus everyone onboard the *Pathfinder* was not a difficult decision. Unfortunate, yes. But not difficult. His job was to save as many lives as possible. And his ship.

"Launch the torpedo."

93

"We're still drifting!" The helmsman turned to Zhirov. "And we can't correct it!"

The overhead lights aboard the *Ghost Sub* went out suddenly and then quickly flickered back on.

"Sir!" another officer yelled. "We're losing power!"

"And our engines are failing!"

"Impossible!" raged Zhirov. *What the hell was happening?!* The room began to dim again, along with all the instrument screens. "How the hell are we losing power?!"

"I don't know, sir!"

"Stop our descent!"

The helmsmen used the instrument pad to halt the ballast tanks and continued staring at his fading screen. "Halted, sir...but we're still descending!"

"Then blow the goddamn things!"

The helmsman complied. A long, massive blast was heard outside as the tanks emptied. "Still sinking!"

Zhirov stared in disbelief. *Were they taking on water? How could they be? There had been no impact. Christ, until only moments ago, no one even knew they were there!*

"All remaining power to the engines!" he shouted. "Get us the hell out of here!"

***

Several hundred yards away, Tay and Lightfoot were watching in fascination as the entire wall before them began to glow more brightly—and not just the area around the drill. The glow continued to spread, beyond the section in front of them, traveling along the entire length of the alien ship's hull. Even the areas covered in coral were now glowing.

Something strange was happening.

The lights surrounding the drill began to fade just as the giant drill bit finally pierced the hull, plunging several inches through to the other side.

"More power!" shouted Lightfoot.

Tay cranked the power up as high as he could, resulting in a horrible grinding sound from the tip of the drill.

The whole wall in front of them now gleamed a brilliant bright white, illuminating every square inch of seafloor around them. At the same moment, both Tay and Lightfoot felt something change. The magnetism that they'd felt earlier became stronger, pulling their gear and their tanks toward the radiating hull.

Both men fought against it. They resisted the force with all their might as their metal tanks twisted them around, toward the giant wall.

"What the hell?!" Tay yelled.

Lightfoot was unable to answer. Instead, he struggled against the pull of his own tank and dive helmet before ultimately losing his grip on the drill and slamming backward against the wall.

As the screeching of the drill loudened, Tay managed to turn his helmet enough to see the spiraled cone drill bit begin to expand, slowly widening its hole in the alien wall.

***

Zhirov stumbled as his submarine suddenly lurched to port. Unable to break away from the erratic sideways and downwards momentum, the boat's entire crew struggled to stay in their chairs.

"We've lost stabilizing control!"

Zhirov looked back to the periscope feed. The screen was black, its camera long since having disappeared beneath the swirling ocean water.

His men remained hunched in front of their displays,

desperately fighting for whatever control they still had. Something was pulling hard on the sub, literally dragging it downward toward the depths of the ocean.

Through intermittent interference, the Russian sonar operator, heard the sound of the splash and braced himself in his chair. The *Sea King's* Mark 46 aerial torpedo plunged through the water, directly toward them.

"Fish in the water!" he yelled. "Bearing one-four-two degrees! Distance six hundred meters!"

"Ali! Ali, can you hear me?!"

"Lee?!" she pressed her buds in tightly. "Yes! I can hear you!"

"Ali, can you hear me?!"

"LEE!" she screamed. "I HEAR YOU! CAN YOU HEAR ME?!"

After a slight delay, Lee's voice returned. "Yes. I — hear you. Barely." He continued. "Ali, listen — me. You have to — out of th — now!"

"What's happening?!"

Alison was struggling to hear him over the static. The transmission sounded faint. As if it was being drowned out by something.

"— fast, Ali! Fast!" There was another pause before Lee's voice faded back in. "—torpedo is coming! — sub!"

Alison froze. Her eyes shot back to the submarine that now appeared to be rolling onto its side. And those last four words were all she needed to hear.

"Sally!" she yelled. "SALLY!"

***

Waiting a few feet away, Sally heard the translation and circled back around.

Alison, I here.

"Sally, we have to leave. Now! Escape!"

An error sounded in her ear.

"We must leave! Now! Or we will die! *Go fast!*"

The translation from the vest seemed to take forever, but there was no error this time. Sally stopped, then immediately turned back around and called again to the other dolphins. This time her signals were very short and very loud.

**

Emerson's sonar officer called out the distance. "Four hundred meters. Three hundred and fifty meters. Three hundred—"

His announcements ceased abruptly. When he didn't continue, Captain Emerson stepped forward.

"What is it?"

The officer was still watching his screen. "It's the torpedo, Captain. Its bearings are changing!"

"Changing how?"

"It's…turning."

"How the hell can it be turning?!"

"I don't know, sir." The officer zoomed in on his screen. "The torpedo seems to be…arcing."

Will Borger moved closer and looked at the display in front of the officer. A three-dimensional map with grid lines outlined the ocean below them. The position of the Russian sub was clearly marked, with the path of the torpedo displayed as a white line moving through the bottom of the picture. At its head, the line was beginning to bend.

"Where the hell is it going?"

"I don't know."

Borger pressed even closer, still studying the screen. Part of the three-dimensional map was an area that he recognized. It was where Tay and Lightfoot were now…with the drill.

"That's the alien ship," he murmured.

"What?"

Borger pointed at the screen. "That's where the ship is buried."

The path of the torpedo curved further into an even wider arc as it passed the alien ship. Its course had now been diverted directly between the ship and the Russian submarine.

Will Borger maintained his fixed stare on the screen. "What's that torpedo made out of?"

"What?"

"I mean what kind of metal?"

Emerson frowned. "How the hell am I supposed to know? The damn thing is malfunctioning."

Borger continued watching the path of the warhead as it began to follow an elongated loop. "Captain. That torpedo is not malfunctioning." He looked at the commander. "The alien ship is magnetic and is *pulling* on its metal casing."

Lee Kenwood stepped in next to Borger. "It looks like a planet when it does an orbit."

Borger nodded. "But the alien ship isn't round. It's oblong, which means that torpedo isn't going to circle it."

It was at that moment that the final piece fell into place for Will Borger. The questions he had about the alien craft but could not answer now made sense—why it was magnetic, and more importantly, why it was so damn big!

It wasn't the ship at all.

The core of the ship couldn't take that kind of damage while traveling through space. It needed to be shielded. What they saw, the giant wall buried deep within the coral, wasn't the main ship. It was the ship's shield! A shield that was designed not to *deflect* the energy of an impact, it was designed to *absorb* it!

The epiphany washed over Borger like a wave, carrying answers that left him breathless along with it. And Will was immediately fearful for Tay and Lightfoot, who were both still on the bottom.

On the screen, in front of all to see, the path of the torpedo began to slow and turn inward.

"Captain," Borger said. "That torpedo isn't going to hit the sub. It's going to hit the buried ship."

Tay and Lightfoot could barely move. No part of the giant wall behind them remained green. The entire massive structure was now bright white.

Why was the whole thing lighting up? It couldn't just be the drill. Tay stared again at the powerful tool, its bit churning deep into the metal and expanding in size. It had now created a huge hole in the craft that appeared pitch-black inside.

Over the whirling, both men heard something through their helmet speakers.

"Tay! Lightfoot! Can you hear me?"

"Borger?"

"Yes. Can you hear me?"

"Barely!" Tay shouted. "We need help. This goddamn thing has us pinned to the wall!"

Borger shook his head. "Listen to me. We don't have time. There's a torpedo in the water, and it's going to strike within a couple hundred yards of you. Maybe closer."

"Jesus Christ!" Lightfoot yelled. "Get us out of here!"

"We can't. There is no time!"

Behind Borger, the sonar officer called to Emerson. "Captain! Impact in ninety seconds!"

Borger's voice came in again over their headsets. "Has that drill punched through the hull?"

"Yes!" Tay shouted.

"How big is the hole?"

Tay looked to his left. "About two feet in diameter. Maybe more. And it's goddamn scary looking!"

"Listen to me," Borger ordered. "Listen! We have barely one minute left. And exactly one option. And you have to do it RIGHT NOW!"

Caught by the increasing pull from the alien ship, the trajectory of the Mark 46 Mod 5 torpedo curved tighter and tighter, until it smashed into the side of the hull with its full force at forty-two knots.

The nearly one-hundred-pound warhead exploded in a concussive blast at more than eight thousand feet per second, directly into the alien wall. The already glowing hull instantly brightened beyond its white color, turning ultraviolet. The impact rippled in all directions, causing waves within the metal itself.

The resulting shockwave raced outward, traveling faster than the speed of sound. Great swaths of coral that were still wrapped around the lower half of the ship were instantly obliterated. Plant life either disintegrated or became flattened under the intense pressure, as did all sea life caught in the devastation.

The wall of devastation could have run for miles without obstruction, but found itself caught in something far more powerful instead. Abruptly, in less than a hundred yards, the shockwave began to slow, simultaneously with the momentary disappearance of all color from the alien hull. At that instant, all light and explosive force began to transform into pure energy.

The outward movement of the shockwave slowed to a sudden halt at which point it froze for a moment before relinquishing its momentum and beginning to recede. Like a vacuum pulling it back into the darkness, the torpedo's deadly force was reabsorbed first, then redistributed through the walls of the alien shield.

In just moments, the devastating blast vanished almost as quickly as it had begun.

97

The blast was heard by every living thing within several square miles, including Junior Sergeant Levin and the rest of his four-man team, all of whom had reached the lowest level of the *Valant* oil platform.

Feeling the shaking of the platform, Levin peered out over one of the rusted railings and down into the dark water but could see nothing. Nothing except the brightly lit *Pathfinder* ship in the distance, where the gunfire continued unabated.

However, unlike Popov and his team, Levin's team met no resistance at all. From what they could see, most of the platform was largely empty. No sound at all could be heard from the bottom level, which was the rig's largest. And aside from just a few lights left on, the entire vessel appeared to be vacant.

Levin signaled two of his men to check the span of the bottom level, while he and the fourth man maintained positions near the stairwells. Their rifles were pointed up, ready for any surprises descending from above.

Several minutes later, the two men returned and signaled that the level was clear. Levin nodded, and together, he and two more climbed to the next level, leaving one team member to secure their escape route.

***

Popov was not aware of the other team's stroke of luck aboard the oil rig. Instead, he and his men continued to press forward, methodically dropping magazines and reloading. Each team member maintained a steady stream of fire.

Popov's own luck, if you could call it that, was being close enough to make it onto the stern of the ship before the Americans were fully ready. The emergence of more American machine guns rang out only seconds after Popov's leap over the side, and he was thankful the timing went in the Russians' favor. The second stroke of luck was having more room to maneuver than some of the sailors above them, two of whom were killed by ricocheting bullets in confined spaces. Three others were killed by inferior training, rather than circumstance— something Popov and his team were relying on.

Still, the remaining Americans continued to fight back, but were forced to retreat to the middle of the ship. This provided the Russian team enough room to move up the ladders, pushing forward toward the science ship's main lab.

Even with his team down to three, Popov eventually managed to force his way to the lab's door. He carefully made his way into the room with a sense of relief, only to find it empty.

The female officer he was looking for had clearly fled. Outside, his men continued to fire in short controlled bursts while Popov's dark eyes scanned the room. The equipment all looked in order. An open drawer and a satellite phone lying atop the counter indicated an abrupt exit.

Popov soon spotted the compact laboratory refrigerator and advanced immediately across the room, where he yanked the glass door open. Stacks of small test tubes lined the top two shelves, all filled with a clear solution exhibiting a slight pinkish hue.

Without hesitation, he withdrew a black neoprene pouch from within his wetsuit and unzipped it along three edges––the inside carefully lined with a silver-coated material. He hastily grabbed a handful of tubes and placed them in a single layer inside the pouch. Then he did the same again, layering the second row over the first.

Popov ignored the machine gun bursts and yelling from outside. He returned the pouch under his wetsuit before checking the room again. He noted three microscopes of varying sizes behind him, two wide computer screens, and several wire cages. He opened a tall cabinet and quickly scanned the shelves before doing the same to the overhead cabinets, but he found nothing else of consequence.

Popov unslung his weapon and yanked the door open again, stepping out behind one of his men.

"To the rig!" he yelled.

***

Below and further back toward the stern, the sound of wet feet slapped noisily across the metal deck before stopping next to one of the fallen sailors. The man lay face down with blood pooling beneath his chest.

Jake Corbin reached down and quietly picked up the M4 carbine. In one motion, he flipped it over and withdrew the magazine, quickly slapping it back into place. He searched the soldier and found a second unspent magazine, tucking it just beneath the top of his suit. Not far away, Alan Beene found a second rifle and signaled back to Corbin.

Still in bare feet, both men moved back to the ladders on opposing sides. And climbed without a sound.

***

It was Popov's only mistake.

They had so effectively cleared the rear of the ship that he simply did not expect more men approaching from the stern. Let alone two Navy SEALs.

When he realized his mistake, it was already too late.

Popov watched both his men go down in front of him in a flurry of bullets as the Americans reached the top of the ladder. The Russians returned fire as they collapsed, wounding Corbin in the shoulder and forcing Beene to jump against an inside wall.

Caught in the crossfire, Popov took the only option he

had and instantly launched himself from the upper deck out over the water. Plunging forty feet into the dark swells next to the ship, he was followed by a hail of bullets. Beene emptied the remainder of his ammo and ran forward, grabbing the fallen Russian's rifle and waiting for Popov's body to reemerge.

98

To Levin, still scouting the *Valant* oil rig, the sudden silence in the distance was not a good sign. The gunfire aboard the *Pathfinder* had stopped too abruptly. Even once in the water, Popov's team would have to continue returning fire until they were far enough away to re-submerge. Which meant they either got under quickly or not at all.

He continued clearing the area on the top platform, including its wide landing pad. They had found no one at all aboard the rig, leaving him both curious and concerned.

They knew the crew on the *Valant* was not large, but what were the chances of the entire group being aboard the *Pathfinder* at the start of the attack? It was possible but highly unlikely.

Finding the top level also empty, he descended again to the crew's living quarters. The rig was old but clearly still functional, as evidenced by the multitude of lights and partially stocked kitchen.

Down another hallway, Levin entered what appeared to be a large office. A metal desk sat near the far wall with two old-style monitors on top and a larger computer underneath. Piles of papers and photographs, along with a keyboard and mouse, littered the rest of the desk. Levin turned to examine an air conditioner on the outside wall, still running and accompanied by a noisy hum.

He returned and watched one of his men shake his head, indicating the rooms were empty. Levin called to the other two team members downstairs over the headset hidden behind his ear.

"Find anyone?"

"No one."

Levin moved back out through the door, where he

peered curiously across the water to the *Pathfinder*. Something wasn't right.

***

Levin's instinct was correct.

Les Gorski was less than twenty feet away, hiding inside the *Valant's* broken elevator. With legs spread wide, balancing atop ledges on either side of the shaft, Gorski's right hand clung to the crossbar behind the doors. His left tightly gripped a rifle.

99

Admiral Langford looked up when his office door opened to see Merl Miller rush in, swiftly reaching back and shutting the door.

Miller remained standing, dressed in a dark blue suit and spotted gold tie. His thin gray hair was neatly combed as always. "Emerson has repelled the attack and currently maintains control of the ship. But his crew has taken heavy losses."

Langford exhaled heavily. He stared at his desk, thinking. "And the team?"

"Most of the team is alive." Miller paused before finally adding, "but Alison Shaw is missing."

"Oh, Jesus."

"She was below the surface when the torpedo struck. As were two of Emerson's men, Tay and Lightfoot. They're organizing a search team now."

Langford nodded solemnly.

"Unfortunately, it's not over. Emerson has lost contact with the *Valant* oil rig. They think it's been seized."

At this, Langford raised his heavy brow. "Is there anything on that rig?"

"Nothing of material importance."

"What about the sub?"

"We've lost it on sonar. Emerson and Lawton think it either sank or escaped."

Langford rose from his chair and leaned forward onto his desk. "Then if the *Valant* has been taken, those bastards are trapped."

"Maybe," Miller replied. "The *Valant* has a landing pad."

Admiral Langford considered it. "You don't think the

sub was their way out?"

"Their sub may be largely invisible, but it's still slow. This team hit the *Pathfinder* to get the bacteria, which means they'd want the fastest exit possible. A sub gives us days to find it."

"You think they'll try to fly it out?"

"It's what we would do."

Langford nodded. He reached for his phone and pressed a button.

After a moment, his secretary's voice could be heard through the speaker. "Yes, Admiral."

"Get me Admiral Collier at Naval Operations."

"Yes, sir. One moment."

It took only seconds for the line to be picked up. "This is Collier."

"Admiral, this is Langford. I have Miller here with me. I understand Captain Emerson still has control of his boat."

"That is correct, sir. We are ready to call off the air strike."

Langford nodded and began to speak, when he suddenly paused.

"Hello?"

He peered up from his desk at Miller before speaking again into the microphone. "One second." He pressed the handset against his shoulder.

Miller raised an eyebrow, expectantly.

"Get Captain Emerson on the phone."

***

An exhausted and bleeding Popov reached the first pillar of the oil rig and after several deep breaths, managed to pull himself up onto the metal platform. He laid there for a full minute before finally rolling over and examining his wound. He was more fortunate than he expected, finding that the bullet had passed clean through his right side. Muscle damage primarily. His breathing was short, more from the pain of inhaling than internal damage. He had suffered worse.

Popov peered up at the underside of the rig, dark and out of the full moon's reach. He then looked at the glowing numbers on his watch and rolled back onto his stomach, pushing himself up.

He examined the control box mounted on the inside of the pillar wall and punched the down button. Overhead and with a clank followed by a loud hum, the utility elevator began its descent.

Popov tried his headset, pressing the tiny button just inside his ear and calling to Levin. There was only silence. He tried again. Still nothing. He pulled the device out and angrily threw it into the water behind him.

Not until Popov reached the lower maintenance level did he dare to remove the pack from inside his wetsuit. It was still there and still sealed, which was all that mattered.

The rest of his men were gone. Popov's only mission now was to reach the landing pad atop the *Valant* before the Yak arrived. He hoped Levin had done his job and cleared the rig.

***

The sound of thumping rotors returned and the fearsome silhouette of the *Sea King* helicopter came into view, rounding the right side of the *Valant*.

Levin and one of his men instinctively ducked back behind two steel beams and watched it pass by before disappearing again. The Americans were doing reconnaissance.

A loudspeaker echoed through the metal halls behind them. "*Valant*, this is *Pathfinder*. Do you copy? *Valant*, this is *Pathfinder*. Please respond."

The broadcast was not a problem for Levin. But the message was. Whoever was calling was clearly expecting someone to respond, which meant the oil rig either was not supposed to be empty…or it wasn't.

Both men jumped when they heard Popov's voice calling out, just one level below them. Levin signaled his man to remain near the hallway opening while he ran for the stairwell and descended.

Not far from him, under the faint glow of an overhead fluorescent bulb, stood Alexander Popov. Both men scanned the open areas behind one another. Tired and cautious, Popov approached.

"Where are the others?" Levin asked.

"It's just me."

Levin's eyes showed surprise but that was all he needed to know. "Did you get the samples?"

"Yes," Popov held up the pack. "What did you find here?"

"No one. It appears empty. But I think some may be hiding."

The helicopter passed by once more, shining a bright spotlight at the rig. Popov and Levin moved hastily out of the path of the light and into the stairwell.

***

From the inside of the elevator, Les Gorski gently pulled the doors open with his fingertips, enough to peer through with one eye.

He studied the lit hallway. There was no movement.

He could hear the repeated calls on the radio several rooms away.

Gorski fought to control his breathing and turned his head, pressing an ear against the slit between the doors to listen.

Nothing. He'd heard two voices before, followed by a pounding down the steps in the stairwell. But he didn't know whether that meant they were going down or more were coming up.

He also couldn't hear any of the distant gunfire coming

369

from the *Pathfinder*, only the sounds of the helicopter circling the rig. That meant whatever had happened over there was over. And now they were here.

In the end, none of that mattered. What did matter was for him to get to the radio. He needed backup. And the crew aboard the *Pathfinder* needed to know what was waiting for them on the *Valant*.

All he needed was thirty seconds. Just enough time for one message to warn them. A quick trip down the hall and back.

Gorski took a deep breath and pried the doors further apart. Once wide enough, he stepped forward with one foot and braced the left door open with his boot and shoulder. Then the second foot, forcing the right door back until both doors were separated. Once it was far enough for him to position his rifle between them, he propped them open. He had nothing else to use, which meant he would not only have to do it quickly but unarmed as well.

He stared down the hall and counted.

One. Two. Three!

***

Near the other end of the hall, Levin's man stood waiting, casually shifting his weight. It was now less than ten minutes until the Yak aircraft arrived.

The loudspeakers of the radio echoed again, while outside the American helicopter continued to circle. And even though the message was in English, the Russian soldier still made out a few faint words. It was a language that all Spetsnaz troops had recently been instructed to learn.

Curiously, the soldier stepped into the mouth of the hallway then inched gradually further, listening intently to the broadcast. It was only then that he was close enough to hear the footsteps.

***

The sudden gunfire startled Popov and Levin, leaving them scrambling up the metal stairs, then out the rusted door of the stairwell.

Levin's rifle went instantly to his shoulder as both men ran into a large room before the ringing of the shots completely disappeared. They rounded the corner into the wide hallway.

He whistled to his man who promptly answered.

"Down here!"

The soldiers ran down the hall, passing several rooms, until they reached the doorway where their teammate was standing. Intensely focused with his rifle aimed downward, he towered over the crumpled figure of Les Gorski.

Levin stepped aside to make room for Popov, who then also looked down into the eyes of Gorski. The front of the American's shirt was covered in blood and spreading.

Just a few feet away, the radio blared again. This time with a different message. "I repeat, roger that. If you still copy, evacuate the vessel immediately! Repeat, *immediately*!"

It was clear from the Russians' expression that they didn't fully comprehend the message. Too bad for them. Les Gorski leaned his head back against the wall and smiled up at all three men, the blood seeping between his teeth. With his last breath, he extended his middle finger.

***

Two minutes later, Popov reached the top deck and walked out onto the landing pad. Something was not right. He waited several seconds before he was sure: the sound of the helicopter was gone. Replaced by something else. A low, distant rumble. No, not a rumble. A roar.

It rapidly grew louder until the thunder could be heard clearly. It was the scream of a jet engine. And the pitch did not sound Russian.

It was the last thought Sergeant Alexander Popov ever had.

100

The explosion was massive. Engulfing the entire rig in a gigantic ball of flame, huge areas of the vessel were ripped apart by a blast so powerful and so hot that many pieces of the walls and flooring melted in midair. The wreckage plunged over a hundred feet into the sea below.

Two towering cranes stood desolate amid the *Valant's* flames, powerful and unshaken until their supports beneath finally turned to molten steel, collapsing. As each crane was brought down, it smashed upon the disintegrating platform and broke into pieces.

***

The flames lit up the dark sky like a miniature sun, from which clouds of thick black smoke billowed upward and disappeared.

It was a display that could be seen perfectly from the *Pathfinder*, where many of the crew were already caring for their wounded and fallen sailors.

But what no one noticed against the bright burning backdrop of red and orange was a tiny silhouette moving across the top of the water—a short distance away but swimming directly toward them.

It was the outline of a dolphin. Dirk. Pulling the unmoving figure of Alison Shaw.

101

Clay approached Caesare in the early morning darkness, as his friend sat propped up against a large rock. When Clay got to within ten feet, Caesare spoke softly, resting his head back against the stone and his gun across his lap.

"Morning."

Clay stopped in front of him. "Time to switch."

"Oh-three-hundred already?"

"Mmm hmm."

Caesare inhaled before gripping his gun and standing up, haphazardly dusting off his pants. "Time flies."

"Hear anything?"

"Nah. Just some animals. They're keeping their distance. I'm sure they can smell us."

Clay grinned. "And we don't even smell that bad yet."

He could see Caesare smile in the darkness. "Yeah. We've sure smelled a hell of a lot worse. Remember Panama? Hiding waist deep in a swamp for four days. Talk about stink."

Clay chuckled and looked around. "Makes this place feel like a resort."

"I do still miss some of it," Caesare mused. "Not so much the conditions, but the team. Being with a group of guys that would do anything for one another. Whatever it took to keep each other alive." Caesare looked out into the darkness. "God, we were a force to be reckoned with." He turned back. "You ever stop to think, Clay, just how much we've done? And how much crap we've seen?"

"Hard to remember until you step back."

"It's true," Caesare nodded his head, his smile returning. "Remember jumping out of that C-130 loaded with all that gear? Christ, with that launcher you couldn't even stand up."

"Hahn and Pidilla had to help lift me."

"I can still see you standing in that doorway. I was laughing so hard. But I'm guessing that jump is what really did in your knees."

"Well, one of 'em."

"It's funny how so many people think of the military as careful and calculating. But they pushed us to do things that were just insane. I can't believe any of us can still walk."

"Yeah, we were all beginning to feel like crash test dummies in the end."

Caesare put his hands on his hips and looked up at the moon, crawling closer to the horizon. "I thought things were political back then. It's even worse now. Things are messier."

"Right and wrong were easier to discern back then. Even when we were ordered to do the wrong thing, it usually seemed like it was for the right reasons. Today, everyone seems to have their own agenda."

Caesare's smile disappeared in the darkness. "I don't know how much longer we can contain this thing, John. All of this. And now here," he said looking around. "This feels too easy. Like we're missing something."

Clay nodded. "I agree. Let's hope we're just getting lucky," he said. "And be ready if we're not."

He took the gun from Caesare and motioned toward the tent. "Get some sleep. We can't stay here much longer."

Without a word, Caesare nodded and walked away. He lowered himself onto the ground not far from the tent, where he could hear DeeAnn's breathing. And Dulce's snoring. How a three-year-old gorilla could make that much noise, he would never know.

He shifted his bag behind himself and leaned his head onto it. Glowing wisps of clouds trickling in front of the full moon was the last thing he remembered before drifting off.

***

Sunrise over the Congo and the mountains of Rwanda was a stunning sight to behold. Rising over the distant plains of Kenya and Tanzania left a fully unobstructed view of the sun as it emerged slowly from the edge of the Earth. Thin clouds allowed the morning sun to pass through beautiful layers of red, pink, and orange before finally moving into the soft blue background of the African sky.

The colors and the sounds of the waking world left John Clay with a deep, if only brief, sense of calm as he took in the scene around him. It was one he would try to remember for a long time.

Once the sunlight had crawled over the stretches of trees before him and finally reached their camp, Clay turned to find Ronin sitting up from under his thinly-lined blanket, resembling thick Mylar. The shorter man rose to his feet and moved silently to the base of the boulder, which Clay was standing on.

"You are awake."

"It was my shift." Clay dropped down onto the ground. "Did you get some rest?"

Ronin nodded. He studied the forest around him, marveling at how far it stretched. "This is what our planet looked like. Parts of it, before the event. Fortunately, we still have many images to remind us."

Clay followed his gaze, thinking. "I once saw your base underwater here. In our ocean. Before you left." He turned to Ronin. "I remember seeing more than just the water. You were rescuing many of the sea creatures as well."

Ronin faced Clay. "That is true. It was not just the water. The animals, both on land and off, are important parts of the ecology. As I said, it is more complex than any of us had appreciated. Delicate. Losing even one species can create a ripple effect larger than you would expect. Losing many creates a wave that is difficult to stop. Your sea creatures are different than ours. But we are trying to compensate and to allow evolution to find a new balance. It is all we can do. And they will be more protected on our planet."

Clay frowned. "I guess we still have a lot of challenges here."

"You think you do." Ronin grinned wryly.

"What do you mean?"

"You think you have problems. But you do not."

"Well, there's an awful lot of people on this planet that might disagree with you."

With a bleak shake of his head, Ronin looked back at the trees. "Believe me when I tell you—all of your differences, your cultures, your laws, and your pride. They are merely barriers. Politics and favors and corruption are not unique to your world. They are present, in some form or another, in every species with any intelligence. These attributes are deeply ingrained and closely related to an individual's survival. Nothing more."

"You're not painting a hopeful picture here."

Ronin turned back and smiled once again at Clay. "Human nature changes when it must change, John Clay. Never sooner. And nothing will change it more than when the survival of an individual group is surpassed by the survival of one's entire species. When your entire human race is threatened with extinction, politics and fighting no longer matter. Another lesson we were forced to learn, as you say, the difficult way."

"How did you get here? To Earth?"

"With great struggle," Ronin answered. "We are told that our scientists succeeded in creating portals shortly before the event. Crude, but the ability was there. Made possible by an energy source your world has yet to discover. A new element, I believe."

"And that's how you did it?"

"No," Ronin kindly smirked. "That is what made it possible. The scientists, some of whom are still alive, were able to establish a portal with one end that could be moved.

377

With increasing amounts of energy generated on our planet, it could stretch to yours. But this new element is rare and in limited supply. We nearly exhausted all that we had to keep the tunnel open until our ship could make it to your planet. And we have very little of it left."

"You can't find this element somewhere else?"

"Thus far, they have only found it in two places. Our planet. And yours."

Clay looked at him with surprise.

"And it was decided not to strip you of yours."

"I'm sure we're going to appreciate that."

He nodded. "The ship that we built to travel here was the only one of its kind. And only with great sacrifice did the crew make it. Most did not survive." Ronin paused. "They have been immortalized as heroes."

"You seem to know quite a bit."

"I don't know the science involved. What I tell you are details known to all my people. History. Not unlike your moon anchorage."

"Landing," Clay corrected.

"Yes."

"So when did you get here?"

"Our arrival, though perilous, was not ideal. We landed in the middle of your great war."

Clay dropped his head forward. "Wait. You mean World War Two?"

"Yes. That is it."

"You're kidding."

"I am not. It presented many difficulties for us."

Clay shook his head, considering the ramifications of what Ronin had just told him. His head suddenly stopped shaking, staring at the visitor. "Wait. Did you...intervene?"

"In your war?"

"Yes."

Ronin's face remained placid. "I was not there. The decisions were not mine to make."

102

"I miss anything?" Caesare asked, approaching the other two.

Clay nodded. "A bit."

"Good, you can fill me in on the way. Time's a ticking. We've got to wake up DeeAnn and the kids and get moving."

***

Inside the tent, DeeAnn awoke to a noise and rolled over to see what was rustling behind her.

Her eyes focused to find Dulce standing behind her. Two long hairy arms snaked through the neck of DeeAnn's khaki shirt, leaving both sleeves draping to the ground. When she frowned, Dulce snorted and chortled through a large toothy grin. In the corner, the smaller Dexter was wearing a sock on his head like a night cap.

DeeAnn dropped her head back down onto the pillow and rolled her eyes. "Ugh. I should have gone into medicine."

Dulce climbed on top of her playfully and stared down into her face. She grunted and motioned with her hands but DeeAnn could not understand.

"Sorry, honey. No vest," she replied, causing Dulce to cock her head and make what sounded like a human sigh. At that, DeeAnn grinned and rolled her own head to one side. "And Steve's right. We need to carry some breath mints for you."

***

Emerging from the tent, DeeAnn combed a few fingers through her disheveled hair before extending her arms into a wide stretch.

Everything was repacked, and the men were clearly waiting for her. Steve Caesare stepped forward with a blue metal mug. "Coffee?"

Her eyes widened with excitement, and she reached appreciatively for the cup. "You know, Steve, sometimes you can really surprise me."

Caesare laughed. "It's just coffee, Dee."

She winked playfully. "Still."

From several feet away, Ronin peered at the two curiously before turning to Clay.

"Their relationship," Clay replied, "is like a brother and sister who always thought the other was the favorite."

"I don't understand."

"It's okay. Just remember they don't *dislike* each other as much as they sometimes pretend to."

Ronin nodded and continued studying the two, while Caesare coaxed Dulce and Dexter out of the small tent, then rolled it up.

***

They continued west, in the direction of Borger's coordinates. There was no existing path, forcing them to forge their way through the dense shrubbery and slowing their progress. Most of the forest consisted of tall, densely-leafed mahogany trees, rising high overhead and dotted with occasional oil palms—the red bunches of kernels stood out against the vast greenery like giant eyes.

After several slips in the moist soil, DeeAnn tred more carefully and began stepping within the impressions left behind by Caesare, now directly in front of her. Dexter rode on Caesare's shoulder and Dulce scampered along next to her.

Ronin moved silently behind her, followed by Clay who

traveled almost as quietly, holding his gun in both hands.

They had traveled almost a full mile before reaching another large clearing. Abruptly, Caesare halted.

He had stopped before, assessing their direction, but this time was different. The clearing was wide open, resembling a prairie covered in tall grass, its far side still glowing under the rays of the rising sun.

Rather than continuing, Caesare spoke in a low voice.

"Dee?"

"Yes."

He didn't respond. Instead he continued peering across the grass.

"What is it?"

Caesare motioned forward and DeeAnn stepped around him, following his gaze. Clay pressed in closer to look over his shoulder.

Something stirred on the far side of the clearing over a hundred yards away, beneath the trees. Over a hundred yards away where it resembled a dark shadow.

After a moment, it moved again.

Then the shadow ambled forward, out to the edge of the trees where its shape became clearer. It was the frame of a massive silverback gorilla, leaning forward onto two powerful arms that made Caesare's look scrawny by comparison.

The gorilla stopped at the edge of the sunlight, staring across the small field at them. His face was black and unmoving.

"Shhh," DeeAnn whispered to the others.

Then more movement appeared in the shadows on the other side, behind him. Moments later, another gorilla emerged, just as large as the first—also staring at them.

Then a third. And a fourth. The last of which was even larger. All males. The rest "black backs."

Dee gasped, unable to hide her uneasiness. "Don't...move," she whispered. But her vest was not facing Dulce, and the small gorilla never heard her words of caution.

Instead Dulce walked forward and straight out in front of Caesare. She peered across the grass, fascinated. And that is when the male gorillas reacted.

Upon seeing Dulce, their eyes widened intensely and each immediately rose onto its legs. The one in the front began growling, followed by the others on either side.

"Oh my God," DeeAnn whispered, louder. "Drop your guns! Both of you. Slowly!"

Next to her, Caesare nodded and slowly lowered his gun to the ground, where he let it fall with a thud onto the soft dirt.

Clay did the same and eased himself back up.

"Steven. Put Dexter on the ground. Gently."

He nodded and lifted the small capuchin off his shoulder, lowering him down next to Dulce.

"Now," DeeAnn said, "everyone very calmly turn sideways and step *back* from them."

Across the grass, the group of massive gorillas moved forward, still growling. And spreading out.

"Further!" DeeAnn cried in a hushed tone. "Further back!"

They all took several more steps backward.

But it didn't help. All at once, the four gorillas roared furiously and burst forward into a run, directly toward them.

DeeAnn screamed and extended her hands in a panic, watching the gorillas rapidly cover the ground between them.

"Don't run!" she yelled. "DON'T RUN!"

"Then what the hell *do* we do?!"

DeeAnn froze only for a second, not wanting to answer. But she had no choice. "Get your guns! Pick them up!"

Both Clay and Caesare leapt forward and picked them back up. The gorillas were no less than fifty yards away and moving at top speed.

"Oh my God," DeeAnn cried and put her hands over her mouth. "Stop! Please stop!"

They did not. The giant gorillas continued toward them. "Shoot over their heads!"

Caesare instantly raised his Beretta M12 and released a burst of bullets over their heads.

But it did not stop them. The display only enraged the gorillas further, opening their mouths and baring their giant teeth. They howled and ran even harder.

Twenty yards.

DeeAnn shook her head in desperation. She couldn't believe she was going to say the words. But there was no other way. "SHOOT!"

But before they could aim, little Dulce unexpectedly burst forward out into the open toward the advancing males. She stopped, and without hesitation, stood up onto her tiny legs, lifting her arms high into the air.

And she screamed. One word, as loud as she could. Over and over. Waving frantically.

FRIENDS! FRIENDS! FRIENDS!

The translation repeated through DeeAnn's vest. And kept repeating in unison with Dulce's screams.

Still in mid-run, the gorillas' eyes locked onto the smaller animal in front of them, waving her arms.

FRIENDS! FRIENDS! FRIENDS!

The gorillas cocked their heads sideways at the words, and they dug their hands into the ground, rumbling to a stop only feet in front of her.

The males studied the petite female for several long moments before looking past her, at DeeAnn and the others. Dexter ran forward and stopped next to Dulce, hidden nearly completely in the grass with only his small dark head visible.

The silverback stared at the humans and let out a bone-chilling scream but did not move.

"Drop your guns!" DeeAnn whispered.

Once again, both men let their weapons fall to the ground.

"Now step back again!"

In front of Dulce, the giant gorillas remained still. Their powerful chests heaved steadily with bursts of hot breath visible in the morning air.

No hurt! Dulce said. *No hurt.*

All four towered endlessly over the two smaller creatures, continuing to heave and watching the humans.

No one moved. They remained frozen, waiting. Until something else moved. Not the four males, but behind them—over the stretch of grass and in the shadows.

Slowly, still more gorillas gradually emerged from beneath the trees. They were all females and infants.

103

"Okay," Caesare said, "I don't want to sound dramatic, but that was a little frightening."

"SHHH!" DeeAnn snapped. "Quiet!"

In front of them, across the grass, a large group of females emerged, moving cautiously. The smallest infants clung to their mother's backs and those who were older walked next to them.

They slowed repeatedly, watching the males, before resuming their approach across the plain.

One of the males glanced back at them before swinging around to look at Dulce. His heavy breaths were still blowing intermittently through his large nostrils.

Dulce dropped from her standing position and sat nervously back on the grass. Dexter, still next to her, moved backward a few steps.

All four males continued studying the two newcomers, dubiously, before their dark eyes rose to examine the humans again.

***

No one moved for an uncomfortably long time.
Finally, DeeAnn watched as the males relaxed and lowered themselves into a near-sitting position. When she stepped around Caesare and into the sunlight, the females in the distance stopped again before continuing once more, even more cautiously now.

DeeAnn eased forward sideways, toward Dulce and Dexter's spots on the grass. She kept her eyes lowered and calmly lowered herself onto her knees, sitting quietly. Then she waited.

The silverback gorilla watched her intently, leaning forward onto a set of massive, powerful arms.

DeeAnn did not move.

Finally, he ambled his way forward and closed the distance, dropping into a sitting position within arm's length of them.

DeeAnn lowered her head and spoke softly. "We are friends."

When the vest translated her words, the silverback in front of her leaned backward in surprise. He studied her and then the strange device on her chest.

"Friends," DeeAnn repeated.

This time the gorilla didn't move. Instead, he stared more intently at the vest and leaned forward until he was within reach again. The giant primate eyed her suspiciously before reaching forward with his long arm and extending his finger, gently touching the hard surface of the vest. He quickly withdrew his hand then eventually reached out once more and poked at it.

"Friends," she repeated.

The silverback squinted at the strange contraption, pondering it for a moment, before motioning with his arm and pointing to himself. *Gorilla.*

DeeAnn smiled and nodded. "Yes. Gorilla. Me no gorilla. I am friend."

Now the other males moved past Dulce and approached, all staring curiously at DeeAnn as the words sounded from the device.

Friend.

"Yes. Friend."

No hurt.

She shook her head. "No hurt."

DeeAnn slowly reached up and muted the microphone, then turned over her shoulder, calling as calmly as she could to the men behind her.

"Come out here and sit down behind me. Just like I did. Single file with no weapons. And slowly."

Clay, Caesare, and Ronin looked at each other in unison then calmly followed one another toward her. Softly. One by one, they each stopped and knelt down, approximately three feet apart and well behind DeeAnn.

"Now what?"

"Shhh," she whispered. "Bow your heads and just sit there. Don't say anything."

She reached up and turned her mike back on. "We friends."

The gorillas studied the men one at a time. The silverback looked back to Dulce then turned to the rest of the band behind him, waiting little more than fifty feet away.

Dulce grabbed DeeAnn's arm with her black hands. *Friends. Come.* Dulce's eyes looked at three of the smaller gorillas waiting with the group of females. All three were peering curiously back at her.

One of the youngsters suddenly leaped forward and scampered halfway across the grass, where it stopped again.

An excited Dulce responded immediately and ran out across the grass, each meeting the other. There they both stood, hunched forward and examining one another closely.

Finally, Dulce spoke. She was too far for the vest to capture the translation, but this time DeeAnn didn't need it. She recognized the familiar gestures. *Me Dulce.*

104

Clay, Caesare, and Ronin remained seated, weary, until DeeAnn eventually turned back around and spoke to them. "Sorry. This may take a while. Just try to be patient, and don't make any sudden movements."

"Don't worry," Caesare joked in a loud whisper. "Me and the big one will be best friends before we leave."

DeeAnn laughed under her breath and turned back around. "Believe me...you don't want to know how they become best friends."

***

It took almost twenty minutes before the rest of the band finally closed in and sat behind the males, facilitated primarily by the playful interaction between Dulce and the rest of the youngsters.

For his part, Dexter watched until the other gorillas got closer, but soon retreated to safety behind DeeAnn.

One of the female gorillas, sitting next to her mate, appeared utterly fascinated and continued to press for answers.

How you talk?

DeeAnn pointed at her vest. "I use the metal."

The female blinked and continued examining the rest of her contraption.

Why metal?

DeeAnn frowned. "I don't know what you mean."

After her words were translated, the female asked a different question.

Where go?

"We're looking for something special. A place."

You no bad.

"No, we're not bad."

She shook her head. *You no bad.*

DeeAnn smiled. "No."

The female then turned back around, following Dulce with her dark eyes. *How you Dulce?*

"I don't understand."

How you Dulce?

"I don't—"

How you with?

"Oh," DeeAnn mused. "She was…lost. And I found her. I take care of her."

A few of the gorillas looked at each other but none replied. The inquisitive female scooted a few inches closer and gently handled DeeAnn's vest, tugging on one of the straps.

"No, no. It has to stay with me."

She let go and pursed her giant lips before slapping a hand onto her head.

"Dee," Caesare voiced hesitantly from behind them, "I know this is kind of amazing and all, but we do need to keep moving."

DeeAnn turned slightly to the side and nodded reluctantly. She looked back at the female gorilla and her mate. "We have to go."

Go you place.

"Yes. To the place."

The silverback, followed by the other males, stood up, remaining protectively in front of the band.

When DeeAnn rose, to her surprise, the female rose with her.

Go place. Come back.

DeeAnn smiled and looked at Dulce, happily playing in the grass with the others. "We'll try."

When they reached the far side of the grass, they turned

around to see the band of gorillas fixed where they were, all watching them.

Ronin was the first to speak. "I found that very interesting."

DeeAnn couldn't help but chuckle. "Yeah. Me too."

Together, they continued. None of them, not even the gorillas, were aware they were being watched.

***

The climb toward Mount Bisoke was steep, and the southeastern side was particularly difficult to navigate. The forest became increasingly dense from the higher volumes of rainfall, which left the group struggling for their footing. Nevertheless, they pushed through heavy vegetation that towered above them.

Finding the faint remnants of a footpath, Caesare ducked under branches and continued trudging through what was left of the trail. He grasped a large branch from a nearby bush, using it to steady himself up one of the more slippery sections. He then held it out until Ronin took the branch and passed it to DeeAnn.

When they stopped to rest, her eyes drifted to Ronin's sleeve, at something she spotted earlier. "What do you have on your arm?"

He glanced down and pulled the sleeve back. Attached to his right forearm was a long band of silver metal, covered in what looked to be faint etchings of circuitry.

Caesare studied the device. "What is that?"

Ronin paused, thinking. "It is hard to explain. It is part of my…equipment, as you would say."

"What does it do?"

This time Ronin frowned. "That is harder to explain. It is my energy source."

Caesare raised his eyebrows at Clay. "Nifty."

Clay looked as though he was about to say something but instead checked his watch, stepping past them just as

Ronin lowered his sleeve. He marched forward through the knee-high bushes, toward a widening in the trees, and peered down at the slope below them. He then looked back at Caesare and DeeAnn. "Any idea how close we are?"

"From the directions I read in the journal, we should be very close."

Caesare removed Borger's photographs from a large pocket and checked his GPS unit. "Same here. Shouldn't be more than another half mile, tops. That way." He pointed in the same direction down the slope.

Clay nodded wittingly and turned back toward the trees. "Take a look at this."

Pushing forward one by one, they all stopped next to him. Through the widening, a small valley lay below. Bathed briefly in the sunlight, below the mountain's cloud cover, groups of many large plants could be seen. What was unusual was that, unlike the rest of the mountain, this small pocketed area was packed wall-to-wall with what appeared to be the same plant. Perhaps a half mile in width, the sea of giant green plants interspersed with millions of small dots of red.

DeeAnn squinted in bewilderment. "What is that?!"

Before anyone could answer, Ronin stepped forward and made a small wave with his right arm. The air in front of them began to waver, and the distant image suddenly grew larger.

"What the hell was that?!"

"A closer view."

"That's not what I meant," Caesare said incredulously. He stared again at Ronin's covered armband. "*How* did you do that?"

The shorter Ronin looked back at the image shimmering before them. "Manipulating energy holds more potential than any other technology. You will find this as well."

"No kidding."

Clay turned back to the shimmering air before them and looked closer at the image. "I think those are poppy plants."

"You mean poppy plants...as in narcotics?" DeeAnn asked.

"As in opium and heroin." Clay stepped to the right, looking through the air and further up the mountain. "There's a lot more up there. And those plants are big. Bigger than they should be."

The air suddenly began to vibrate, and the magnified image proceeded to evaporate.

"It does not last long," Ronin offered.

Clay nodded and looked back to DeeAnn whose expression conveyed that she had already grasped what they had just found. "My God. This is it. This is what Dian Fossey found."

"I think so."

"A valley of drugs," she whispered.

"Not just any drugs. The most addictive and deadly."

Caesare shook his head. "Just like Afghanistan."

"But these plants are bigger than they should be. Much bigger."

"Which probably means they've had *help*."

Clay nodded. "Like the plants in Guyana."

"So there's something in the water here too," DeeAnn said.

"It looks that way. Likely leaking out of the second vault and someone else discovered it, like this Ngeze person—"

"Then this is what he's been protecting," Caesare finished. "The biggest, and maybe the most powerful, poppy plants in existence."

"A drug trade that no one else in Africa could match."

"This is why?" DeeAnn placed a hand over her mouth. "This is why Dian Fossey was really killed, because of drugs?"

"Probably. If it is in the water, then this is a place that would probably grow anything Ngeze planted here. And why he kills anyone who comes near it."

"But if that's true—" All of a sudden, DeeAnn was interrupted by Dexter unexpectedly leaping and scrambling up a nearby tree trunk. She stopped and watched as he neared the top and looked out over the other trees. *And began screaming!*

She immediately covered her ears as protection from the high-pitched screeches and whirled around to Dulce, clearly concerned. "What? What is he saying?!"

Dulce studied him in the tree. *He say humans here. Many humans.*

105

It was all Clay and Caesare needed to hear.

"Get down!" they yelled together over Dexter's screaming, pushing DeeAnn and Dulce forcefully to the ground.

In a flash, Ronin jumped over them and faced the same direction the small monkey was looking. He waved his arm again, causing the air to waver before another magnified image appeared. At least a dozen figures, highlighted in red thermal silhouettes, could be seen above them. Together they formed a half circle around the area.

"Son of a bitch!" Caesare growled, crouching down. He looked to Ronin. "How far?"

"Perhaps a few hundred yards."

Clay faced Caesare gravely. "Maybe within earshot."

Small explosions suddenly hit the trees around them as bullets ripped into the bark. Others zipped by and tore through the foliage behind them, barely preceding the sounds of gunfire.

All three men hit the ground. "And clearly within shooting range!"

The noise quickly escalated into a barrage of gunfire from dozens of rifles, all shooting together.

Instantly, Ronin moved again, waving at a much larger area in front of him. This time the air exploded in flash of bright light and the shots became muffled. The wide expanse of air seemed to solidify, and several clusters of bullets appeared frozen before them in midair—stopped as though in a thick, invisible glass.

"It won't last!" Ronin yelled. "Run!"

Clay and Caesare were immediately on their feet, pulling

DeeAnn and Dulce off the ground like rag dolls. Dexter screamed and jumped to the ground where Caesare scooped him up with his free hand. Lowering his head and surging headlong into the wall of thick bushes, Caesare quickly plowed a path for the others to follow.

They made it almost fifty yards before Ronin's wall evaporated, and the thunder of shots returned. A fresh hail of bullets continued zipping through the forest, destroying everything in their path, searching for the Americans who were now blindly running as fast as they could.

106

Above them on a small ridge, Amir Ngeze watched as the trees and vegetation below shook wildly under the heavy barrage, trunks splintering and branches falling violently to the ground.

Finally, Ngeze held up his hand, halting the attack. He waited while the last of the echoes faded in the distance.

There was no movement beyond the few trees left swaying after the bombardment. There was no return fire. Nor any screams or cries for help.

Ngeze couldn't keep himself from grinning. They had caught the Americans completely off guard. He motioned several of his men forward to check the area and watched them descend slowly down the embankment. The small group headed through a sparse swath of trees before disappearing again into heavy foliage.

Ngeze waited impatiently for confirmation. He didn't know why the Americans were here, and frankly, did not care. They'd gotten close enough to his poppies to tell him that they were interested in more than the Fossey woman after all. He had to expect they were after his secret.

And since the Sentwali boys had indicated that two of the men may be soldiers, Ngeze was not about to take any chances. It was far easier to simply bury their bodies and pay off people in town to tell a fabricated story, if asked.

Judging from the continued silence, some of Ngeze's remaining men slung rifles over their shoulders and prepared to descend and clean up the mess. It was something they had done many times before.

But as they took their first steps forward, one of the men below reappeared. He peered back up the embankment and shook his head.

The rest of the men, now unsure, turned and awaited a response. Ngeze broke the silence and yelled. "What! How many dead?"

With another shake of his head, his man yelled back in Kinyarwandan. "Nothing. No one."

Ngeze's eyes flared. "Impossible!" He stormed downhill, followed quickly by the rest. The messenger waited at the bottom until they got closer, finally turning back into the foliage with Ngeze on his heels.

Once through the trees, the Hutu commander looked around carefully. It was impossible! They'd heard the Americans talking and fired directly on them.

"Eminence," one of his men called to him.

Ngeze crossed through the low brush and stopped where the other man was standing, staring down at the ground. On top of the trampled leaves lay dozens of spent bullets grouped together in a curved line.

***

"Anyone hurt?" Clay demanded.

DeeAnn checked the primates and shook her head, when Clay turned to Caesare.

"How many would you guess?"

"Maybe two dozen," Caesare answered pointedly, peering intently back into the trees.

"Same here."

Behind them, and without a word, Ronin dropped the pack from his back and withdrew a thin, silver-colored rifle. As he wrapped his hands around the barrel, it automatically grew and extended itself several more inches. A light flashed on both the weapon and his armband indicating they were linked.

"That was a quite a trick back there," Caesare commented over his shoulder. "What else can that thing do?"

Ronin raised his gun. "Many things."

Clay grinned. "Good. Got any more of those in your pack?"

"I do not."

"Worth a shot." He turned to DeeAnn. "We're going to need to split up and get you somewhere safe. There's too many of them for you to stay with us."

"Where is safe?"

Clay pointed along the eastern side of the mountain. "That way. Ronin, can you get them up there? Should be safer."

"Yes."

"Good. Get to higher ground. If they get through us, at least you'll see them coming." Clay turned to DeeAnn. "Still have your phone?"

She checked her pocket. "Right here."

"Good." He pulled out and checked his magazine before sliding it back into the bottom of his M12.

Next to him, Caesare unzipped both bags and handed Clay more magazines, which he stuffed in the side pockets of his pants. Together, they each hefted their packs over both shoulders.

Caesare raised a camouflage Boonie hat and pulled it firmly down over his black hair. With a grizzled expression, he turned to DeeAnn. "Get going. We don't have much time."

DeeAnn hesitated. "Steve…"

"I know, I know, you're gonna miss me. Me too, now get out of here." He then patted Dulce on the head, only to have her lunge forward and wrap her arms around his leg. "Time to go. Run fast, Dulce!"

With sad eyes, Dulce looked back and forth between the men, signing something DeeAnn's vest could not hear.

"Go," Caesare said firmly. "You'll be safe."

Both men watched briefly as the four took off running, led by Ronin, and disappeared into the bushes. Then the two promptly turned back around.

Clay squatted, scanning what he could see from his view

through the trees. "Looked like they were curved around that small ridge."

"What I wouldn't give for a squad of Marines right now."

"You and me both," Clay replied dryly.

"At least we have good cover. But these Berettas aren't much good for distance shots. We gotta stay in tight."

"Agreed." Clay turned and scanned the thick foliage behind them. "And slowly draw them out."

"Try and break 'em up."

"Right." Clay looked at Caesare with steadfast blue eyes. "You ready?"

"As I'll ever be."

***

Ngeze and his men were more militia than anything else. Paid killers, many formerly serving in the Rwandan Patriotic Army, or RPA, now employed by Ngeze to maintain his stranglehold over nearly everything west of the Ruhondo. And what they lacked in experience, they made up for in ruthlessness. They had yet to have someone discover their secret poppy plants and live. Instead their remains were buried in shallow graves after being thoroughly interrogated, until they were sure word had not spread.

For now, Ngeze's men focused their search near the bottom of the ridge, glancing ahead through openings in the forest for signs of movement.

Ngeze himself emerged from the bushes and slowly climbed another small incline, followed by one of his men named Boshoso.

Muscular and dark-skinned, Boshoso was almost a foot taller. The man was Ngeze's right hand, an officer in the RPA before being discharged under "unfavorable circumstances."

As he approached, Boshoso's eyes moved through the trees and back to Ngeze, who merely shook his head.

Boshoso was surprised. He'd never seen anyone escape such an onslaught, nor bullets clustered on the ground like that. Something very different was happening here.

"We are dealing with something else here," his boss said.

"I agree."

"We must be careful. Especially if these are American soldiers."

Boshoso did not answer. Instead, he faced the forest again and allowed his lips to spread into a tight grin. Fighting and killing soldiers was more than just a thrill to him. It was about beating an adversary who had been *trained*. Another predator. And American soldiers were even better. The head of an American soldier was a *trophy*.

***

What Boshoso was blissfully unaware of was that the "trophies" he sought were not common soldiers. Even ex-SEALs remained some of the best trained fighters on the planet, trained to dominate in virtually any terrain. Including areas similar to the one they were now in. And in a heavy forest like Ngeze's, SEALs could not only attack and move in the blink of an eye, they could damn near disappear altogether.

It was a dire realization that came all too soon, when the Americans suddenly opened fire on the first of Ngeze's men. Seemingly from nowhere, the ambush dropped them with a short burst that ended as quickly as it began.

Yelling erupted as the rest of Ngeze's men turned and immediately scattered for cover.

Clay and Caesare were already moving. Retreating and repositioning, they found new cover seconds before several of their attackers rose, opening fire into the thick brush in front of them.

The echoes of the barrage faded into silence while Ngeze's men braced for return fire.

But none came.

Abruptly, Boshoso began shouting at the top of his lungs. Driving the men forward with another salvo, he screamed for them to spread out.

Behind him, Ngeze raised his own rifle and lowered himself behind a boulder. He popped his gun up to eye level and listened.

Another burst of fire erupted, short and controlled. His men began yelling again, before their own fire resumed.

***

Clay and Caesare relocated, now spreading out from one another. This time they waited longer, not only for Ngeze's men to stop shooting, but to eventually press forward in the increasing hope that their fire had finally struck the Americans.

Both Clay and Caesare quietly replaced their magazines. The M12s, while deadly, were no match for the range and accuracy of the AK-47s. Their game had to be as much mental as physical. Their strategy was to lure Ngeze's men closer, within range, where they would strike again and retreat further. A cat and mouse approach. Until all the mice were dead.

They counted six men down, and pressed themselves lower when they heard someone yelling more orders. The unleashing of a new hail of bullets followed, even closer this time.

Dozens of rounds ripped through the large leaves and fronds around them, while others tore huge chucks of bark from nearby trees. One round ricocheted, tearing through Caesare's upper calf. He gritted his teeth and pressed tighter against the boulder in front him.

"Dammit!" he grimaced. "You hear me, Clay?"

"You okay?"

"I'm hit. In the leg. I can still move but I'm under heavy fire!" He tried to look around the rock. "My left is no good and I have no more cover behind me."

"Come towards me," Clay's voice sounded over the radio in Caesare's ear. "Say when."

"Now!" Caesare leaned out and unleashed a blast into the trees where one of Ngeze's men made it to within ten yards of him before being hit in the chest.

Clay rose and joined in, running through his entire magazine to give Caesare enough time to escape.

Sliding down a mound of dirt and surging through a thicket of towering bushes, he found a line of rocks and slid in low behind them.

"You see me?"

"Yeah," Caesare nodded, pulling out an empty magazine and replacing it with another. "One more down."

***

Further back on the ridge, Ngeze was still listening. He could hear the fire from the Americans. Longer bursts now, and moving. There were only a few of them, steadily retreating backward.

Ngeze slowly rose with his own rifle and advanced stealthily along a small ridge to his left. He wound behind a dense group of trees where the terrain then dropped further into the brush and near to where the Americans were shooting from. If he could move quickly, Ngeze might be able to come around far enough to get an angle on one of them.

***

Chunks of the tree exploded behind Caesare, forcing him to duck again. Dozens of 7.62 rounds pelted the ground around him, ripping through branches and spitting dirt into the air.

Hidden from view, Clay emptied his magazine and instinctively reached for another, but this time his hand found nothing. Under fire, he glanced down to find the thick pocket in his pants ripped open, leaving only frayed fabric. He patted the pocket and confirmed it was empty. His extra magazines were gone.

Desperately searching the ground, Clay visually traced his steps backward through the bushes. He couldn't see them. He then checked his spent magazines, hoping for a few unfired rounds. Nothing.

Clay peeked quickly under the fallen tree he was leaning against when several flashes appeared and the ground around him exploded. He instantly pulled his pack off and ripped it open. Finding another magazine, he grabbed it and slapped it in. "I'm getting low."

"Same here."

"Let's smoke 'em!" Clay reached back into his pack and retrieved a small green canister. He yanked the pin, activating the fuse, and threw it as far as he could. With a flash and thunderous bang, a thick stream of gray smoke began filling the air.

***

Almost a hundred feet to the right of Clay, Ngeze hit the ground and tried to catch his breath. He squirmed forward and parted a set of branches with his left hand, scanning. A dense section of vegetation separated him from the Americans' location. To his right, a gray cloud of smoke began billowing upward, gradually cutting off visibility for rest of his men.

His rifle in hand, Ngeze continued moving slowly and slid head first over a rock-strewn embankment. And calmly disappeared into the dense bushes ahead.

***

After throwing his own smoke, Caesare reached for his last remaining magazine. The shots abated briefly, and he could hear the yelling of Ngeze's men drawing closer.

**

Still yelling orders, Boshoso watched the smoke fill the air in front of them. It was spreading quickly. And once it reached them, the murky gases would leave him and the rest of the men too blind to shoot for fear of hitting one another. They had to pick a side, and quickly. He pointed in Caesare's direction.

"Through the smoke! THROUGH THE SMOKE! NOW!"

Simultaneously, the eight remaining men jumped to their feet and ran hard toward Caesare. They continued through the veil of smoke, yelling and opening fire once again.

**

Caesare sought cover behind a severely splintering tree. Bullets continued pummeling deep into the trunk in front of him, drilling, as if trying to make it out the other side.

He focused past the disintegrating tree to see Ngeze's men advance through the smoke and resume firing.

"I've got trouble, Clay!" he yelled.

Caesare's eyes darted backward, looking for a way out. But there wasn't enough cover. They were too close. He wouldn't make it more than a few feet.

The ground was still exploding around him when he double-checked his magazine, verifying it was in, and took a deep breath.

"I think it's time to spray and pray."

With that, he fingered his trigger and twisted onto a knee, ready to leap.

**

Ngeze could now see Clay through the trees. He was

404

close enough to make the shot, given a better line of sight. He inched sideways through the towering bushes, looking for a better angle. He could see part of the American, lying on the ground, still firing at his men—barely fifty feet away.

Easily within range.

He slowly propped himself up onto his elbows, looking to place the American in his sites.

He slowed his breathing, trying to relax. A soft breeze ruffled the fronds next to him, continuing past and through to the plants behind him.

Ngeze stopped, waiting a moment for the wind to settle. The breeze faded, but the leaves behind him were still moving. What started as a low rustling sound gradually grew louder.

Curious, he began to turn when a movement suddenly exploded behind him. In an instant, Ngeze whirled around with his gun, making eye contact with a set of dark eyes. They belonged to a large silverback gorilla, now standing over him.

Powerful eyes that spotted his rifle and immediately became enraged.

***

John Clay whirled to his right, raising his gun the second he heard it—a deeply terrifying, animalistic roar. The awful sound was then followed by a bloodcurdling human scream.

***

Boshoso and his men all turned toward the scream. The voice was unmistakable. It was Ngeze, somewhere in the distance. And when the sounds stopped, they did so with a deadly gargle.

The surviving men all turned to Boshoso, who remained frozen, staring in stunned silence through the trees. Their weapons were still pointed in the direction of the

Americans, the faint wisps of smoke rising faintly from their barrels.

They never noticed the smoke cloud that had passed over and was now fully behind them. Or the glimpses of movement materializing from the other side.

It was not until one of Ngeze's men looked back again at Boshoso that he saw the impending danger. And tried to warn the others.

Behind them, emerging from the smoke, were silverbacks. Dozens of them. All running while leaning forward in attack position, atop powerful arms, and baring huge, terrifying teeth.

Before Boshoso could speak, the gorillas exploded forward into a blur of speed and strength, closing the short distance in an instant.

107

Ronin stepped into view as Clay and Caesare emerged from the cluster of boulders below him, lumbering in their steps and with Caesare limping slightly. Their weapons were nowhere to be seen and their packs now bounced loosely upon their backs with each step.

The shorter Ronin wore little expression. Still, he kept his own weapon pointed past them until they climbed high enough to where he stood. "Are you injured?"

"Not too bad. Could've been a hell of a lot worse."

DeeAnn slowly rose into view from where she was hiding, her eyes wide with concern. "What…happened?"

Both men looked at her, then each other, pausing for a moment before Clay shook his head. "Don't ask. Let's just say the coast is clear…for quite a while. Are you guys all right?"

"Yes," Ronin responded. "We are unharmed."

Clay merely nodded.

Dulce and Dexter gradually appeared as well, poking their furry heads up slightly to the left of DeeAnn, but remaining cautiously at a distance. They had all obviously heard the chilling sounds from below.

Clay lowered himself onto a rock, still breathing heavily. No one spoke until Caesare broke the silence, while staring further up the mountain. "Uh…Clay," he uttered, motioning with his head, "look familiar?"

Clay raised his head to see Caesare peering uphill at several large boulders—reminiscent of what they had seen in South America.

108

When the giant vault was finally opened, the entry looked nearly identical to the one they'd found in Guyana. A smooth, sheared face of cliff wall hosted a door several feet as thick as it was wide, cut into solid rock. Even the electromagnetic switch worked the same.

Inside, several inches of thick dust covered the rock granite floor where hundreds of huge glass pillars had stood for more than a millennium, each full of a green liquid swirling around chains of tiny spheres.

But what was different about this vault was that it was bigger. Much bigger. The sunlight from the doorway lit only a small portion of the cavern, but it was obvious to both Clay and Caesare that this one held more.

And the walls looked...different.

At a point just before the light's rays faded back into darkness, the southernmost wall revealed some sort of carving. It appeared to be a set of symbols with lines, or seams, down each edge. As if it was some of kind of rectangular panel. Or cover.

"Oh my God," whispered DeeAnn. "This is what you found before?"

"Yes."

She approached one of the green glass pillars and studied it. "What are those things—" Her sentence faded before she could finish it. She looked closer and nodded thoughtfully. "Those are the embryos."

Clay turned around and looked at Caesare. "This place is definitely bigger."

"Yep."

"You see this on the wall?"

Caesare squinted and peered at the strange markings. "I

didn't see that in the other one."

"Neither did I."

They found themselves interrupted by another voice from the doorway. The voice was similar to Ronin's and one which all three of them recognized.

"You have done well, John Clay."

They turned to see several distinct figures, partially silhouetted by the sunlight outside.

Clay's lip curled upwards as he stepped away from the wall. "Well, hello there, Palin. Nice to see you again."

"As it is you," the older man replied. "And of course, Mr. Caesare and Ms. Draper."

Caesare stepped closer and shook his hand with a smile. "I guess we should thank you for sending Ronin."

Palin peered at his soldier. "It was not entirely magnanimous, I'm afraid."

"No, I suppose it wasn't."

Palin looked away and studied the giant pillars, reaching high toward the rock ceiling. "This is what you found with your first vault?"

"More or less."

His eyes eventually returned to Clay. "We are grateful to you. You have again come through in our hour of need."

Clay grinned. "Well, it wasn't entirely magnanimous."

"So what now?" Caesare asked, leaning on his good leg. One of Palin's men moved past, kneeling down behind him, examining his bandaged leg.

"Now our work continues," Palin answered. "We will keep trying to save what's left of our planet. Hopefully we can achieve a greater foothold by studying and replicating the liquid that you found. Your last location was destroyed too quickly."

"You can take that up with the Chinese."

Clay glanced back to the pillars. "Why did they do it, Palin? Why would an alien race leave behind such a large supply of their DNA?"

Palin considered the question. "I do not know. Perhaps

409

as a safety net for their own future. Or perhaps something else. Whatever the reason, you would do well to remember what I told you. Your Earth is unique. It is not the only habitable planet, there are many thousands, but your planet contains some unique properties."

"We know, the water," Clay replied.

"The amount of water," Palin corrected. "Yes. That is one. Both of our planets are also on the edge of the galaxy, where looming astronomical threats are rarer. And each with an evolution that is still relatively immature, particularly yours. Because of these things, your planet is valuable. A water world ripe for the picking." Palin glanced down at Dulce as she and Dexter both peeked out curiously from behind DeeAnn.

Palin continued. "Your Earth is a beacon. It has been for a very long time. What has been left here should come as no surprise. And is likely not the only one. Your planet is sure to have been noticed by many other races. Some more capable than others of reaching it."

Caesare glanced at Clay. "Wait. You're saying there's more?"

Palin shrugged. "Most likely."

Clay nodded thoughtfully. "So…what do you need from this vault?"

Palin looked back at his men. "We will not disturb it. It does not belong to us. We will study it only."

"And try to reverse engineer the liquid?"

"Ideally. Our evolutions are not so far apart as you might expect. Only one or two hundred years. The liquid you found here is an advancement, even to us."

"A hundred years doesn't seem like much."

"It is not," Palin mused. "But more than enough for many more mistakes. Ones which you have yet to make."

"Well, let's hope we can learn from you," Clay replied.

"Perhaps. Unfortunately, neither of our races seems to learn lessons as well as we should. It is why history, for both of us, repeats so frequently."

Clay thought about Palin's words. "We need to hide this, Palin. Better than we did before. And stop the leaking."

With hands behind his back, Palin nodded. "No one shall find this."

"We'll also need a way to contact you."

"Other than waiting for you to follow us," Caesare joked.

Palin grinned. "Of course." He nodded at Ronin. "You will no longer have difficulty contacting us."

There was a short silence and just as Clay was about to respond, Caesare's satellite phone rang. He stepped closer to the doorway and slid the pack off his back to fish it out.

"Hey, Will. Is that you?"

Caesare paused, listening. As he did, the cheeky expression suddenly disappeared from his face. He looked immediately to Clay. "The *Pathfinder* was attacked."

"What!"

He continued listening. "There were casualties," he added somberly.

Clay's first thought was instant: *Alison.*

Caesare's eyes softened. He pulled the phone away from his own ear and reached forward, offering it to Clay. "I think you'd better take this."

A look of panic washed over Clay, and he immediately grabbed the phone. "Will?"

There was a rustling on the other end before another voice spoke. It was weak.

"Hey, handsome."

"Alison! Are you okay?"

"Yeah, I'm okay. Just suffering from some decompression sickness."

"How bad?"

"Dr. Kanna doesn't think there's anything permanent. But I'm going to need a lot of rest."

Clay pressed his hand over his mouth with relief. "Thank God."

411

"No, thank Dirk," she joked faintly. She paused before continuing. "John, I need to ask you a question."

"Anything."

On the other end, Alison glanced wearily up at Will Borger, now sitting next to her bed. "How fast do you think you can get to an airport?"

Clay's eyes turned intently to Palin, who stood before him, listening. "I'd say pretty damn fast!"

It was under the bright glow of his headlights that Vic Mooney saw the outline. As he drew nearer, the image crystallized and confirmed his first impression. It was the image of a person sitting on the side of the road, leaning against a tree.

Had his truck been full, he would never have been able to stop in time. But instead, his air brakes shuddered and smoked as he slowed the red semitrailer truck down enough to get a clearer picture—just as the figure passed beneath his side mirror and out of view.

After another two hundred feet, Mooney's brakes brought the semi to an abrupt stop at which point he immediately turned on his emergency lights. He flung the door open and jumped down onto the pavement. Trotting to the back of his rig, he found with a sudden sense of dread that the person had not moved.

In the distance and under the glow of flashing yellow lights, he could clearly see it was the figure of a teenage girl––with her head down.

He raised his baseball cap higher onto his balding head and eased closer to examine the girl. She wasn't moving. He reached out and gently shook her.

No response.

He shook her again. This time the girl's head stirred.

***

Li Na Wei rolled her head and squinted almost imperceptibly at the man staring down at her from above. His complexion looked western, maybe like an American.

The only word she could manage was "help."

Vic Mooney was not American. He was a *Canuck*. Or more commonly known, a Canadian.

A forest planner by trade, Mooney was born and raised in British Columbia. There, he later retired and signed on as a contractor with one of the country's largest shipping companies. He now spent six months out of the year driving trucks in Northeastern China and the other half fishing giant white sturgeon along Canada's famed Fraser River.

Just an hour after stumbling upon Li Na, he stood in a shabby hallway, facing a small office with a clear glass window.

"So, what the hell are we supposed to do?! Call the police? Or a hospital?"

Sixty-one-year-old Mooney stared at his friend and fellow Canuck, Brian Armsworth, without an answer. "The girl needs help."

"We don't even know who she is!"

Mooney looked at him sarcastically. "Do you know who *anyone* in China is?"

Armsworth, slightly shorter with a full gray beard, frowned. "Not really."

"Look, man. I don't know who she is either. But the girl needs help. Look at her."

Armsworth glanced again through the glass at Li Na, lying still on a ratty couch. "Okay, so she's lost. And hungry."

"Are you kidding? I found her on the side of the road for Christ's sake. Unconscious. So, unless you want to take her back—"

"Fine! Fine," Armsworth said, shaking his head. "So

what did she say?"

"She said her father was murdered. And someone is trying to kill her too. Been chasing her for days."

"And how do you know that's true?"

"I don't. But she's scared to death and stinks to high heaven. What kind of conclusion would you draw?"

"Where is she from?"

Mooney shrugged. "No idea."

"What's her name?"

"Li Na."

"Li Na what?"

"Don't know."

Armsworth frowned suspiciously at Mooney. "So why are you making this my problem?"

"Because the *Jasper* is leaving tonight."

Armsworth's eyes suddenly shot open. "Oh, hell no! No way!"

"What?"

"Not on my ship!"

"Brian, look at her," Mooney motioned through the window again. "Look at her! This girl's in trouble. Do you think she'd be looking like that for fun?"

"Who the hell knows with kids these days? Maybe she's on crack."

"Maybe she's not."

Armsworth was still shaking his head. "Then who's chasing her?"

"She said some soldiers. The Army, maybe?"

"The government?! My God, you're out of your gourd! You want to get mixed up with the government? And not just any government, the *Chinese* government?"

Mooney shrugged again. "She's got a passport."

"Oh, well, that's different then. If she's got a *passport*!"

"And she's willing to pay her way."

"I don't care."

Mooney folded his arms. "Yes, you do."

"No, I don't."

"Yes, you do."

Armsworth shook his head.

"I'll tell you why you care. Because you know she's in trouble. Just like I do. And just like me, you've seen some really shitty things over here. Bad things that make your damn skin crawl."

Armsworth didn't answer.

"And you know why else? Because you have daughters."

Armsworth looked sternly back at Mooney.

"You have daughters, just like me. Grown and moved out, or in college. Where we can't protect them." Mooney stared hard at his friend. "Now you stand there and you tell me that if one of *your* girls was in trouble, and I mean real trouble, that you wouldn't be *praying to God* for someone to help them. To help your little girl if they were able to."

Armsworth tried to shake his head.

"Say it. Say that you would rather have your daughter fend for herself. Against who knows what? And over here, of all places."

The aging captain stopped shaking his head and stared again at Li Na through the glass.

"Christ, she's unconscious."

"She comes and goes. I think she's exhausted." Mooney raised his hand and showed Armsworth a wad of Chinese Yuan. "She can pay."

"Get that out of my face," Armsworth growled.

"If you get caught, all you have to say is that she's a stowaway. Sneaking aboard some random cargo ship. Plausible deniability."

Armsworth turned and looked out of another much larger window, one that faced out over the endless shipping docks of Shenyang. Dozens of people moved back and forth, many pushing pallets of supplies. None were paying attention to them in the small office.

"This is insane."

Mooney raised his eyebrows. "Is it? Do we really have

416

that much to lose?"

Armsworth was not amused. "That's what people usually say right before things go horribly wrong."

There was very little known about China's new Shijian 16 satellites. Thought by most western analysts to enhance the communist country's electronic eavesdropping efforts, the true capabilities of China's growing number of spy satellites were anything but clear.

The unfortunate truth was that the satellites were far more powerful than China's adversaries suspected. And one of them had just been commandeered by the Ministry of State Security in an attempt to find out exactly who had picked up Li Na Wei on the side of the road.

The girl had already been granted her first stroke of luck in being picked up before Peng and his team could reach her. The second was *when* it happened—at night, when even the best satellite technology was much less effective.

It would take hours to not just discern the vehicle, in this case a truck. Then to attempt to follow its signature through the vast maze and glaringly bright lights of Shenyang's shipping docks, scattered along the mouth of the Liaohe River, would be a painstaking process.

It would need to be carried out frame by frame, by a team of the MSS's sharpest technicians. But find it, they did. And hours later, MSS agents descended upon the Canadian shipping dock and all of its workers. Including a stunned Victor Mooney.

Sheng Lam peered down through the helicopter's side window at the ship below, steadily growing larger upon a sea of blackness. The *Jasper's* navigation lights were clearly visible at a distance, as was the muted yellowish glow from the ship's deck lights and wheelhouse.

Inside the aircraft, Lam glanced at his watch. It was far later than he'd hoped. It took several long hours but the MSS had found her. Not just the dock where the truck had stopped, but the ship itself—now trying to escape Chinese waters, and failing.

This time there was nowhere to go. Nowhere for her to run.

Lam turned to see the squad's leader watching him. His intuition easily interpreted the message in Peng's tired, unblinking eyes. Once they had the girl, Sheng Lam would not be aboard the flight back.

***

Captain Armsworth was standing in front of his wheelhouse in the brisk air, watching the helicopter approach and then hover over the only open area of the ship. Landing the Mi-17 helicopter was also a tight fit, but the pilot managed to touch down expertly with a small controlled bounce. At that point, two of Armsworth's crew ran forward quickly with heavy chains to secure the aircraft.

No sooner had the helicopter's bounce faded than the green door was slid open and armed soldiers began exiting.

***

Followed by his first officer, Armsworth calmly descended the two decks and reached the main. The Chinese soldiers approached with guns raised.

Peng spoke directly to Armsworth's first officer, who was of Chinese descent but was a man who had little sympathy for or loyalty to the Chinese government.

"Where is she?" Peng shouted over the wind.

"What is the meaning of this?!" the officer demanded. "Where is who?"

"The GIRL!"

"What girl?"

Peng's eyes raged. "Do not play games with me! The teenage girl you brought aboard in Shenyang!"

"There are no females aboard."

Armsworth listened to the garbled exchange and moved his eyes from soldier to soldier, stopping on Lam. The smaller, wirier man seemed especially agitated. Even angry.

His first officer immediately grew quiet when Peng pushed the barrel of his rifle into the man's chest. "I *know* she is aboard!"

The officer turned silently to Armsworth who also raised his hands. "There is no one like that aboard. Search the ship."

"I WILL search the ship!" growled Peng. "And when I find her, you will be arrested for treason!"

Without a word, both men stepped aside, allowing the soldiers to pass. Peng shouted orders to his men and pointed at the cargo holds.

The two calmly watched as all six soldiers disappeared. They remained where they were standing, looking at one another. When Peng's voice finally faded, Armsworth looked at his own watch.

The Chinese soldiers would find nothing. Not because they had hidden her. But because they were exactly thirty-eight minutes too late.

420

113

The UH-60J was a variant of the Mitsubishi H-60 twin-turboshaft helicopter and designed specifically for search and rescue missions for the Japan Air Self-Defense Force. It was also somewhat fitting that the white UH-60J they were on, speeding less than twenty feet above the ocean swells, was based on the United States' *Sea King* helicopters.

Li Na's unconscious body was laid out across the rear of the cabin, held steady by Steve Caesare, while John Clay readied the syringe.

"Now just like I said…" The voice they heard over their aviation headsets belonged to Amir Kanna, the ship doctor aboard the *Pathfinder*. "First the bolus injection *then* the maintenance infusion."

Clay followed the doctor's instructions carefully, administering both. Caesare then assisted by activating the small multichannel infusion pump to control the delivery. Together, they watched a portable EEG monitor and waited for the brain wave pattern described by Kanna.

"Okay," Clay finally announced. "We're beginning to see the pattern."

"Good," Kanna replied. "Now listen, the thiopental slows the metabolic rate of the brain tissue, but it also depresses blood pressure. Tell me what it is now."

Caesare inflated the sleeve and counted. "Ninety-one over sixty."

"Okay. Keep monitoring and tell me if it falls significantly below that. How long until you reach Busan?"

Clay looked at his watch. "About fifty minutes."

"Good. We'll have a team standing by."

***

On the other end of the call, Kanna stared across the table at Neely Lawton, who looked just as worried.

"Do you think it will work?"

He shook his head. "I don't know. It's a long shot."

It was more than a long shot. Medically induced comas were typically little more than last ditch attempts to save a patient's life. And it was literally the only idea they had to save Li Na—to shut her brain down and force it to rest.

"The problem," Kanna said, "is that keeping someone under for too long brings on more problems—worse than just low blood pressure. Under a coma, the entire body begins to deteriorate quickly. If this bacterium she has cannot counterbalance that…"

"It may not be enough," finished Neely gravely.

"Correct." Kanna leaned into the phone. "Gentlemen, keep monitoring. I'll call you back in ten minutes."

***

"Roger that." The call ended and both men leaned back.

Clay stared down at Li Na, then continued watching the monitor before finally turning to Caesare. "How do you think he knew?"

"How who knew what?"

"How did Borger know she was on that ship?"

Caesare blinked, thinking, then shook his head. "Beats the hell out of me."

114

Alone in her lab, Neely sat on a metal stool in silence, staring at the empty refrigerator. It had been the only way she could think to limit the attack on the ship, to end the Russians' search and keep them from killing more of the ship's crew.

Let them have the bacteria. Leave it in plain sight and let them have it all. At least then they would stop looking.

And they did. They took it and fled to the *Valant*, where it was subsequently destroyed, along with the entire Russian team. And where Les Gorski lost his life.

Through the window, she watched the fire, still raging. Blanketing the entire area beneath an eerie yellow glow.

Outside, the rest of the crew moved about the ship, assessing the damage. The lights of two Navy battleships approached steadily in the distance.

Neely exhaled and gently reached into her pocket, where she pulled out a flat, round object—a sealed petri dish filled with a pink culture.

She held the container up and studied it under the light. The Russian soldiers might have noticed if some of the test tubes were missing. But they would never have looked for her petri dishes.

***

When the sun rose that next morning, Neely was still in her lab, now studying a large monitor on the table in front of her. What she found was muted by the somber mood throughout the ship, leaving her staring quietly at the readout for a long time.

On the stern, Alison sat quietly with her legs gently

dangling over the starboard edge. With both a safety line and arm wrapped around a large stanchion, she stared out over the glimmering water. The crew worked behind her, repairing their largest winch. She ignored the loud clanging of metal and smiled as some of the first dolphins appeared above the water.

She never moved, not even as Neely approached and sat down beside her.

"You okay?"

Alison nodded.

"Waiting for Dirk and Sally?"

She nodded again. After a long silence, Alison spoke with a soft voice. "How's Li Na?"

"Still stable. For now."

"Good."

Together the pair sat, appreciating the tranquility, as the dolphins played. After several minutes, Neely broke the silence.

"So…there's something interesting."

"What's that?"

"I got back some of the sequencing results for the mice."

"The ones that all died?"

"Yes."

Alison looked at Neely expectantly. "And?"

"Some of their DNA is different."

"That's significant, right?"

Neely nodded. "Several genes that are normally dormant were changed. Most likely by the bacteria."

"Changed how?"

"Instead of remaining dormant, like in other mice, they appear to have been reactivated, or switched back on."

"But without them being alive—"

"I don't know what those genes did," acknowledged Neely. Thoughtfully, she continued staring out over the water. "But I'm wondering if the same thing has happened to Li Na."

Alison had just turned to look at her, concerned, when

some of the dolphins began speaking to her. She spun back to see Dirk and Sally peering at her from the water.

She reached down and turned on her vest.

"Hello, Dirk. Hello, Sally."

Hello Alison.

Sally swam closer. *You hurt.*

Alison managed a grin. "I'll be okay. Thanks to Dirk."

Dirk promptly rose up out of the water, slapping his flippers before falling backward. *Me love Alison.*

From the edge of the ship, she peered at him curiously. He had never said that before. "I love you too, Dirk. And Sally too."

Alison looked down to see Sally still watching her. "What is it, Sally?"

Me tell Alison.

Alison wrinkled her brow. "Tell me what?"

What Sally said next took both Alison and Neely by surprise—something neither one had expected, but in hindsight, would seem quite obvious. *Me mother.*

115

Captain Zhirov moved through the hatches in near-total darkness, feeling his way along the familiar metal corridors until he reached the control room. The emergency lighting was barely functioning and what little remained of their reserve power was dwindling rapidly. Which meant the ship was completely paralyzed.

Nothing was working. The engines were dead, communications and sonar gone. Even the ventilation systems could no longer scrub the deadly carbon dioxide from their air. It was as if all the energy had been completely sucked out of the sub. They were stuck to the bottom of the ocean floor, unable to move and now facing a death sentence if they did not begin emergency evacuation immediately.

The effectiveness of their submarine escape training would prove to be the difference between life and death. And Zhirov was thankful they were not any deeper.

Several of his officers were already in the control room, awaiting the order they all knew was coming—to abandon ship.

Zhirov opened his mouth to speak but stopped when he heard the noise. It was a loud and slow scraping sound, coming from above. The sound of metal against metal.

The Russian crew all peered up, listening. After a short silence, another series of sounds reverberated through the sub's hull—bumps and bangs followed by more scrapes.

It was the Americans.

After a couple minutes, a much more distinct pattern began to resonate, loudly and repeatedly. They were using Morse code.

Several of the officers began deciphering the letters, forming words in their head until the short message ended. Clear and concise, and sarcastic.

Knock knock. Guess who.

116

Several hours later, Dima Belov sat pensively, somewhat uncomfortable in his cold metal chair. His hands were cuffed behind his back.

In front of him sat a young American officer and his interrogator, flanked on both sides by three captains, judging by their insignias.

After a barrage of questions, Belov had revealed nothing. Not even his name. Instead he wore a bemused expression, studying the men in front of him. They were inconsequential. The real interrogation would begin later, when he was transported off the ship. For now, he was merely buying time.

He needed more leverage. He already had information the Americans would undoubtedly find valuable—he knew that. But nothing that would keep him out of prison.

What he needed was something better. Something he would soon have, with just a little more time.

After another twenty minutes had passed, the old man finally leaned forward and spoke in a thick Russian accent.

"What day is it?"

The captains looked at each other for agreement before nodding to the younger officer.

"Friday."

"What time?"

"About three thirty."

"Morning?"

The younger man shook his head. "Afternoon."

To that, Belov simply nodded. It was all he needed to know, and those would be the only words they would get from him. For now.

Because what none of the men sitting before him

realized was that Belov knew much more than anyone thought. He knew all about the *Pathfinder* ship, the original discovery, and the bacteria. He knew about the *Valant* acting as a decoy. But he knew much more. He also knew about the team secretly reporting to their Joint Chief of Staff, Admiral James Langford. He knew of the men named John Clay and Steve Caesare, and more importantly, he knew about Puerto Rico.

He knew about the research center and the computer system they were hiding—the one that allowed them to speak to the dolphins. And how integral that computer system and its data were to the Americans' secrets.

He also knew that, in a matter of hours, they were about to lose it.

***

Ironically, the team was not Russian. They were German—former members of CASCOPE. Mercenaries, unattached and hired out to the highest bidder. And utterly ruthless in their indifference.

They had been hired by Belov to commandeer a computer system at a civilian facility, and by the looks of it, one that was poorly guarded.

They had already studied the location several days before. And now, lacking any word from Belov, they had their signal to execute.

As evening fell, the moving van pulled into the empty parking lot and stopped near the side entrance. Two of the Germans rolled the cargo door up, jumping down onto the cracked asphalt as the truck began backing up. Slowly and silently.

One of the men held up his hand, and the truck lurched to a stop. Two more immediately exited the cab carrying rifles, while the first two grabbed theirs from inside the cargo area.

They were through the door in twelve seconds, easily

disabling the alarm on the other side. Without a word, they moved smoothly and efficiently down the hall, quickly reaching the computer area.

There, all four stopped and stared into the dimly lit room, then looked at each other. Dozens of vertical server racks lined the entire wall, all firmly bolted into place.

But each one...was empty.

117

Will Borger shoved the gearshift into second, causing the truck's giant engine to roar as the vehicle lurched, climbing the windy road of Highway 10. With a steep mountain on one side, the narrow shoulder completely fell off on the other. There was only darkness, dotted by the faint flickering lights of Puerto Rico's western coastline. Ahead, the truck's headlights illuminated the winding road, which only seemed to steepen the further they drove.

In the end, it was not Borger who figured out where to hide IMIS. It was Lee Kenwood, the twenty-five-year-old computer engineer sitting next to him in the passenger seat.

And even Borger had to admit, the solution was brilliant.

"So, kid," he said, shifting gears again, "you study any astronomy?"

"Um, not too much," Lee responded. "A little."

The older Borger nodded. "You ever hear of the Drake Equation?"

Lee shook his head. "No."

"It's a logistical argument made by a guy named Frank Drake back in the sixties. An argument to realistically estimate the number of intelligent civilizations in the universe."

"That sounds interesting."

Borger nodded, gripping the large steering wheel with both hands. "It is. The bottom line is that there's predictably a *lot* of alien life out there. And a lot of it has probably been around for a while."

"Makes sense."

Borger grinned at his companion across the darkened cab. He liked this kid. "So then answer this—if there's so damned many, why haven't we seen any...until now?"

Lee thought about the question. "A lot of people think they have."

"Maybe some. But most of 'em are quacks," Borger retorted. "Some events, like that Nome Alaska thing, may be true. But for the rest, there's no definitive proof. No evidence. Except what *we've* just found. Any of that strike you as a little odd?"

"Uh…"

"What I'm saying is in all this time, and with all these civilizations out there, how can we have only been visited by one or two?"

"You mean the vaults."

"Right. Two official footprints out of everything out there. To me, that means either they're the only ones to have come here…or those are the only two we've found."

Lee looked at Borger as he slowed and navigated a tight turn. "You think there's more?"

"What I think," he replied, "is that humans have been crawling all over this planet for an awfully long time. We can't be the first ones to find something. I mean, look at those vaults. They've apparently been here since our ancestors were the same as Dulce's. Could they really be the *only* things?"

"It doesn't seem like it."

"No, it doesn't. The reason I'm bringing this up is because of what you were able to do not too long ago, having your IMIS system decipher some of those old hieroglyphs. The ones that helped us locate the first vault in Guyana."

"Right. The Mayan symbols."

"So," Borger continued, "what if there are more finds out there, still hidden? And we just haven't found them yet. And what if other discoveries *were* written down by people or cultures that were here a long time ago?"

"I hadn't thought of that."

Borger motioned toward the back of the truck. "And if there are, maybe this computer system of yours can find them."

Lee was now staring at Borger, fascinated. "I think it could."

"I was hoping you'd say that. And there's something else too."

"What's that?"

"Ancient writings are a good place to start. But there are a lot more secrets out there than that. Things not nearly as old."

Lee raised an eyebrow. "I don't think I'm following."

"What I mean is that there are all kinds of secrets in this world. Would you agree?"

"Of course."

"And who has more secret data buried than anyone else?"

Lee thought for a minute. "The NSA?"

"Bingo."

"You want to break into the NSA?"

Borger grinned. "Break-in is such a negative word. I was thinking more like…perusing."

"You want to peruse the NSA's data?"

"Well, it's not that easy. The NSA's data is encrypted."

"Then I'm not following again."

"What a lot of people don't know is that for years the NSA has been in the business of collecting everything on the internet. Calls, text messages, emails, *everything*. And they've been doing it for a long time. Forty years almost."

"Okay."

"Like I said, it's all encrypted. But here's the thing— encryption, just like any technology, evolves. So what we have today is not what we had before. Computers, networks, cars, light bulbs, everything."

"Including encryption algorithms," added Lee.

"Exactly. The encryption these days is uncrackable."

This time, Lee smiled. "But not the encryption used decades ago."

"Right again," Borger nodded. "Even the encryption

used ten years ago is not nearly as strong."

"So, a lot of the NSA's data is not crackable," Lee said.

"But an awful lot of it *is*."

"And you want to know if IMIS can do it."

"No," Borger replied. "I want to know if IMIS can be *taught* to crack it."

Lee was silent, staring out the windshield into the darkness as they drove. Borger shifted in his seat, waiting for Lee's answer.

"Yes. I think it can. With enough computing power."

Now Borger was the one smiling in the glow of the truck's dashboard. "Have you heard of Hewlett Packard's new computing platform called *The Machine*?"

"No."

"It's powerful. *Really powerful.*"

A wide grin spread across Lee's face. After several minutes of silence, he looked at Borger. "So what's the plan?"

"First off, we'd need some help."

***

The international terminal at Puerto Rico's Luiz Muñoz Marín Airport was busy. It wasn't surprising for a Friday evening. Thousands of passengers were walking briskly to and from the dozens of gates in what could only be described as a controlled mob—trying either to make their flights or thankful to finally be off one.

One such person, twenty-something and wearing wrinkled clothes, looked up and down the wide corridors for signs pointing to baggage claim.

His straight, dark hair hung disheveled and down past matching eyebrows, stopping just short of his tired but youthful eyes. The young man patted his jacket to make sure the passport was still there and fell in behind a throng of people headed in the same direction.

The Chinese passport listed his real name as Yong

Yang—a name that had been thoroughly scrubbed from China's government records. But not by them, by Yang himself. In an attempt to save his own life.

It was his only option left. To disappear. He knew too much—about the Chinese government. About their secrets, and about their search for Li Na Wei—the daughter of General Wei.

After all, he was part of the group who had been searching for her and was one of the best hackers China had ever seen. Until they forced him to flee for his own survival. Leaving the young man known by the rest of the hacker community as *M0ngol* with a new agenda.

Now that he was on western soil, his first priority was to locate the man known as Will Borger—the one to whom M0ngol himself had revealed Li Na's location, aboard the Canadian container ship.

∗∗∗

Lee Kenwood glanced at the shadowy hills crawling past them, illuminated only by a soft glow of moonlight shining diligently between the scattered clouds above them.

Ambient light made both Lee and Will Borger thankful as they now attempted to navigate an even tighter, and much windier, dirt road. With the headlights off, the two peered intently through the windshield, using the faint moonlight to keep them on the treacherous road.

The screen on Lee's phone illuminated and he looked down to check the incoming message. With a frown, he turned to Borger.

"They found Mr. Lightfoot's body."

Will Borger dropped his head solemnly. "What about Tay?"

"No word on Mr. Tay yet."

Borger shook his head, disheartened. Will focused instead on keeping the truck's speed under ten miles per hour, reducing as much of the bouncing and shaking as he could. The IMIS servers in the back were heavy, yet extremely sensitive to sudden jarring.

They rounded another small turn, continuing stealthily along the perimeter of the giant complex. Fortunately for them, this was the one federal site in Puerto Rico that would never have floodlights.

The project's construction had begun in the 1960s, funded by the U.S. Department of Defense, and built to study the planet's ionosphere. The famed Arecibo Observatory was repurposed into a national research center in 1969 after being taken over by the National Science Foundation. It relied not only on the uniqueness of Puerto Rico's limestone sinkholes, but also the island's proximity to the equator. Not only did it hold the record of being the largest single-dish radio telescope on Earth for the last four decades, it also had the honor of producing some of the most historic radio-based observations in human history.

After almost twenty minutes, the truck wound its way through the last turn and slowed when it saw the huge chain-link fence standing twenty-foot-tall. Stretching across their path, the fence was constructed with strands of barbed wire across the top, and what appeared to be a small, narrow maintenance entrance in the center. The thick poles on each side of the double gate reached the full height of the fence, all topped with more barbed wiring.

Below, at ground level, a human shadow stood just inside the fencing. Lee glanced at Borger before opening the passenger door and sliding down onto the ground. He walked past the truck's hood and idling engine as he approached the gate.

When he got close, the shadowed figure pulled one side of the gate open and stepped out. As Lee drew near, he stopped just a few feet from the older man, whose gray and white hair was easily visible in the moonlight. A dark-blue hat matched the rest of his uniform.

Lee grinned. "Hello, Mr. Diaz."

The guard smiled and closed the gap between them.

"Good evening, Lee." The man embraced him and then looked past to the truck with Will Borger sitting in the driver's seat. "I was beginning to worry."

"Sorry, sir."

Diaz frowned. "I told you, no more sir."

"Right. Sorry."

"Is this everything?"

"It should be."

Diaz nodded approvingly and motioned Lee in the direction of the complex. Together, they pushed both large chain-link gates all the way open, providing a path for Borger and the truck.

Borger eased forward, rolling slowly past them before the two promptly closed the gates behind him. Diaz locked them again and walked to the front of the truck where Borger was rolling down his window.

"Keep your lights off and follow me." Without another word, the senior man continued forward and climbed into a nearby Ford Explorer.

Next to Borger, Lee gently pulled his door closed and watched keenly as they accelerated.

***

Their destination was less than a quarter mile away. It was one of a dozen of the complex's maintenance buildings, standing twelve feet tall and made of thick concrete walls for improved insulation. The place felt surprisingly cool when the three men finally stepped inside.

"Used to have a bunch of outdated weather equipment running out here," Diaz said. "Until a couple years ago, when a few of the buildings were cleaned out. Rumor has it that the old equipment was getting too expensive to operate. None of these buildings have been used since. And this one's the furthest away."

Using their phones as small flashlights, both Will and Lee scanned the walls, noting the power circuits near the floor.

It was the perfect location. The biggest challenge in moving the IMIS system had not been finding a secure facility. There were thousands of places they could have hidden it, tucked away from prying eyes or from all of civilization, for that matter.

Nor was it electricity. That had been easy too.

Their biggest problem was connectivity—having a communication link to the system. Even though Borger could bundle enough satellite links to make it work anywhere, the signal would still be traceable. And relatively easily for someone with the right skills.

This made Arecibo the perfect camouflage. It housed a three-hundred-meter dish, used twenty-four hours a day, nonstop. Numerous pieces of equipment, including the interferometer signaling and several more radio and optical observatories located around it. All of these devices receiving and transmitting different signals and frequencies would make it easy for Will and Lee's satellite link to be lost in the noise. The frequencies would never interfere, and even *if* noticed, would likely be written off as residential bleed-over from a nearby cabin or motorhome.

The perfect place to hide IMIS was in plain sight. And all made possible by one of the facility's senior security guards named Luis Diaz—the father of their lost friend and colleague, Juan Diaz.

118

President Carr finished scribbling his signature on several documents before glancing up after the door to the Oval Office opened. Short and stocky, his chief of staff, Bill Mason, entered without a word. He was followed by Admiral Langford and Defense Secretary Miller.

The president sat up and placed his pen down; he then watched as all three men approached and took seats around his desk. Langford leaned forward and slid a large, sealed manila envelope over the desktop, which Carr picked up and opened. He slid the papers out, placed them on top of the envelope, and began reading in silence.

After a few minutes, he raised his eyes and looked heavily at Langford and Miller. "You're joking."

"No, sir."

The president placed his hands on his desk. "You're actually serious. A marine preserve?"

Langford and Miller both nodded.

"That's how you plan to hide this alien ship, in the ocean, by turning it into some kind of sanctuary?"

"That's right."

"Are you two *that* short of sleep?" Carr asked. "This is what you've come up with?"

Langford didn't flinch. "There are hundreds of marine and coastal preserves already. Each sitting president in the last twenty-five years has dedicated funds to increase that number. You would be no different."

"Wouldn't that attract attention?"

"Not really. The newest and largest preserve is the Pacific Remote Islands Marine National Monument south of Midway. It now covers an area that is three-quarters of a million square miles. We would only need a tiny fraction of that near Trinidad."

The president shook his head. "And what exactly would we be protecting?"

"Turtles," Miller answered.

"Turtles?"

"Several species of turtles are endangered in the Caribbean Sea. Loggerheads and Hawksbills primarily."

"And these turtles are in the same location as our ship?"

"No."

"No?"

Langford shrugged. "We don't need them to be. We merely need to claim that they are."

Carr thought it over, leaning back in his chair and folding his arms. "Well, it's damn big ocean. I'm sure there's *got* to be a few turtles somewhere in the area."

"How much money?" the chief of staff asked.

"Not much. Maybe fifty million. Enough to make it appear legitimate."

"And you think *this* will keep everyone away?"

"We think it will attract the least amount of attention," Miller replied. "It will also make the environmentalists happy and allow them to focus their energy elsewhere. While we continue our work."

President Carr exhaled. "This is the best idea we have?"

"This is the only idea," Langford said. "The ship cannot be moved, at least not now. We need more time to get attention away from the area. It would also provide a logical reason for us to have a research vessel permanently located there."

Mason shook his head. "I don't like it. Those are international waters. We don't have the authority to commandeer that area. It's likely to start a political fight that we don't need right now."

Langford stared at the chief of staff. "Well, we're all ears for your idea."

Mason did not answer.

"Look," Langford turned back to the president. "These

are small islands we're talking about. If we must incentivize a few countries, then we incentivize them. We can more than make it worth their while."

"And Venezuela?"

"They need help more than anyone right now. *From* anyone. If we make the offer attractive enough, they should jump at it."

The president pressed his fingers together in front of himself, thinking. He looked at Mason. "It may not be the worst idea."

Mason merely shrugged.

"Okay," Carr said to them both. "Make it happen. But your job is to keep this operation as small as humanly possible, without raising suspicion. Understood?"

Both Langford and Miller answered together. "Yes, sir."

"And we'll need to be ready for the Russians wanting to know what the hell happened to their new submarine. But for now, your first order of business is to come up with an explanation of why we have an oil rig burning in the middle of our new marine preserve." Carr looked at his watch. "You have thirty minutes."

119

Raindrops began forming dots on DeeAnn Draper's shirt as she sat on the ground, watching Dulce play in the tall grass. She looked completely at home, running and tumbling with the other young gorillas.

Accompanying the early hints of rain was a cool breeze continuing to strengthen across the top of Mount Bisoke.

DeeAnn's tan shirt rippled gently, and the tall grass around them rippled in waves across the clearing. Of course, none of the gorillas seemed to notice the weather changes.

Behind her, Ronin stood solemnly, looking on and admiring the green hills which stretched in every direction. They exhibited a vast lushness that he had never seen on his own planet.

At least not yet.

After searching the second vault, they had also found and stopped the leak. The same seepage which had been providing the former warlord Ngeze with enriched water for his prized opium fields, would now be removed. The vault itself had been well-camouflaged, hidden from view, by Ronin's people. It would remain that way until Clay or his team returned.

The visiting soldier, standing motionless, moved only his eyes when he noted DeeAnn raising her arm to check her watch. It was almost time.

***

DeeAnn took a deep breath and rose onto one knee. She faced the vest toward Dulce and called to her.

The young gorilla paused in her playing and stood up to

peer over the grass. Her dark fur blew softly in the wind. She abruptly turned and knuckle-ran a dozen yards back to DeeAnn.

DeeAnn's eyes were red with tears.

"Dulce, it's time for me to go."

The small gorilla studied her sadly.

Go now?

"I'm afraid so."

Come back?

DeeAnn frowned and slowly shook her head.

Dulce turned and looked at the rest of the gorillas—children and mothers. The larger males sat further out, protecting the band.

"Dulce," DeeAnn said. The lump in her throat suddenly grew, and she struggled to speak. "I have to go. But you don't. You can stay. If you like."

Dulce turned back around. *Me stay?*

DeeAnn pursed her lips and simply nodded.

You no stay?

She shook her head. "I can't. I have to go home."

This home.

DeeAnn's voice began to waver. "This isn't my home. It's your home."

Without a word, Dulce raised her hands and wrapped them around DeeAnn's. After a long silence, she let go and stepped backward in the grass.

DeeAnn began to cry. She watched in silence as Dulce made a very slow turn and proceeded to walk back toward the others. One of the mothers opened her arms and welcomed Dulce in closer to her. All the while, Dulce kept peering across the grass at DeeAnn, sadly.

DeeAnn immediately raised her hands and covered her face. She wept into them, unable to contain her emotion, her shoulders shuddering as she cried.

She turned away, not wanting Dulce to see her like that. She wanted Dulce's last memory of her to be a happy one. But nor could she bear to see Dulce happy without her, knowing she'd never see her baby again.

With her back turned, DeeAnn's vest could not translate anything more. Still sobbing, she reached down to pick up her bag. She prayed Dulce would be happy. The little gorilla had given DeeAnn so much. Much more than she knew. And helped her heal in ways she would never understand.

Now Dulce was free. Back where she belonged. And with a new family that would take care of her.

Now she had to leave. And be strong. It was not the goodbye she wanted. But it was probably easier. For her *and* for Dulce.

She kept her back turned and began walking toward Ronin. Neither she nor her vest could see Dulce, or the female gorilla, or their exchange. Nor did she see when Dulce turned and came bounding back through the grass.

It was only Dulce's enthusiastic grunts that allowed her to turn in time for the small gorilla to jump up and into DeeAnn's arms. Where she wrapped her long arms tightly around and squeezed.

When Dulce leaned back and peered up at DeeAnn, IMIS translated every word.

You me mommy. You me home.

120

It was pitch black. No light at all. And no sound.

The only sensation Tay had when he opened his eyes was touch and the hard surface beneath him. It was so dark, he could not even be completely sure his eyes were open.

Tay moved his right arm across the smooth, cold metal and nearly screamed in pain. But he could at least move it. He then tried his left, followed by both legs. All excruciating, but functional.

His fingers found his face, where he could feel dried blood covering most of it. Rolling his head from side to side, he could see absolutely nothing in the darkness. *Where in God's name was he?*

Tay tried to play back his last memories. Patchy and jumbled. Panic, with water swirling around him, as he and Lightfoot tried to detach the drill from the ship. But he couldn't remember why.

Tay retrieved a glimpse of himself making his way to the back of the drill, desperately trying to throw the giant motor into reverse. And then the violent bucking of the drill, smashing into them.

And finally, the massive surge of water sucking them toward the wall.

His bearings slowly returned like a continuation from his last memory. He turned and again tried to peer through the total darkness. He couldn't see anything at all, at first. But then something appeared. Something distant and dimly lit. Glowing softly.

***

It would take a long time for Tay's panic to subside. He

was trapped inside the ship. But unlike Lightfoot, he was alive. He was still alive, and more than that…Elgin Tay was an engineer.

ABOUT THE AUTHOR

Michael Grumley is a self-published writer who lives in Northern California with his wife and two young daughters. His email address is michael@michaelgrumley.com, and his web site is www.michaelgrumley.com.

MESSAGE FROM THE AUTHOR

It's funny. As a teenager, I realized at a certain point that I owed a lot of who I was to my parents, naturally. As a man, I came to accept that I'm nothing without my wife and daughters. And now as an author, I know that I'm nothing without my readers.

I've learned an awful lot over the last few years since starting the Breakthrough series. One is that writing a book is much harder than it seems. Another is that many things determine success, not the least of which is some degree of luck. And perhaps most importantly is that no one is an island. In the end, we all need the help and support of others, in anything we do. And for that, I would like to say thank you.

Thank you for investing your precious time with me, and of course with Dirk, Sally, Alison, John Clay, and the others. I could never have dreamed how many people the Breakthrough stories would affect, and how many readers would in turn affect me. I suspect any author worth his or her salt would agree that their readers have touched them as much as they have touched the readers. And for that, I am eternally grateful. I simply would not be writing these stories without you, and I am deeply grateful.

I truly hope you have enjoyed Ripple. There are some

big concepts laid out in this story line, and if you've enjoyed it so far…just wait until you see what happens next.

In the meantime, please visit my website at www.michaelgrumley.com to get a FREE copy of "Genesis" if you haven't already. It's an unpublished Breakthrough novella, which tells the story of Alison Shaw's run-in with the Navy, how she came to meet Dirk and Sally for the first time, and how the IMIS project was born. I think you'll like it.

And finally, if you could please spare a minute to leave a review for Ripple, I would be extremely grateful. Many readers may not be aware of how essential reviews are to the success of a self-published author. I would really appreciate it if you could help let others know.

Thank you very much.
Michael

Made in the
USA
Monee, IL